BLACK OPS

When MI5 Agent Spider is asked to assume the identity of the contract killer hired to take out President Vladimir Putin, he knows he'll become a wanted man. And things are about to get more complicated: Spider is told that his MI5 controller and close friend Charlotte Button has been running an off-the-books assassination operation, taking vengeance on the men who killed her husband. Spider owes his life to Button — but this discovery will stretch his loyalty to the limit. Because he is told to betray her. Worse, he's asked to cooperate with his nemesis at MI6, Jeremy Willoughby Brown, in taking Charlie down. And he will have to cross the assassin Lex Harper, currently on the trail of two Irish terrorists, who may be able to lead him to his ex-boss . . .

SPECIAL MESSAGE TO READERS

BLACK OPS

STEPHEN LEATHER

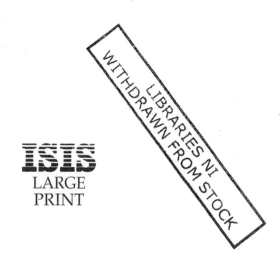

ISIS
LARGE
PRINT

First published in Great Britain 2015
by
Hodder & Stoughton

First Isis Edition
published 2019
by arrangement with
Hodder & Stoughton
An Hachette UK company

A catalogue record for this book is available
from the British Library.

ISBN 978–1–78541–778–8 (hb)
ISBN 978–1–78541–784–9 (pb)

Published by
F. A. Thorpe (Publishing)
Anstey, Leicestershire

Set by Words & Graphics Ltd.
Anstey, Leicestershire
Printed and bound in Great Britain by
T. J. International Ltd., Padstow, Cornwall

This book is printed on acid-free paper

For Laura

Rob Tyler wanted a beer, but he was working and on a point of principle he never drank on the job. He was sitting in a house in Queens, about ten miles from the towering skyscrapers of Manhattan. The house was in a quiet cul-de-sac, and probably worth a couple of million dollars. Three bedrooms, a nice yard, a garage easily big enough for two cars and a hot tub on a terrace leading off the main bedroom. He was sitting on an Italian sofa and on the marble coffee table in front of him was the rope that Tyler would use to hang the man who was expected home at any moment.

Tyler was dressed for murder. He was wearing white forensic overalls, paper covers over his shoes, and a shower cap. There were blue latex gloves on his hands, and in the kitchen was a black garbage bag into which he'd put all the protective clothing once the job was finished. The job specifications had been clear. The man was to be killed by hanging and everything had to point to suicide. That didn't necessarily mean a note — it was a fallacy that all suicides left a note before killing themselves — but it did mean that the marks on his neck would have to be consistent with hanging and there would have to be rope fibres on his hands. Tyler had already selected the perfect spot for the hanging — the bannisters around the main hall would do just fine.

Tyler had carried out more than a dozen killings that had looked like suicides. Hanging was the most popular but he had also slit the wrists of a woman in a bath and had done a couple of overdoses. Overdoses were messy. The best way was to force a liquid down the victim's throat with a large syringe and then follow up with tablets when they were unconscious. The overdoses were two-man jobs, Tyler doubted that one man could do it on his own. He'd done hangings on his own but this time the job had been assigned to two contractors. Tyler wasn't overjoyed at working with another contractor, especially one he hadn't worked with before, but the woman seemed professional. She'd said her name was Leila and was vague about where she'd come from and hadn't given much away. She was pretty, with mahogany brown skin and the blackest eyes he'd ever seen, short, curly hair and a body that wouldn't quit. She was wearing high heels and a short skirt that showed off a pair of awesome legs and a low-cut top with a cleavage that he couldn't stop looking at. From her dark skin and hair Tyler suspected Guatemala or Nicaragua but her accent was a puzzle. Her English was perfect but her accent was slightly off, as if she'd been born overseas. He'd tried speaking to her in Spanish but she hadn't replied. Tyler assumed she'd been hired because of her looks — she was the perfect honey for a honey trap.

Leila had made contact with the target and had been to the house with him the previous night. The target

2

was divorced, she said, and had jumped at the chance of getting between her legs. He'd been so enamoured that he hadn't realised she had copied his key and noted the burglar alarm code.

Now they were in the house and waiting for him to return. It was seven in the evening and they had been inside for the best part of four hours. Tyler had jokingly suggested that they visit the bedroom to pass the time but she had smiled sarcastically and said that he wasn't her type. Tyler wondered if that were true. He was a little over six feet and was in the best physical condition of his life, better even than when he'd been in Delta Force. He wondered if it was worth trying again, after the target was dead. Killing could be the ultimate aphrodisiac, with the right kind of girl. He realised he was staring at her breasts again and that she was looking at him. He smiled and looked away.

"How long have you known Mercier?" he asked.

Mercier had hired them for the job. Tyler was getting a hundred grand for the gig. He didn't know how much the girl was being paid. He'd be doing most of the work. As soon as the target turned up, the girl would cover him with her gun. He'd already brought a quilt down from upstairs and laid it behind the sofa. He'd wrap the target with the quilt and then place the noose around his neck and pull it tight until he was dead. That way there would be no signs of a struggle. Once the target was dead it would be easy enough to attach the rope to the bannister and set the scene. Tyler had already selected a dining-room chair. He would put the

3

target's fingerprints on the back and make it look as if the chair had fallen to the side.

"A couple of years."

"Done many jobs for him?"

"A few."

"Anything I might have heard of?"

She tilted her head on one side and scrutinised him with her jet black eyes. "Do you always ask this many questions?"

"I'm just curious."

"Well you know what curiosity did to the cat." She checked the action of her gun.

"You do that a lot," said Tyler. "Check your gun."

"I like to be sure," she said.

"You always use a Glock?"

"For close-up work, sure. You can't go wrong with a Glock. Plus there's a lot of them about so they're harder to track down."

"They kick their cartridges everywhere though."

"If you dump the gun, that's not an issue." She shrugged. "Horses for courses."

Tyler nodded. "And what did they tell you about me?"

She wrinkled her nose. "Not much."

"And you didn't ask?"

"Why would I ask?"

"Not curious?"

She laughed. "You're the curious one, Robert. I don't have a curious bone in my body."

"But when they said there'd be two people on the job, didn't you ask for details?"

4

She shook her head. "No." She tilted her head on one side again and fixed him with her eyes. "You asked about me?"

"Of course," said Tyler.

"And Mercier told you?"

"He just said that you were very pretty and I should keep my cock in my pants."

"Good advice," she said. "That's all he told you?"

"Why, does that worry you?"

"I'd have hoped there would have been some sort of confidentiality. I wouldn't want an employer to start giving out my personal information to a . . ."

"Stranger? But I'm not a stranger. I've worked with Jules for many years. And it's not as if he gave me your real name. Other than that he told me nothing."

She walked over to the window and looked down at the street, then at her watch. "So what do you want to know, Rob?" She reached into her pocket and took out a bulbous suppressor and screwed it into the barrel of her Glock as she continued to look down into the street.

Tyler shrugged. "You're a pro, that's obvious. But you're young. What are you? Twenty-one? Twenty-two?"

She smiled. "Twenty-four."

"That's still young. How did you get the experience?"

"Israeli Army," she said. "Signed up at eighteen."

"You're Israeli?"

"My parents moved there before I was born."

"So you're Jewish?"

"Is that a problem?"

Tyler laughed. "Of course not. Wow, I wouldn't have put you down as a former soldier."

"It's compulsory in Israel, national service for everyone. Three years for men, two years for women. But only half go into the military. And a lot of kids duck it if they can. But I enlisted. I wanted to serve."

"And you got a taste for it?"

"For what?"

"Combat?"

"There wasn't much combat. But there was a lot of training. Then I joined Mossad. The Israeli equivalent of the CIA."

"What did you do for them?"

"That's classified. But between you and me, pretty much the same as I'm doing today."

"You were a government assassin?"

She smiled tightly. "Like I said, it's classified."

"And now you do it for money?"

She nodded. "A lot of money. And you were what? A Navy Seal?"

"Delta Force," said Tyler.

"Were you one of the ones that got Bin Laden?"

"I'd gone private before then," said Tyler.

"How many jobs have you done?"

"In total? A couple of dozen."

"You don't know for sure?"

"To be honest, once a job is done, it's done. I don't dwell. It's like women. I have absolutely no idea how many women I've fucked over the years. A hundred. Two hundred." He shrugged. "I can't remember their faces, never mind their names. It's the same with

6

targets. Mind you, there's one coming up that I'm never going to forget."

She looked at him, intrigued. "Tell me more."

"I can't," he said.

"Is it for Mercier?"

"No. Someone else. It'll probably be my last job. For a while, anyway."

"It's big?"

Tyler grinned. "Very big. The biggest."

She smiled and locked eyes with him. "You can tell me," she said.

He shook his head. "I can't tell anyone. That's one of the downsides of this job, you know? It all has to stay secret. Otherwise you're fucked."

"You can tell people you trust," she said.

"Yeah, but who can you trust?" he asked. "You can't trust anybody." He looked at his watch. "Why is he running late?"

"What do you mean?"

"The target. Where the hell is he?"

"He's here already," said the girl.

Tyler frowned. He was about to reply when he realised what she meant. He started to raise his gun but it was too late, way too late. Her Glock was already pointed at his chest and he barely had time to open his mouth before the first shot smashed into his chest, followed closely by a second. He was barely aware of the muffled pops of the suppressed shots and the bullets felt like nothing more than punches to his chest. He fell backwards and was dead even before the third shot hit him in the face and his brains and skull splattered across the wall behind him.

Lex Harper tapped his pool cue on the side of the table and tried to focus on the balls. "Remind me again, am I big or small?"

The three men sitting on bar stools to his left groaned as one.

"He's pissed," said a big man wearing a Singha beer vest and baggy shorts.

"He's taking the piss, that's what he's doing," said the man sitting in the middle of the three. He was tall and thin with a beard that compensated for a rapidly receding hairline. "Lex, mate, time to go home. And don't use the bike. I don't want to be visiting you in the ICU."

"I'm fine," said Harper, struggling to focus on the table. He frowned. "Just tell me, big or small?"

"Small," chorused the three men.

The barman put down fresh bottles of Heineken in front of them, each protected with a foam tube stamped with the logo of Noy's Bar, a red lipstick kiss on a St George's Cross. The bar was open to the air and even with the large fans playing down on them from the ceiling, the beer wouldn't have stayed cool for long without insulation. Noy's Bar was just off Pattaya's Walking Street. Most evenings Walking Street was packed with tourists eyeing up the red light area's bars and hookers, but Noy's Bar was off the beaten track enough for Harper and his pals to be able to enjoy a quiet game of pool and a few beers without being disturbed by crocodiles of Chinese and Korean tourists snapping away with their smartphones. Though in Harper's case it had been more than a few beers along with half a dozen tequila chasers. It was just after 8p.m. but the four men had been drinking and playing pool after an extended lunch in the Pig and Whistle and all the signs were that the drinking at least was going to continue into the early hours.

As Harper leaned over the table to play his shot, he felt a vibration from his denim hip pack. Night or day Harper always had the pack around his waist. It contained one of the many mobile phones he used, an Irish passport and two credit cards, and 50,000 baht in cash. The pack, together with the heavy gold neck chain he always wore, meant that he could get out of Thailand or anywhere else he found himself at a moment's notice, leaving by the airport, by boat or travelling overland to a neighbouring country. He had a larger bug-out bag under the bed in his apartment and another in the back of his SUV, but all the essentials for a fast escape were in the hip pack. Much as he loved Thailand, his unbreakable rule was never to be so fond of a place that he couldn't leave at a moment's notice, without a backward glance.

His companions groaned as he straightened up, took out his phone and read the three-word text message from a UK number: *YOU HAVE MAIL.*

"Guys, I've got to go," he said, slotting his cue into a rack on the wall.

"He's on a mission," laughed Singha shirt. "It's that dancer from Anglewitch, the one with the tits."

"To be fair, they've all got tits," said Harper. "Real or fake. Okay, I'm off."

"Take a taxi, Lex."

Harper nodded and waved a thanks for the advice. He was just sober enough to know that he was too drunk to be riding his Triumph Bonneville home. Pattaya's streets were a death trap at the best of times, but being drunk on a powerful motorcycle when pretty much everyone else on the road was either equally intoxicated or high on drugs was a recipe for disaster. He headed off down the road in search of an Internet café. The nearest was run by a middle-aged former go-go dancer called Rose. Rose was still a stunner, so much so that at least four foreigners had given her the money to start her own Internet café-cum-print shop. Two of her backers were British, one was Australian and one was an Indian. The Indian and one of the Brits thought they were married to Rose, having gone through a traditional Thai ceremony in her home town of Udon Thani. Rose had never followed up with the paperwork, which meant she was free and single and open to offers.

All four of her backers lived overseas and, so far at least, had never decided to holiday in Pattaya at the same time. They all deposited regular sums into her bank accounts and sent her presents to prove their devotion and in return received daily Skype calls where she would shed a tear and say how she loved them and missed them.

When Harper walked in she was sitting at one of her terminals helping a pretty teenage girl with a tattoo of two Japanese koi on her back compose an email to an overseas sponsor.

"Tell him you cannot dance because you miss him so much," said Rose, pointing at the screen. "And tell him your mother has to go into hospital soon. Don't say what's wrong with her. Wait for him to ask. And don't ask him for money. Wait for him to offer."

The girl frowned. "What if he doesn't offer?"

Rose smiled. "He will," she said, patting the young girl on the leg. "They always do."

"Can I use a computer, Rose?" asked Harper.

"No problem, Mr Lex," she said. "Take any."

Harper sat down at the furthest terminal from the counter and logged on to Yahoo Mail. He had memorised the email address and password, but had never sent a single email from the account. Its sole use was for communications with his MI5 handler, Charlotte Button, the only other person who knew the password. They sent messages to each other using the drafts folder — a technique first developed by al-Qaeda terrorists, allowing instantaneous communications that bypassed even the most hi-tech surveillance systems. The National Security Agency in the States and GCHQ in the UK had the capacity to eavesdrop on every phone call and email anywhere in the world, but using the drafts folder trick meant that the emails were never actually transmitted and therefore could not be flagged up by anyone monitoring his communications. Only if a spook had discovered the existence of the email account and hacked into it would the messages in the drafts folder be compromised, and even then, they'd have to be quick because Button and Harper's SOP was to delete every message as soon as they had read it.

A single message had been added to the drafts in the last couple of hours: *LOCATION ONE. SOONEST. TEXT ME WHEN IN SITU.* Harper smiled to himself as he deleted the message. Even if someone really had hacked into his account, the message wouldn't tell them much. Location One was London. He waved over at Rose. "Rose, coffee, black. Two sugars."

"Coming, Mr Lex."

"And a bottle of water."

Harper went back online. There was a KLM flight due to leave Bangkok at two thirty in the morning. He booked himself a business class seat and a connecting flight to Dublin. Rose brought him his coffee and Harper thanked her.

"And when I've finished this one bring me another, and another. In fact, if you can put me on an intravenous drip, that would be great."

Rose frowned, not understanding.

"Just coffee, Rose, and keep it coming."

He sighed and looked at his watch. At this time of night it wouldn't take much more than an hour to get to Suvarnabhumi airport. He had plenty of time to get a couple of coffees under his belt before heading home to grab what he needed.

There were two of them sitting in the back of the van, and the ventilation wasn't the best. The air quality wasn't helped by the continuing flatulence of Jamie Brewer, Spider Shepherd's number two on the surveillance operation.

"I'm sorry, mate, really," said Brewer after breaking wind for the third time. "I had a curry last night."

Shepherd wrinkled his nose in disgust. "That is awful. Really."

"Mate, I'm sorry."

Shepherd would have loved to open the rear doors but that wasn't possible, not when it was packed with transmitting and recording equipment. The van they were in had the livery of a courier company and sitting in the front seat was a brunette in a beige uniform. Her cab was sealed and they had to talk to her via an intercom.

Shepherd stared at one of the four flatscreens on the side of the van. It showed an electronic map of the area around them along with six flashing red dots. Above each of the dots was a number from one to six, representing the six watchers on the operation. The watchers had been tasked with following Ahmed Khalaf, a twenty-three-year-old former medical student who had ended his studies early and travelled to Syria to fight alongside the jihadists of ISIS, the Islamic State of Iraq and Syria. Khalaf had been easy enough to track as he had posted numerous photographs on his Facebook page. He had been allowed back into the country but MI5 had kept him under surveillance from the moment he had arrived at Heathrow. It was clear from the way that Khalaf behaved once he was back in the UK that he had been well taught by ISIS. He didn't

13

have a mobile phone and he didn't own a computer. He made calls from phone boxes and twice a day he went to one of several Internet cafés. It was clear he was up to something and MI5 put him high up on their list of priorities. There were three teams of five assigned to Khalaf, working eight-hour shifts. Shepherd had been assigned to monitor the teams and he took it in turns to do ride-alongs. Surveillance was a difficult job at the best of times and long-term surveillance was especially demanding, hour after hour of sitting outside buildings followed by short bursts of frenetic activity. As days turned into weeks and even months, the job got that much harder. Surveillance teams would start to make assumptions and let down their guard. A target might leave the house every day at the same time, walk down the road and turn left. He might do that every day for a hundred days. But on day one hundred and one he might turn right and disappear. Shepherd's job was to make sure the teams didn't lose their edge.

For the first couple of weeks of surveillance Khalaf did nothing out of the ordinary. He spent most of his time in a bedsit in Stoke Newington, venturing out only to pray at a local mosque. MI5 had two men in place at the mosque and they were able to ascertain that Khalaf spoke to no one while he was at prayers. He would occasionally shop for food and once a day he would take a walk through the thirty-one acres of Abney Park garden cemetery.

The cemetery was always a difficult venue. There were dozens of paths winding between the 200,000 or so graves and while there were always some people wandering around, it was difficult to stay close without being seen. Dogs were always a good cover and the teams could call on more than a dozen offered up by volunteers prepared to allow MI5 to borrow their pets.

During the third week Khalaf visited Stoke Newington public library in Church Street. On the first visit he had wandered around the bookshelves for ten minutes before leaving. A few days later he visited again, this time making use of one of the library's six computers. The visit to the library then became a daily event, and each time he would spend up to an hour on one of the computers. The surveillance teams installed keystroke programs on all of the machines and they were able to keep track of his Internet activities. Immediately they saw what he was doing the teams went on to full alert. Khalaf was reading articles on the mass jihadist killings in Iraq, Kenya and India, and spent time studying online newspaper articles about the murder of British soldier Lee Rigby who was hacked to death near the Royal Artillery Barracks in Woolwich. During the fifth week of surveillance, Khalaf went to the place where Fusilier Rigby was murdered and spent more than an hour walking around.

During the sixth week of surveillance, Khalaf opened a Yahoo email account and sent an email to an address that was traced to a library computer in Ealing. Khalaf used a drafts folder for the account to contact a British-born Somalian later identified as Mohammed Mahmud. Like Khalaf, Mahmud had broken off his studies and travelled to Syria to fight with ISIS. He had somehow managed to travel there and back without attracting the attention of the security services. From the messages that piled up in the drafts folder it was clear that the two men were planning a beheadings rampage in the London area. In the sixth week they were joined online by a third London-based jihadist who was also a member of ISIS. The third man had been harder to track down, he went online using a pay-as-you-go smartphone and was rarely active for more than a few minutes at a time and changed his SIM card every week.

A second five-man team, also under Shepherd's guidance, had put Mahmud under the microscope. Like Khalaf, he lived alone, leaving his small flat in a terraced house only to shop, visit a local mosque and the library.

During the eighth week of Khalaf's surveillance, both teams converged on the Abney Park cemetery. When it became clear that the two men were going to meet, Mahmud's team pulled back.

The two men sat together for more than an hour on a bench close to the Gothic church in the centre of the cemetery. Three watchers walked by during the time they were together but none was able to hear even a fragment of their conversation.

There was no doubt that the men were planning a major terrorist atrocity and Shepherd had recommended that they be arrested and charged. His boss Charlotte Button had agreed with him but they had been overruled — the surveillance was to continue until the third man was identified. That had been three weeks ago and they were no closer to finding out who he was.

The surveillance had turned up another cell, however; this one in Bradford. Khalaf had gone to a second email address draft folder and began communicating with another potential ISIS soldier, a British-born Pakistani who was about to fly out to Syria. Through him they managed to trace and identify another four would-be jihadists.

Meanwhile Khalaf was also using Google Earth to look at the roads around several shopping centres and railway stations in London, and visiting websites for large shopping malls, including the giant Westfield mall in White City and Stratford. Mahmud was just as active on the Ealing library's computers, spending hours looking at websites that detailed the construction of IEDs.

As the two men continued to research and plot, the surveillance teams increased their hunt for the third jihadist, but his habit of only using a pay-as-you-go phone and constantly changing his SIM card meant he was impossible to pin down. The teams drew up more than a dozen possible suspects from the people that Khalaf and Mahmud met, but they couldn't get any concrete proof of who the elusive third man was.

Shepherd had joined the surveillance team at eight o'clock in the morning, just as they had taken over from the night shift. Outside the vehicle were three watchers, codenames Whisky One, Whisky Two and Whisky Three. Whisky One and Whisky Two were on the pavement and Whisky Three was kitted out as a bicycle courier. All were in position outside Khalaf's building. He wasn't expected out before ten o'clock.

It wasn't until after eleven that Khalaf appeared. He was wearing a black Puffa jacket with the hood up and he had a grey North Face backpack slung over his shoulder.

"That's new," said Brewer, nodding at the screen showing the view from the CCTV camera mounted under the van's rear-view mirror. It could be moved using a small joystick on a panel in front of Brewer.

"He's had a backpack before, right?"

"Smaller than that. Adidas."

"Tango is on the move," said Shepherd. He was wearing a Bluetooth earpiece connected to the transceiver on his waist.

"Whisky Three, I have eyeball. He's going back behind the house."

Shepherd and Brewer watched on the screen as Khalaf disappeared behind the house. There were a dozen occupants, each with their own room, though they shared two bathrooms and a kitchen. The rubbish bins were at the rear but Khalaf hadn't been carrying any rubbish.

"What's he playing at?" said Brewer.

The mystery was solved soon enough when Khalaf reappeared pushing a bicycle, an old-fashioned type with a wicker basket fastened to the handlebars.

Brewer cursed. "Where did that come from?"

"Whisky Three, you need to stay on him," said Shepherd. He nodded at Brewer. "Get the driver moving."

"He's never done this before," said Brewer.

"It'll be okay," said Shepherd. He looked back at the screen. Khalaf was pedalling down the street. "Whisky Two, Whisky One, you need to get mobile and head south. Taxi or bus. Over."

"Whisky One, roger that."

"Whisky Two, roger."

Shepherd picked up his mobile and called the supervisor of the second surveillance team, over in Ealing. Her name was Lisa Elphick and like Shepherd she was sitting in the back of a van. "Dan, hey, we're a bit busy here," she said.

"Us too. Our Tango's on a bike. Heading south. He's never done that before."

"Ours is running what looks like counter surveillance, and he's never done that before. I'm down to one eyeball at the moment."

"You've got a guy on a motorbike, right? I'm looking to borrow him for a while."

"That's not going to happen. He had a car stop for him, turns out it's an Uber cab. Normally he takes the bus so we were on foot. The bike is the only eyeball I have at the moment." She swore vehemently. "He's just got out of the cab on The Broadway. Bravo Two stay close. If necessary, dump the bike. Bravo One, Bravo Three, where the hell are you? Dan, sorry, we've lost him, I'll have to call you back." She cut the connection.

Shepherd brought Brewer up to speed.

"You think they're up to something?" asked Brewer.

"Could be a coincidence."

"Both out of character at the same time? That sets alarm bells ringing."

"Do you want to call for backup?"

"I'd be happier," said Brewer.

"Whisky One, I'm in a cab."

"Good man. Stay on him."

"Whisky Three, I have eyeball."

Shepherd looked at the screen showing the positions of the watchers. They were all moving. "I'll see what I can do," he said. Then he called up the Head of Mobile Surveillance and got through to his number two. Shepherd quickly explained what he needed and the officer agreed to get two surveillance bikes in his area as soon as possible. Shepherd asked for a time frame and was told five minutes, possibly ten. It was better than nothing. Shepherd ended the call. "Help's on the way," he said.

The van lurched to a halt. "Sorry," came the driver's voice over the intercom. "Red light."

"Whisky Three, we're held at lights. Do you still have eyeball?" asked Shepherd.

"Whisky Three, affirmative. He's heading south on Essex Road. I'm about a hundred yards behind him. He's taking it easy and isn't looking back. Over."

"Whisky One, are you still in the cab? Over."

"Whisky One, passed him about fifty yards back. Over."

Shepherd looked at the map. "See if you can get the cab to wait at City Road. Over."

Shepherd looked at the screen showing the forward video feed but Khalaf was too far ahead to be seen.

"Has he ever done anything like this before?" Shepherd asked Brewer.

Brewer shook his head. "Never. He always goes to the same place. The mosque. The shops. The library. The cemetery."

"There was no indication that they were getting ready to go," said Shepherd. "That new backpack is a worry."

His phone rang and he looked at the screen. It was Lisa. "We lost him," she said. "He was on foot and we couldn't get to him on time."

"Could he have got to a Tube station?"

"Ealing Broadway? Possibly."

"What are you doing now?"

"Canvassing the area. If he did go down the Tube then we really have lost him. Sorry."

"Any chance of you sending your bike my way? Our target is on a bicycle and we're having trouble keeping up with him."

"You think something's up?"

"Maybe. There was no chatter, though. I could do with your bike, Lisa."

"It'd mean I have one less pair of eyes on the ground."

"I get that, but a bird in the hand and all that."

"Your call. I'll send him over."

"Our target is heading south down Essex Road to City Road. Brown coat, bicycle with a wicker basket on the front."

Shepherd ended the call just as the van started moving again.

The van sped south. Shepherd watched the progress of the watchers on the screen. Whisky One had stopped close to the junction of City Road and Essex Road. Whisky Two was still in Stoke Newington. Whisky Three was moving slowly down Essex Road.

"Whisky Two, what's your situation, over?" asked Shepherd.

"Whisky Two, still on foot, sorry. No bloody cabs for love nor money. I might grab a bus. Over."

"We need you on City Road, Whisky Two. Do what you can. Over." He looked up at the video feed. The traffic was moving slowly and there was still no sign of Khalaf.

Shepherd scowled at the digital map. Whisky Three was getting close to City Road. At the junction Khalaf could turn west or east or continue south on the A1. "Whisky Three, stay with him, over," he said.

"Whisky Three, I'm about fifty yards behind him. I have eyeball. Over."

Shepherd looked over at Brewer. "He's never gone this way before?"

Brewer shook his head.

Shepherd called up Lisa on the phone again. "Any joy?" he asked.

"No sign of him, sorry," said Lisa. Her professional pride was obviously hurt. Losing a target was the worst thing that could happen to a watcher. "The bike is heading your way. What do you think? Do we have a problem?"

"I'm not sure," said Shepherd. "Did your guy have a backpack?"

"Yes. But that's not unusual. More often than not he has a bag of some kind."

"Our target has a different bag to his usual one. And he's never used a bicycle before."

"Shit. I'm sorry."

"Don't sweat it. Just keep sweeping the area, he still might turn up." He ended the call. "Mahmud's gone," he said to Brewer. "And he had a backpack. Might not be significant . . ."

". . . or it might be," said Brewer. They looked at the video feed. In the distance they could see Whisky Three, weaving in and out of the slow-moving traffic.

"Whisky Two, I'm in a black cab and heading south on Essex Road, but the traffic's bad. Over."

Shepherd looked at the digital map and pointed at the flashing light that signified Whisky Two's position, well back from where the van was.

"Whisky Two, be prepared to head west or east on my word. A rat run might save you some time. Over."

"Whisky Two, roger that. Over."

The van had slowed now. Shepherd glanced at the video feed. The traffic was heavier and Whisky Three had disappeared into the distance.

"Whisky One, I have eyeball."

"Soon as you see which way he's headed, let me know, Whisky One. Is your cab okay to follow?"

"Whisky One, all good. Over."

Shepherd looked at the digital map. Whisky Three was getting close to Whisky One which meant that Khalaf would be somewhere in between.

"Everyone on full alert, he could go anywhere at the junction," said Shepherd. He looked at the map. The van was a couple of hundred yards away from City Road.

"Whisky One, he's off the road. He's pushing the bike along the pavement and heading west."

"Out of the cab, Whisky One. Follow on foot."

"Whisky One, going on foot. Over."

"Whisky Three, what's your situation?"

"Whisky Three, I'm on the pavement."

Shepherd looked at the digital map. Whisky Two was still stuck in traffic, a mile or so behind the van. The van came to a halt. Shepherd looked at the video feed. The traffic was bumper to bumper ahead of them. "I'm going on foot," he said. "They need help out there."

"No problem, I'll mind the shop," said Brewer.

Shepherd pushed open the door and jumped out. He began jogging south along Essex Road, keeping at a reasonable pace so as not to attract too much attention.

"Whisky Three, he's left the bicycle by some railings."

"Stick with him, Whisky Three."

"I'm having trouble with the bike."

"Dump it," said Shepherd, increasing his pace. "Whisky One, do you have eyeball?"

"Whisky One. Just lost him. Wait. Yes, I have eyeball. He's outside the Tube station. He's looking at his watch."

"Is he heading in?"

"Not sure, he seems to be waiting."

Shepherd ran faster, not caring now who was looking at him. His feet pounded on the pavement. Ahead of him he saw the junction with City Road. Angel Tube station was to the left. The traffic was barely moving so he ducked between two cars and crossed the road.

"Whisky Three, he's going inside. Over."

"Whisky One, I have eyeball. I'm following him inside. Over."

"Whisky Control, see if you can fix up a feed from the station's CCTV," said Shepherd.

"I'm on it," said Brewer.

"Whisky One, I've lost eyeball. Repeat. I've lost eyeball. Over."

Shepherd cursed. "What's happened, Whisky One?"

"Loads of people just came through and then I didn't see him on the escalator. He must have gone down the stairs."

"After him, quick as you can. Whisky Three, where are you? Over."

"Just at the entrance, I'm going in. Over."

Shepherd ran as fast as he could, his arms pumping at his side, the transceiver banging against his hip under his jacket. He slowed as he reached the entrance to the station and had to weave through the exiting passengers. "Does anyone have eyeball?" he asked.

"Whisky Three, negative."

"Whisky One, negative."

"Don't do this to me, guys. Find him."

Shepherd didn't have an Oyster card so he jumped up and over the ticket barrier. A uniformed Tube employee shouted for him to come back but made no effort to chase after him. As he hurtled down the escalator he pushed the earpiece of his transceiver into his ear and clipped the main unit to his belt. He reached the bottom of the escalator. "Whisky One, Whisky Three, where are you?"

"Whisky Three, southbound platform."

"Whisky One, same. Southbound platform."

"Do you see him?"

"Whisky Three, negative."

"Whisky One, no eyeball."

Shepherd cursed and ran towards the northbound platform. The tunnel opened midway onto the platform. He looked right and left. There were several dozen people waiting for the train.

"Jamie, what's happening?"

"Negative on the CCTV feed," said Brewer. "Where are you?"

"Northbound platform," said Shepherd. He looked up at the electronic announcement board. "The next train is one minute away. Whisky One and Whisky Three are on the southbound platform."

Shepherd turned left and walked down the platform, scanning faces. A middle-aged man with a briefcase. An Asian woman with two young children. A teenage schoolboy, his eyes glued to an iPhone.

"What are you going to do, Dan?" asked Brewer.

"Play it by ear," said Shepherd.

Two black guys in long coats, one carrying a guitar case. An old Asian lady in a sari with a Harrods carrier bag. Two women in full burkhas, one of them with a toddler in a pushchair.

"You think he's going to get on a train?"

Shepherd could feel the wind on his face. There was a train heading his way.

"I don't know. What's happening up top?"

"All quiet here."

"Whisky Three, still no eyeball."

"Whisky One, no eyeball."

"If the station was the target he'd have started by now," said Shepherd.

A young man with a backpack was eyeing up a pretty blonde girl in torn jeans. She seemed to be deliberately avoiding eye contact with him.

Shepherd's heart was racing. The target had to be on one of the platforms, there was nowhere else for him to be. He reached the end of the platform. There was an old man in a heavy overcoat, mumbling to himself, and a woman sitting on a bench eating a sandwich. Shepherd turned and started to jog back down the platform. He could hear the train now, roaring through the tunnel behind him.

"The train's coming," he said. "Can you stop it, Jamie? Get them to say there's a mechanical fault."

"I'll try."

The train burst out of the tunnel and the brakes screeched as it drew up at the platform. The doors opened and passengers poured out.

"What's happening, Jamie?"

"Negative on the stopping," said Brewer. "They've got me on hold."

"I'm going to have to get on the train," said Shepherd. "Whisky One, Whisky Three, give me a sit-rep, over."

"Whisky One, no sign of target. Train's just pulling in. Over."

Shepherd cursed under his breath. Three followers. Two trains. One target.

"Stick with your train, stay in touch with Jamie as best you can. Over." The transceivers were functioning just fine in the station but he had no idea how they would perform in the tunnels.

The flood of exiting passengers was over and the passengers on the platform were now making their way on to the train. Shepherd reached the halfway point of the train. "Jamie, I'm getting on the northbound train. See if you can get backup at the next station. Same with the southbound train. Over."

"I'm on it. Over."

The doors began to close and Shepherd jumped on board. He quickly scanned the passengers. There were four Asian males but two had long beards, one was wearing a long frock coat and the remaining one was with a pretty Indian girl. He moved down the carriage towards the front of the train, weaving between passengers who either ignored him or glared at him for invading what they saw as their personal space.

The train lurched forward and within seconds had rattled into the tunnel.

Shepherd continued to scan faces. Another Asian male, but this one bearded and engrossed in his smartphone. Two Japanese tourists squinting up at a Tube map on the carriage wall. Two girls in school uniform, sitting with their heads together, sharing a pair of earphones.

Shepherd reached the end of the carriage. He looked through the windows of the connecting doors into the next carriage. His breath caught in his throat as he saw the target, standing by the door halfway down.

He turned away and held the microphone close to his lips. "I have eyeball on Tango One, over," he said. There was no answer. "Jamie, can you hear me?" There was nothing in his earpiece, not even static. Shepherd turned back to look through the window again. Khalaf was looking at his watch and shifting his weight from foot to foot. He was gearing up for something, Shepherd could tell.

Moving from one carriage to the other involved opening the two heavy connecting doors and stepping across the gap between the two carriages. It would be noisy and attract a lot of attention. It would be better to wait until they reached the next station and then change carriages.

Khalaf had turned his back to the door and was now looking down his carriage, towards the front of the train. Shepherd realised he was looking at another Asian man. He could have been Khalaf's brother. Tall and thin, wearing baggy jeans and a grey hoodie with the hood up, his eyes hidden behind impenetrable sunglasses. On his back was a North Face backpack, the same style as Khalaf's but his was red. Like Khalaf he was agitated, swaying from side to side. The two men looked at each other and Khalaf nodded. The other man flashed Khalaf a tight smile and Shepherd's stomach lurched as he realised there wouldn't be time to switch carriages. His mind raced. There had been no intel that Khalaf's cell had access to bombmaking equipment but the backpacks were a worry. If there were bombs in the backpacks then a double explosion in a confined space would be deadly. He ran through his options, but truth be told there weren't many. He could pull the emergency switch and stop the train, but he didn't see how that would help. He could shout a warning but that would only serve to start a panic. If he'd been armed then he could pull out his gun and try to take them out before they commenced their attack but that was pure wishful thinking because he didn't have a weapon. He could wait until the train reached the next station but from the way the two men were behaving it was clear they were getting ready to act. Or were they? Nothing they had seen during their surveillance had suggested that they were going to attack a Tube train. And the choice of target made little sense. If they were suicide bombers then a carriage was the perfect target as the confined space meant guaranteed casualties. But if it was a knife attack then a carriage would serve to limit casualties, and block off any means of escape. Was he reading it wrong? Were they getting ready to attack now or were they just tense?

He looked up at the Tube map on the side of the carriage. The next stop was King's Cross St Pancras. The mainline station and London home to the Eurostar. That had been one of the places Khalaf had visited on Google Earth.

The train began to slow as it approached King's Cross. Shepherd glanced through the window. The two men were now ignoring each other and seemed more relaxed. Shepherd had come around to the view that there was no risk of an explosion on the Tube. It wouldn't make sense to have two suicide bombers in the same carriage. That meant they were en route to the target, or it was a knife or gun attack. Guns were unlikely because there had been no chatter about firearms, but then the bicycle had caught them all by surprise.

The platform flashed by and the train stopped. Shepherd started moving towards the door but took a quick look over his shoulder and saw that Khalaf wasn't moving. Passengers poured off but Khalaf stayed where he was. So did the other guy with the backpack who was now studiously avoiding Khalaf's gaze.

"Jamie, can you hear me?" whispered Shepherd, covering his mouth with his hand.

"Affirmative."

"Tango One is on the northbound train, now at King's Cross. Over."

"Roger that. Over."

"I don't think anything's going to happen on the train. There is another Tango with him. Repeat, two Tangoes on board. Tango Two is an IC6 male, tall and thin, grey hoodie, baggy jeans, sunglasses and a red North Face backpack. Over."

"Roger that."

Passengers were now getting on to the train. Khalaf moved further into the carriage to make room at the door. Shepherd tensed and took a step closer to his door just in case Khalaf made a last-minute dash for the platform.

31

"Euston is the next mainline station, then it's south to Charing Cross," whispered Shepherd. A middle-aged businessman with a briefcase was looking at him curiously but Shepherd couldn't turn away because he had to keep Khalaf in sight. "Get Alpha Romeo Uniforms to both locations ASAP."

"Roger that," said Brewer.

Getting Armed Response Units to the station would take a few minutes at least, possibly longer depending on traffic. But it was the best way of dealing with any attack.

The doors to the train rattled shut. "We're moving again, I'll be losing my signal soon," said Shepherd. The train lurched forward and within seconds they were back in the tunnel.

Shepherd kept glancing at the next carriage, but the two men made no moves to open their backpacks. Khalaf kept looking at the Tube map by his head. Once he looked over at the other man and nodded. The other man smiled thinly and nodded back. Shepherd was tense, knowing that if at any point they began to mount an attack he would have only seconds to get into the next carriage.

As the train began to slow, signalling its approach to Euston, Khalaf turned to face the doors. So did the other man. They were preparing to get off. Shepherd moved to his door, his heart racing. The train burst out of the tunnel and the platform flashed by. Shepherd peered through the window, looking for the exit. He had to know whether he would be in front of Khalaf and the other man, or behind them.

The train stopped and the doors opened. Shepherd took a quick look across at the next carriage. Khalaf was getting off. The woman behind Shepherd decided he wasn't moving quickly enough and nudged him in the back with her shopping bag. Shepherd stepped out on to the platform. The exit was to the left. Khalaf was striding towards it, the bag slung over his shoulder. The other man was about twenty feet ahead.

"Jamie, can you hear me?"

"Loud and clear," said Brewer.

"They've exited at Euston," said Shepherd.

"There's an ARU on the way."

"How far?"

"A few minutes. I'll update you as soon as I know for sure."

Khalaf turned into the pedestrian tunnel that led to the escalators. Shepherd hurried after him. "Heading for the escalators now," said Shepherd.

"What do you think they're up to?"

"I don't know, it could just be they're here to catch a train. Maybe off on a training day. Tell the ARU to approach softly, softly. If they're just passing through the station we don't want them to know they've been spotted. The second Tango is on CCTV here so make sure you get the feeds."

"I'm on it."

Shepherd turned into the tunnel leading to the escalators. Khalaf was already on one. He was walking slowly and steadily up. Shepherd followed him. Khalaf was showing no signs of checking for a tail, but then he had never performed any counter-surveillance techniques all the time that he'd been followed.

"Heading up the escalator now," said Shepherd.

"ARU is two minutes away," said Brewer.

Khalaf reached the top of the escalator. He seemed sure of where he was heading and strode purposefully towards the mainline station. Shepherd carried on walking up the stairs. He put his hand over his mouth as he walked past a woman in a fur coat with a Louis Vuitton wheeled bag. "Tango One is heading into the main station. Over."

"Roger that," said Brewer.

Shepherd stepped off the escalator and hurried after Khalaf.

The station concourse was busy. Dozens of travellers were standing around staring up at the electronic screens waiting for their platform numbers to be announced. Those lucky enough to know where their trains were hurried towards their platforms. Two British Transport Police officers were standing outside a coffee shop, deep in conversation.

Shepherd looked around but couldn't see the man who had been in the carriage with Khalaf. "I've got eyeball on Tango One but I've lost eyeball on Tango Two," said Shepherd.

"Whisky One and Whisky Three are on the Tube heading north," said Brewer. "Whisky Two is coming your way in his taxi."

"I'm sticking with Tango One," said Shepherd.

Khalaf was heading towards the podium in the middle of the station above which was the massive four-sided sign indicating the exits, platforms and toilets. When he reached it, Khalaf stopped and began to remove his backpack.

"Jamie, he's taking his bag off. I think it's about to kick off."

"ARU is one minute away, and there's another en route," said Brewer.

"I can't wait," said Shepherd, breaking into a run.

"Be careful, Spider," said Brewer.

Khalaf bent down and placed his bag on the floor and unzipped it.

Shepherd ran behind a woman in a dark suit and realised too late that she was towing a wheeled cabin bag behind her. He swerved, clipped it with his left leg and stumbled, arms flailing. He managed to recover his balance but narrowly missed colliding with a pensioner with a walking stick who glared at him aggressively, even though he was in his eighties.

Khalaf was tying something around his head. Shepherd sprinted again, his arms pumping like pistons.

Khalaf straightened up. He'd tied a strip of white cloth around his head on which was Arabic writing in black. His eyes were wide and staring and he was muttering to himself. He looked as if he was high on something, amphetamines maybe, taken to give him the energy to do what he was about to do. In his right hand he was holding a machete, at least two feet long with a wooden handle and a strap that he'd wrapped around his wrist so that it wouldn't slip from his grasp. In his left hand he had a combat knife, almost a foot long with a serrated edge on one side.

Everything seemed to be moving in slow motion as the adrenaline surge kicked through Shepherd's system. Khalaf stood up and held his weapons high. No one was paying him any attention. Passengers were either concentrating on the announcement boards, fiddling with their smartphones or were too wrapped up in their own thoughts to be aware of what was going on right under their noses. Two businessmen in suits were so engrossed in their conversation that they walked within feet of Khalaf without noticing him.

Shepherd was about fifty feet away from Khalaf when he threw back his head and screamed, "Allahu Akbar!" at the top of his voice. There was an echo from the far left of the station, but Shepherd realised immediately it wasn't an echo, it was Tango Two. And half a second later there was a third yell, then a fourth, and a fifth.

The passengers nearest Khalaf began to scream and run like sheep suddenly startled by a snapping dog. He raised his machete and sliced at a man in a green anorak holding a tennis bag, catching him on the arm. Blood spurted and the man screamed. He tried to run but seemed to have lost all his coordination and his left leg collapsed and he fell. A woman let go of her suitcase and screamed. Her hands flew up to cover her mouth, her eyes wide and staring. Khalaf turned to look at her and raised his machete again. The man on the ground was screaming in pain and clutching at his injured arm.

The woman backed away, still screaming, and Khalaf took a step towards her. "Allahu Akbar!" he yelled.

He was side on to Shepherd. Shepherd sprinted faster, knowing that he had only a second to act. There was no time for anything fancy, no grabbing or kicking or throwing. He ran full pelt at Khalaf, twisting his shoulder and hitting him in the right side with all his weight. They both went flying, the combat knife clattering to the ground. Shepherd hit the floor and immediately went into a roll, down on to his shoulder and up again, using his momentum to carry him back to his feet. Khalaf was less coordinated and hit the ground like a sack of potatoes. The machete slipped from his grasp but stayed tied to his wrist. As Shepherd stood over him, Khalaf cursed and groped for his weapon. The woman finally regained the use of her legs and began to run, still screaming, for the exit.

There were more shouts of "Allahu Akbar" off to his left amid all the screaming and crying.

Khalaf had the machete in his hand now and murder in his eyes. His fingers tensed around the handle but Shepherd didn't give him the chance to move, he stepped forward with his left leg and kicked the man hard in the head. The skull snapped to the side and the spine snapped like a dead twig. Shepherd knew from the sound and the angle of the neck that Khalaf was dead. He bent down, picked up the combat knife, and began running across the station concourse.

People were running everywhere, mainly towards the exit, but there were some passengers rooted to the spot and unbelievably some were taking videos on their mobile phones.

Shepherd heard frantic screaming off to his left and he started running in that direction, weaving through the panicking crowds. He saw a machete rise and fall followed by the screams of a woman in pain. The attacker was dark skinned and had a strip of cloth around his forehead. He had the same manic look in his eyes that Khalaf had had, and like Khalaf held a machete in his right hand and a knife in his left. He was bearded and wearing a waistcoat over a traditional shalwar kameez, a long grey shirt and baggy off-white pants. The woman he had just slashed was writhing on the ground, her blouse glistening with blood. She had gone into shock, her mouth opening and closing like a stranded goldfish, her eyes staring up at the station roof.

The man with the machete roared in triumph and started running after a businessman in a long coat and heavy briefcase. The businessman realised he was being chased and he turned and shrieked as he threw the briefcase towards his attacker. The case hit the man on the knees but he was so drugged up on amphetamines and adrenaline he didn't register any pain. He jumped over the briefcase and stabbed the businessman in the chest. The businessman fell back, his arms flailing. The machete went up and came slashing down, slicing through the businessman's left sleeve. The businessman turned and tried to run but the machete slashed down again, catching him in the shoulder.

Everyone in the vicinity was screaming now and the attacker was chanting, "Allahu Akbar, Allahu Akbar!" at the top of his voice.

The businessman took a couple of steps and then fell to his knees. The attacker raised his machete again, getting ready to separate the head from the body. Shepherd was a dozen or so feet away and moving fast. He yelled "Police!" more to get a reaction than to identify himself, he just wanted to distract the man. It worked, the man turned to look at him, the machete still held high.

Shepherd had the knife in his right hand and he held it low, moving in close before stabbing upwards. The man stumbled back and slashed down with the machete, narrowly missing Shepherd's wrist. Shepherd's left hand managed to grab the man's sleeve and he pulled him towards himself as he struck with the knife again. This time he felt the knife penetrate the man's clothing and he pushed harder, feeling the blade separate the ribs. The man's mouth opened but no sound came out, then Shepherd grunted and pushed harder, driving the knife upwards towards the heart.

Off to his right Shepherd was aware of the sound of shots being fired and more screams.

The man began to shake and the knife he had been holding clattered to the floor. His weight pitched forward against Shepherd, forcing himself down on the blade. The machete slipped from the man's fingers and swung free on the strap around his wrist. Shepherd felt warm blood gushing over his hand and he gave one final push and the struggling ceased as the blade pierced the heart.

As he pulled out the knife and stepped back, he heard more shots and shouts of "Armed police!" The man fell face down at Shepherd's feet and blood pooled around him as Shepherd stood and looked around. He heard more rapid-fire shots to his left and at the far end of the station he saw three armed police officers shoot down a young Pakistani guy in a blue tracksuit. The rounds smacked into the man's chest and for a second or two seemed to have no effect — the man continued to charge at the officers with his machete held high above his head, but then he suddenly collapsed like a stringless marionette and fell to the ground, shuddering for a second or two before going still.

"Spider, what the hell's happening?" asked Brewer in his ear. "The ARUs are there."

"I see them," said Shepherd. "All good."

"Armed police, drop your weapon now!" The shout came from behind him and Shepherd turned to see two armed policemen dressed all in black walking towards him, their carbines up at the shoulders, fingers inside their trigger guards. "Armed police, drop your weapon!" repeated the one nearest him. The guns were Heckler & Koch G36 assault rifles with thirty-round curved magazines, one of the Metropolitan Police's weapons of choice, but Shepherd had never been a fan. It had a tendency to overheat during firefights, taking a toll on its accuracy with the result that it became pretty much ineffective above a couple of hundred metres.

Announcing they were "armed police" seemed a bit unnecessary considering what they were pointing at him, but Shepherd complied, tossing the knife on to the ground. He knew there was no point in identifying himself, no point claiming that he was one of the good guys, no matter what he said they would have to follow protocol. He sighed and put his hands behind his neck, then knelt down, making no sudden movements.

"Down on the floor!" screamed the second officer.

"I'm already down," Shepherd muttered under his breath.

"Armed police, down on the floor!" screamed the first officer.

Shepherd realised they meant face down so he sighed, slowly took his hands away from his neck and eased himself down, turning his head so that he could watch them approach. They still had their weapons trained on him and their fingers on the triggers.

He heard the pounding of boots and more shouts of "armed police" and Shepherd said a silent prayer that the cops wouldn't put a bullet in him, just to be on the safe side. It wouldn't have been the first time that he had been shot by the cavalry.

Harper arrived in Ireland just before two o'clock in the afternoon. He took a taxi from Dublin airport up to Belfast. There were no checks at all between the north and the south of Ireland and barely any sign that he had crossed a border of any kind. Once at Belfast airport he paid cash for a one-way ticket to Heathrow using a British driving licence as ID. Barely twenty-four

41

hours after receiving the text message in Pattaya he was walking out of Heathrow airport and over to the line of waiting black cabs. A chunky East European woman in a fluorescent jacket asked him where he wanted to go.

"Somewhere hot and sunny," he said.

She frowned. "What?"

"Where are you from?" asked Harper. "Bulgaria? Romania?"

"Where do you want to go?" she asked, ignoring his question.

"She's from Romania, mate," said the driver of the cab nearest to Harper. "Just tell her where you want to go or you'll be there all day."

"Here's the thing," said Harper. "I don't know her, so why should I tell her where I'm going? It's none of her business."

"She just wants to make sure that it's not local. I've been here for three hours waiting for a fare and I don't want to be dropping you down the road."

"You won't be," said Harper. He pulled open the door and climbed in. "Drop me near King's Cross."

"You got a train to catch?"

"Bloody hell, is everyone going to be asking me what I'm doing today?"

The cabbie laughed. "I'm guessing you had a long flight," he said, pulling away from the kerb. The woman in the fluorescent jacket glared after him, muttering under her breath.

Harper had the driver drop him close to King's Cross station. He had a small holdall and he swung it over his shoulder as he walked around for half an hour to make absolutely sure that he wasn't being followed. He used the time to buy three cheap mobile phones and half a dozen SIM cards. Only when he was satisfied that he was clean did he rent a room for cash in a grubby, no-questions-asked hotel. He sent a single text message from one of the new phones and then shaved and showered and changed into a clean shirt before parking himself at the window overlooking the street.

The redevelopment of the hinterland around King's Cross had pushed the prostitutes and the sleazy hotels and bedsits that had catered for them there even further towards the margins. Watching from the window of his room, Harper smiled to himself as he saw Charlotte Button picking her way through the litter in the street and skirting a prostitute negotiating with a furtive, balding man in a city suit. A few moments later, he heard her footsteps on the stairs and a light tap at his door.

He opened the door and ushered her in. She looked around the room and shook her head. "I'm sure you choose places like this just to make me feel uncomfortable," she said.

"I prefer to stay below the radar," he told her. It was starting to get dark so he switched on the light. Button drew the curtains, then looked disdainfully at the dust on her hands. She went through to the cramped bathroom and washed them under the cold tap, looked at the grubby towel and thought better of it, and flicked her hands dry as she walked back into the main room where Harper was sitting on the edge of the bed.

She took off her coat and put it on a hook on the back of the door before she sat down on the one chair in the room. As usual, she was immaculately groomed, with not a hair out of place and dressed in a black Chanel suit with a slim gold Cartier watch on her left wrist.

He had never managed to place her age — she could have been anywhere from early thirties to late forties — but whatever her age she was a bloody attractive woman.

"So, let's get straight down to business," Button said as she rested her briefcase on her knees, clicked open the locks and took out a file and a thick envelope. "As usual, this is completely off the books. On completion of your task, your fee will be paid into your offshore account. Meanwhile . . ." She showed him the corner of a thick wad of notes. "Here's ten thousand dollars in cash for expenses. If you need more, contact me through the drafts folder."

Harper took the envelope from her and made as if to start checking the cash.

"It's all there," Button said, unable to stop the edge in her voice from revealing her irritation.

He grinned as he continued to check the notes. "You can't trust anyone these days, Charlie, you know that." He slid the envelope into his pocket.

"I'll need receipts and —"

Harper interrupted her. "I'll try," he said, "but as you know, in the circles I move in, that isn't always possible."

"I know that — drug dealers, gangsters and terrorists aren't exactly known for their tidy paperwork, are they? And I've never quibbled over the expenses claims you've submitted but, wherever possible, I need receipts to back them up." She gave a self-deprecating smile. "Even spooks have accounts departments to answer to, you know."

"Fine, but you haven't told me what — or who — you want me to do in return for Her Majesty's generosity."

She studied him for a moment. "How much attention have you been paying to the UK news recently?"

He smiled. "As much as I usually do: practically none."

"You really should try to get beyond page three of the *Sun* occasionally, Lex, you'd find it very educational."

"Oh but I do," Harper said. "I always read the sports pages too."

Button had to smile, despite herself. "Anyway, had you been following the news, you'd know that the New IRA have been becoming increasingly active, both in Northern Ireland and here on the mainland."

"The IRA? I thought HMG had followed Lyndon Johnson's famous advice and had got Adams, McGuinness and their boys all inside the tent, pissing outwards, these days."

"They are, but that's only the Provisional IRA. There were — and are — always factions and splinter groups who held out against the peace process. The Real IRA

45

is pretty much defunct now but the New IRA are another story. Two members of the Police Service of Northern Ireland have been shot in recent weeks, a bomb was detonated in Londonderry, killing two people, and a device was left in a backpack at the bus station in Birmingham last week. No warning was given and it was only by a miracle — and the vigilance of an off-duty bus driver — that it was found and destroyed in a controlled explosion. Had it gone off, as it was timed to do, during the rush hour, scores of people might have been killed.

"The New IRA are very well funded and, as a result, are increasingly well supplied with weapons and explosives. And as usual, the various agencies here, in Northern Ireland and in the Republic often seem to be more interested in marking out their turf, scoring points off each other and protecting their sources than they are in actually eliminating the problem. So, we've decided to bypass the usual channels." She fixed him with her cold gaze. "We need to cut off the supply route of funds and weapons to the New IRA at source."

"So my task is?" Harper said.

"You are to dispose of two targets. Their real names are Declan O'Brien and Michael Walsh but to keep it simple let's call them Mick One and Mick Two." She opened the file and began sliding surveillance photographs and police mugshots across the table towards him. The first was of a solidly built man who looked to be in his early forties, with thinning sandy-coloured hair and a face that bore the marks of heavy drinking and a few fist fights, if the clumsily set broken nose was anything to go by. "Declan O'Brien . . ."

"AKA Mick One."

". . . is a New IRA activist," Button said, ignoring the interruption. "He is a key figure on their Army Council and eager to establish himself as the Gerry Adams for the twenty-first century, but the only way he's going to achieve that is with a significant escalation of the New IRA's campaign against British rule. Our past successes in penetrating the organisation and raiding their arms caches left them with few remaining weapons or explosives but, as I said, they are now very well funded and O'Brien is actively scouting the illegal arms trade, looking for a variety of weapons and explosives, including heavy weapons."

"And the source of their funds?"

"Is your second target. They are being funded in the main by Michael Walsh — Mick Two," she said, as she saw Harper poised to interrupt again. She passed him another photograph, this time of a paunchy, grey-haired but still young-looking man in a sharp business suit. "He's a Boston Irish-American multi-millionaire and idealist, who imbibed all the IRA myths with his mother's milk, and is now using his wealth to try to make them come true. He's been actively fundraising in the US and getting his rich Irish-American friends to chip in. Although he's your second target, his American citizenship makes this an especially sensitive operation, so to avoid any possibility of our being implicated, the op must take place well away from the UK and without any identifiable trace of a UK connection. The way that

O'Brien's death is perceived is less important — though any evidence or even suspicion of a UK connection will inevitably lead to the New IRA attempting a 'spectacular' by way of reprisal — but we'd prefer that Walsh's death appears to be a falling-out among thieves, not an assassination."

Harper nodded. "Let's see if I can set it up in Germany then. Anything that makes the Yanks pissed off with the Krauts has got to be good news for you, right?"

Button held up a hand. "Where you carry out the op is up to you, I don't need or want to know the details. But if you do carry it out in Germany, just make sure the German intelligence agencies don't get the slightest whiff of what's happening either before or after the event. Not only would that catastrophically damage our relations with them, but the German agencies are also as leaky as a rusty sieve and penetrated by US agents at every level." She paused. "Why Germany?"

"I've an acquaintance there — a friend would be stretching it — who might prove very useful. She's ex-Stasi and not only knows where all the bodies are buried, but some of the weapons too."

"Just be aware," Button said, "that while you have your 'Get Out of Jail Free' card as far as all the UK agencies are concerned, that does not extend to any of our European partners. If you get picked up by the Bundespolizei, the Federal Intelligence Service or the Military Counterintelligence Service in Germany or indeed those of any other allied or hostile country, you're on your own and, if challenged, we'll deny any knowledge of your existence."

"Understood," Harper said.

"This isn't just about the two men, Alex. We need more. A lot more."

Harper nodded. "I'm listening."

"We need the organisation damaged, ideally damaged beyond repair. We want you to hit them financially, we want them in-fighting, not knowing who they can trust, we want them crippled as a terrorist organisation."

"Bloody hell, Charlie, you're not asking much."

"Money's no object and you can subcontract out as much of it as you need. With all that's going on in the world just now, the last thing HMG needs is trouble in Ireland again. This needs to be nipped in the bud, and by nipped I mean killed. One more piece of information that may be useful." Button passed another photograph across the table to him, this time of a heavily made up, twenty-year-old woman with her half-undone blouse revealing part of a tattoo at her cleavage, and an inch of black hair showing at the roots of her peroxide blonde hair. "O'Brien has a daughter."

"Not bad looking in a rugged sort of way. I suppose we'll have to call her Mick One And A Half."

Button again ignored the interruption. "Her name's Bridie and she works for the London end of the family business, collecting cash for the boys, but she's eager to do more for them. We've had her under observation for quite some time. She's a bit of a loose cannon, a hard drinker like her father, a borderline alcoholic in fact, but she's chafing at her slow rate of progress up the New IRA food chain. Her dad loves her, of course, but the rest of the New IRA's Army Council see her as a bit of a spoilt daddy's girl. She's always trying to find ways to improve her reputation with them but she's also perpetually short of cash and constantly looking for opportunities to make some money on the side. She could be your way in. But she's not a target."

Harper nodded. "Understood. But we're missing a trick, aren't we? What if we not only eliminate your two problems but find a way to put a serious hole in the New IRA's existing funds as well?"

Button studied him for a moment. "Go on."

"We make my legend that I'm a major criminal, a gang boss and arms dealer, a Swiss citizen, but of unknown East European origins, and if they can persuade me to do business with them, I'm just the man to supply anything they need."

"And if they start asking awkward questions about your background?"

Harper smiled. "Seriously? I'll just do what any gang boss and arms dealer would do in those circumstances: I'll tell them to fuck off. Come on, Charlie, do you think the New IRA men would answer any questions about their origins if I was dumb enough to ask any? They'll do some checking of my legend, of course, but if your people are up to their job, that won't throw up any red alerts, will it?"

He waited for her nod of assent before continuing. "I use the promise of supplying weapons as bait to draw them in, but instead of killing them straight away, I'll set up a deal with them." He paused. "Actually, make that two deals. I'll make it a condition that I supply them with some lesser weapons first — shorts, semi-automatics, that sort of thing — to establish trust on both sides. They'll all be ex-Soviet or East European and untraceable, and I'll plant tracking devices so that you can follow them to wherever they're hiding their arms. That deal will cost them some modest funds but I'll then do the big deal with them for some serious kit: plastic explosive, heavy machine guns, mortars, missiles, whatever they want basically."

"Sounds to me like you're over-egging the pudding."

"You want to hit them financially, then there has to be a con. And a good one. This way we get to take a serious chunk of money from them. And you get to bust all their arms caches."

Button frowned. "I don't know, it's risky. The more layers you add, the greater the risk of compromise or cock-up."

"And the greater the rewards when it pays off. This way, you get exactly what you want. You're not just eliminating a terrorist and his money-man, you're also giving the New IRA a whole savage kick in the balls. As well as the key people they'll lose, you'll hit their funds, empty their weapons caches and sow an atmosphere of mistrust and paranoia among the survivors. They'll be wondering how were they betrayed, who grassed them up? It could make the whole organisation implode." He studied her expression for a moment. "Relax, Charlie, like any other good con, the marks will sell themselves on the deal because they'll be desperate to get their hands on what they think I've got to sell."

There was a long silence. Button's brow furrowed as she thought through the implications and pitfalls. Harper merely leaned back with his hands behind his head and waited.

"Okay," she said eventually. "Tell me what you need."

Harper grinned and leaned forward. "A Swiss passport in a generic East European name — Müller would do — and two credit cards, one Amex and one Visa because, contrary to their advertising slogans, Amex doesn't always do nicely. If you want to throw in a debit card backed by a pleasingly well-lubricated account, I wouldn't say no either, because this job is going to need a lot of walking around money. And some of your comms wonder kit would be handy too, providing you're still sure the Yanks can't crack it."

"That's all doable. How many sets will you need?"

Harper did a quick mental calculation. "I'll need a research and surveillance team of four people, to cut my time on the ground and identify the routines and weaknesses in the targets' security and locate and screen the locations we'll need to use, so five sets including mine — no wait, make it six," he said, studying the photograph of O'Brien's daughter again. "There's someone else who might be very useful."

Button passed him four more photos. "There are a few more people you need to be able to ID." They were all thickset, tough-looking men, in their mid-thirties to mid-forties.

"Nice-looking boys," Harper said. "I'm guessing they're the muscle."

She nodded. "Some or all of them will probably be body-guarding the targets."

"So, no dramas if any of them get caught in the crossfire?"

"None at all," Button said. "They've all got form: bombings, knee-cappings, shootings, arson. Nasty pieces of work, one and all."

"Right, it'll take me forty-eight hours to sort out a plan and brief my team," Harper said. "Then we're in business."

As Button snapped her briefcase shut, they heard a furious argument erupting down the hallway, with a woman screaming obscenities and a man's voice swearing back. A door slammed with a violence that made the walls shake and they heard heavy footsteps going down the stairs. Button gave a weary shake of her head. "Right, I'll have a Swiss passport in the name of Müller and the rest of your legend delivered to you by this time tomorrow. Same place?"

"Why not?" Harper, said with a broad smile. "It's already starting to feel like home."

Button put her coat back on, flashed him a tight smile, and left. Harper stood at the window, peering through a crack in the curtains to watch her go. He saw her pull three anti-surveillance moves as she headed down the road and he nodded his approval. She might well be behind a desk most of the time, but Charlie Button had never forgotten her tradecraft.

Harper waited fifteen minutes then put on his coat and took a walk to a nearby park, a patch of urban wasteland with its patchy grass strewn with litter, broken glass and blackened patches where fires had been lit. A group of half a dozen youths in hoodies gave him curious looks and muttered to each other, but Harper stared at them until they looked away. He made four calls on one phone and then removed the SIM card, broke it in half, and tossed it into an overflowing waste bin.

They took Shepherd to Islington Police Station in the back of a windowless van with his wrists bound together with plastic ties. Two hard-faced specialist firearms officers sat in the back with him, cradling their carbines. That seemed like overkill and he doubted that they'd even be able to get a shot off in the confines of the van, but he said nothing. There was nothing he could say. They were just cogs in the machine and weren't able to make any decisions that would affect the outcome of what was happening. Even if he could convince them that he was an MI5 officer they didn't have the authority to release him. Shepherd just went into shutdown mode, sitting quietly with his head down as he waited for it all to be over. They had taken the transceiver off him, and the earpiece, but he'd had just enough time to tell Brewer that he was about to be taken into custody.

The armed cops said nothing; they just stared at him stonily. Even if he spoke to them he doubted they would reply. He hadn't been cautioned or charged which meant that anything he did say would only cause them problems down the line. They knew that everything had to be done by the book, which meant that any questioning had to comply with the Police and Criminal Evidence Act.

The van stopped and he heard a metal gate rattle back then the van moved forward and stopped again. He heard muffled voices and then the rear doors opened and a uniformed officer in a stab-vest unlocked the cage to allow one of the armed officers out. The second armed officer motioned for Shepherd to get out. Shepherd shuffled along the bench seat and stepped down. He was grabbed by the arms by two more officers and pulled roughly away from the van. He blinked in the sunlight. There were half a dozen armed officers all pointing their weapons at him. He was in a police car park and from the windows of the main building, dozens of faces looked down.

They bundled him a few yards to a ramp that led to a grey door where there were two more armed cops. They hustled him down a corridor and into a custody suite where a grey-haired sergeant stood behind a computer terminal. The sergeant was wearing glasses but he looked over the top of them to scrutinise Shepherd.

"This is him?" he said. He had a West Country drawl that suggested haystacks and cider. His workstation was raised about a foot off the ground so that he was able to look down on Shepherd, even though he was several inches shorter.

"It's him," said one of the armed cops.

There were half a dozen uniformed officers standing by a door, all staring at Shepherd. One of them was an inspector. He was in his late twenties and had fast-track graduate-entry written all over him, his uniform neatly pressed, his hat on perfectly straight, his hands clasped behind his back as if he were on parade.

"Name?" the sergeant asked Shepherd.

Shepherd ignored him. He looked over at the inspector, the highest-ranking officer in the room. "Can I have a word, inspector?"

The inspector frowned. "What?"

"I need to talk to you in private."

"That's not going to happen," said the officer. He jutted his chin up as if to reinforce his decision.

"I have some information that you need to hear."

"I would suggest that you do not say anything until you have a solicitor present."

"There's no need for that," said Shepherd. "This is all going to be sorted out in the next hour or so. Just put me in a room or a cell if you'd prefer and I'd really appreciate a cup of coffee and a sandwich if you could grab one from the canteen. I haven't eaten for a while."

The inspector looked across at the custody sergeant. "I think we need the doctor in here to assess his mental condition," he said.

"Look, I'm just trying to make this easier for you," said Shepherd. "Within the next hour someone is going to come and take care of this. They'll be accompanied by a senior officer and he's going to want to know what you did in the way of processing. And trust me, the more you do now the more you're going to have to undo down the line. Just let me sit in a cell for an hour and I'll be out of your hair."

The inspector looked at Shepherd coldly for several seconds, then nodded at the sergeant. "Fingerprint him, DNA him and bag his clothes."

"Fine," said Shepherd.

"Name?" asked the custody sergeant.

Shepherd stared at the officer but didn't reply.

"We can do this the easy way or we can do it the hard way, but the end result is going to be the same."

Shepherd still said nothing.

The sergeant waved a constable over. "Turn out his pockets," said the sergeant.

The constable pulled a wallet from Shepherd's back pocket. He took out a driving licence and compared the photograph to Shepherd's face before handing it to the sergeant. The sergeant pushed his spectacles further up his nose and smiled as he examined the licence. "Craig Brannan. Date of birth, July fifteenth 1975." He smiled down at Shepherd. "See now, that wasn't too difficult, was it?"

Shepherd continued to stare at the sergeant but kept his mouth shut. He'd done all he could do, said all he could, now it was just a matter of waiting for it to be over.

"Ever been in trouble with the police before, Mr Brannan?" asked the sergeant. He tapped away on his computer for several seconds and then smiled thinly. "Apparently not." He looked at the constable. "Anything else in his pockets?"

The constable fished out Shepherd's keys, two sets, one for his flat and one for his car. He put them down on the counter. "That's everything."

The sergeant looked down at Shepherd. "Your driving licence has your current address, does it, Mr Brannan?"

Shepherd stared sullenly at the sergeant but didn't reply.

The sergeant smiled. "Well, we'll know soon enough, won't we." He nodded at the constable. "Right, let's process Mr Brannan as quickly as possible, shall we? I'm sure the antiterrorism boys will be wanting a word with him soon enough."

Shepherd spent just thirty minutes in the cell. They had taken a DNA swab from the inside of his cheeks, scrapings from under his fingernails, swabbed the palms and backs of his hands, removed his clothing and given him a white paper suit and paper shoe covers for his feet. They had made him place his hands on the LiveScan fingerprint recognition screen and taken his prints and photographed him from the front and sides including a full body photograph. They didn't give him a coffee or a sandwich but every five minutes or so an eye would appear at the peephole to check on him.

Eventually the door opened and the custody sergeant waved for him to stand up. "You're free to go," he said. He avoided eye contact with Shepherd as he motioned for him to leave.

Shepherd stepped out of the cell where a uniformed chief superintendent was standing next to a man and a woman. She was blonde and pretty. She wore a black suit with a white blouse and had a large Prada black leather bag over her shoulder. Shepherd doubted she could have been older than twenty-five, but she carried herself with more confidence than the chief superintendent who was probably twice her age. Her companion was in his early thirties, his hair slightly too long to be fashionable, in a dark brown leather jacket and carrying a black leather holdall. The audience that had been gathered in the custody suite before — including the uniformed inspector — had gone, as had the armed cops.

"We're sorry this has taken so long," said the girl, offering a well-manicured hand with scarlet nails. "Katy."

Shepherd doubted that Katy was her real name, but he shook hands.

"This is Bernard."

Bernard nodded and shook hands with Shepherd.

"Ms Button sends her apologies," said Katy. "As I'm sure you can understand she's a bit busy at the moment."

"Not a problem," said Shepherd.

Bernard handed him the holdall. "Your clothes are already being processed so it'll take us time to get them back. In the meantime there's a change of clothes in there and we've got a car outside to run you home."

Shepherd unzipped the bag and looked inside. Black jeans, a blue polo shirt, socks and underwear, and a pair of Nikes. He looked at the training shoes and smiled when he saw that they were his size. There were times when MI5 could be so bloody efficient, and other times when they couldn't organise the proverbial piss-up in a brewery.

"There's a room over there where you can change," said the chief superintendent. "We'll have your belongings in a minute or two." He looked uncomfortable, as if he wished he were anywhere else but in the custody suite at that moment.

"Thanks," said Shepherd.

The chief superintendent extended his hand. "If you don't mind, I'd like to shake your hand. What you did out there, you saved a lot of lives. I'm sorry for the way you were treated."

Shepherd shook his hand firmly. "No problem, your men were just doing their jobs."

"I appreciate your understanding," said the officer. He turned to address the custody sergeant. "This lady and gentleman are to have full access to anything they want, including the CCTV footage. Whatever they want, they get. Understood?"

The custody sergeant nodded. "Yes, sir."

Bernard went behind the counter and started tapping on the custody sergeant's keyboard. Katy took Shepherd over to the room where he could change into his clothes. "We'll be here for a while removing all trace of you from the system," she said. "Your car is in the car park, the driver knows where to go. Ms Button said she'd call you later this evening."

Shepherd smiled. "I'll look forward to that."

The MI5 car dropped Shepherd outside his apartment in Battersea. The two-bedroom flat had impressive views over the Thames and was some compensation for the fact that he had been away from his Hereford home for the best part of three months while overseeing the surveillance operation. He took the lift up to the ninth floor and let himself in. The burglar alarm began to beep and he tapped in the four-digit code before heading to the shower to wash the smell of the cells off him.

Later he cooked himself a steak and ate it with a salad and a bottle of lager as he watched the various news channels cover the Euston station attacks. Sky News seemed to have the best police sources as they had already identified Khalaf and had sent a camera crew to his address in Stoke Newington. They had also managed to get hold of footage from half a dozen of the mobile phones that had been filming the events at the station. The images were shaky and blurred but gave a good indication of the panic that the attackers had caused. There was one video of one of the attackers slashing at a teenage girl with his machete, his face contorted with anger, then the attacker had turned towards whoever was holding the phone and the picture shook and went blank. Sky showed the short videos again and again with various commentaries provided by the presenters.

The BBC's coverage seemed to be concerned mainly with so-called terrorist experts, mainly academics, pontificating about the spread of Islamic fundamentalism and making wild guesses as to what the authorities would do in the wake of the attack. There were interviews with Muslim groups who were placing flowers at the scene and a statement from the Muslim Council of Great Britain saying how they deplored the attacks. CNN had managed to find two American tourists who had been at the station and ran the interview with them at least twice an hour even though they had fled as soon as the attacks had started.

The station had been closed for several hours and armed police had appeared at all mainline stations, which had caused travel chaos that had spilled over into rush hour and there were still long delays getting commuters out of the capital. The Mayor of London had given a short press conference, appealing for calm and thanking the police for their sterling work. "Londoners will not be intimidated by random acts of violence," he had said, and went on to say that he took pride from the fact that London was one of the most ethnically rich cities in the world, and that would remain its strength.

The Met's Commissioner also gave a press conference saying that security would be increased at all transport hubs in the capital but that he did not expect any further attacks. Shepherd hoped that he was right, but he knew that MI5 was tracking at least a dozen other groups like Khalaf's in the capital. He wanted Londoners to carry on as usual, but to be vigilant.

It wasn't until late evening that his phone finally rang.

"Spider, so sorry, as you can imagine it's been a bit hectic here." It was Charlotte Button, his MI5 boss.

"There's a lot of flack flying around, I suppose."

"Not as much as you'd think. Anyway, how are you?"

"Fine and dandy."

"No injuries?"

"Luckily the Met's finest managed to keep their impulses in check and not shoot me. But yeah, it did get a bit frantic and I was standing there with a bloodstained knife in my hand."

"Have you been watching it on the TV?"

"Sure. They're not showing any CCTV from Euston station?"

"No, and they won't be until we've been through it. Don't worry, you'll be edited out of it."

"I hope so," said Shepherd. "The last thing I need is to be on Sky News and plastered over the tabloids. That would put a real damper on my undercover career."

"It's being taken care of as we speak. Anyone who saw what you did has been tracked down and approached and they've all agreed to keep it to themselves. You met Katy and Bernard? They took care of everything at Islington. You're out of the system there now. Look, we need to meet, obviously, but I'm going to be flat out for the rest of the night. We've got a briefing with Number Ten and there's a Joint Terrorism Analysis Centre meeting after that. I'll be here until the early hours. Why don't you get some sleep and I'll see you tomorrow?"

"Saturday?"

"This is important and there is some time pressure. Let's make it morning so that you can head back to Hereford before lunch."

"Do I come to you?"

"I'm out and about tomorrow, let's make it outside of Thames House. I'll text you the location. Sweet dreams." The line went dead.

Shepherd put down his phone. He doubted that his dreams would be sweet. The adrenaline was still coursing through his system and images of what had happened at Euston station were constantly flashing through his mind. He looked at his watch. Ten thirty. It was late, and running at night in London wasn't the most pleasant of experiences, with drunks shouting advice and encouragement and pedestrians constantly fearing that pounding feet signified an impending mugging. There was a well-equipped gym in his building that was open all hours so he changed into a T-shirt and shorts and headed down for an hour or two's exercise.

A double-knock on the hotel door woke Harper from a dreamless sleep. He wrapped a towel round his waist and padded across the threadbare carpet and peered through the security peephole. It was an anonymous grey man in a dark suit, carrying an aluminium briefcase. Harper opened the door. The man scrutinised Harper's face for a couple of seconds as if satisfying himself that he had the right man, then handed over the briefcase. Harper took it and closed the door. He sat on the bed, opened the case and checked the contents. There was the passport in the name of Müller, the comms kit he had requested and the necessary backup to his legend: credit cards, driving licence, a receipt from a Geneva restaurant, and a

Photoshopped and carefully cracked and crumpled snapshot of "Herr Müller" and a blonde woman in front of the Kremlin.

Harper stowed the briefcase under his bed, then showered, shaved and changed into a clean shirt and jeans. He went outside, bought a copy of the *Sun* and found a café down a side street that served him a full English breakfast and half-decent coffee. He polished off the eggs, bacon, sausage, fried bread and mushrooms and drank three cups of coffee as he read the paper, spending most of his time on the sports pages. As he'd told Button, Harper wasn't generally concerned with politics or world affairs. So long as he and his friends were okay, he didn't really care what was going on in the world around him. He had never voted, he hadn't paid tax since leaving the army, and even if pressed he doubted he'd be able to name more than a handful of the men and women who ran the country.

After finishing his third cup of coffee he paid his bill and spent a couple of hours wandering around London, keeping an ever-watchful eye out for tails. On the way back to his hotel he stopped off at a Pret A Manger and bought a dozen sandwiches and five bottles of water.

Shepherd paid for his takeaway coffee and tea and took them outside, then jogged across the road taking care not to spill them. The door that led to the upper floors was between a florist's and a charity shop. It had been a while since Button had summoned him to the location for a meeting and the last time he'd been there the charity shop had been a butcher's. The main door had been repainted, too. It had been white but was now a pillar-box red. The three brass nameplates were still at the side of the door, as was the entryphone with three buttons. Shepherd pressed the middle button and waved up at the CCTV camera that monitored the entrance. The door buzzed and Shepherd went inside. Button had the door to the office open as he climbed the stairs. She smiled at the cups he was holding.

"You are so sweet," she said.

She was wearing a dark blue suit with a skirt cut just above the knee and matching blue high heels. He handed her the tea and she ushered him inside and closed the door.

"Wasn't this a SOCA safe house?" he asked.

"For a while," she answered. "But not any more. The NCA doesn't have much use for safe houses."

The National Crime Agency took over from the Serious Organised Crime Agency in October 2013 to become the UK's equivalent of the FBI, supposedly leading the fight against organised crime, human trafficking, drugs and cyber crime as well as being the main point of contact with international agencies such as Europol and Interpol. SOCA had been a spectacular failure and as far as Shepherd could see the NCA didn't appear to be doing much better.

The office was lined with filing cabinets and volumes of tax law. There were four desks, one in each corner of the room, and a door leading to another office. Button went through the second door and sat at a high-backed executive chair behind a large oak desk. "I know you're never comfortable in Thames House," she said.

"It's not about being comfortable, it's about being recognised," he said as he sat on one of the two wooden chairs on his side of the desk. "You never know who's going to see you coming and going. And as I'm undercover a lot of the time it's better I don't get seen by the staff there."

"I absolutely understand," said Button. "And I prefer to get out of the office myself." She looked around and smiled. "Of course, all I've done is swap one office for another. I would have suggested a nice lunch but of course then we wouldn't be able to talk freely. So, job well done yesterday."

Shepherd shrugged. "I'm not sure that allowing a terrorist incident to go ahead counts as a job well done."

"There were no indications that it was about to kick off; we were still at the intel-gathering phase," she said. "Nothing they had done or said suggested that they were ready to move."

"Maybe we missed something."

"Maybe we did. But at the end of the day we stopped them and I think we both know it could have been so much worse," she said. "We have a dozen walking wounded and four in intensive care. But at the end of the day no one died, and that's down to you."

"Four people died," said Shepherd. "And I killed two of them."

"Let me rephrase that then," said Button. "No one who matters died. I hope you're not shedding any tears over four dead jihadists."

"I'm not."

"I'll happily arrange sessions with Caroline Stockmann if you want," she said. "You're almost due your biannual psyche evaluation anyway."

Shepherd shook his head. "I'm fine. What about the one who's still alive?"

"Under armed guard in University College Hospital. As soon as he can be moved he'll be in Belmarsh and we'll start questioning him. But as you know, these days we're not allowed to raise our voices or hurt their feelings, so I doubt he'll say much."

"Do we know who they are? I recognised Khalaf but I've no idea who the other one was. He was a totally new face to me."

"The one still alive is Mahmud, the Somalian from Ealing. The dead ones are cleanskins, not known to us and, so far as we know, have never been abroad."

"How did we miss them?" asked Shepherd. A cleanskin was someone not known to the security services, a terrorist who had somehow managed to stay beneath the radar.

"We think the second guy you took out was the guy that Mahmud and Khalaf were talking to online. We've got our technical boys working on his phone as we speak. So Khalaf and Mahmud spoke to the third guy, the one you took out, and the third guy spoke to the cleanskins. They're copying the terrorist cell model that the IRA used so well during the Troubles."

"We were lucky," said Shepherd.

"We have to be," said Button. "There are dozens of cells planning similar atrocities every day of the week across the UK. We can be as professional as we want but at the end of the day sometimes it comes down to luck. If you hadn't been on surveillance yesterday it could have all gone down very differently. Still, as I said, no civilians were killed, four of the jihadists are dead and one is in custody, so it's drinks all round."

Shepherd shrugged. "I guess so." He sipped his coffee. "I don't understand why they do it, these guys. Why attack civilians when there are so many high-profile targets? Track down Tony Blair and hack him to death — that I could understand. Go for the politicians. Go for the army, that I understand. But why attack civilians? I just don't get it."

"The clue's in the name," she said. "They're terrorists. It's about inspiring terror. If they kill a soldier in uniform then the public can convince themselves that it won't happen to them. But a truly random attack scares everyone."

"But achieves nothing. It makes no sense to me. I don't think it ever will. What do they want? Sharia law? The UK turned into an Islamic state? That's never going to happen. Troops out of Iraq and Afghanistan? They've got that. At least with the IRA you know what they wanted. A united Ireland. This lot? It's like they just want to hurt people." He sipped his coffee and shrugged. "I'm overthinking it, right?"

"There's no easy answer," said Button. "That's the problem. All we can do is be vigilant."

"Well you say that, Charlie, but maybe we should stop British citizens from flying into these war zones because they're sure as hell not going as tourists.

They're going to be trained and this is what happens when they get back."

"They hadn't all been to Syria, Spider. And so far as we know, none of them had been for training in Pakistan. There's something else at work here and frankly I'm as confused about it all as you are." She forced a smile. "Still, ours not to reason why." She swung her briefcase up on to the table. "Anyway, there's a job that requires your undercover talents in a more traditional area," she said. She opened her briefcase, took out a file and pushed a photograph across the table towards him. It was a black and white surveillance picture, taken with a long lens. A small man, balding and with round-lensed spectacles, was climbing into the back of a limousine. Another man, taller and wearing a dark coat, was holding an umbrella over the man to keep off the rain.

"This is Max Jansen. His daughter was on Malaysia Airlines Flight Seventeen."

"Shit."

"Yeah. She was eighteen and was flying to Bali with a couple of friends for a gap year. They were going to work for an animal charity."

Shepherd grimaced. Malaysia Airlines Flight 17 had been shot down in the sky above the Ukraine-Russia border in July 2014, killing all 298 passengers and crew. Shepherd remembered seeing television footage of the aftermath of the crash near Torez in the Ukraine. It was heartbreaking seeing the personal belongings scattered among the wreckage, the larger body parts covered by sheets. The Ukrainian forces refused to let air crash

70

investigators near the site but seemed to have no problem in allowing Ukrainian peasants to sift through the wreckage looking for valuables.

"Jansen blames Putin for the attack. He holds him personally responsible."

"Sounds reasonable," said Shepherd. It was generally accepted that the passenger plane had been shot down by pro-Russian separatists using a Buk surface-to-air missile. The Russians had blamed the Ukraine forces for the attack, but the Ukrainian government claimed the missile had been launched by Russian troops under orders from the Russian government. Shepherd tended to believe the Ukrainians.

"Jansen was involved with a Dutch campaign to force the Russians to accept responsibility for the incident, but he recently fell out with them," said Button. "According to the AIVD, Jansen has decided to take matters into his own hands."

"In what way?" The AIVD was the Algemene Inlichtingen en Veiligheidsdienst, which translated as the General Intelligence and Security Service, the Dutch equivalent of MI5.

"He wants to hire an assassin to take out Putin."

Shepherd laughed out loud. "Oh come on, he's delusional."

"He's got the money. He's got all the money he needs. He set up a software company that Microsoft paid millions for in the nineties and he used that to launch a video games and app developer that is now one of the biggest companies in Holland."

"Never heard of him."

"You won't have heard of most of the really rich," said Button. "Not the smart ones, anyway. They keep a low profile. You wouldn't find Jansen buying a football club or building a super yacht. But trust me, he's worth billions. And he's in the market for a contract killer."

Shepherd smiled and shook his head. "You don't take out a man like Putin with a contract killer," he said. "It doesn't work like that. He's better protected than the US President."

"US presidents have been shot," said Button.

"And the Secret Service has learned lessons from it. But Putin is . . ." He shrugged. "He's untouchable. He knows how hated he is and he does what's necessary to make sure no one dangerous gets anywhere near him. He and the rest of the men who run Russia are protected by the Federal Protective Service. There are thirty thousand men and women in the FPS and their only mission is to protect Putin and about thirty others. In contrast there are about five thousand in the American Secret Service and they have to protect the president and the vice-president and their families, every former president and their families, plus visiting heads of state. Literally hundreds of people. And they have to deal with currency counterfeiting. But it's not just about the numbers, Charlie. Putin runs Russia with an iron fist in a steel glove. A hired killer can't just ride into Moscow and take a pot shot at him. I'd say he's probably the best protected man in the world."

"Putin's coming to London next month," said Button. "It's a long-standing fixture, a meeting with the prime minister."

"Ah," said Shepherd.

"There will be an FPS unit with the delegation, of course. But slimmed down from what he's used to, and unarmed of course."

"If the threat is real, cancel the visit."

"The threat is real, but cancellation isn't an option. How would it look if we had to admit that we couldn't protect a visiting dignitary?"

"A darn sight better than if a visiting dignitary was assassinated here."

Button flashed him a cold smile. "We're hoping it won't come to that, obviously. Holland isn't exactly choc-a-bloc with assassins, so he's looking further afield."

"Looking how, exactly? Advertising on Craigslist?"

Button didn't bother smiling this time. "He's using a middleman in Amsterdam. Guy by the name of Lucas Smit." She handed him another photograph, this of a slightly plump man in his forties with sandy hair. "Smit's an underworld fixer. He's been asking around in Berlin and Paris and recently he approached a contract killer in London who apparently turned the job down."

"How do you know this?"

"Which bit?"

"The fact that the job was turned down."

"The AIVD have a surveillance team on Smit. He's very careful but someone in London slipped up and left a message on his voicemail, saying they weren't interested."

"Who turned the job down?"

"The AIVD don't know. Smit was calling a throwaway mobile in London. They have a voice but voice-matching hasn't come up with anything."

Shepherd exhaled slowly. "There's not many would take on a job like that," he said. "There'd be a manhunt like there's never been before."

"It would be a retirement job," said Button. "A last hurrah."

"It's all very short notice, though."

Button gave him another photograph. A man in his early thirties, square-jawed and with slabs of white teeth that suggested American dentistry. "Robert Tyler. Former Delta Force. Went private a few years ago, initially for a US black company but for the last two years has been totally freelance, working for guys like Smit. We think he accepted the Putin contract six months ago but he was killed last week."

"By the Russians?"

"We don't know. The cops found his body in a house in Queens. Two shots to the chest, one to the face. No forensics. It looks like a professional hit."

"Getting killed is an occupational hazard, it goes with the job. Do the Russians know that there's a contract out on Putin?"

"If they do, we didn't tell them."

"But they could have found out on their own and taken care of it."

"True. But then wouldn't you have expected them to have taken out Smit as well? Or cancelled Putin's visit?"

"You could always ask them," said Shepherd.

74

"I assume you're joking," said Button. "We're not in the business of sharing intel with the Russians, and vice versa. We're not even sure that Tyler was connected to the Putin contract. It's purely circumstantial. But the facts are that immediately after Tyler's death, Smit went into overdrive."

"Did this Smit mention a number?"

Button shook her head. "He's far too careful to be caught discussing money but we're assuming millions."

"Tens of, I would have thought. And even then . . ." He shrugged. "I can't see contractors lining up to take the job. You'd get the Walter Mittys and the chancers, the guys trying to make a name for themselves, but the real professionals would see too much downside."

"AIVD want us to come up with someone," said Button quietly.

"I'd already figured that out," said Shepherd. He smiled. "But come on, what would my way in be? I call up Smit and say that I've heard he's looking for an assassin?"

"There's a network of middlemen like Smit right across Europe, and beyond. I think we can get you into the loop."

"Charlie, at that level it's all word of mouth. You need to know someone who knows someone who knows someone."

"We think we have a way in. There's a guy in custody in Ras al-Khaimah, in the Emirates, who was caught trying to kill a minor royal. The prince had fallen out with another prince and it all got nasty. The guy they caught is behind half a dozen high-profile kills over the past ten years. He's never been identified, no one knows what he looks like. You become him."

"That's hellish risky. I won't know who knows him."

"No one knows him. And certainly Smit doesn't, and that's all that matters."

"And how do you get me next to Smit?"

"A middleman in London who sometimes works for Five."

"This is getting very, very messy, Charlie."

"It's a bit complicated, but there's a logic to it. The killer's known only as The Dane."

"Because he's from Denmark or because he's a big dog?"

Button smiled coldly. "I know you're trying to lighten the moment, but this is complicated enough as it is. No, he's not Danish. At least he doesn't have a Danish passport. When they caught him in Ras al-Khaimah he had Irish, Canadian and Australian passports. Their police liaised with Interpol and they ran his prints and DNA through all the EU databases but they drew a blank. The passports all had his photographs but different names so no one knows his real name or where he came from."

"What if The Dane gets out?"

"He won't," said Button. "They were going to take off his head and that still might happen. But until then he's in a tiny concrete box being fed through a hole in his door. No visitors, no doors, just the occasional beating to break up the monotony."

"But what if word gets out that he's being held there?"

Button shook her head. "It won't. The request for help from Interpol was made at a very high level. There's probably fewer than a dozen people who know that he's been caught, and all of them are good guys."

"So the plan is to get your man in London to introduce me to Smit and then Smit puts me in touch with the father?"

"Basically, yes."

"And will the London guy know that I'm not The Dane?"

"Probably not."

"Probably not?"

"If we can have the London guy believe you are The Dane, his recommendation would carry more weight."

"And how do we do that?"

"We're working on it," said Button. "I'm hoping that in a few days we'll be ready to move."

Shepherd nodded. "I'll need all the intel on The Dane, obviously."

She opened her briefcase and passed him a grey thumb-drive. "Everything you need is on there," she said. "I'll get a legend drawn up and provide you with all the documentation you need."

"How does The Dane operate?"

"You mean, how does he kill? Always at a distance. That's his trademark. So sniping or bombs. He's a crack shot with a sniper's rifle and an expert bombmaker. That's why until Ras al-Khaimah, he'd never been caught or even identified. His bombs have been especially productive. One of his kills in the States used a bomb with a timer to make it active, cross referenced with a GPS signal from the victim's phone. The bomb was in place for more than a month until The Dane activated it and then when the target arrived . . . bang!"

"Then I need to get up to speed with explosives and get to know my way around a sniping rifle again."

"I can get you a briefing from one of our experts on the explosives front," said Button. "And I'm sure you can brush up your sniping skills in Hereford."

Shepherd nodded.

"Are you okay? You look a little . . . perturbed."

Shepherd pulled a face then sipped his coffee. "Don't you think that Putin deserves a bullet in the head?" he said eventually.

Button's jaw dropped. "I can't believe you said that."

"Someone should take responsibility for what happened to that plane. Almost three hundred people died."

"I rather think some sort of proof is needed before you make a statement like that," said Button. "It's not an absolute certainty that the Russians fired the missile that brought the plane down. Or that Putin gave the order."

"You don't think it was the Russians? Seriously?"

"It wasn't the first time that a plane was shot down over the Ukraine," said Button. "The Ukrainian military shot down a Siberia Airlines flight over the Black Sea in 2001, killing seventy-eight. They never officially admitted liability but eventually the government conceded that it was probably the result of an errant missile fired by its armed forces."

"Errant missile? That's like the old chestnut of collateral damage, isn't it? I seem to remember the Ukrainians paid out just two hundred thousand dollars per victim."

"Your memory never fails you, does it?" She drank her tea.

Shepherd shrugged. "You don't need a trick memory to know that the Ukrainians pretty much got away with murder then. Now Putin's managing to pull the same trick."

"The point I'm making is that if the Ukrainians did it then, they could have shot down the Malaysian flight. And I have to say I hope you're not serious about Putin being a valid target for assassination."

"I'm just saying, if my son had been on the flight, I'd be wanting to hold someone accountable. And if it looked as if that wasn't going to happen, then maybe I'd be looking to take matters into my own hands."

"Are you saying you don't want this mission?"

"I'm not saying that. I'm just saying that I can empathise with the father. Maybe even sympathise. Wouldn't it be easier just to shut him down?"

"Shut him down how, exactly?"

"Send someone around to warn him off. Tell him we know what his intentions are."

"The Dutch want him arrested and charged."

"So don't tell the Dutch. I'll make a call."

Button tilted her head on one side as she looked at him with narrowed eyes.

He laughed and threw up his hands. "Don't look at me like that," he said.

"Like what?"

"Like you're thinking of charging me with being an accessory before the fact."

"We don't charge people in Five, you know that. I just find your attitude surprising, that's all. He's planning to fund an assassination and you seem to think a verbal warning is punishment enough."

"I won't mention it again," said Shepherd.

"And don't forget Lucas Smit. The world will be a safer place with him behind bars."

"No argument there," said Shepherd. "Okay, when do I start?"

"I need to get my ducks in a row; why don't you go and do what you have to do in Hereford, I'll fix up an explosives expert and then we'll get you up and running."

The four members of Harper's team were in his hotel room by two o'clock on Saturday afternoon. The last one to arrive was a pale, intense-looking man in his mid-thirties, dressed all in black and wearing black leather gloves. His nickname was Hansfree — an ironic reference to the fact that the man was missing most of both arms below the elbows. Both his hands were prosthetic, but he was so proficient with them a casual observer would have no idea of his disability. He'd lost his hands during an IED incident in Bosnia, after which he'd left the army and set himself up as a freelance researcher. With his prosthetics and voice recognition software he was as quick if not quicker than any able-bodied computer user.

Hansfree sat on the bed next to a pale, dark-eyed brunette in her thirties who tended to use the name Maggie May when she was working.

Harper stood by the window. The curtains were still drawn and the lights were off. "Apologies for the venue but this is all at short notice and I didn't want to do the briefing in a public place, for obvious reasons." He nodded at the sandwiches and water on the dressing table. "Refreshments there if you need them. Right, glad you could all make it. Time to have some fun and make some money. I've worked with you all individually before but I think this is the first time you've all met each other and for security purposes, it's likely that we won't do so again in the future. I'll do the introductions, it'll save time." He nodded at the only female member of the group. "The lovely lady is Maggie May, at least that's her working name. She's a surveillance professional, one of the best. Sitting next to her is Hansfree, one of the best researchers and computer men in the business."

Hansfree raised his right hand in salute. Harper gestured at the small, unassuming man with mousy hair standing by the bathroom door. "That's Billy Whisper, AKA Bravo Whisky. He was secret squirrel in Northern Ireland during the later stages of the Troubles — and also spent a couple of years seconded to the cousins over the water."

"Why Billy Whisper?" asked Hansfree.

"Because people say that I talk too quietly," said Billy, though hardly anyone heard what he said.

Hansfree laughed. "I get it."

"Billy's a linguist by training," said Harper. "He speaks fluent Arabic, German, French and Russian, and has a working knowledge of Farsi and Pushtu as well. He can do a cracking Northern Irish accent when necessary."

"So I can," said Billy Whisper.

"And, last but not least, is the gentleman on my right, variously known as BB, Bravo Bravo or Billy Big, and sometimes, behind his back, as Brick Shithouse."

The powerfully built figure next to him looked up and raised a hand in salute.

"Billy Big is ex-SRR — Special Reconnaissance Regiment, the successor to the Fourteen Int Company that Billy Whisper worked for." He smiled. "And better at intelligence gathering than they were too. The SRR is based in Hereford like the SAS. Right, now we know who everyone is, it's time to get down to business. Comms procedures: we'll be using these smartphones." He pulled the briefcase out from under the bed and opened it. "They're protected by a GCHQ super code that — unlike Angela Merkel's phone — is not breakable by the NSA in the States. So we can communicate by text, mobile and email and they're all guaranteed secure, and just to make sure that they stay that way, all transmissions will automatically self-destruct after twelve hours. However, as they invented the code, self-evidently GCHQ can listen in, and since this op is off the books, we need to keep comms neutral-sounding and avoid trigger words — weapons, bombs, et cetera, et cetera — that might spark attention."

Harper spent the next hour laying out the main points of the plan he had been formulating and gave each of them their designated tasks. When he'd finished he gave them a final warning. "Like I always say, no plan ever survives contact with the enemy," he said. "We need to be flexible and ready to adapt quickly to changing circumstances. I'll be using an intermediary to make first contact with the principal target's daughter and, if we all play our parts right, she'll open the doors to her father and his rich friend. The set-up will be in Monte Carlo, so your first assignment is to find the right location and carry out the necessary surveillance on it, but the pay-off will probably be in Germany. You'll have generous expenses, no receipts required, and your fees on completion can be paid in cash or into any bank account, anywhere in the world, as you prefer. Questions?" All four shook their heads. They were professionals and all knew what was expected of them. "Good, then we'll speak as necessary but you need to hold yourself in readiness at all times."

They left the room one at a time at five-minute intervals. Harper stood at the window and watched them go. Maggie May was the last to leave. "How's your boy?" asked Harper. She had a six-year-old son, the reason that she was now working freelance. She had been working for MI5's surveillance section when she had made the mistake of falling pregnant. That wouldn't normally be an issue at MI5, but the mistake had been compounded by the fact that the father was her boss, and was married.

"He's growing up fast," she said.

"Who's looking after him while you're with me?"

"My parents," she said.

"And his father?"

"Still with his family. Still refusing to pay me a penny and still dodging a DNA test."

"If ever you need a helping hand . . ." said Harper.

She grinned. "I'm not that desperate yet, Lex."

"I'd do it pro bono."

"It's not the money. It's the fact that no matter how much of a bastard he is, he's still the father of my son."

"I hate my father," said Lex. "Just because you carry someone's DNA doesn't mean you owe them anything."

"Well, you sort of do, Lex. If it wasn't for the DNA, you wouldn't be alive, would you?" She hugged him and pecked him on the cheek. "You take care, you hear?"

"And you, babe."

Harper stood at the window and watched her leave. She stopped at the street corner and turned, then blew him a kiss. Harper chuckled as she walked away.

Shepherd checked his phone as he walked over to his BMW SUV and groaned as he realised the battery had gone flat. He had a charger in the car so he plugged it in before starting the engine and heading for Hereford. He pulled into a service station after an hour and checked his phone on the way to buy a coffee. There were two text messages from Katra asking him to call her urgently. He rang and could tell from her voice that she was upset.

"Where are you, Dan?" she asked.

"On my way to Hereford," he said. "I won't be long. What's wrong?"

"Liam's in trouble at school," she told him.

Shepherd's stomach lurched. "What do you mean? Is he okay?"

"I'm not sure. They called and said he was in trouble with the police."

"The police? Katra, what's going on?"

"I don't know. The school phoned this morning and asked to speak to you. They said the police were talking to Liam. But they wouldn't tell me what it's about. They said they had to talk to you."

"I'll call them now," he said. He ended the call and scrolled through his phone's address book looking for the school's number. He realised he didn't have it and called Katra back. She gave him the number and he tapped it into his phone. He eventually got through to the headmaster's secretary after being put on hold for a couple of minutes.

"Mr Shepherd? Would it be possible for you to come to the school?"

"When?"

"As soon as possible."

"Today? Saturday?"

"It's a boarding school, Mr Shepherd. We never close."

"Can you tell me what's happened?" he asked.

"I think the headmaster would rather tell you in person," she said.

"Is my son okay?"

"He's fine. But there has been a problem that we need to talk to you about."

"My au pair said the police have been to the school."

"Yes, that's true," she said. "There was a problem with Liam's locker. Mr Shepherd, really, it would be better if you came and spoke to Mr Turner."

"I'll be there as soon as possible," said Shepherd. He ended the call and hurried back to his car, thoughts of coffee forgotten.

He arrived at Liam's school on the outskirts of Harrogate at just after three o'clock in the afternoon. It was an impressive sandstone building with two large wings either side of a turreted tower from which flew two flags — one the Union flag, the other the school crest. Off to the left were extensive playing fields and to the right were tennis courts and an Olympic-sized swimming pool. Shepherd found a parking space in the staff car park and hurried inside the main building. It was, he realised, only his third visit to the school. He found the main office wing and was directed to the headmaster's office where his secretary, a prim young woman with her hair pinned back, asked him to wait on one of a line of hard-backed chairs. "Mr Turner is on the phone. As soon as he's done I'll tell him you're here," she said. Shepherd spent several minutes studying a collection of framed photographs of various school sports teams and trying to quell the rising sense of panic that kept threatening to overwhelm him.

Eventually the door to the headmaster's office opened and the man appeared. He was in his fifties, tall and thin and wearing a shabby brown cardigan over brown corduroy trousers.

"Mr Shepherd, come on in," he said. "I apologise for my casual attire but I'm not usually in the office on a Saturday."

The headmaster's office overlooked the school's playing fields. There was a large desk that looked antique, on which sat a keyboard and a computer monitor. There was a leather high-backed chair behind the desk and two wooden chairs facing it. The wall behind the desk was lined with books and framed certificates and degrees hung on the wall by the door.

"Please, sit down," said Turner, waving at the wooden chairs. As Shepherd sat, Turner walked around the desk and slid into his executive chair. "Can my secretary get you a tea, or a water?"

"I'm fine, thank you," said Shepherd.

The headmaster nodded at his secretary and she closed the door. "Well, we don't often get to see you at our school, Mr Shepherd, I'm just sorry that it couldn't be under better circumstances."

"I don't really understand what's happened," said Shepherd.

Turner frowned. "No one's told you?"

Shepherd shook his head.

Turner sighed. "I'm afraid a quantity of cocaine was discovered in Liam's locker. A not inconsiderable quantity as it happens. Half an ounce, pretty much."

Shepherd's jaw dropped. "I'm sorry — what?"

"Half an ounce of cocaine was found in Liam's locker this morning. The police were called and he has already been questioned."

"Why the hell wasn't I told?" said Shepherd.

"We tried to contact you, several times. The phone number we have for you seemed to be switched off and there was no voicemail. We phoned Liam's main contact number, a lady by the name of Katra, I believe?"

"Our au pair, yes."

"Well, we explained that we needed to talk to you as soon as possible."

"You didn't tell her about any drugs."

The headmaster looked pained. "There is a problem in that she isn't a family member or a legal guardian. There are data protection issues."

Shepherd nodded. He was still flustered and his mind was going around in circles. "Where is he?"

"He's in with one of our student councillors. I'll bring him in as soon as we're finished."

Shepherd frowned. "Finished?"

"You have to understand that the school has a zero tolerance policy when it comes to drugs."

"You're expelling him?"

"Our hands are tied, Mr Shepherd. As I said, we have a zero tolerance policy."

"There has to be some mistake," said Shepherd. "Liam doesn't take drugs. He's not that sort of lad. They must have belonged to someone else."

"Liam has already admitted that he knew the drugs were in the locker."

Shepherd sat back in his chair and sighed. "I don't believe it."

"We were surprised, I must say. Liam has never been in trouble before. But the facts are beyond dispute. He had half an ounce of cocaine in his locker and as such ..." he shrugged. "As I said, we have a zero tolerance policy."

"But there has to be an explanation," said Shepherd.

"He told the police he was holding the drugs for a friend."

"When did the police talk to him?"

"Before lunch. We called them as soon as the drugs were discovered."

"How did you know they were in his locker?"

"We conduct regular random searches," said the headmaster.

"Does the school have a drugs problem?"

"No, we do not. We make it clear that we conduct regular searches and that we remove anyone found with drugs from the school."

Shepherd shook his head. "This is a nightmare," he said. "Was Liam charged?"

"I don't believe so."

"You don't know?" snapped Shepherd.

"I wasn't present during the questioning."

"Where did they talk to him?"

"They used an office here. We thought that better than taking him to the police station. Liam admitted everything, and the police are now deciding what action to take."

"Presumably they don't know for sure it was cocaine?"

"The police seemed sure, but they are having it tested."

"Who was with him when the police questioned him?"

"One of Liam's teachers."

"What about a lawyer?"

"It wasn't felt necessary."

Shepherd frowned. "Who didn't feel it was necessary?"

The headmaster squinted at Shepherd. "I understand the police said he could have a solicitor present if he wanted, but Liam said he was happy to answer their questions."

"I'm not sure that should have been his decision to make. He's a child."

"He's seventeen, Mr Shepherd. Anyway, I think it probably best that you talk to Liam. And then perhaps you could take him home."

"Excuse me?" said Shepherd. "What do you mean, take him home?"

"As I've already explained, we have a zero tolerance policy."

"But he's innocent until proven guilty, surely?"

"Mr Shepherd, Liam has already admitted he knew about the drugs. He's hardly innocent."

"So that's it? He has to leave?"

"I'm afraid so, yes." He stood up but Shepherd stayed where he was.

"Look, Mr Turner. Liam's a good kid, you know he is. And he's had more than his fair share of problems. His mum died when he was very young and I've been away a lot. I was in the army, and then the police. I wasn't around much . . ."

The headmaster sat down again. "I understand that, Mr Shepherd. But a lot of our pupils come from broken homes . . ."

"I didn't say Liam came from a broken home," interrupted Shepherd. "He lost his mum. What I mean is that I'm the one to blame, I wasn't around enough while he was growing up. Isn't there some way you could give him a second chance?"

"It's called zero tolerance for a reason, Mr Shepherd."

"I get it. And I'll punish him. We can both punish him. But it can't be right ruining his education because he made one mistake. This could ruin Liam's life."

"You'll find another school, Mr Shepherd."

"I don't want to find another school. I want Liam to stay here."

"I'm afraid that isn't possible."

Mr Turner stood up again and walked over to the door. He opened it and waited for Shepherd to leave. Shepherd could see there was no point in arguing; he sighed and stood up.

"Thanks for your time," he said. "And I'm really sorry this happened."

Mr Turner forced a smile. "You and me both, Mr Shepherd." He walked through to the outer office and Shepherd followed him. "Laura, could you take Mr Shepherd along to see Liam? And please give him the card the detectives left. I'm sure he will want to talk to them."

Shepherd shook hands with the headmaster and went with the secretary down a corridor, across a quadrangle and along another corridor. She knocked on a door with a sign saying "STUDENT SUPPORT AND WELFARE" and opened it. Liam was sitting on a chair by the window and he jumped to his feet when he saw Shepherd.

A middle-aged woman in a dark suit was sitting behind a desk. "Mr Shepherd?" she asked.

Shepherd nodded. Liam was shaking and seemed close to tears.

"I'm Sarah Weinstein," she said. "I'm Liam's guidance counsellor."

"I didn't realise he had a guidance counsellor."

"All the students do," she said. "Now, I've got some papers for you to sign and then you can take Liam home. The school will forward you a cheque for the portion of the school fees that aren't applicable."

Shepherd glared at Liam and the boy folded his arms and averted his eyes.

"Ms Weinstein, is there anything that can be done? I really don't want Liam to leave."

She smiled sympathetically. "I'm so sorry," she said. "The school has a zero tolerance policy when it comes to drugs."

"So I've heard," he said. "Fine, show me where I have to sign."

Shepherd said nothing as he walked to his SUV. Liam walked half a pace behind him, towing the wheeled trunk that contained all his belongings. Shepherd was holding two carrier bags of clothing that wouldn't fit into the trunk and a tennis racket. They loaded the stuff into the rear of the vehicle in silence and then climbed into the car. It was only when Liam slammed his door shut that Shepherd turned to him, eyes blazing. "What the hell were you thinking?"

Liam stared into the footwell and bit down on his lower lip.

"I asked you a question, Liam."

Liam looked up, his eyes brimming with tears. "I'm sorry."

"Sorry doesn't cut it," said Shepherd. "What were you doing with drugs in your locker?"

"A friend gave them to me."

"A friend gave you half an ounce of cocaine? Do you have any idea how much half an ounce of cocaine is worth?"

Liam shrugged. "I dunno. Fifty quid."

"More likely three times that. Why would anyone give you a hundred and fifty quid's worth of drugs?"

"He said it was cannabis."

"Who did?"

"Roger. My mate."

"And you told the police this? You told them that this Roger gave you the drugs?"

Liam nodded.

Shepherd ran a hand through his hair. "Even if you thought it was cannabis, what were you thinking?"

"I don't know."

"Someone gives you drugs and you just say thank you very much and put it in your locker."

"He said he didn't want to be walking around with it. He was going to a rough pub, he said."

"You know how serious this is, right? You're not a kid any more. You're playing Big Boys' Games now, and Big Boys' Rules apply. As of next year you'll be an adult, and the way things are going you'll be an adult with a criminal record." Shepherd shook his head. "What the hell were you thinking? Cocaine, Liam? You could go to prison, you know that?"

"Dad, I thought it was cannabis."

"Oh, that makes it better, does it? Cannabis is a Class B drug. You can still go to prison for it."

"Not for small amounts. It's been decriminalised."

Shepherd's eyes narrowed. "Are you telling me you smoke cannabis?"

"Everybody does, Dad. It's no biggie."

"No biggie!" Shepherd looked up at the roof of the car and fought the urge to scream at his son. He took a deep breath and forced himself to stay calm. "Liam, not everybody smokes cannabis. And those that do are breaking the law, no matter what you say about decriminalisation. It's a gateway drug. It leads to other things."

"Dad, I smoke the odd bit of puff. I'm not going to start injecting heroin, if that's what you're afraid of."

"What I'm afraid of is you going to prison, Liam, because that's on the cards at the moment. You're being charged with possession of a Class A drug with intent to distribute. That could put you behind bars and kill off any chance of a decent career."

"Dad, I thought it was dope. Roger said it was dope. I was just holding it until the weekend."

"Who is this Roger?"

"Roger Flynn. He's a mate."

"He goes to the school?"

Liam shook his head. "I met him outside."

"Outside? What do you mean, outside?"

"I met him at a party."

"A party? Where?"

"Leeds."

"The school lets you go to parties in Leeds? Since when?"

"Dad, look, everyone does it. Roger has a car, he runs us there and back."

"How old is he?"

"Our age. Pretty much."

"How old is he, Liam? Don't go all vague on me. You're in big trouble and I need specifics."

"He's eighteen. Nineteen maybe. He's got a driving licence. And he never drinks and drives."

"Does he sell drugs to the kids at the school?"

Liam shrugged. "Maybe." Shepherd pointed a warning finger at his son's face. "Yes. I think so."

"And you've been buying drugs from him?"

Liam shook his head. "No. Of course not."

"But you've taken drugs, right?"

"I smoke pot now and again. And Roger gives me the odd tab of E."

"Ecstasy?"

Liam nodded. "So this guy is a drug dealer, not a mate. Now did you tell the police it wasn't yours?"

"I had to. They said if I didn't they'd take it that the drugs were mine. But now Roger's denying it's anything to do with him."

"Well he would, wouldn't he?" Shepherd ran a hand through his hair. "This is a hell of a mess, Liam."

"I know, Dad. I'm sorry. I'm really sorry."

Shepherd forced a smile. "Okay, one step at a time," he said. "The school won't have you back, so we'll have to get you in somewhere else. You're going to have to help me with that. Go on to Google and see what boarding schools are available. Come up with a list."

"I don't have to go to boarding school, Dad. There are schools in Hereford. I can live at home. Katra's there, it won't be a problem."

"I thought you liked boarding?"

"When I was a kid and you were away all the time, sure. But I can take care of myself now. One more year and I'll be going to university." His face fell as he realised he was making plans that might well never come to fruition. "You know what I mean," he said. "Hereford would be a better bet for me. And cheaper for you."

Shepherd nodded. "Okay, I'll get that sorted for you, I'll see what schools are available. Second, we need to get you a lawyer. You didn't have one when the police questioned you, did you?"

"They said I could have one but I said it wasn't necessary. I figured I hadn't done anything wrong. Was that a mistake?"

Shepherd pulled a face. "It depends. Sometimes you can clear things up by just telling the truth, but you had Class A drugs. A lawyer might have been a good idea. But there was an appropriate adult with you?"

Liam nodded. "Mrs Grainger, from the school. She's one of my teachers."

"And she didn't say you should have a lawyer?"

"She didn't say much, actually. The police did most of the talking. She just said that I should tell the truth."

Shepherd sighed. Sadly it wasn't always true that honesty was the best policy, especially when dealing with the police. "And what exactly did you tell them?"

"The truth. That Roger gave me the package to hold for him until the weekend. He said it was cannabis and he'd let me have some at the party."

"And why did Roger give it to you?"

"He said he was having problems at home and didn't want his mum to find it. It wasn't the first time."

"What?"

"He's done it a few times in the past and there's never been a problem."

"I don't see why anyone would think it was a good idea to take drugs into the school in the first place. And how were you going to get to this party?"

Liam looked away, embarrassed.

"You were going to sneak out of school?"

"Everyone does it, Dad."

Shepherd shook his head in frustration. "I'm sure that's not true. You were sneaking out for drugs and booze, is that it?"

"For parties, Dad. Didn't you go to parties when you were a kid?"

"I didn't take drugs when I was your age," said Shepherd. "Or any age," he added quickly.

"But you didn't wait until you were eighteen before you had a beer, right? No one does."

Shepherd held up his hands. "Liam, this isn't about you having the odd bottle of beer or even the occasional joint, this is about you being caught with a Class A drug. But none of this would have happened if you'd just followed the rules."

Liam nodded. "I'm sorry."

"I know you're sorry. But unfortunately being sorry isn't going to count for anything." He shook his head. "I can't believe how stupid you've been."

He got out of the car and looked at the card the headmaster's secretary had given him. It belonged to a Detective Sergeant Paul Drinkwater and had a landline number and extension, and a mobile. He called the mobile but it went straight through to voicemail. He left a short message and then called the landline. That extension also went through to voicemail. This time he didn't leave a message. He called back on the main station number and was told that DS Drinkwater had left the station and wasn't expected back until Monday. Shepherd went back to the SUV and climbed in. Liam was wiping away his tears as he stared out of the window. Shepherd hated his son being so unhappy but knew that the lad had brought it upon himself. "I'll have to talk to them on Monday," he said. "Meanwhile you're grounded in Hereford. And I mean grounded. No TV, no PlayStation, no phone."

Liam nodded but didn't look at him. "I thought you'd be angrier than this," he said.

Shepherd forced a smile. "I am angry, Liam. I'm furious. But getting angry isn't going to fix anything."

He started the engine and put the SUV in gear. "Let's see what I can do."

Harper picked up a rental car from an independent firm run out of a railway arch in the East End of London. He paid cash and didn't have to show his licence. The car was a nondescript Ford Mondeo, three years old with almost 100,000 miles on the clock. Harper had picked up a UK street atlas at a newsagent. He never used SatNav. While SatNavs made navigation easier, they also provided a permanent record of where the car had been.

He left London and drove north, keeping just below the speed limit. By early evening he was sitting in the far corner of a service station car park on the M6 west of Manchester. Harper flashed his lights as he saw a silver BMW cruising around the edge of the car park. It parked in the next bay and a few seconds later, Jony Hasan slid into Harper's passenger seat.

Harper knew the British-born Bangladeshi well and had bought untraceable weapons from him on several occasions.

"Shit car, bruv," Jony said. "I thought you had better taste than that."

"I do. Sometimes it's better not to draw attention to yourself, but you wouldn't know anything about that, would you?" He looked him over. "Jesus, Jony, you look more like a throwback to the 1950s every time I see you. All you need is a quiff and a guitar."

Jony broke into a broad grin. "I'll take that as a compliment, bruv." He was in his mid-twenties, dark skinned and with slicked-back hair that was always glistening with gel, and as usual he had turned up dressed in his "uniform" of black leather jacket and black jeans with pointed, silver-tipped black boots. He passed Harper a cigarette, lit one himself, and lowered the window a couple of inches. He blew a plume of smoke out into the gathering darkness and then glanced across at Harper. "So what's it to be, bruv? Need a handgun, one careful lady owner, no history?"

"Not this time, Jony. I'll be needing stuff for this job that even you can't supply. But I've got some work for you just the same, if you're interested. A little bit out of your normal run and you'll have to base yourself in London for a few weeks, but there's some serious money in it. Five grand a week and you won't even have to get your hands dirty."

"You just played my favourite tune. I'm in."

"Don't you want to know what the job is first?"

"Nah, it doesn't matter," Jony said. "For five grand a week I'll do anything short of murder." He frowned and flashed Harper a worried look. "It's not murder, is it?"

Harper grinned. "It's not murder, I just need you to bait a trap for me."

"And who's the victim?"

Harper passed him the photo of O'Brien's daughter. "She's called Bridie. Bridie O'Brien. I need you to chat her up."

Jony started laughing. "Not bad. Blonde, pretty, twenties; she's just my type. If her dad owns a brewery I might be in love."

Harper grinned. "Come off it, Jony, we both know they're all your type."

"All right if I fuck her then?"

"Be my guest, just as long as you take care of business first."

"And you ain't going to pay me just for chatting her up, right?"

"That's the easy part. You've got to pose as a dodgy wheeler dealer, though that shouldn't be too much of a stretch, should it?" he said. "You're selling knock-offs of one sort or another — hot phones, booze, whatever — from the back of a van. She's always in her local getting pissed, and is always strapped for cash, so it should be fairly easy for you to chat her up and then hire her for a couple of cash jobs, driving you around while you make deliveries."

"And you're sure she'll do it?"

"Like I just said, she's always strapped for cash, so yeah, why wouldn't she? Then you need to find a way to let her accidentally catch sight of a couple of weapons."

"Whoa, bruv, that's putting me right in the frame."

"She and her dad are hardcore, Jony. She's not going to be trying to grass you up, but she is going to try and buy some weapons from you."

Jony put his head on one side. "And?"

"The first time she asks you, you're going to clam up. When she persists, you tell her you're just the delivery boy. Your boss is a very big wheel in the illegal weapons trade, an East European guy who's got contacts in all the old Soviet bloc countries and can get anything from a pistol to a nuclear bomb. But he never comes to this country and is very, very wary about new customers. When she persists — and she will — you'll reluctantly agree to ask your boss."

"Which is where you come into the picture."

"Eventually, yes, but you need to knock her back the first couple of times she asks."

"Gotcha," Jony said. "That's it?"

"Except that you need to be very cautious around her. Make sure you keep plenty of distance on her and don't let slip your real name or anything about you that would allow her — or her heavy friends — to identify or trace you. She's not a real player herself, she's just a foot soldier, but her dad is the genuine article — the boss of a seriously dangerous organisation, real hardcore. You don't want to be messing with them and you sure as hell don't want them knowing your contact details or anything that could help them track you down, because if they get the slightest hint that you've been playing them, you're dead meat." He paused. "And when they realise they've been conned, they will definitely try to find you."

Completely unfazed, Jony gave a broad grin. "They'll have a job; we all look alike to you white guys, right?"

Harper laughed and handed Jony a thick envelope. "That's your first couple of weeks' payment and a bit extra for expenses. The address of her local's in there as well; she's there practically every night of the week apparently, but don't be too quick to chat her up. Let her clock you a couple of times and catch sight of you shifting a few dodgy phones first. Softly, softly, catchee monkey."

★   ★   ★

Shepherd and Liam arrived back at Hereford after dark. They had driven the whole way in silence. When they eventually pulled up in front of their house Shepherd turned off the engine and looked at his son. "As soon as we get inside, pack a suitcase and I'll drive you over to your grandparents."

"Why can't I stay here?" asked Liam. "Katra is here, she can take care of me."

Shepherd shook his head. "I don't trust you, Liam. I'm sorry, but that's the way it is."

"I'll be good, Dad. I swear."

"Then you need to prove that to me. You need to earn my trust again."

Liam put his hands over his face. "I can't face them, Dad. I can't tell them what I did."

"You have to own up to your mistakes," said Shepherd. "That's what men do."

"I'm sorry, Dad. I'm really sorry. But please, don't tell Granddad and Grandma. Can't we just say I wanted to come back to Hereford?"

"Lying is never a good idea," said Shepherd.

"You lie, when you're working. When you're undercover, you lie all the time."

"That's different. Don't try playing that game with me, Liam. When I'm undercover I'm pretending to be someone I'm not. It's my job. You're talking about lying to people who love you."

"I can't tell Granddad. I can't. And I don't want Grandma looking at me knowing what I did. Please, Dad, I won't lie but can't I just say I'm changing schools and leave it at that?"

Shepherd thought about it for several seconds. "Okay. You can say you wanted to come back to Hereford. But no lying. And you're on a seven p.m. curfew every night, weekdays and weekends. And when you go out you tell them where you're going and when you'll be back."

Liam nodded. "Okay."

"I'm serious, Liam. This is your one chance to get back on the straight and narrow."

"Dad, I made a mistake. I won't do it again."

"Okay." He opened the door and climbed out. "And we're still not out of the woods on this, remember? I'll do what I can but you might still end up in court, and if that happens there'll be no way of stopping Granddad and Grandma from finding out." He opened the rear door of the SUV and helped Liam take out the trunk.

Katra had the front door open for them as they walked up the path. She hurried out and hugged Liam. "You get bigger every time I see you," she said. She had her blonde hair tied back in a ponytail and was wearing a pink sweatshirt over cut-off denim jeans.

She smiled at Shepherd. "I'll get his room ready," she said. "Then I can cook. I've got steaks."

"Steaks would be great, but no need to get his room ready," said Shepherd.

Liam manhandled his trunk up the stairs. Katra went to help him but he waved her away and told her that he could do it himself.

Katra followed Shepherd through to the kitchen. He sat down while Katra made coffee. He explained what had happened and why Liam was no longer at the boarding school.

"Drugs?" she said. "Not Liam."

"I'm afraid so," said Shepherd. "So he's going to stay with his grandparents. I'm pretty sure I can get him a place in the Hereford Academy in Redhill. Do you know it?"

Katra nodded.

"You can drive him there and back, but I want him staying with his grandparents."

"He can stay here. I can take care of him."

"I don't think I can trust him, Katra."

"I'll watch him like a hawk."

Shepherd smiled. "I'm sure you would. But he was sneaking in and out of school to go to parties. I don't want him doing that here."

"I'll sleep outside his door," said Katra, and Shepherd laughed. "I'm serious, Dan," she said. She put a mug of coffee down in front of him. "This is his home. It doesn't make sense for him to stay somewhere else."

Shepherd sipped his coffee. "You might be right," he said.

"I'll get up before him and I won't go to sleep before he sleeps," said Katra. "I won't let him go out unless he checks with you first."

Shepherd smiled at her enthusiasm. Katra had been his au pair for almost ten years and she was part of the family. "Maybe," he said. "How about you get started on the steaks?"

As Katra busied herself cooking, Shepherd sipped his coffee. He realised that Katra had been with him for three years longer than he'd been married to Sue, Liam's mother. Not long after Sue had been killed in a senseless road traffic accident, Shepherd had hired her to take care of Liam. She was barely out of her teens at the time, and spoke reasonable English but with a heavy Slovenian accent. Over the years her English had improved and her accent had evened out. If anything she had picked up a slight Australian accent from all the Australian soap operas she watched. He found it difficult to imagine life without her. Over the last few years she had spent far more time with Liam than his grandparents had. She was family now, and she was right, the house was his home. It was where he belonged. "I'm just going up to talk to Liam," he said.

He went upstairs and knocked on the door to Liam's bedroom.

"Yes?"

Shepherd pushed the door open. Liam was sitting on the bed and from the redness in his eyes it was clear he'd been crying. "Are you okay?"

Liam nodded. "I'm nearly packed. I can leave some stuff here, right? This is still my home, isn't it?"

"Of course it is," said Shepherd. He walked over and hugged his son. "We just have to get this sorted out, that's all."

"I'm really, really sorry, Dad," said Liam. He sniffed, then released himself from Shepherd's hug and wiped his eyes.

"Look, I've been thinking about you staying with your grandparents. If you promise to not let me down, it'd be all right if you stayed here."

"Really?"

Shepherd nodded. "I've spoken to Katra. She can take you to and from school and do any cooking you need. But I'll talk to her every day and if you put a foot wrong you go to your grandparents and I let them know why."

Liam nodded solemnly. "I won't let you down, Dad."

"And keep your iPhone on and charged all the time."

"You're going to track my phone?"

"I just want to know where you are. And if I call you and you don't answer, there'll be hell to pay. Understood?"

"Yes, Dad," said Liam quietly.

Shepherd ruffled the boy's hair. "We'll get through this, I promise."

Just before Katra served up their steaks, Shepherd phoned Major Gannon at the Stirling Lines barracks at Credenhill, the SAS headquarters that were just a short drive from his home. "I need a favour," he said.

"And I'm just the genie to grant it," said the Major.

"I'm going to be a contract killer."

"Well, you wouldn't be the first member of the regiment to follow that career path, but I did have higher hopes for you."

Shepherd laughed. "I should have been more specific," he said. "I'll be playing the part of a contract killer and I could do with being brought up to speed on sniping, and explosives."

"Sniping's not a problem, but what were you thinking about in terms of bangs?"

"Charlie's going to fix me up with one of her experts, but I figured it wouldn't do any harm having a demolitions refresher. It was never my field, though like everyone else I did the basics."

"And you still have all your own fingers, which is always a good sign," said the Major. "What's your time frame?"

"Days rather than weeks," said Shepherd. "I'm in Hereford now and I'd like to strike while the iron's hot."

"Pop around after breakfast," said the Major. "I'll have something fixed up for you. How's young Liam, by the way?"

"Don't ask."

Shepherd arrived at the Stirling Lines barracks at RAF Credenhill just before nine o'clock. He brought his BMW to a halt in front of the barrier and handed his Home Office ID to a uniformed guard. "Dan Shepherd, here to see Major Gannon."

The guard studied Shepherd's ID, consulted a list on a clipboard and handed the ID back. "Do you know where to go, sir?" he asked. A second guard had walked around the BMW, examining the underside with a mirror on a stick.

"Oh yes," said Shepherd.

The guard raised the barrier and Shepherd drove slowly by the green featureless metal-sided buildings that made up Credenhill, home to the SAS since 1999.

The Major had arranged to meet him by the armoury. As Shepherd drove up he saw him standing by the entrance. He was wearing a black Adidas tracksuit and army boots and had a small backpack slung over one shoulder. He'd put on a bit of weight since Shepherd had last seen him, but he thought better of mentioning it as he shook hands and bumped shoulders with him. Even without the extra weight the Major was a big man, broad-shouldered with a nose that had been broken several times.

"This is all short notice, isn't it?" asked the Major as he pulled open the door and ushered Shepherd inside.

"Yeah, I was only told yesterday."

"I've asked Pete to get a few rifles ready and he can talk you through them. Sniping was never one of my specialities. Are you okay to wait a day or two for the explosives briefing? Our best guys are off base at the moment."

"No problem," said Shepherd. "I've got some business to take care of in Leeds tomorrow anyway."

Sergeant Peter Simpson, grey haired and stocky, grinned as the Major and Shepherd walked up to his counter. "The proverbial bad penny turns up again," he said in a gruff Geordie accent. Simpson was a member of the Royal Logistic Corps, which in SAS slang made him a Loggy. He had been a standard feature in the armoury for all the years Shepherd had been in the regiment and no one knew more about arms and ammunition.

Simpson and Shepherd shook hands, then the sergeant took him and the Major down a corridor lined with wire-mesh cages. He led them into a room at the far end where a number of rifles had been arranged on a wooden trestle table. "I thought I'd run through the weapons here and then you can take whatever you want out on to the range."

"Sounds good," said Shepherd.

The Major stood by the door, his arms folded.

"Right, as you know, the regiment favours the Barrett M82, the HK PSG1 and occasionally the Dragunov." Simpson picked up a rifle and handed it to Shepherd. "But this, as you probably also know, is the standard sniper rifle throughout the British Army."

Shepherd nodded. "The Accuracy International L96A1."

"Got it in one," said Simpson. "It's been the rifle of choice since it replaced the Lee-Enfield L42A1 series in the mid-eighties. Adjustable butt, integrated adjustable bipod and static iron sights, it was designed to achieve first-round hit at six hundred metres but is capable of some pretty serious harassing fire up to eleven hundred total metres. It fires an 8.59mm round, heavier than the usual 7.62mm sniper's round so is less likely to be deflected over extremely long ranges. It comes with a free-floating stainless steel barrel that can be changed in the field in just over four minutes. In fact, it's so simply put together that even the average squaddie can carry out most repairs themselves. It's practically idiot-proof." He nodded at the weapon. "You can strip it?"

"Sure." Shepherd broke the gun apart into its separate components quickly and efficiently.

When he'd finished, Simpson nodded his approval. "That trick memory of yours comes in handy, doesn't it?"

"To be honest, it's muscle memory rather than memorising a check list," said Shepherd. "I replaced the barrel in complete darkness once, in the desert and under fire."

"Let's see you put it back together then," said the sergeant.

Shepherd grinned and reassembled the weapon almost as quickly as he'd taken it apart.

Simpson took it from him and put it back on the table. He picked up a second rifle. "This is the L96's big brother, arguably the best sniping rifle in the world," he said. "The L115A3. There aren't too many of these in service because of the price — a hefty twenty-three grand. Most half-decent snipers can hit a man at up to one thousand five hundred metres and even at that distance the round hits with the equivalent energy of a .44 magnum fired close up. One hit, one kill, pretty much. Because of the longer range, it comes with Schmidt and Bender day sights that magnify up to twenty-five times, compared with the L96's twelve times."

"Nice bit of kit," said Shepherd approvingly.

"Fired one?"

Shepherd shook his head. "I think we applied for one but it never came, at least not while I was in the regiment. The five-round magazine seemed a good idea. Lets you get off a handful of shots without reloading but a small enough magazine so it doesn't get in the way. And the folding stock makes it that much easier to put in a backpack in a hurry."

"It's one hell of a gun," said the Major. "There's a corporal in the UK Household Cavalry now who holds the world record for a confirmed kill using one of those."

"That's right," said the sergeant. "Corporal Craig Harrison. He shot and killed two Taliban static machine gunners at almost two and a half thousand metres in Afghanistan in 2009. Then went on to take out their machine gun. All confirmed by GPS because at first the Yanks wouldn't believe it. They held the record prior to that and were a bit miffed that a Brit could out-shoot them."

"That'd mean the round was in the air for three seconds, thereabouts," said Shepherd.

"Makes you think, doesn't it. If you knew it was coming, you'd have all the time in the world to get out of the way."

Shepherd rubbed his shoulder. "Yeah, but life's not like that unfortunately."

"That's right, you were hit by a sniper out in Afghanistan, weren't you?" asked the sergeant.

"It was a regular AK-74 so the damage was survivable," said Shepherd.

"You were lucky," said the sergeant.

The Major chuckled. "If Spider had been lucky, he wouldn't have been shot in the first place."

Simpson pointed at the third weapon on the table. "I wasn't sure if you wanted a PSG1, as I know you weren't a fan," he said.

"I could always take it or leave it," said Shepherd. "The Präzisionsschützengewehr, German for 'precision shooter rifle', but really it's only good up to eight hundred metres or so. Personally I was never happy beyond six hundred."

"To be fair, it was designed more for multiple targets than for range," said the Major. "H&K came up with it in response to the massacre at the 1972 Munich Summer Olympics. The cops couldn't take out their targets fast enough and it all ended badly. So H&K were asked to come up with a high-accuracy, large-magazine-capacity, semi-automatic rifle and that's what they did. It's terrific for taking out a number of targets at five hundred metres or less, not so great for long shots." He shrugged. "Horses for courses."

"I never liked the fact that it doesn't have iron sights," said Shepherd. "If you lose your scope, you're screwed. Plus, it kicks out its casings up to ten metres. That's fine for the cops, but it's a bloody liability for a sniper."

"So what exactly are you looking for?" asked Simpson.

"Basically to familiarise myself with the main sniping rifles and to get in some practice."

"I've got one of our top snipers waiting at the range," said Simpson. "How familiar do you want to get with the guns here?"

"I need to be able to field strip them all, and know the characteristics backwards."

"I've got all the specs written down for you," said Simpson. He picked up the fourth weapon on the table.

"How about we start with this?" he said. "Any sniper worth his salt has picked up a Dragunov at some point. The squad support weapon of choice for most of the former Warsaw Pact. More for marksmen than snipers, hence the ten-round magazine, but there's a lot of them about."

Shepherd nodded and took the weapon from the sergeant. All the Dragunovs he'd handled had been wooden with a skeletonised stock but this one was made from a black polymer.

"It's designed so you can use the iron sights at the same time as a scope, so you can take out distant and close targets at the same time," said Simpson.

"Yeah, the sight can be adjusted to a maximum range of twelve hundred metres, but I've never heard of anyone making a kill shot at more than half that."

"Think you can strip it?" asked Simpson.

"No problem," Shepherd replied. He began to quickly and methodically break the rifle down into its component parts. He grinned over at the sergeant. "Like riding a bike," he said.

Shepherd spent two hours stripping and reassembling the sniper rifles under the watchful eye of the sergeant and the Major.

Shepherd decided to use the L115A3 for his sniping practice. He carried it and a box of ammunition to a Land Rover parked outside the armoury. The Major drove them the short distance to the outdoor range. They parked by the entrance and the Major took a red flag from the back of the Land Rover and ran it up a flagpole to show that the range was live while Shepherd took the gun and ammunition inside the brick-built shelter that was open to the target area.

A trooper dressed in black fatigues was standing in front of a wooden table examining paper targets. He turned and nodded at Shepherd. "You Spider?" he asked. He had unkempt red hair and a sprinkle of freckles across his nose.

Shepherd nodded. The trooper held out his hand. "Chris Hawkins. They call me Happy."

They shook hands. "You're the sniper?" Shepherd asked. Hawkins looked as if he was barely out of his teens, though he must have been in his early twenties.

"Indeed he is," said the Major, walking up behind him. "Happy here is the best in the regiment."

"How the hell did you get the nickname Happy?"

"One of the directing staff gave it to me while I was on selection," said Hawkins. "It was just one of those things. I did it during winter and it was bloody freezing and pissing down, but the worse it got the more I kept grinning. I think I was in shock, to be honest, but by the end of it I was Happy Hawkins." He shrugged. "It could have been worse. What about you?"

Shepherd grinned. "I ate a spider once. A big one." He put the rifle on the table.

"My favourite," said Hawkins. "You fired one before?"

"In my day the budget wouldn't run to it."

"Yeah, I think strings were pulled to get a couple."

The Major laughed. "Strings? Bloody ropes, more like. Happy can run you through the basics, but I'm sure your muscle memory will kick in. We can't do more than a hundred metres or so here but as soon as you're ready we'll go out to the Brecon Beacons for some distance work."

"Sounds good," said Shepherd. "Let's get started."

After hours on the range getting a feel for the rifle, the Major, Shepherd and Hawkins piled into the Land Rover and the Major drove them the forty miles or so along the A438 to the middle of the Brecon Beacons National Park. The Major took the Land Rover off road for a couple of miles until they were in a bleak valley that was well clear of any walking trails.

"We've used this area before for sniping practice and we've never had any problems," said the Major. He pulled a black nylon kitbag from the back of the Land Rover. "You two get set up, I'll arrange a few targets. What do you think, Spider? A thousand metres?"

"Sounds about right," said Shepherd.

The Major shouldered his bag and jogged off across the rough terrain.

Hawkins looked around for a good vantage point. "How about up there?" he asked, pointing to the left. There was a small plateau about halfway up the slope.

"Looks good to me," said Shepherd.

They had packed the rifle in a waterproof case and Shepherd unzipped it and slung it over his shoulder. Hawkins grabbed a blanket. "Might as well make ourselves comfortable," he said. He pocketed a box of ammunition. "So you were in Afghanistan?"

"When it first kicked off," said Shepherd. "You?"

"Half a dozen times, right up until they pulled out. Was it a shambles when you were there?"

Shepherd chuckled. "Nothing changes, huh?"

"It's as if the politicians want to start wars but don't have the balls to win them." Hawkins shook his head. "Mind you, what the hell were we doing there in the first place?"

"To be fair, that was where al-Qaeda was training its terrorists."

"So we should have just gone in and destroyed the camps. Bombed them. That's what we have an air force for. Or send in the regiment to do the job properly. But the idea of invading a country like Afghanistan was doomed from the start. If the Russians couldn't control the place, what chance did we have?"

"Ours not to reason why," said Shepherd. "You sound pretty disillusioned."

Hawkins snorted. "Not with the regiment. I love it. Can't imagine being anywhere else. But disillusioned with the politicians who run our country? How can you not be? Especially with the way they fucked up Iraq and Afghanistan. It was different for you, maybe. You went in at the start when everyone was gung-ho. I was there towards the end, and it was obvious it had been a major '-up. The Afghans hated us, the Taliban were just waiting for us to leave and the public had had enough." He grinned. "Sorry, didn't mean to rant."

"Nah, I understand completely. I've been on missions before where you have to wonder if the top brass knew what they were doing."

"The Major said you left the regiment because you had a kid."

Shepherd nodded. "Liam. He's seventeen now."

"Will he join the regiment?"

Shepherd laughed harshly. With a drugs conviction Liam would be hard pressed to follow any half-decent career, but he figured it best not to tell too many people until he'd had a chance to sort it out. There was still a possibility that he could persuade the cops not to charge his son. "I don't think so. He's never shown any signs of wanting to sign up. I guess I wasn't the best role model while he was growing up. I was away a lot and when I was with his mum there were always arguments."

"She didn't want you to be in the SAS?"

"She wanted a husband, not a voice over the phone, which is what I was for most of our marriage." He shrugged. "What about you? Married?"

Hawkins shook his head. "A girl in every port," he said. "Actually, that's bollocks. The odd passing ship, maybe, but no one steady. Who has the time?"

"Married to the regiment?"

"You know what it's like. We can be sent anywhere at short notice, we can't tell anyone where we are or what we're doing. Not many will put up with that." He gestured at the plateau. "Let's get set up."

He led the way up the slope. It was steep in places and Shepherd had to scramble up on all fours. The plateau was about eight feet wide and twelve feet long. Hawkins threw down the blanket. He opened a leather

118

case and took out a pair of powerful binoculars. "Let's see how the Major is getting on."

Shepherd unslung the rifle and flipped out the bipod and the folding stock before placing it on the blanket. There was a bulbous suppressor on the end of the barrel to cut down on the flash and noise.

"You'll like this," said Hawkins, passing the binoculars to Shepherd. Shepherd scanned the bleak countryside and found the Major. He was about a kilometre away, placing a watermelon on the ground. The Major then straightened up and put a transceiver to his mouth. The transceiver on Hawkins' waist crackled. He picked it up.

"How's that, Happy? Over."

"Looks good, boss," said Hawkins. "But what have you got against fruit?"

The Major went back to his kitbag and pulled out a second watermelon. He placed it to the right of the first one. The next item he pulled from the kitbag was yellow and smaller than the watermelon. Shepherd laughed. It was a honeydew melon, about half the size of the watermelon. It was followed by a mango, a grapefruit and an apple. Shepherd handed the binoculars back. "I hope he doesn't start putting out grapes."

Hawkins laughed. "We could ask him to do a William Tell."

"Best not," said Shepherd, lying flat and putting his eye to the scope. "You know why snipers got called snipers?"

"Snipers snipe, I thought that was all there was to it."

"It's from the bird, the snipe. It's one of the hardest birds to hunt. They're hard to find and almost impossible to creep up on, and when they fly they have this erratic way of flying that makes them hard to target. Back in the day when hunters sold their kills at the market, only the best shooters would bring in snipe. So they became known as snipers."

"I didn't know that," said Hawkins.

"You learn something new every day," said Shepherd.

"That's true. Then you die and forget it all."

Shepherd chuckled. "Happy really is a terrific nickname for you," he said. He got himself into position. He shoved a rolled-up piece of cloth under his shirt around his right shoulder then he used his left hand to support the butt of the rifle, placing it next to his chest and resting the end of the rifle butt on it. By balling his hand into a fist he could raise the butt, and relaxing his hand would lower it.

Hawkins put the transceiver to his mouth. "Boss, we're ready here, over."

"I'll give you plenty of room, over," replied the Major.

Shepherd placed the butt of the rifle firmly in the pocket of his shoulder. The cloth pad he had placed there would minimise the movement from his pulse and breathing. He gripped the pistol grip of the stock with his right hand, using his bottom three fingers to keep the stock pressed firmly against his shoulder. He slipped his thumb over the top of his pistol grip. Only when he was completely happy with his grip did he place his index finger on the trigger.

He took several breaths to calm himself, then wiggled his elbows until he felt completely relaxed. He rested his cheek against the stock.

"Okay," said Hawkins. "Just follow the same procedure as you did at the range. Visualise. Focus. Relax. Aim. Breathe. Count one, two, three, shoot. Control the trigger. Follow through."

Shepherd didn't reply. He was totally focused on the target, the watermelon on the far left. He had to find his NPA, the Natural Point of Aim. He kept his head in the same position but looked away from the scope, to the right. Then he looked back. The crosshairs had drifted slightly. He adjusted his position and repeated the move, looking away and back. The drift was less this time. He corrected his position. This time the crosshairs remained on the target.

"You're holding your breath," said Hawkins. "Only hold your breath when you're ready to take the shot."

Hawkins was right, Shepherd realised. It was the tension kicking in. He allowed himself to breathe again as he focused on the watermelon. The crosshairs rose and fell as he breathed in and out.

He mentally prepared himself for the shot. The trigger had to be pulled when the sight picture was perfect and done in such a way that the rifle didn't move. And the trigger had to be squeezed so that the balance of the rifle wasn't compromised. So many things could go wrong that he had to be totally focused. A poor marksman anticipated the recoil by moving his shoulder forward when the trigger was pulled. Jerking the trigger was another fault — it had to be pulled back smoothly, and the action had to be continued after the shot was fired. Flinching was another problem, where the whole body overreacted to the sound of the shot, to the point where sometimes the sniper closed his eyes.

The follow-through was as important as actually firing and Shepherd ran through every step in his mind, visualising everything that needed to happen to make the shot perfect. Even after the shot had been made, Shepherd had to keep his cheek pressed against the stock. The finger had to stay on the trigger until all the recoil had dissipated. He had to keep looking through the scope. He had to stay totally relaxed. Actually pulling the trigger was only a small part of what was necessary to be a successful sniper. It was a process, and every part of that process was vital. He blinked, looked away, and then looked back through the scope. The crosshairs were centred on the watermelon. He took a breath and concentrated, focusing on the target and nothing else. All that mattered was the target, he had to zone out everything else. He exhaled, breathing tidally. His finger tightened on the trigger. He inhaled, exhaled halfway, then held his breath and began counting in his head — one, two, three.

As he got to three he slowly started to apply pressure on the trigger. He made the movement smooth and firm, knowing that the slightest jerk would throw the shot off. The cartridge exploded and the stock kicked against his shoulder. Even though the shot had been made he continued to squeeze the trigger until it was fully back, and then released it slowly.

He saw the round slam into the ground to the left of the watermelon and kick up a small divot of earth.

"Three inches to the left," said Hawkins, watching through his binoculars. "Slightly down."

Shepherd smiled thinly. There was nothing to be ashamed of in missing with the first shot with an uncalibrated weapon. There were two knobs on the scope. The top one zeroed the point of impact vertically, the one on the side compensated for windage and affected the POI horizontally.

He adjusted the top knob first, by one click. That would put the next round slightly higher, hopefully by six inches. Then he adjusted the side knob, which would move the next round to the right.

He relaxed, breathed tidally, and looked through the scope again. His second shot kicked a large chunk out of the side of the watermelon. "Not bad," said Hawkins. "One click should do it."

Shepherd clicked the side knob and prepared to make his third shot. It smacked into the centre of the watermelon and it disintegrated into a mass of red and green pulp.

"Confirmed kill," said Hawkins.

Shepherd took aim at the second watermelon and hit it dead centre. His fifth shot destroyed a honeydew melon, then he reloaded.

"Fruit cocktail anyone?" laughed Hawkins.

"I'm surprised I got up to speed so quickly," said Shepherd.

"Nah," said Hawkins. "It's like riding a bike. You never lose it."

Shepherd drove to Leeds first thing on Monday morning. He had phoned ahead and DS Drinkwater hadn't been around but another detective on the case, DC Shaun Allen, had agreed to see him at eleven o'clock. Shepherd had to park on the street a short walk away from the city centre station and, after a brief wait on a plastic chair in reception, a side door opened and a man in a grey suit waved him over. "Mr Shepherd?"

Shepherd nodded. "Dan," he said, figuring it would be better to get on first-name terms with the detective.

"Detective Constable Shaun Allen," said the detective. They shook hands. Allen was in his mid to late thirties with blond hair cut short and the start of a paunch that was straining at the jacket of his suit. "Come on through." He led Shepherd down a corridor to an interview room where a second man was waiting for them. He was in his late twenties, a few inches taller than Allen with receding dark brown hair and black square-framed spectacles. He was sitting on the far side of a table with a closed file in front of him and simply watched as Shepherd followed Allen into the room. "This is Detective Sergeant Paul Drinkwater," said Allen. "He's in charge of Liam's case."

"Pleased to meet you," said Shepherd. "And thanks for seeing me."

Drinkwater didn't get up or offer to shake hands. He just waved dismissively at the chair on the other side of the table. "We would have been interviewing you at some point anyway," said Drinkwater.

"Why's that?" said Shepherd, sitting down.

"Your son is about to be charged with possession of a Class A drug with intent to supply." He adjusted the cuffs of his shirt.

"Liam isn't a dealer," said Shepherd.

"He did have sixteen grams of cocaine in his possession," said Drinkwater, opening the file in front of him. "I doubt that a seventeen-year-old would have that much for personal use."

"He didn't know it was cocaine," said Shepherd. "He thought it was a bit of cannabis. And if it had been cannabis he'd have been let off with a caution."

Drinkwater shook his head. "The guidelines are clear. A person found in possession of one form of drug, believing it to be another form of drug should be charged with the substantive offence of possession of the actual drug. He should not be charged with attempted possession of the drug he believed it to be. That's what the CPS says." He sounded as if he were reading from a textbook.

"But you're allowed some flexibility, surely? Liam's just a kid; he was holding something for a friend. Someone he thought was a friend. He didn't open the package, he didn't use, he didn't sell. All he's guilty of is stupidity."

"His guilt or innocence isn't up to me," said Drinkwater. "That's for a court to decide. But the charge will be possession of a Class A drug with intent to supply."

"Even though he wasn't supplying? And didn't intend to?"

"Again, intent is down to a court to decide."

Shepherd held up his hands. "Okay, yes, you're right. Look, I'm as anti-drug as the next man, and believe me I've read the riot act to my son, but he's not a drug dealer. He's just a kid who made a bad choice. He trusted the wrong person. And from what I understand, he's already told you who that person is."

Allen nodded. "Roger Flynn. Yes. But Mr Flynn isn't prepared to corroborate your son's story."

"It's not a story. It's what happened. Look, Liam isn't the bad guy here."

"Actually he is, Mr Shepherd," said Drinkwater. "He was caught with sixteen grams of cocaine."

"But it wasn't his, he didn't know what it was, and didn't intend to sell it."

"Then he can tell that to the court. Did you know that your son took drugs?"

Shepherd didn't reply.

"Do you understand the question, Mr Shepherd?"

"Yes, I understand the question. I'm damn sure that Liam hasn't taken cocaine."

"What about other drugs? Ecstasy? Cannabis?"

Shepherd didn't answer.

"What about alcohol? Does your son drink, do you know?"

"What does that have to do with anything?" asked Shepherd.

Drinkwater leaned across the table towards Shepherd. "Your son has admitted to us that he smoked cannabis and attended parties where alcohol was consumed."

"He's a teenager."

126

"So do you condone his behaviour?"

"Of course not. I'm not happy about him drinking or smoking cannabis, but he's an adult next year. Look, he made some bad choices but he's not a criminal."

"Again, you say that, Mr Shepherd, but by definition someone who breaks the law is a criminal. And your son has broken the law."

"Do you have kids, Paul?"

Shepherd could see from the way the detective's jaw tightened that he didn't appreciate being addressed by his first name.

"My status isn't an issue," said Drinkwater.

"You can't watch them all the time," said Shepherd. "You have to give them space, and sometimes they make bad choices. That's part of growing up."

"Your son was found in possession of a Class A drug. That's more than just a bad choice."

Shepherd sighed. "Look, I used to be in the job. I was an undercover cop with the Met. Is there anything you can do to make this easier on Liam?"

Drinkwater's eyes narrowed. "What are you suggesting, Mr Shepherd?"

"I don't know, professional courtesy. I was in the job. I'll make sure he stays on the straight and narrow from now on. And he's already told you everything he knows."

Drinkwater took out a ballpoint pen and a small black notebook. "How exactly would this 'professional courtesy' work, Mr Shepherd?"

"Forget it," said Shepherd.

"No, I'd like to know what you were implying. Some sort of special treatment, perhaps?"

"I'm sorry if that's the impression you got," said Shepherd. "I just hoped there was a way of resolving this without my son ending up in court, that's all."

"Your son will be treated in exactly the same way that any member of the community would be if they were found in possession of a substantial quantity of a Class A drug. I hope you understand that, Mr Shepherd."

Shepherd gritted his teeth. "I do. Yes."

The detective put his hands palm down on the table. "So, I want to thank you for coming in, Mr Shepherd, but I'm afraid there is nothing we can do to help you. You'll have your chance to speak in court, of course. And I suggest you get a good lawyer for your son."

Shepherd opened his mouth to speak but then realised there was nothing he could say that would change the outcome. He stood up and offered his hand. "Thank you for your time, anyway, sergeant."

Drinkwater shook his hand but clearly wasn't happy with the physical contact.

"I'll show Mr Shepherd out," said Allen. He opened the door and took Shepherd down the corridor towards the reception area. He pressed the button to open the door and pulled it open. He looked at his watch. "My shift finishes at six," said Allen. "I'll probably stop off at The Grapes for a pint on the way home."

"The Grapes?"

"It's a pub. Turn left and it's a hundred yards down the road. You have a nice day."

★   ★   ★

128

Shepherd was sitting at the main bar in The Grapes with a Jameson and soda in front of him when DC Allen walked in. He was wearing a dark blue raincoat and had a red scarf around his neck. He looked around the bar, spotted Shepherd and walked over, taking off his scarf. The barman came over and Shepherd ordered a pint of bitter.

"Busy day?" asked Shepherd.

"Every day's a busy day," said Allen. "But it's mainly paperwork and emails; I probably spend twenty per cent of my time doing real police work." He scowled. "The job's changed, you know that."

"It was changing while I was there," agreed Shepherd.

"Then you know what it's like. And if anything it's getting worse by the day. You can't just do the right thing any more. You have to be seen to be doing the right thing. But it's worse than that. You have to report anyone who isn't doing the right thing. And if you don't, you're as guilty as they are."

"You have to spy on each other?"

"It's worse than the KGB, Dan."

The barman put down Allen's pint. Shepherd reached for his wallet but Allen shook his head. "I'll get it."

"Don't want to be seen accepting a bribe?"

"Don't want to be seen, period," said Allen. He paid for his beer and the two men headed over to a corner table. Allen sat down, took a long drink of his pint, and stretched out his legs. "Paul's fast-track, I'm sure you gathered that. He plans to be a superintendent within ten years, who knows after that. He's got a degree in economics, and never puts a foot wrong. So he plays it by the rules, has done from day one. Second day of training at Hendon he reported a guy for admitting that he had smoked dope."

"So he's a snitch?"

"It's not as clear-cut as that. The guy could have been a plant. The Met plays tricks like that. The plant boasts about smoking dope. Anyone who doesn't report him is off the course. Anyone who does report him gets a pat on the back. We all know that's how it works."

"You're saying he had no choice?"

Allen shrugged. "I'm saying he knows how to play the game. And that's why I can't help you. And neither can he. Those days are gone. If he didn't report it he'd be out on his ear. So he won't take that risk."

"Unless you both agree to help?"

"Then he'd have something over me for the rest of my career and vice versa." He took another long pull on his pint. "It's a minefield."

"Yeah, I can see that."

"I've got kids myself, Dan. I know what it's like."

"Teenagers?"

"Boy's twelve and the girl's eight. She's all sweetness and light but my son . . ." He shrugged. "They grow up so early, you know?"

"Tell me about it."

"I don't know if it's the fault of the schools or the Internet but they know too much. They're exposed to too much. You have to watch them twenty-four seven."

"Liam isn't a dealer, you know that."

"He was caught with a dealing quantity, Dan. Bang to rights as they say in all the old cop shows. Can't say that any more, of course. Everything that comes out of our mouths, on duty or off, has to be approved by PACE."

"He thought it was cannabis."

"That's what he says. But even if it's true, he still gets charged with possession of a Class A drug. Like Paul said back in the factory. The CPS guidelines are clear."

"Can't you get the charge down to simple possession?"

"If it was up to me, probably. But Paul won't have it. And I understand why. He has to go for the higher charge wherever he can. If it came out that he'd gone for a reduced charge because Liam's dad was a former cop . . ." He sipped his beer again. "You're not really Home Office, are you, Dan?"

"Why do you say that?"

"You've got a spook's eyes."

Shepherd laughed. "I'm not sure that's true."

"I'm just saying. A little honesty might not go amiss."

Shepherd grimaced. "If I was a spook, I wouldn't be able to tell you, you know that. But I can tell you I was in SOCA for a bit."

"SOCA? Waste of time that was. Overpaid and underworked, too many cooks and not enough Indians or whatever the most damning metaphor is."

"That's pretty much how I found it, yeah."

"And what were you doing for SOCA?"

"Undercover work, mainly."

"What sort of cases?"

"Drugs. Terrorism. Organised Crime. You name it."

"Not sure I could work undercover."

Shepherd shrugged. "Not everyone can do it, that's true. It's a bit . . . stressful."

"And now?"

Shepherd grinned. "Yeah, my job now is stressful, too."

Allen took another long pull on his pint. "I had a thought," he said eventually.

"I'm listening."

"Paul isn't going to drop the charges against your boy. Looking at it from his point of view, he can't. He can't even reduce the charge. He has to play it by the rules as he sees them. But maybe you could offer him something else."

"Something else?"

"He needs a big score to make the next move up the ladder. Something high profile. A career maker. Liam's conviction isn't that, it's just a bread-and-butter case. Now, he needs those to meet his targets, but he also needs something bigger to make his mark. Something to get him noticed. Now, you were a cop. You worked undercover. Maybe you could bring him a bigger fish."

Shepherd swirled his drink around his glass. "You mean do Paul's job for him?"

"Paul's backed up with paperwork and admin the same as me. He doesn't have the time to put together anything major."

"And I do?"

"I'm just saying, Dan. If you want to help your lad, give Paul something bigger to get his teeth into. Liam was holding the drugs for Roger Flynn. Roger Flynn won't tell us who he got the drugs from. And why should he? Flynn is going to walk and Liam gets charged. We've got nothing on Flynn other than Liam's word and he knows that. But Flynn must have got the drugs from someone, someone higher up the food chain. And that someone must have got the drugs from someone else. And at some point there'll be a big fish. You give that big fish to Paul and Paul will probably drop the case against your lad." He sipped his beer, watching Shepherd over the top of his glass.

"I've got no jurisdiction here, you know that?"

"You'd have to be careful, sure. But all we'd need is intel. A call that so-and-so has five kilos of whatever and we'll do the rest."

"And that will get Liam off the hook?"

Allen nodded.

"I have your word?"

"I'm not going to put anything in writing, Dan. But you give us a decent collar and I can guarantee that any charges against Liam will disappear."

Shepherd noticed that Allen was no longer talking about it being solely Drinkwater's collar. Now it looked as if both detectives would be taking the credit. He had the feeling that they were playing him, but under the circumstances he didn't see that he had any choice other than to be played. "Okay," he said, "I'll give it a go."

Allen reached inside his coat and pulled out a computer printout. "Roger Flynn is the youngest in a family of toerags. Basically he's a drug dealer and graffiti artist, and like most of his family he's quick to use his fists. He's been cautioned half a dozen times but to be honest he's more of an irritant than anything. But his family is involved in all sorts of shenanigans. Car theft, mail-order fraud, illegal fags, counterfeit DVDs, and drugs, of course. But they're hardly the Corleones, it's all low-level stuff. The dad has been inside half a dozen times, mainly for assault but did five years a while back on a drugs charge. Roger's two elder brothers have both been inside, assault and GBH, and it's only a matter of time before young Roger goes away." He handed the printout to Shepherd.

"So it's the dad you want?" said Shepherd, flicking through the typed sheets. "Aidan?"

"Aidan Flynn's a pain in the arse, but his drug dealing is small time. He sells to the guys who stand on the street selling twenty-quid wraps of coke or heroin. Doubt that he has more than an ounce or two at a time. And he's not stupid. He rarely has the gear himself. He gets others to hold it."

"Like Liam?"

Allen nodded. "Like Liam. But we're not looking to target the Flynns. We want their suppliers. Though even they might not be big enough. We might need the suppliers to their suppliers."

"You're not asking for much, are you?"

"It's not anything you haven't done before."

"Sure, but then I'd have been part of a major operation. You're asking me to go it alone."

"All we need is intel, Dan. And it's your call. If you don't want to do it . . ."

Shepherd sighed. "I'll do it," he said.

"Okay. Well I know the CPS is swamped at the moment, so I'll sit on the paperwork as long as I can, and then it'll be a few weeks on some lawyer's desk at the CPS before anything happens. But the sooner the better, yeah? The further up the chain it goes, the harder it'll be to derail it."

Shepherd shook hands with the detective. "Thanks. I mean it."

"It's professional courtesy," said Allen. "Just because the DS doesn't know what it means doesn't mean it doesn't exist."

Bridie O'Brien's local was a dingy pub in the back streets of Kilburn. The surrounding Victorian houses might once have been family homes but were now all divided and subdivided into flats and bedsits, housing a drifting, transient population. Many were on benefits, the remainder mostly manual labourers or petty criminals. There were plenty of Irish among them, but twenty or thirty other nationalities too, and people kept themselves to themselves, asking few questions and giving even fewer answers.

Jony found Bridie perched on a stool at one end of the bar. He had a couple of pints of Guinness but largely kept himself to himself, though he made sure that when he went to the bar for a refill he stood next to her while he was being served. As he picked up his pint, he winked at her, and said, "All right, darling?" but then sat down at a table across the room and left as soon as he'd drunk his pint.

He was back the following evening, this time having arranged for a couple of stooges to be there as well, sitting in different parts of the room. They were fringe figures from Manchester's criminal underworld, willing to do anything for cash, no questions asked. Having made sure that Bridie was again there to witness the performance, he strode across to one of them, pulled a bulky package from inside his leather jacket and handed it over. After a furtive glance around the room, the other man peeled some notes from a thick wad in his pocket, passed them to Jony and then hurried out.

Jony's other mark had positioned himself just along the bar from where Bridie was sitting. Jony stood next to him without acknowledging or looking at him and ordered a pint. Out of the corner of his eye he made sure that Bridie was looking in his direction, then took a top-end smartphone from his pocket and put it on the bar. Under cover of taking a drink from his pint, the man next to him slid the phone into his pocket. He drained his glass and walked out, but as he brushed past Jony, there was the faint rustle of paper money changing hands.

When Jony looked up, Bridie was watching him. "That guy just nicked your phone," she said, smiling.

Jony grinned at her and flashed her a handful of notes. "Good thing I picked his pocket, then." He paused. "Buy you a drink?"

He was not alone when he went back to his bedsit that night, and Bridie went with him when he made a couple of "deliveries" the next day. They again spent the night together — "perks of the job," Jony said when he reported in to Harper — and the following day, as they were once more nursing a drink in the pub, Jony played his next card. "I've a bit of a special delivery today," he said. "I need someone I can trust to keep watch for me. It's worth a monkey if you're interested."

"Five hundred quid? Of course I'm feckin' interested," she said.

He drove her out to an industrial estate off the North Circular, parking at the far end of a piece of waste ground. They had been there for ten minutes when a Mercedes with blacked-out windows drove up and parked about fifty yards away.

"That's them," Jony said. "Swap seats with me and then keep your eyes peeled. Any sign of anything unusual, any other people or cars appear, beep the horn."

He got out, walked round to the passenger side and peeled back the carpet in the footwell. The exposed steel floor looked perfectly normal until he took a knife from his pocket and drew it along an almost invisible line on the floor, revealing the lid of a hidden compartment. Inside the compartment were two packages, and as he lifted them out, Bridie could see the outline of gun barrels through the thick plastic wrapping.

"Keep alert," he said, and set off towards the Mercedes. Harper, in the driving seat, winked at Jony as he handed the packages in through the open window. "All good?"

"All good, bruv," Jony said. "She practically gave birth when she caught sight of these."

"Then all we need now is for her old man to take the bait and then you can bow out and go back to the day job." He handed Jony a Jiffy bag. "The next instalment — don't spend it all on wining and dining your lady friend."

"She's a cheap date, bruv. No fine dining, just Guinness, Irish whiskey and crisps."

"And a few shags as well?"

"Bruv, I'm shocked," Jony said with a grin. "Didn't you know an English gentleman never kisses and tells?" He winked, then stood back as Harper swung the Merc around and disappeared back up the road in a cloud of dust.

Jony drove back into London in silence, waiting for Bridie to make the first move. "You sell a lot of guns then?" she said at last.

"A few."

"I might be able to put some business your way, that's all. My da's organisation is looking for supplies."

"I don't supply them, I just deliver them for my boss and he's very choosy about who he deals with."

"What sort of stuff can he supply?"

"Are you serious?"

"About what? About my da? Sure. He's in the market for stuff, really."

Jony flashed her a sideways glance. "I can get my hands on pretty much anything. Handguns, rifles, explosives, even heavy weapons. But like I said my boss doesn't deal with people he doesn't know. He's ultra paranoid about his security and with good reason — a lot of cops right around the world would pay good money to find out who he is and where he is."

"It wouldn't hurt to ask though, would it?" she said, placing her hand on his thigh.

"I can ask, but I'm telling you, the answer will be no."

He pulled over to the side of the road, got out and faked a phone call as he paced up and down the pavement. A moment later he got back into the car, slamming the door behind him. "He said 'No', and I got a right bollocking for even mentioning his existence to someone he doesn't know."

"Look, I made a call myself while you were talking to him," she said. "My father's very interested. He runs a serious organisation and he's got the financial backing to get some serious gear. So go back to your boss and ask again."

"He'll only give me the same answer."

"Please, baby. Try again. For me."

Jony shrugged. "All right, I'll try him again, but don't hold your breath. And I'm not calling him back tonight; one bollocking a day is plenty."

Major Gannon arranged for Shepherd's explosives training on Tuesday morning. He had an early egg and bacon breakfast with Liam, and even managed to get more than a few monosyllabic answers from him about how he was getting on at his new school. The headmaster was a good friend of the SAS and had agreed to push through Liam's enrolment without waiting for the required paperwork.

Shepherd didn't raise the drugs incident with Liam. There was nothing to say. He was fairly sure that Liam had learned his lesson and he wouldn't be able to do anything until the following day. Going up against drug dealers was best not done alone so he had phoned Jimmy Sharpe who had arranged to take Wednesday off and go to Leeds with him.

Shepherd dropped Liam off at school and drove to Credenhill. The same guard checked his ID against the list on his clipboard with the same intensity as he had on Sunday, while another guard examined the underside of the car again, slowly and methodically.

The Major was waiting for him in front of the regimental clock, which had been moved from the previous Stirling Lines barracks when they relocated in 1999. The tower was where the regiment honoured its dead and the Major was watching as a man in blue overalls was adding the name of another trooper who had failed to beat the clock. At the base of the clock was a verse from the "The Golden Road to Samarkand" by James Elroy Flecker, a poem that had been adopted as the regiment's creed.

We are the Pilgrims, master; we shall go
Always a little further; it may be
Beyond that last blue mountain barred with snow,
Across that angry or that glimmering sea.

★ ★ ★

"What happened?" asked Shepherd.

"He was on attachment to the Colombians, helping to take down one of the cartels. We don't know how but his cover was blown and they tortured and killed him."

"If you're putting together a team, count me in."

"I'll keep you posted," said the Major.

"Wife? Kids?"

"Thankfully, no. But his mum hasn't taken it well."

He turned away and led Shepherd over to a featureless green metal building. "I've got one of our top dem guys here today," he said, putting his arm around Shepherd's shoulders. "I wasn't sure how far you'd want to go."

"I don't need to actually blow anything up, but I need to know the whys and wherefores."

"Contract killer, you said, so I suppose you don't really need to know how to blow up the big stuff."

The SAS were experts at infiltrating enemy areas and blowing up assets, everything from buildings and bridges to ships and military bunkers. But those sorts of skills weren't really applicable in the world of contract killing.

"I'm thinking IEDs, cars, booby-traps. I need to be brought up to speed on explosives and detonators, what goes where and what the pitfalls are."

"Well Bunny is the man for that. I don't think anyone knows more about the stuff that goes bang."

"Bunny?"

"Bunny Warren. He was doing some very secret stuff in Iraq, playing their bombers at their own game. He'd go in and booby-trap their IEDs. When they went to

141

check, they'd end up on the receiving end of their own devices. Hoisted by their own petards, and good riddance."

The Major took Shepherd into the building where a short man in green fatigues and gleaming white Nikes was waiting for them. Bunny Warren was in his thirties and had the typical SAS physique — wiry rather than well-muscled, average height, and with the ability to blend into a crowd. Warren was the perfect grey man, there was nothing noticeable about his face — he had regular features, skin slightly sunburnt, mousy brown hair that was parted on the left. No jewellery, not even a wristwatch. The Major introduced the two men and they shook hands. Warren had a firm grip and his brown eyes were measuring Shepherd up.

"The boss says you want a full dem briefing so I've put out samples of pretty much everything," he said, waving at two trestle tables loaded with equipment. "We weren't sure what you'd want in the way of demonstrations but we've got an area cordoned off if needed."

"I'm more into the technicalities at the moment," said Shepherd. "At some point I'm probably going to be tested on my technical knowledge so I want to be sure that I'm up to speed."

"No problem," said Warren, rubbing his hands together. "Let's get started."

"If you don't mind I'll hang around for a while," said the Major. "Like Spider, my demo skills are a little rusty."

He pulled up a chair, sat down and stretched out his long legs. For the next two hours Warren went over the various types of explosives on the market, from simple dynamite and TNT to the more complex RDX and

142

PETN. He went into great detail about ammonium nitrate fertiliser, how it could be mixed with TNT to produce Amatol or with diesel fuel oil to produce ANFO — Ammonium Nitrate Fuel Oil mixture — often the IRA's explosive of choice for car bombings and the like. Warren paid particular attention to the methods of detonating the various explosives. "You can have the most efficient explosive in the world, but if you can't get it to go bang you're wasting your time," he said. While it was doubtful that Shepherd would need to be making an ANFO car bomb, Warren talked him though every step of the process.

They broke for lunch and in the canteen, over fish and chips and several mugs of coffee, Warren talked Shepherd and the Major through composition explosives that were mainly designated by acronyms such as C-1, C-2, C-3, C-4, C-A, and C-B, made from mixing explosive such as PETN and RDX with plasticisers, waxes and oils, each recipe producing different ignition and explosive characteristics.

Back in the building, Warren spent the rest of the afternoon showing Shepherd and the Major how to set up detonating circuits for various composition explosives, paying particular attention to Semtex and C-4, the explosives of choice for most of the world's terrorist organisations.

He had a block of brick-orange Semtex H for Shepherd to handle, along with a block of the more reddish Semtex 1A and the brown Semtex 2P.

"Invented back in the fifties by a Czech chemist, but it didn't go into production until 1964," Warren told them. "No doubt you know that seven hundred tons of Semtex was shipped to Libya in the seventies; a lot of that was sent on to terrorist groups around the world, including the IRA of course. Since 2002 all Semtex sales have been controlled by the Czech government and these days production is down to about ten tons a year, most of it for domestic use. The manufacturers have cut the shelf life down to just five years but there's still an awful lot of it slopping around, especially among the jihadists."

Warren also had a block of C-4 to show them, off-white and malleable like putty, which was what the SAS generally used for its shaped charges. He tossed it to Shepherd.

"These days terrorists are more likely to be using this, for car bombs and IEDs and the like," he said. "The Yanks call it C-4, we call it PE-4. It's totally stable — as you know, when you're pushed for hot water you can set fire to a small piece and it'll burn quite nicely. Even shooting it won't set it off. For it to go bang you need a detonator or a blasting cap. A quarter of a pound will easily kill several people and a pound will take out a truck. Are you sure you don't want to set off a block or two?"

Shepherd could see that Warren was itching to create an explosion or two so he laughed and nodded. "Yeah, what the hell, let's blow some shit up."

Harper had arranged to meet Jony outside a pub in Leytonstone, east London. He got there first and read through the *Sun* as he waited for him to arrive. Jony parked his BMW next to Harper's car nose to tail and the two men wound down their windows.

"All good?" asked Harper.

"She's hot to trot," said Jony. "Says her dad is as keen as mustard. Wants to meet."

"Excellent," said Harper. "We're going to do that offshore." He passed over a piece of paper. "Give her that."

Jony looked at the name and address on the piece of paper: *Müller. Hotel de Paris. Monte Carlo. 3p.m. Thursday.*

"Monte bloody Carlo?"

Harper grinned. "How the other half lives," he said. "Give her that, then soon as you can, get the hell out of Dodge."

"No sweat, bruv. I lost interest in her some time ago." He waved, wound up the window and drove off.

Harper stopped off at an Internet café on the way back to central London. He paid for a coffee and an hour on a terminal and went through to the draft folder. He left a short message. *YOU THERE?* And sipped his coffee.

Within ten minutes a message had appeared in the drafts folder and for the next couple of minutes they went back and forth in a conversation that no one in the world — not even GCHQ or the NSA — could monitor.

IT'S ON. I'M ARRANGING TO MEET THEM IN MONTE CARLO.

After a few seconds a new message appeared in the drafts file. *BECAUSE?*

Harper typed quickly. *BECAUSE YOU WANTED IT DONE OUTSIDE THE UK AND BECAUSE I KNOW THE PLACE WELL. AND BECAUSE I HAVE A COUPLE OF BANK ACCOUNTS THERE.*

FINE.

AND JUST SO THERE ARE NO UGLY SURPRISES I SHOULD TELL YOU THAT I'VE BOOKED THE BEST SUITE AT THE HOTEL DE PARIS, A SNIP AT JUST OVER 5,000 EUROS A NIGHT. A LITTLE OTT FOR MY TASTE BUT THE IMPRESSION IS THE THING.

WHATEVER IT TAKES TO GET THE JOB DONE.

Harper sat back and grinned at the final message. He was supposed to be a mega arms dealer and he wouldn't be giving the right impression staying in a two-star bed and breakfast in Marseille. The whole thing hinged on them believing that he didn't give a shit whether the IRA boys bought weapons from him or not.

He went back into the draft folder a final time and was surprised to see another message from Button. Just two words. *BE CAREFUL.*

He smiled and raised his coffee cup to the screen. "Always," he said, then typed a smiley face and logged off.

Shepherd had just dropped Liam off at school when his mobile rang. He took the call on his Bluetooth. It was Charlie Button.

"How are things in Hereford?" she asked.

"I've brushed up on my sniping and I'm up to speed on explosives," he said.

"Excellent. I've arranged for you to see one of our technical boys on Friday. He can talk you through the latest IEDs. And I'm hoping by then we'll have fixed up an intro to the London agent who knows Smit. Can you be in London Friday morning and I'll talk you through it? It looks as if we'll be able to do something on that evening."

"No problem. Just let me know where."

"It'll be north London so keep the Battersea flat up and running. I'll get all the data changed for your new legend. Anyway, there's nothing that needs doing until Friday, so take the next couple of days off. I'd say put your feet up but knowing you you'll be out running."

"Something like that," he said. He waited until he was back home before phoning Jimmy Sharpe. "Razor, are you still free for a run to Leeds today?"

"Are you buying the beer?"

"Whatever it takes," said Shepherd. "One snag, I'm in Hereford. Can you get the train to Leeds and I'll pick you up? I'll drive you back to London when we're done."

"Can I play with the siren?" said Sharpe.

"I don't have a siren, Razor."

"I was joking."

Harper flew to Prague on Wednesday morning. The seat next to him in business class was empty and he spent the flight reading through a file that Hansfree had put together for him, containing a mass of documentation on the capacity and black-market prices of a range of Russian- and Czech-manufactured handguns, semi-automatics, machine guns, ammunition, explosives and detonating cord, and even surface-to-air and ground-to-ground missiles. If he was going to be convincing in his role as a big arms dealer, it was the sort of information that he had to have at his fingertips.

After landing in Prague, he took a cab into the centre of the city. He bought a bag full of toiletries from a pharmacy, picked up a Czech hardback book and a couple of magazines, and then spent a couple of hours drinking beer and eating Bohemian food at U Flekù. He took another cab back to the airport and flew to Nice, where he rented an S-Class black Mercedes. He drove along the coast towards Monte Carlo and it was late afternoon when he pulled up outside his hotel. It was in the heart of the city, overlooking the harbour and within yards of the casino. Its facade, pierced by marble colonnades, balustrades and wrought-iron balconies, was so elaborately decorated that it could have been a wedding cake. Harper jumped out and dispensed the first of a succession of €50 notes to the parking attendant, the doorman, the bellhop, the reception clerk who checked him in, and the barmen and waiters who served him. By the end of the evening, there was probably no one on the hotel staff who did not know that their new guest, Herr Müller, was a lavish tipper.

The hotel wasn't the sort of place Harper enjoyed — all chandeliers, ornate plasterwork and gilt and cherubs by the bucket-load — but it suited the legend he had adopted. He wanted somewhere that would overawe the IRA men, putting them on the back foot from the start.

Harper unpacked his Czech toiletries in his suite. He opened them one by one and emptied out part of each one, squeezing out half the toothpaste and squirting some of the shaving foam down the toilet. He opened the Czech magazines in a few places, cracked the spine of the hardback book and riffled through and thumbed some of its pages, and then put it next to his bed. His legend was that he was an East European arms dealer who never travelled to Britain, and if the IRA men searched his room and found a washbag full of toiletries from Boots or a receipt for a Marks and Spencer prawn sandwich, his cover would be blown and his life in immediate danger.

That evening, he dressed in an Armani suit paid for with one of his new credit cards and ate in the hotel's Michelin-starred restaurant before strolling across the square to the casino. As he entered, he slipped a €100 note into the doorman's gloved hand.

"My name's Müller," he said. "I'll be staying in Monte Carlo for the next week or so. Look after me and my guests well, won't you?" He played a little roulette, gave more lavish tips to the croupier and the waiters, and as he walked out into the square to the hotel, he smiled to himself as he heard the doorman call after him, "Good night Herr Müller, sir."

"Explain this to me again," said Jimmy Sharpe. "It seems hellish complicated."

Sharpe and Shepherd were sitting in a rented Mondeo parked outside the Coach and Horses, Aidan Flynn's watering hole of choice, a short walk from his four-bedroom council house on the Seacroft council estate to the east of Leeds. It was one of the country's largest council estates, with a reputation for crime, violence and drugs.

"We pick him up and get him to tell us where he gets his drugs from. Best way to do that is let him think he's got a problem and we're here to help him."

"Why don't we do it the easy way?" asked Sharpe. "Beat the crap out of him until he agrees to get his son to take the fall. The drugs belonged to his son, the son tells that to the cops and your boy walks."

"Yeah, well the simplest way doesn't always produce results," said Shepherd. "For one, even if the Flynn boy does cough, it doesn't help Liam. Liam was holding the drugs, there's no getting away from that. I need to give the cops a bigger fish. And for two, Flynn is a scumbag but even scumbag dads will do whatever they have to do to protect their kids. He won't want his son going down, so no matter how much pressure we put him under, at some point he'll go to the cops and tell them what's happened. It won't take them long to realise that it was me and then I'm screwed."

"What the hell was your boy doing holding drugs anyway?" asked Sharpe.

"He thought it was cannabis, not that that's an excuse. I'm sure if he'd known it was cocaine he'd have said no. But that's not the point."

"How old is he? Still sixteen, right?"

"Just turned seventeen. He's been going to parties where there's been drink and drugs."

"And girls, I hope."

"Cheers, Razor."

"Come on, Spider. How old were you when you had your first pint? Fifteen? Sixteen?"

"Fifteen," said Shepherd.

"Yeah, well we're made of sterner stuff in Glasgow. I was thirteen when I had my first drink. Cider. And I puked my guts up afterwards. And I'd been smoking for a year before that."

"Didn't know you were a smoker."

"I gave up years ago. But I stuck with the drinking. And it's never done me any harm."

"Cannabis and cider aren't the same thing."

"Well, I'm no fan of drugs, but you have to face the facts — health-wise alcohol does a lot more damage than cannabis any day of the week. I'm not saying that cannabis is a good thing and I know it can lead to harder drugs, but no one ever smoked two joints and went looking for a fight. In fact there's a lot to be said to giving cannabis to any scrote that wanted it. It'd keep them quiet."

"Razor . . ."

"Okay, I'm being facetious. But with cannabis users not even getting a caution these days, it seems a bit unfair sending people to prison for holding half an ounce."

"Yeah, well unfortunately it wasn't cannabis in Liam's case. So stick with my plan, yeah?"

Sharpe threw him a sarcastic salute. "*Jawohl, mein Herr,*" he said, in a parody of a German accent. "I vill obey your orders."

"I'm starting to regret asking you along."

"Yeah, like you were spoilt for choice," said Sharpe. He looked around at the shabby council houses, rusting cars and potholed streets. "Here's what I don't get. Your lad's at a posh boarding school and his mate's living in this place?"

"They met at a rave or whatever they call them these days. A party."

"The school let him out to party?"

"They were sneaking out. Flynn's son had a car; he's a year older. Turns out he was selling drugs to the kids at the school."

"Do you think your boy knew that?"

"He says not."

"Here we go," said Sharpe, pointing out of the window. "Is that him?"

Shepherd looked over at the pub doorway. A big man was standing there, swaying slightly as he lit a cigarette. He was wearing a long black leather coat with the collar turned up. As the lighter flared it illuminated the man's goatee and hooked nose, then the flame went out. "That's him all right," he said. Flynn was a big man, well over six feet with wide shoulders and hands the size of small shovels.

"Big bugger," said Sharpe. He unfolded a printout that he'd taken from the police national computer. There was a picture of Flynn taken three years earlier when he'd been arrested and charged with assault. His arrest record had started when he was a teenager, mainly assault and petty theft, and had continued throughout his adult life.

"You know what they say," said Shepherd. "The bigger they are, the harder they —"

". . . hit," Sharpe finished for him.

"I was going to say fall," said Shepherd. "Anyway, we're only going to talk to him."

Flynn began to walk unsteadily down the street, the lit cigarette in his right hand. Shepherd switched on the engine, pulled a slow U-turn and came up behind him. Flynn looked around. Sharpe wound down his window and flashed his warrant card. "Get in, Aidan," he growled.

"Who the fuck are you?" asked Flynn, squinting down at Sharpe.

"The fucking tooth fairy," said Sharpe. "Get in the back."

"Are you arresting me?"

"Do I look like I'm fucking arresting you?" He put away his warrant card. "If you make me get out of this warm comfortable car I'll not be best pleased. Now get in the back."

Flynn climbed into the car.

"And put your seat belt on," said Shepherd. He kept facing forward; he didn't want Flynn getting a look at anything other than the back of his head.

Flynn muttered and did as he was told as Shepherd put the car in gear and drove off.

"Does someone want to tell me what's going on?" asked Flynn.

"Aidan Flynn, right?" asked Sharpe.

"You fucking tell me."

Sharpe twisted around in his seat. "Show me some ID."

Flynn looked as if he was going to argue but Sharpe's baleful stare took the wind out of his sails and he sighed and took out his wallet. He fished out a driving licence and gave it to Sharpe. Sharpe looked at both sides and handed it back. "Your name came up in an investigation in Glasgow."

"I don't do fuck all in Glasgow," said Flynn, putting his licence away.

"Will you shut the fuck up and listen," said Sharpe. "We've had a group of Romanians under surveillance for the past three months. Nasty bastards, Aidan. Real nasty. They've been ripping off drug dealers, stealing their cash and drugs and not caring too much about the damage they do along the way. Mainly knives, but they're tooled up and not afraid of pulling the trigger. They've hit at least six times but the nature of the victims means they're not queuing up to fill out a police report. What we have got is two neds in intensive care and another one in the morgue. Now to cut a long story short, your name came up during a surveillance operation."

"You're barking up the wrong tree, I've never been to Scotland," said Flynn.

Sharpe sighed and looked over at Shepherd. "If he had another brain cell or two he might be dangerous," he growled. "I'm starting to think we're wasting our time."

154

"We could always just throw him to the wolves," said Shepherd. "No skin off our nose."

"Look, what the fuck is going on?" asked Flynn.

"What's going on, my stupid little friend, is that the Romanians have started doing their thing south of the border. And your name has been mentioned."

"I don't have enough drugs to be worth robbing," said Flynn. "I'm not big time."

"No, but you have a supplier. What we heard was that they were going to tail you to your supplier when you go to make a buy. It's your supplier they're after."

Flynn frowned. "I buy from a Turkish gang," he said. "They can take care of themselves."

"Yeah? You think? Well I can show you two guys in Glasgow Royal Infirmary who thought they could take care of themselves, too. No mate, we're here to stop a bloodbath."

"So you're just giving me a tip-off, yeah?" Flynn grinned. "Well I appreciate that, officers. Good to see the boys in blue helping the community. Now if you could drop me around the corner from my house, that would be great."

"These Turks, who are they?" asked Shepherd.

"Don't worry about that, I'll tip them the wink," said Flynn.

"Like fuck you will," said Sharpe. "We don't want them tipped off. We're going to be putting them under surveillance. Then when the Romanians move in, we grab them."

"The Turks won't be happy about being used as bait," said Flynn.

"Which is why we won't be telling them," said Sharpe. "Look, we've done you the courtesy of letting you know what's happening. You tell us where the Turks are and we'll do the rest."

Flynn scratched his chin. "How I do know you're not setting me up?"

"For what?" said Sharpe. "If we wanted to bust you we'd just go around to your house."

"No drugs in my house," snarled Flynn.

"Really? What about cash? You know these days if you can't prove that any cash you have isn't the proceeds of crime, we can take it off you. Shall I get a warrant and get some feet on the ground?"

Flynn held up his hands. "Okay, okay, I was just asking a question. No need to bite my head off. They run a kebab shop in Church Street. The minicab office above the shop is also theirs. They sometimes use the cabs to deliver the gear."

"Is that what you do?"

"Sometimes. Sometimes I send one of the lads around to get kebabs and some gear. Great kebabs."

"Good to know, next time I want food poisoning," said Sharpe. "How do you arrange a delivery? Do you call?"

Flynn nodded. "Sure."

"I'll need that number," said Sharpe.

"You gonna tap their phone?"

"Best you don't know," said Sharpe. "Just consider yourself lucky. If the Romanians had turned up while you were there you could have been the one in the ICU."

156

Flynn took out his mobile and read out a number. Sharpe tapped it into his own phone. Shepherd pulled in at the side of the road. "You won't be hearing from us again," he said to Flynn. "Just keep your head down and find another supplier and you'll be fine."

Flynn climbed out of the car and Shepherd drove off. "That went better than I thought it would," he said. "I was worried we might have to get a bit physical."

"Nah, he's stupid but he thinks all cops are even more stupid. He reckons he's come off best in that deal." He held up his phone. "Now what? You tell your pals to turn the Turks over and your boy is free and clear?"

"Let's see how big they are, first," said Shepherd. "Flynn is small time. The Turks might not be much bigger. Are you okay to hang around for a day or two?"

"I've taken a week's leave," said Sharpe. "I'm happy to help." He grinned. "It's just like the good old days."

"Except that we've got no jurisdiction here. This is totally off the books."

"We're putting bad guys away, that's what counts," said Sharpe. "Now, are you up for a drink?"

O'Brien and Walsh and the two IRA thugs they had brought with them as security arrived just as the sun was going down. Harper watched from the balcony of his suite at the Hotel de Paris as they arrived in a grey Audi saloon. He acknowledged the call from reception to say that his guests had arrived, but left them cooling their heels in the lobby for another ten minutes before he went down to meet them. The desk clerk, doorman, concierge and valet parking attendant all greeted Harper with a chorus of "Good evening, Herr Müller," as he strolled through the lobby and shook hands with the Irishmen and Walsh.

Declan O'Brien, red-faced, with sandy, thinning hair and jowls overlapping his shirt collar, was sweating profusely in a cheap suit that looked to be at least ten years old and two sizes too small for him. His gaze was shrewd and calculating, but he had the look of a heavy drinker and the undigested alcohol on his breath as he greeted Harper confirmed it. The money man, Michael Walsh, was dressed in a sharp suit with a Brooks Brothers shirt and gleaming loafers. His handshake felt boneless and he looked as round and plump as a Pillsbury Doughboy as he stared around him, taking in the lavish decor. The goons with them were two of the IRA thugs whose photos Button had shown him. Harper noted that both were heavyset, with the stern, suspicious expressions that nearly all amateur bodyguards adopted.

He led them to seats in the far corner of the lobby, settled himself in a chair facing out over the room and ordered vintage champagne from a hovering waiter. When the waiter returned Harper tipped him with a €50 note and told him, "Make sure we're not disturbed again."

"Just before we start," O'Brien said, "I'll have to insist on a little precaution, I'm afraid. One of my men here is going to need to check you for hidden microphones. Nothing personal," he said hastily as he saw the look in Harper's eye. "But as you'll appreciate yourself, you can't be too careful in this line of business."

"You're not patting me down in public," said Harper.

"It's not about not trusting you," said O'Brien.

"Of course it is," said Harper. "And that goes both ways. I've already looked into both your backgrounds and, rest assured, if I'd found anything to cause me concern, this meeting would not have taken place and you gentlemen would have met with a very unfortunate accident on your way here from the airport. But okay, yes you can pat me down if I can do the same to you. But not here. Let's just go to the Gents, yeah? At the risk of looking like a couple of queers going for a quick one. Your security can stay put."

Harper headed for the men's room with O'Brien and Walsh in tow. The facilities were as opulent as the lobby, with gilded mirrors and elaborate fittings. Harper opened his jacket and undid his shirt and allowed O'Brien to pat him down. Then the two men did the same and Harper frisked them. "You realise this is a waste of time," said Harper.

O'Brien frowned. "What do you mean?"

"Transmitters these days are the size of a pin. And mobiles can be used to record and transmit even when they're switched off. For all I know you could have a fake tooth capable of recording everything it hears within ten feet. It's all James Bond these days. So patting each other down doesn't really prove a thing." He shrugged. "Just so you know."

"Let's just say I feel a bit safer," said O'Brien.

"Then we're all good," said Harper, patting him on the back.

They went back to their table and sat down. Harper noticed that one of the bodyguards had gone. He was probably checking Müller's room.

"You have no security, Mr Müller?" O'Brien asked, looking around.

Harper smiled. "The fact that you can't see it doesn't mean it isn't there."

"And you speak very good English," Walsh added, "almost perfect to my admittedly American ear." His tone was even and his smile bland, but there was no mistaking the veiled query and implicit threat behind his words: are you really who you claim to be?

Harper gave a self-deprecating smile. "Most Germans do. And I went to an international school in Switzerland and university in the UK." His expression remained unchanged, but his gaze locked with the American's. "Now, if there are no further questions you need resolving?" He paused and took a sip of his champagne. "So, gentlemen, to business: what exactly is it that I can do for you?"

Walsh shot a nervous glance around them as O'Brien leaned forward. "Your man told my daughter you were able to supply all kinds of equipment. We're looking for big stuff."

Harper nodded. "I can supply you with almost anything, for a price. The question is, how big is big? Since the Soviet Union fell apart there is some very big stuff around. I could probably get you a submarine if

160

you wanted one. Mortars or ground-to-ground missiles, easy as pie."

"Missiles would be good," said O'Brien, nodding.

"Are you familiar with the Katyusha rockets? They're ex-Soviet weapons, originally introduced during the Second World War but regularly upgraded since then. The Soviets fired them from a multiple launcher holding up to forty rockets. It was nicknamed 'Stalin's organ' — not because they resembled his genitals but because a bank of them looked like organ pipes — but they can be fired from any sloping track, even a length of guttering would do. Hezbollah fired off hundreds during the 2006 war in Lebanon and they're still used in Palestine by Hamas and Islamic Jihad militants firing rockets into Israel. A salvo of them will obliterate everything within a square kilometre, but even a single rocket can cause carnage. The howling sound they make in flight also increases the terror they generate. They're not one hundred per cent accurate, but used against concentrated enemy forces . . ." He paused and cocked an eye at them. ". . . or densely populated urban areas, they can be devastating. And the lack of precise accuracy might even increase their potential as terror weapons, if that's what you're looking for."

O'Brien's expression did not change an iota, though Harper was sure he was offering him something beyond his wildest dreams. "And the price?"

Harper was equally impassive. "One point five million dollars each."

He saw O'Brien exchange glances with his backer, and the faint nod from the American.

"I work on phased payments," Harper said, "fifty per cent in advance, fifty per cent on delivery to any destination in mainland Europe, packaged and crated as pipework, machine tools, refrigeration equipment, or whatever you prefer. Shipping to Britain or Ireland, or wherever you want after that, will be your responsibility."

"Half in advance?" Walsh said. "I'm not handing over that kind of money up front, without anything to show for it. How do we know we can trust you?"

"You don't. But more importantly from my point of view, I don't know if I can trust you. You came to me, remember? So here's what I suggest we do. First, we'll do a small deal, and establish whether we can trust each other. I will supply you with some small arms — Kalashnikovs, ammunition, maybe even grenades or plastic explosive — but no heavy weapons at this stage." He held up a hand as O'Brien started to protest. "It'll be in the nature of a test. You'll get some weapons you can use and if everything goes smoothly and both sides are happy, then we can talk about a shipment of more serious and specialised equipment. You tell me your requirements and I'll give you a price within a couple of hours at most and deliver the goods within a week."

The two men held a whispered consultation and then O'Brien gave a reluctant nod. "All right then, I'll give you a list." He reached into his pocket for a pen, but Harper stopped him at once. "I don't ever want anything in writing. Just tell me what you want."

There was another whispered consultation between the two men then O'Brien nodded. "We want ten

AK-47s, five thousand rounds of ammunition, twenty grenades, detonators, det-cord and fifty kilos of Semtex."

Harper shrugged. "The plastic explosive might be Semtex but we also source it from Russia, France, Greece and Poland, and sometimes American C-4 or British PE-4 comes my way, would that be okay?"

"The origin doesn't matter," O'Brien growled. "Just so long as it does the feckin' job when it detonates."

"Give me a few minutes," Harper said, rising to his feet, "and I'll have a price for you for the other stuff."

Harper went out on to the terrace and took out his phone. He paced up and down as he faked a phone call for several minutes, then walked back into the lobby and sat down, facing the men. "The supplies are no problem, the price is two hundred thousand dollars."

O'Brien raised an eyebrow. "That's a lot more than we were expecting to pay."

"The weapons are guaranteed untraceable and they are genuine military supplies, not poor quality copies and knock-offs. You can get AK-47s cheaper elsewhere — you can pick them up in the bazaars of Peshawar for a few dollars, I believe — but to get them to Europe would cost multiples of that in bribes and be done at considerable risk to yourselves. Grenades are less readily available and plastic explosive is really hard to get. The days when you could buy a few kilos from some disgruntled Czech or Russian soldier trying to top up his pay are long gone. So there's a scarcity value as well as the risk factor."

He paused, trying to read their body language. "Anyway, the price isn't negotiable," he said. "Like I said, you came to me. I don't have to go around drumming up business. Take it or leave it."

He sat and watched the people filing through the lobby while the two men held yet another whispered consultation and finally O'Brien said, "All right."

Harper reached into his pocket and handed him a BlackBerry. "This is encrypted. It cost me two grand so treat it with respect. There is one number programmed on this phone. You will communicate with me only on that number, using only this phone, and you will not give the number to any other person in your organisation, no matter who they are. Nor do you ever speak to anyone else using this phone. And I will speak to one person and one person only. So . . ." He looked from O'Brien to Walsh. "You two had better decide who's in charge."

"I'm in charge," O'Brien said.

"And any breach of any aspect of this," Harper said, "and not only is the deal off but I'll come looking for you."

O'Brien's expression showed his anger. "You think you can threaten me?"

Harper shrugged. "I'm sure you're quite a big shot in your organisation. But this is my domain; my game, my rules, as I believe you British like to say."

"We're not feckin' British," O'Brien hissed.

Walsh hastily intervened. "We appreciate your precautions and we realise that you are protecting our security as well as yours."

"Fine, at least we're on the same page," Harper replied. "Now enough of business, I'm sure you'll want to freshen up after your journey. I've booked suites for you here and I've reserved a table for dinner in the restaurant here, it's Michelin starred and the chef is one of the best in France. And afterwards, I'd like you to be my guests at Monte Carlo's famous casino." He gave his best smile. "Who knows, you might win enough to pay for your shipment."

Sharpe snapped away with his long-lensed camera as a Turkish man in a long black coat came out of the door that led up to the minicab offices. The man walked a short way along the street and climbed into a Toyota and drove off.

"They're busy enough," said Sharpe.

They were sitting in their rented Mondeo a hundred yards or so from the kebab shop in Leeds. They had been there for an hour and had photographed a dozen different drivers. The kebab shop was open for business but it was late morning and there had been few customers. Sharpe lowered his camera and looked at the computer printout on his lap.

"The taxi firm and the kebab shop are in the name of two brothers, Yusuf and Ahmet Yilmaz. Yusuf is older by a couple of years. Yusuf has two sons and four daughters. Ahmet isn't married."

"You know Turkish family names are a relatively new invention," said Shepherd. "Started in 1934. Before then most male Turks used their dad's name followed by *oglu*. It means son of."

"Aye, we had something similar in Scotland," said Sharpe. "Neither of them have criminal records, they've done a good job of staying below the radar. Using the taxis to deliver is a smart move. And the kebab shop and the taxi business are both cash businesses so there's no problem getting their ill-gotten gains into the bank. I'm guessing they funnel money back to Turkey, too. They keep a relatively low profile here. They drive second-hand cars, their houses are nothing special."

"Smart," said Shepherd.

"How much longer do you want to sit here?" asked Sharpe. "All we're getting is photographs of drivers and cars."

"It's all grist to the mill," said Shepherd. "The more we give the Leeds cops, the better."

"I could do with a drink."

"Let's give it another hour."

An hour later, Shepherd and Sharpe were sitting in a pub about a mile away from the kebab house. Sharpe had a pint in front of him, but Shepherd was driving so had ordered a coffee. Shepherd took out a pay-as-you-go phone and tapped out the number that Flynn had given him. It was answered with a growl.

"Yusuf?"

"Who wants to know?"

"I'm a friend of Aidan Flynn. He said you were the go-to guy for a decent amount of blow."

"I don't know you."

"Nah, but I've got cash and I'm looking for an ounce and I need it now."

"Where are you?"

"Pub called the Royal Oak. In High Street."

"Okay, there'll be a minicab outside in fifteen minutes. The driver'll send you a text when he's there. Get in the back, hand over the cash and the driver will give you the gear."

"How much?"

"Eight-fifty."

"How pure is that?"

"It's good stuff."

"Yeah, well if you're selling it for eight-fifty it's been cut to fuck. I want it as pure as you get it. An ounce before you cut it."

There were a few seconds' silence before he spoke again. "Fifteen hundred."

"I'd be happier with twelve."

"Fourteen or you can fuck off."

"Fourteen it is," said Shepherd. One thousand four hundred pounds for twenty-eight grams of cocaine worked out at about £50 a gram but that was still too cheap for the cocaine to be pure. Street cocaine was generally cut by ninety per cent so that just ten per cent was the real thing. Pure cocaine, if you could get it, was closer to £100 a gram. "And if your gear's as good as Aidan says it is, I'll be back for more."

The line went dead and Shepherd nodded at Sharpe. "All good. One thousand four hundred."

"Have you got that on you?"

"I will have if we hit an ATM. I've got a few cards on me. There's one down the street. You get another drink in while I get the cash."

"What are you going to do with the gear once you've bought it?"

"I hadn't thought that far ahead."

"You'll have to dispose of it. Which means a grand and a half down the drain."

"I don't see I've got any choice, Razor," said Shepherd. "Make mine a Jameson and soda."

Sharpe had just ordered himself another pint when Shepherd's phone buzzed to let him know he'd received a text. *YOUR CAR IS OUTSIDE. BLACK VAUXHALL ZAFIRA*. He nodded at Sharpe. "We're on."

"Shall I come with you?"

"Best not. It'll look strange, two up on a drugs buy. But I'll keep my phone on so you can listen in." He called Sharpe's number and Sharpe answered. Shepherd slipped his phone into his jacket pocket as he stood up.

"What happens if anything goes wrong?" asked Sharpe. "They know you'll have nearly fifteen hundred quid in your pocket."

"I'll be fine."

"I hope so."

Shepherd nodded and headed out of the pub. The black Vauxhall Zafira was parked down the road. He walked along to it and climbed into the back. The driver seemed to be Turkish but it was hard to be sure because he had a flat cap pulled down over his face. "You got the money?" he growled.

168

"Sure," said Shepherd. He handed over a thick roll of twenty-pound notes.

The man counted them with gloved hands and then nodded. "Okay. Get out. Another car will come and give you the gear."

"What?"

"Two minutes. He'll give you the gear. I have to go now."

"Fuck that for a game of soldiers," said Shepherd. "I paid you. I want the gear now."

The driver sighed and shook his head. "I don't have the gear. I take the money. The next car gives you the gear. That's how we do it."

"And how do I know you won't drive off with my cash?"

"Do you want your money back? You can have your money back. I don't care. I'm just the driver."

Shepherd stared at the back of the man's head, then realised he didn't have any choice. "Two minutes?"

"Maybe less."

"Okay."

Shepherd climbed out and as soon as he slammed the door shut the taxi drove off. He looked around and couldn't help but chuckle. If he had just been ripped off, Sharpe was never going to let him hear the end of it. He shoved his hands into his pockets and turned to look into a shop window. Electrical equipment, solar-powered lights, lava lamps and radio-controlled cars. Shepherd was squinting at a radio-controlled drone that came with a TV camera when he heard a car drive up. He turned and saw another Vauxhall, this one blue, with a driver who was wearing a matching flat cap to the man who'd taken Shepherd's money. The driver's side window wound down as Shepherd walked over to the car. The man's hand appeared holding a small padded envelope. Shepherd took it and almost immediately the car sped off down the street.

Shepherd went back into the pub. "Bingo," he said, sitting down at Sharpe's table and sliding the envelope towards him.

"Congratulations," said Sharpe. "Be a laugh if I arrested you for possession, wouldn't it?" He peered inside the bag. "Do you want to test it, or should I?"

"Could you, without raising a red flag?"

"I wasn't planning on sending it to the lab," said Sharpe. "The taste test'll do the business."

"Are you serious?"

"Spider, sometimes you have to do what you have to do. Don't play the innocent with me, you've done enough drug deals in the past. You pull out a test kit and your card is well and truly marked. Sometimes you have to bite the bullet and put a bit up your nose." He laughed and sipped his pint.

Shepherd didn't say anything, but he knew that Sharpe was right. Undercover cops weren't supposed to do anything illegal during the course of an investigation, but if you were surrounded by heavies with guns and everyone else had sampled the merchandise, a refusal could be fatal.

"Give me a minute," said Sharpe. He stood up, slid the envelope into his pocket and headed to the toilets.

Shepherd took his phone out and killed the call to Sharpe's phone, then called Liam. He answered on the third ring. "Where are you?" asked Shepherd.

"Home. Downstairs. I'm doing some homework."

"How is the school?"

"It's actually okay. Better than I thought it would be. I'm trying out for the football team tomorrow."

"So it's working out?"

"I think so."

"And what are you telling them when they ask why you moved schools."

"Just that I hated boarding. I tell them I thought I was going to Hogwarts but it was more like Borstal. It gets a laugh."

"I'm glad you've got something to smile about," said Shepherd.

"Dad, I'm sorry."

"I know you are. I'm trying to get this sorted and then I'll be back in Hereford."

"Any idea how long?"

"Sooner rather than later, I hope. How's Katra?"

"She's good. Keeps forcing food on me. I think I've put on a kilo already. She was bored with no one here."

"Don't give her any problems, Liam."

"What do you mean?"

"You know what I mean. No curfew breaking, no sneaking out."

"Dad, I'll be as good as gold. I swear."

"I hope so. Okay, good night. God bless." Shepherd ended the call as Sharpe came back and sat down. He tossed the padded envelope across the table. "All good?" asked Shepherd.

"I'm no expert, but it's definitely coke. Now what?"

"Now I take this to the cops and that should be the end of it."

Harper was at his most expansive over dinner, keeping up a stream of conversation and making sure both men's glasses were well topped up. He made a show of filling his own glass each time as well, but he was drinking little, merely sipping from his glass. Walsh also drank sparingly, but O'Brien was guzzling his wine down, swallowing first growth vintage claret as if it were water. Nor did he hold back from wolfing down every scrap of the five-course meal that Harper had ordered for them.

After dinner, they strolled across the square to the casino, where the doorman fell over himself to greet Herr Müller and his honoured guests, signalling frantically for a hostess to escort them into the gaming rooms. Herr Müller then led them to the roulette table and gave both men a stack of €100 chips. "Please," he said, as the American fumbled for his wallet. "Tonight you're my guests." His smile was unforced; he was imagining Button's face when she saw the bill for his expenses, almost all of them without a receipt.

O'Brien continued to drink steadily, growing more red-faced, sweaty and irritable with each glass. While Walsh won a small amount of money, O'Brien was losing on almost every spin of the wheel. Harper played shrewdly, placing his chips as if he hadn't a care in the world, but betting only on odd or even or red or black to minimise his losses. When O'Brien was cleaned out, Harper bought them both vintage cognacs as a nightcap but then excused himself.

When he got back to his suite, the first thing he did was to turn back the carpet next to the bed and the wardrobe. He had placed a few cornflakes on the floor under the carpet that morning and they had been crushed to fragments. The "Do Not Disturb" sign would have kept housekeeping out so, although nothing had been taken and everything was apparently just as it had been, he was sure the room had been thoroughly searched. He smiled to himself. They were definitely on the hook, all he had to do now was to reel them in. And for that he'd need more help. He picked up his phone and called a number in Germany.

Shepherd left London in his BMW SUV early on Friday morning. He had programmed the address Button had given him into his SatNav but the place was still difficult to find. It was listed as an Agricultural Research Station, close to where the M1 intersected the M25, but there were no signposts and it took Shepherd half an hour of driving around narrow roads before he found a single-track lane that led to a wire fence. At a gate with a security barrier, his ID was checked and then he was waved through.

The "Agricultural Research Station" turned out to be a two-storey pre-war brick-built office block with metal grilles over all the windows. There were half a dozen cars parked by the main entrance including a large black Vauxhall Insignia with a suited driver in the front who was watching a movie on an iPad.

There was an intercom by the side of the entrance and he pressed the single button. The door clicked and he pushed it open. Button was already walking down a corridor towards him, her heels clicking on the tiled floor. She had her hair held up with a gilt clip and was wearing a dark blue blazer over a Burberry skirt.

"Perfect timing," she said. "Our explosives expert is just setting up, but before I take you to see him there's someone else you need to meet."

She took him back along the corridor to a windowless office where a tall man in a black leather jacket over a grey shirt and tight black jeans was sitting on a desk, swinging his legs back and, forth.

"This is Neil Murray, he's Five but he's been on attachment to the NCA for the last couple of months in an operation that's been targeting a south London gang. They're a nasty bunch, the south London equivalent of the Addams Family. Drugs, protection, extortion, and extensive money-laundering operations."

"How are you doing?" said Murray. He slid off the desk and shook hands. Shepherd noticed that his nails were bitten to the quick and the fingers were stained with nicotine. Nail biting and chain-smoking were common among undercover operatives, though Shepherd had never succumbed to either vice.

"All good," said Shepherd. "How are you enjoying the NCA?"

"Better than I thought I would," said Murray. "I was worried it would be a SOCA-like bureaucracy but they seem to know what they're doing." He looked across at Button, obviously just remembering that she and Shepherd had both worked for the now-defunct Serious and Organised Crime Agency. "No offence," he said.

Button smiled. "I was never a fan of SOCA either," she said. "Too many chiefs and not enough . . ." She grimaced. "Whoops, can't say that any more. Let's just say it was top-heavy admin-wise." She turned to look at Shepherd. "Neil has been posing as a contract killer and has done several jobs for this family. He's not actually carried out the contracts, obviously. We talk to the targets and they agree to cooperate by going into hiding for a few weeks. We fake a photo to show that the deed has been done and Neil gets the credit. The NCA is close to tying everything up and Neil will be moving back to us soon, so the timing is good. He knows the London agent I told you about, the one with connections to Smit in Amsterdam."

"His name's Timmy Owolade, parents from Nigeria but born and brought up in west London," said Murray. "Nice guy as it happens and great fun in a karaoke bar. His brother is a crim in New York and that connection helps him with tit-for-tat contracts, stranger-on-a-train stuff, you know? A contractor from the US comes over to do a killing in the UK, Owolade sends someone from the UK to New York. Nice little operation. The NCA are getting ready to take him down so he's the perfect patsy to get you close to Smit."

"Sounds good," said Shepherd.

"I'm meeting him tonight at the Mayfair Hotel."

"And you want me there?" Shepherd pulled a face. "It's a bit on the nose, isn't it?"

"We thought we'd just have you passing through," said Button. "You can be popping in for a drink, you say a quick hello to Neil because you know him. You shake Owolade's hand and then go. Neil can then fill Owolade in and hopefully he'll bite."

"And if he doesn't?"

"Then we'll try again another day," said Button. "I've already given Neil a file on everything we know about Fredrik Olsen, which frankly isn't much. You can have a look at the file later."

"If he bites, I'll give him your number," said Murray. "Then it's up to you."

"Okay, that sounds as if it might work. But what am I doing in the Mayfair? A Danish contract killer having a quiet drink in London?"

"I'll fix you up with a date," said Button. "Faith Savill-Smith. You met her at Islington police station."

Shepherd recalled the pretty blonde who'd got him out of the cell. She'd used the name Katy then, but Faith suited her better.

"I'll give you her number before you go. Any questions?"

"What name are you using?" Shepherd asked Murray.

"Same first name. Surname Morris."

"How did we meet?"

"Let's say we worked on a job together. There's one in the file about a hit in Milan. I'm very familiar with Milan so let's stick with that. We don't need too much backstory, but anything I tell Owolade I'll run by you afterwards."

Button looked at her watch. "Right, let's let Neil get back to London and I'll introduce you to Dr McDowall."

"I'm getting a medical?" Shepherd gave Murray a wave as he followed Button out of the office and down the corridor.

"That's Doctor as in PhD. Two PhDs actually."

Dr McDowall, double PhD, was barely out of his twenties, his skin as white and unlined as porcelain. He had a mane of black hair that emphasised the paleness of his skin and was dressed like a student who was having trouble making ends meet. He was wearing a stained Oxford University sweatshirt with the sleeves rolled up, khaki cargo pants and plastic sandals. He had on spectacles that looked as if they had been supplied by the NHS and a plaited leather bracelet around his left wrist instead of a watch.

"Ben is our explosives and IED expert," said Button, by way of introduction. "I've asked him to give you a briefing, basically everything a contract killer needs to know about explosives and their use."

McDowall nodded enthusiastically. "I'm just back from the CIA's testing facility in Langley, Virginia, and have some stuff that really is hot off the presses," he said. "I'm planning to go through some circuit diagrams before we get on to the practical work. You might want to think about taking notes. Some of the circuits are quite complex."

"That's okay. I've got a photographic memory."

"Eidetic? Me too." He frowned and pushed his glasses higher up his nose. "So why didn't you pursue an academic career?"

Shepherd grinned. "That's a very good question."

Harper met O'Brien and Walsh at breakfast. Over perfectly cooked eggs Benedict he explained what the two men needed to do. He kept his instructions terse and to the point.

"You should return to Ireland or wherever it is that you base yourselves but be ready to fly to Paris at a few hours' notice. You will be met on arrival at Charles de Gaulle airport and given further instructions. When you reach the place where the items are stored, you will have an opportunity to inspect them and satisfy yourself about their quality. The items will then be placed among some equipment in appropriately labelled crates and once payment has been handed over, you can take them away. For an extra payment I can also arrange for them to be delivered to the docks at a suitable port, and loaded on to a ship for Dun Laoghaire or any other port you may care to nominate. You'll need to handle the Irish end, customs-wise."

Walsh shook his head. "We'll be making our own arrangements for shipping. We don't want to be handing our money over to you and then arriving at the docks to find that by an amazing coincidence someone's tipped off the gentlemen in uniform, now do we?"

"Suit yourself," Harper said. "So much the better, it saves me the trouble and expense of arranging the shipping myself."

After breakfast, Harper settled his bill with one of the credit cards Button had given him, then flew to Berlin where he used the credit card again to buy a top-of-the-range BMW motorcycle. He rode to a small town in what had been the heartlands of the DDR — the German Democratic Republic in the Communist era — and booked himself into a Gasthaus. He phoned Zelda Hoffmann and arranged to meet her at ten o'clock that night.

Zelda was in her late forties, but still a glamorous woman, a blonde-haired, blue-eyed German stereotype, though half a lifetime of perpetual disappointments had etched stress lines into her face and forehead. A former Stasi agent in Communist East Germany, even though more than twenty years had passed since the fall of the Berlin Wall, she still burned with anger that all her hopes of a future in the best seats in the house had disappeared with the collapse of Communism. Her father had been a senior figure in the Stasi and East German politics, and Erich Honecker, the Leader of the DDR, had attended her naming ceremony when she was a child. Zelda had remained a friend of his right up until his escape to Russia when the brutal apparatus by which he maintained his iron control of his state began to crumble and topple down around his ears.

Harper knew Zelda of old and had obtained weapons from her before for below-the-radar jobs in Eastern Europe. She had helped the Stasi stash weapons away after the fall of the Berlin Wall, hiding them before the West German Bundeswehr could arrive to claim them, in the hope that one day the East would rise again. According to Zelda, although the Bundeswehr had found some of the Stasi caches, many others remained undiscovered: an arsenal not merely of small arms and ammunition, but of heavy machine guns, mortars, grenades and rocket launchers as well. "If we could have dug holes big enough to bury tanks we would have done that too," she had once boasted. She also had considerable influence among other disaffected apparatchiks from the old regime and could produce a number of hard-faced former Stasi men to act as observers, bodyguards or thugs as the situation demanded.

He had already phoned her from Monaco and explained the basics of what he wanted, but he went through it in more detail as he sat with her at a table in a bar near the town's derelict steelworks.

"I'll need some people, Zelda," Harper said, "but more important, in addition to the weapons I've already told you about, I'm going to need something a bit more specialised. Can you still get access to those Katyushas?"

She glanced around the bar and then lowered her voice, a needless precaution since it was deserted apart from them. The owner was in the back room, where the flicker of a TV screen and the sound of an over-excited commentator showed he was watching football. "I can do that," she said. "Among the weapons I helped to hide, there was a stock of Katyushas. We sealed them in air- and watertight containers." She shot him a crafty look, involuntarily licking her lips as she did so. "But they are very precious to us."

Harper gave a broad smile. "Don't worry about the price. Money's no object. My clients are eager to buy some if all goes well on our first deal, but they may wish to examine one first. Would that create problems for you?"

She laughed. "There are no problems that cannot be solved by goodwill and American dollars."

"Then we're in business," Harper said. "So how many American dollars will it take to buy a Katyusha?"

"That's negotiable."

"I was thinking a hundred thousand."

"And I was thinking we need to negotiate."

He grinned and placed a hand on her arm. "Do you trust me?"

She held his gaze, trying to read his expression and then gave a slight shrug of her shoulders. "Of course. We go back a long way, Lex."

"How about this? I'll pay you seventy-five per cent of the money I get from my clients, with payment to be made immediately after they take delivery of the rockets. You will be responsible for organising an inspection of the rockets if necessary and for delivery from wherever they are stored to a location that we shall agree between us, but probably to the south or south-west of Berlin. I will sort out the arrangements for the handover. Deal?" He held out his hand.

She hesitated, then nodded. "Deal. But in Germany we seal a deal with a kiss, not a handshake."

It was not a German custom that Harper had come across before, but she was still a good-looking woman, so it would be no hardship to humour her. He leaned forward and kissed her. At once her arm snaked around his neck and she kissed him back passionately, sliding her tongue into his mouth.

"Hold on, Zelda," he said, gently disengaging himself. "Let's save the celebrations for when the deal is complete!"

She shrugged. "If you say so."

"Just a couple more things. I will need a semi-automatic pistol, a shoulder holster and a dozen magazines of 7.62 short ammunition for myself."

"You're expecting trouble?"

"I'm always expecting trouble. That way I'm fully prepared to deal with it if it arises. I'll also need a range of other weapons — not for sale, just as window dressing."

Zelda gave him a puzzled smile. "What is this window dressing?"

"It's like when department stores put things in the window to lure in the customers. So as well as the weapons you're already supplying, I'm going to need some more things for show — a few handguns, more AK-47s, machine guns, RPGs, mines and maybe a mortar or two. I don't want my clients thinking that they're the only ones I've got. I'll give them back, unused, when the show's over. And pay you a rental fee too, say ten thousand dollars."

"All right." She paused, moistening her lips with the tip of her tongue.

"Tomorrow?"

She laughed. "Of course not. But the day after, perhaps. Now are you sure there's nothing else I can do for you?"

182

For a moment he was tempted but he shook his head. "Thanks, Zelda, but let's keep it strictly business for now, shall we?"

"For now, yes. And afterwards?"

He smiled. "And afterwards, who knows?" He winked and walked out to get his bike.

Shepherd picked Faith Savill-Smith up outside Bond Street Tube station. She looked considerably more glamorous than when he'd met her in Islington Police Station. She was wearing a white Chanel jacket over a pale green dress cut low at the front, impossibly high heels, and had a dark green Chanel handbag over her shoulder.

"Wow, did Charlie let you put the outfit on expenses?" he asked as she climbed into the BMW.

At first she didn't understand what he meant, then she laughed and tossed her hair. "No, this is all mine," she said.

"Does Charlie get you to do stuff like this often?"

"Stuff?"

"Ride shotgun like this?"

She smiled, but he figured he'd struck a nerve by the way her eyes tightened a fraction. "She does, actually." She glanced down at her impressive cleavage. "And she always insists that I have the twins on show."

"Insists?"

"Well, hints."

"What did she tell you about tonight?"

"Just that I'm to be your eye candy, that you're getting close to a bad guy. I'm to look pretty and say as little as possible."

183

"That sounds about right," said Shepherd. "My cover name is Frederick Olsen. Try not to use my name; call me honey or babe or something affectionate. I'll introduce you as Katy. Make eye contact with everyone but not so much as to attract their attention." He grinned. "Though I think the twins will probably attract enough attention on their own."

"They do tend to hog the limelight," she said, doing a little shimmy for him that took his attention from the road for a few seconds more than was safe.

"We'll sit at the bar and have a drink. At some point a guy called Neil will come over and seem surprised to see me. We'll make small talk, he'll introduce me to the guy he's with, then I'll make my excuses and leave. You just follow my lead."

He found a parking spot across the road from the hotel. The doorman cast an admiring glance at the twins as Shepherd followed Faith inside and walked with her across reception to the bar.

They sat on stools and Shepherd asked her what she wanted to drink.

"A Bellini would hit the spot."

Shepherd nodded at a barman dressed all in black and ordered her cocktail and a Jameson and soda for himself. While the barman was making the Bellini and casting sly looks at the twins, Shepherd took a quick look around the bar. Murray was sitting at a table by the window with a large black man with a booming laugh that echoed around the bar each time he let it rip. There was a bottle of Cristal champagne in an ice bucket next to the table and two corks which suggested they were already well into their second. A young blonde girl with a figure to rival Savill-Smith's was sitting next to Owolade and rubbing the back of his neck. Owolade was deep in conversation with Murray, a conversation that was punctuated by him slapping the table and laughing loudly.

Their drinks arrived and Shepherd and Savill-Smith made small talk for about fifteen minutes before Shepherd felt a hand on his shoulder.

"Bloody hell, what are you doing in London?"

Shepherd turned, faked surprise, then slid off his stool and hugged Murray. "Neil, wow, long time no see."

Shepherd introduced Savill-Smith as Katy and the two men chatted about old times for a couple of minutes before Murray said he wanted to introduce him to the man he was drinking with. He put his arm around Shepherd's shoulder as they went over to his table.

"Timmy, I want to introduce you to an old friend, Frederik Olsen. We go back a long way."

Owolade didn't get up but extended a gold-ring-encrusted hand that Shepherd shook. "You want a drink, Freddie?" he asked.

"I'm never one to turn down Cristal, but we're going to have to love you and leave you," he said. He patted Murray on the back. "I've got a table booked at Scott's. But we should catch up sometime, lots to talk about." He shook hands with Murray, nodded at Owolade, and put his arm around Savill-Smith as he guided her to the door.

"Do you really have a table booked at Scott's?" she asked as they stepped out on to the pavement.

"Of course," he said. "Deep cover. You have to be prepared to follow through."

"So we're going to eat at Scott's on expenses?"

"Do you have a problem with that?"

She laughed. "It's one of my favourite restaurants, so no, no problem at all."

Harper's team had located a suitable building for the next phase of the operation: a small warehouse in a grim East German rust-belt town a few hours' drive from Berlin. The warehouse was in a steep, winding side street, its cobbled surface covered in ice and semi-frozen slush. Most of the surrounding buildings were boarded up or derelict and the few people braving the biting east wind hurried past without a second look, their chins sunk into their coats. Their faces looked as grey and poor as the town they lived in. While Billy Big made a brew, Billy Whisper and Maggie May showed Harper round the building. Hansfree stayed hunched over his computer. It looked as if the warehouse had stood empty since the Berlin Wall came down and every surface was thickly carpeted with dust. In the Communist era the warehouse must have been the office and store place for some arm of the government or the Party because fading propaganda posters still lined the walls. A sun-bleached image of a demonic American eagle with nuclear missiles for talons menacing a few blonde Brunhildes hung next to a photograph of some East German official handing a beaming worker the keys to a new car.

Harper laughed. "First prize one Trabant, second prize two Trabants!"

At the front of the building, accessed by a door opening on to the street, was a small office, no more than a few metres square, with shelves and rusting filing cabinets lining the walls. The drawers sagged open and a mess of spilled, yellowing papers was scattered across the floor.

"Like the Marie Celeste, only dustier," Harper said.

"But it'll do?" Billy Whisper asked, in a voice so low he could have been talking to himself.

"It'll do," Harper said. He grinned. "Actually it's perfect."

A perilous-looking metal staircase led down into a basement warehouse with double steel doors opening on to a loading ramp in the street at the rear of the building. Harper gave a nod of approval. While the two Billys set off in a hired truck to collect the office equipment they had sourced to "dress" the office, Harper put in a call to Zelda. She turned up within an hour, bringing four of her former comrades to clean the place up, all of them women who were equally solid of body and stolid of expression.

"Now we know what happened to the East German shot-put team," Billy Whisper murmured.

"Okay, let's get started," Harper said. "We've got company coming soon. And can you also find me a couple of big, surly-looking guys to act as guards, Zelda?"

"Of course, what do you need them to do?"

"Nothing really, just stand around looking mean. More window dressing."

She returned later that afternoon accompanied by two hulking men with broad, Slavic features and suspicious-looking bulges in the armpits of their coats.

"They'll do just fine, Zelda," Harper said. "Do they speak any English?"

"No, not a word. Is that a problem?"

"Not really, tell them all they've got to do is guard the doors, open them when I tell them to do so and look thoughtful and nod if I say anything to them whether it's in English or some mid-European gibberish."

With the promise of a hundred-dollar bonus each if they got the job done faster, the cleaning women had already gone through the building like a tornado, dusting, sweeping and polishing. As soon as they'd finished, the two heavies helped Billy Whisper and Billy Big unload the equipment they had brought: second-hand but modern-looking desks, chairs, filing cabinets, telephones, computers and printers. If not exactly pristine, the place now at least looked like a functioning business. The rusting filing cabinets and other old equipment were carried into the back of the warehouse store and covered with a tarpaulin.

Harper added a few finishing touches, including a box of disposable gloves, bottles of vodka and schnapps, and a couple of photographs of him in character, exchanging handshakes with groups of Slav-looking officials and army officers, which Hansfree had Photoshopped and hastily framed. Harper broke off at the sound of an engine and saw an unmarked grey Mercedes van reversing up to the steel double doors at the bottom of the loading ramp. While Zelda's two hired goons stood guard in the street and Hansfree worked on his laptop, Harper, Zelda, the two Billys and the van driver, all wearing disposable gloves, manhandled a series of wooden crates stencilled with the name of a refrigeration company into the building. They placed them against one wall and unscrewed the lids, revealing the arms and explosives inside them: AK-47s, ammunition, grenades, slabs of plastic explosive and lengths of detonator cord.

They then unloaded the additional weapons that Zelda had brought for the window dressing Harper had requested and, still wearing disposable gloves, they spent a few minutes arranging a heavy machine gun, a mortar and a series of pistols, semi-automatics and rocket-propelled grenade launchers against the other walls of the storeroom. She had also brought him the semi-automatic pistol he had asked for, a Soviet-era Makarov with a shoulder holster, spare magazines and 1,000 rounds of 7.62 short ammunition.

After Zelda and her cleaners had left, Harper asked Hansfree to check the registered number on the pistols and research the origin of the ammunition boxes. It took him less than half an hour on his laptop. He called Harper over and kept his voice low so that he couldn't be overheard.

"The registered number shows the Makarov was allocated to the Stasi and the numbers on the base of the ammo show the factory where it was manufactured and when it was made," he said. "Again, records show it was Stasi."

"Bloody hell, good work Hansfree — how do you find out all this stuff?"

"Have you heard of BRIXMIS? In Cold War days the two sides were so shit-scared of starting nuclear Armageddon by accident that they agreed a semi-official form of spying in which a Soviet military mission was allowed access to almost all areas of West Germany to satisfy themselves that there was no secret mobilisation for war going on, while the British Commanders'-in-Chief Mission to the Soviet Forces in Germany, BRIXMIS for short, did the same on the other side of the Iron Curtain in East Germany. They weren't supposed to gather intelligence as well but of course both sides did, and all the information that BRIXMIS gathered, from the most minute details of Soviet bloc equipment to covert infiltration routes, observation post locations and even targets for assassination in the event of war, is gathered in the BRIXMIS files which, astonishingly, are still unclassified."

"Excellent. Can I borrow one of your laptops?"

Hansfree waved Harper to a computer. He sat down in front of it and went through a proxy service to open Button's draft folder. He wrote a message — *THE SUPPLIES HAVE BEEN DELIVERED.*

He sat back and waited. In less than fifteen minutes she was online and leaving a reply.

HOW LONG BEFORE THEY ARRIVE?

TWENTY-FOUR HOURS, Harper wrote. I'VE ARRANGED FOR THEM TO COME THE SCENIC ROUTE TO KEEP THEM ON THE BACK FOOT.

TRACKING DEVICES?

IN HAND. ALL ON SCHEDULE.

KEEP ME INFORMED.

Harper closed the file and logged off the proxy service. He stood up and went to watch Hansfree at work. Hansfree had put an aluminium briefcase on a table and deftly opened it with his metal claws. Inside, neatly stowed in compartments cut in the foam rubber lining, were a series of tiny electronic gadgets and a set of drills, files and brass armourer's tools. Calmly and methodically, working fast but with no appearance of haste, he took each of the New IRA's weapons in turn and disassembled it. He fitted one of the tiny devices into some of them, drilling into the stock, and then sealing the hole and matching the finish so skilfully that it was undetectable. He also made imperceptible alterations to the barrel or firing mechanism of each weapon, and then reassembled them. Harper as always was mesmerised by the skill with which the man used his artificial hands. "You're an artist, mate," he said once when Hansfree looked over at him.

"I wasn't always this good with them," said Hansfree. "I spilled a lot of coffee when I first started."

"Yeah, well now your claws are better than my fingers, no question."

"I'd still swap you, any day."

191

When he'd finished, even Harper's searching examination could see no visible difference in any of the weapons. He gave a nod of approval. "Good job. Now how do I pass the tracking info on?"

"I'll put the details on a thumbdrive," said Hansfree.

Harper went over to talk to Maggie May and confirmed that she was all set to fly to Paris to await O'Brien and Walsh. The two Billys would be spending the night in the warehouse with Hansfree and Zelda's two thugs, though the thugs would be outside on guard duty.

Harper went right through the building, checking it over from top to bottom, looking for anything out of place. At last, satisfied, he rode his motorbike deep into the countryside outside the town and took a dirt track into a dark conifer forest. There was a cottage at the entrance to the track and an old man splitting logs in the yard paused to glance at Harper as he rode past, but looked away almost at once and went back to his work. Old habits die hard, Harper thought to himself — curiosity could be bad for your health in the Communist era; best to look the other way. He rode on for another mile, deep into the heart of the forest, where the track ended in a clearing scarred by the caterpillar tracks of heavy vehicles. A stack of newly felled tree trunks, stripped of their bark and branches, were piled at one side of the clearing, with an industrial wood-shredder at the other in front of mounds of sawdust and pulverised wood, but the foresters had finished work for the day and there was no sign of any activity.

192

Harper cut the BMW's engine, put it on the kickstand and hung his helmet from the handlebars. After the noise of the bike, he gave his ears a couple of minutes to get used to the silence, inhaling the scent of pine resin that still hung heavy in the air, and then made a careful circuit around the clearing, watching and listening for any movement or sound. Satisfied, he returned to the clearing, took the Makarov pistol from his shoulder holster and paced out twenty yards from one of the mounds of chippings. He sighted on a fragment of blood-red bark, exhaled slowly as he took up the first pressure and then squeezed the trigger. There was a spurt of sawdust a couple of inches above and to the right of his mark. He made an adjustment, sighted again, and this time the shot drilled a hole straight through the bark. He spent half an hour there, firing while standing, kneeling and lying prone, and practising fire and movement, shooting, throwing himself to the ground and rolling over a couple of times before firing off another shot. He also practised magazine changes while rolling on the ground.

When he'd finished, he cleaned the pistol and returned it to his holster and then spent a few more minutes gathering up the ejected cartridge cases from the rounds he had fired. Buried deep in the mounds of chippings, the rounds themselves were likely to remain undiscovered until long after Harper had completed his op and left the country. He rode back along the track and past the cottage, though this time there was no sign of the old man, other than a blue-grey wisp of smoke rising from the chimney. He gunned the engine as he reached the road, roaring away towards the town. Harper found a small, anonymous hotel near the railway station and paid for a room with cash. As he settled down to grab a few hours' sleep, in a room with mildewed walls and mouse droppings on the floor next to the bed, he smiled to himself. After his presidential suite in Monte Carlo, normal service had now been resumed.

Shepherd woke at 8a.m. and went for a run around Battersea Park before showering and changing. Neil Murray had telephoned him just after he'd got home the previous evening, having dropped a slightly tipsy Savill-Smith in front of a very expensive mews house in Chelsea that her parents had apparently given her as a twenty-first birthday present. Murray had reported that Owolade was definitely interested. He had pumped Murray for information and persuaded him to hand over a contact number.

"I'm pretty sure it's on," said Murray. "But I've no doubt that Charlie will let me know if it falls through. Anyway, you've got my number — if you need anything, give me a call."

Shepherd made himself a cheese and bacon omelette and was just about to dig a fork into it when his phone rang again. A withheld number. He picked it up and growled, "Yeah?"

"Freddie, this is Timmy, we met last night with Neil. You can't have forgotten me, I was the big black man drinking Cristal."

Shepherd chuckled dryly. "I remember, Timmy. What can I do for you?"

"Did Neil tell you my line of business?"

"He didn't say a thing, just that you were a friend and that you had a huge dick."

Owolade laughed so hard that for a moment Shepherd thought the man was going to have a seizure. "You're a very funny man, Freddie."

"I do my best. So let me ask you again, Timmy, what can I do for you? Did Neil give you my number?"

"I'm about to put some work Neil's way and I could probably do the same for you."

"I'm not looking for work at the moment."

"Everyone is available if the price is right, Freddie."

"I have to say that I'm not comfortable having a conversation like this on the phone, especially with someone I don't know."

"Neil can vouch for me, the same as he vouches for you."

"And I'm even more uncomfortable that he's been giving you personal information about me."

"Freddie, please, let's not get off on the wrong foot here. I'm just a middleman, and I know a guy in Amsterdam who would love to talk to you. I know he's having problems filling a contract and you'd be perfect."

"So why hasn't Neil put himself forward?"

"Because this is big, real big. I can't give you the details but I can put you in touch with the man who can, if you want."

"And what's your interest in this, Timmy?"

"Let's just say, with a contract as big as this there'll be a half-decent finder's fee."

"You're pimping me out, Timmy, is that it?"

Owolade roared with laughter again. "Yes, man, I suppose I am. Here's what I was thinking: I'll get in touch with the Dutchman, and if he's interested I'll put the two of you together and you can hear for yourself."

"And if I take the contract, he pays the finder's fee? Not me?"

"Of course."

Shepherd pretended to think about it. "Okay, I don't see what harm it can do. Yeah, go for it."

"I'll call you back," promised Owolade and he ended the call.

Shepherd ate his omelette and drank two cups of coffee, then decided to go out for a paper. He was on his way back from the newsagent when his phone rang. Owolade was still withholding his number.

"It's on," said Owolade. "There'll be a ticket booked for you on the three o'clock KLM flight from Heathrow. What name do you need it under?"

"Harry. Harry Cartwright. Today?"

"Strike while the iron's hot," said Owolade. "You'll be met at the airport but the guy will be holding a sign that says System Communications. The driver will take you to see Mr Smit."

"That's his name, is it? Smith?"

"Not Smith. Smit. Lucas Smit."

"Never heard of him," said Shepherd.

"Well he's heard of you," said Owolade. "Your reputation precedes you, as they say."

"Okay, I'll be there," said Shepherd. "What about me getting back to you?"

"No need," said Owolade. "If I need your services, I'll call you."

"Is your finder's fee taken care of?"

"That depends on what Mr Smit thinks of you," said Owolade. "Now I wonder if I could ask you a question? The girl you were with last night. Was she a hooker?"

"Why do you ask?"

"No offence, it's just that she was as fit as fuck and if she's an agency girl I wouldn't mind, you know . . ."

Shepherd laughed. "She's a friend," he said. "With benefits, as they say."

"Well, no harm in asking," laughed Owolade. "Good luck in Amsterdam."

Shepherd ended the call and immediately phoned Button. The call went through to voicemail and Shepherd cursed. He was sorting through his wallet to check that he only had Harry Cartwright credit cards when Button called back.

"Smit wants to see me in Amsterdam. Today."

"That's good news."

"It's bloody short notice."

"It shows Smit's keen. What's the story?"

"They're booking me on an afternoon flight from Heathrow."

"I'll get Amar to meet you there. Do you want a team shadowing you?"

"It'll be okay," said Shepherd. "It's just a chat, and they came to me. Doubt they'll be suspicious."

"If you change your mind, let me know."

★ ★ ★

The ticket was waiting for Shepherd at Heathrow. He checked in and went through to the business class lounge, heading straight for the men's room. Amar Singh was already there, dressed in maintenance overalls and fiddling with the U-bend of one of the washbasins. Singh was an Asian in his mid-thirties, one of the top technicians in MI5's technical support section. He was usually dressed in expensive designer gear and he looked distinctly uncomfortable in the scruffy overalls as he stood up and wiped his hands.

"How's it going, Spider?"

"All good, Amar. How are the wife and kids?"

"Nagging the life out of me, but what can you do?" said Singh. He took an iPhone out of his pocket and handed it to Shepherd.

"I'm not a big fan," said Shepherd. "The batteries always seem to run out at the worst possible time."

"This phone you don't switch on," said Singh. "It functions as a recorder, not a transmitter. Everything said within ten feet is recorded on a chip. So long as it's in your pocket it'll record everything. But even an Apple technician wouldn't be able to spot the difference between it and a regular phone."

"Thanks," said Shepherd, slipping the phone into his inside pocket.

The door opened and a middle-aged businessman with a harried expression rushed over to the urinal. Shepherd nodded at Singh and left.

Shepherd cleared Dutch immigration and walked out into the arrivals area. A big man in a heavy coat was holding a sign on which SYSTEM COMMUNICA-TIONS had been printed in capital letters. Shepherd smiled and nodded at the man. The man nodded back and took Shepherd to a multistorey car park where another man was sitting at the wheel of a black stretch Mercedes with tinted windows. Shepherd climbed into the back while the heavy got into the front next to the driver. There was an envelope on the back seat with the word EXPENSES printed on it. Shepherd opened it and flicked his thumb across an envelope containing a dozen or so €500 notes. He smiled and pocketed the envelope. He was sure Button would appreciate the money to offset the expenses of the operation.

They drove for the best part of forty-five minutes before they pulled up in front of a terrace of pretty four-storey houses overlooking a wide canal. The heavy climbed out and opened the door for Shepherd and then ushered him to the front door of a pale green house. The Mercedes drove off as the door opened. Another big man, this one with a military haircut and wearing a brown leather bomber jacket, pulled the door wide open and nodded for Shepherd to go into the first room on the right. It was clearly a security centre with three tables and a couple of sofas. There was a bank of small screens on one wall showing CCTV images of the outside and inside of the house. On one of the tables there was a row of chargers containing transceivers and several mobile phones. Two more men in bomber jackets were lounging on a sofa and they watched as the man who opened the front door ran a portable metal detector slowly over Shepherd, from head to toe. He took Shepherd's two phones, his keys and his wallet and put them in a small tray, then asked him in accented English to remove his coat. That went on to one of the tables.

The heavy who had met Shepherd at the airport motioned for him to follow him up the stairs. The second floor was a room that ran the full length of the building, with book-lined walls and works of art that looked real and expensive, and there was a white grand piano by a window overlooking the canal. There were three dark green leather sofas and a lot of antique furniture.

The third floor had four rooms leading off a central hallway. The heavy knocked on one of the doors, opened it, and motioned for Shepherd to go inside.

The room was windowless and the walls, ceiling and floor had been lined with a grey foam material. On top of that was a wire mesh that effectively created a cage that filled the whole room. There was a wooden raised floor on which stood all the furniture — an ornate Regency desk, four winged leather chairs and a coffee table that matched the desk, piled high with reading material. The only electrical equipment in the room appeared to be a laptop sitting on the desk.

Lucas Smit was sitting in one of the winged chairs. He was a small man with swept-back white hair and cheeks flecked with broken veins. He studied Shepherd with pale blue eyes framed by eyelashes that had greyed with age. He was in his sixties, maybe older, and his hands were dotted with brown liver spots. He smiled, showing yellowing teeth.

"Please sit, Mr Olsen," he said, waving to one of the chairs. "This is not the most attractive room in the house, but it is the most secure."

Shepherd sat down. He had been in secure communication rooms in various embassies around the world and this was on a par with the best. The design meant that all eavesdropping methods were rendered useless.

Smit settled back in his chair and watched Shepherd like a snake contemplating its next meal. "You're very successful at what you do, Mr Olsen," he said quietly.

Shepherd shrugged. "I get by."

"You're very modest. You don't sound Danish, I have to say."

Shepherd shrugged.

"My English is good. Some would say perfect. But most people would realise that I am not a natural-born speaker and quite a few would know that I was Dutch."

"Your accent sounds good to me," said Shepherd.

Smit smiled without warmth. "You flatter me, Mr Olsen. But that's not your real name, is it? Any more than you are Danish." His eyes bored into Shepherd's for several seconds, then he smiled. "That's very clever. You make the world think you are Danish so they start off on the wrong track. That's why no one really knows who you are, or where you come from. And why you've never been photographed."

"There are advantages to having a low profile, obviously," said Shepherd, and Smit chuckled. "But you approached me, remember? These days I don't tout for work. Work finds me."

Smit nodded. "I appreciate that, but whenever I work with someone for the first time, I am obviously somewhat apprehensive."

"That's understandable. But you have to appreciate that I can hardly supply references."

Smit put up an apologetic hand. "I'm sorry if I come across as suspicious. It's the nature of our business. Do you mind if I ask you a few questions?"

"Not if you don't mind if I don't answer them." Shepherd smiled. "Go ahead."

"How many kills have you made?"

"Twenty-seven as a freelance contractor."

"Do you care about the nature of your targets?"

Shepherd frowned. "In what way?"

"Men, women, children?"

Shepherd shrugged. "A target is a target."

"Do you care why a target has been selected?"

"These are very strange questions," said Shepherd.

"Some men are choosy about which contracts they accept."

"I'm not. If I had reservations, I couldn't do the job."

"What about collateral damage?"

"It's messy and best avoided. But if the only way to take out a target is to involve others, then sometimes it's necessary. But as I said, best avoided."

"Suppose you were asked to shoot a friend?"

"Is that what this is about? You want me to kill someone I know?"

Smit laughed dryly and put up a hand. "No, the contract I have in mind for you is not a friend of yours. I am just trying to get a feel for your mindset."

"I'm a professional. I'm good at what I do and I'm paid a premium price for my skills. Would I kill a friend?" Shepherd shrugged. "It would depend on the price, I suppose. But then, I don't have many friends."

Smit nodded and smiled, as if he approved of the answer. "What's your longest kill?"

Shepherd shrugged. "I try not to go beyond five hundred metres. You rarely get the chance for more than one shot and beyond that distance it's a bit problematical."

Smit nodded. "Tell me about the problems with long-range shots."

"Are you serious? You're testing me?"

"I just want you to confirm that you are a professional. I don't think that is too much to ask for before I arrange a contract worth three million euros. Now my question is simple — what are the extra problems with long-range shots, beyond a thousand metres?"

"Fine," said Shepherd. "I assume you're not talking about windage or bullet drop because that's important no matter what the distance. Beyond a thousand metres two other factors kick in, the Coriolis effect and bullet drift."

Smit smiled. "Exactly," he said. "Now how about you explain those to me."

Shepherd shook his head dismissively. "This is ridiculous," he said.

"Humour me," said Smit.

"The Coriolis effect is when the earth's rotation pulls the round either left or right, depending on where the shooter is and the direction of fire. The closer you are to firing east-west or west-east the less the effect."

"And bullet drift?"

"Rounds spin as they move through the air. Up to three thousand times a second. The round will tend to move in the direction it's spinning. It's a very small deviation and up to a thousand metres you can pretty much ignore it."

"And how do you account for it when making your shot?"

"You don't," said Shepherd. "Okay, you can use a ballistic computer but in my experience you're better making a shot and then compensating. Which is why if it's a job, I keep to well below a thousand metres." He flashed Smit a tight smile. "Happy now? Did I pass?"

"You passed," said Smit. "But all you have done is shown that you understand the technicalities of sniping. You can talk the talk, as the Americans say, but can you walk the walk?"

The same two heavies who had picked Shepherd up at the airport dropped him off at the Intercontinental Amstel hotel and returned his phones. Smit had booked a palatial suite overlooking the river and given him the business card of a local escort service. The Dutchman said he had an account with them and that Shepherd could order as many girls as he wanted. Shepherd took off his coat and tossed it on the bed, then phoned Button.

"He wants to see me in action," he told her. "Gave me some crap about walking the walk."

"I suppose that's only to be expected," she said. "You're an unknown quantity. When and where?"

"He says he has a place in Croatia. Tomorrow."

"Can't you persuade him to do it in the UK? We could set something up."

"He's worried about it being a fit-up. The plan is for me to stay here overnight. He's booked me into the Intercontinental Amstel."

"That's a lovely hotel," she said. "You should try the restaurant. La Rive. It overlooks the river and has a Michelin star. Graham and I . . ." She left the sentence unfinished. Graham had been her husband; he had died a few years previously.

"Thanks, but I'm not here for the fine dining," said Shepherd.

"Well it's your call, obviously, as to whether you go or not."

"It's not the safest of places, Croatia."

"I could arrange some sort of backup."

"You could. But that might be the test. To see if I'm being followed. We can't take the risk. If I go, I have to go alone."

"As I said, it's your call."

Shepherd closed his eyes and tapped the phone against the side of his head for several seconds. "I'll do it," he said eventually. "I don't see that I've got a choice."

"You've always got a choice."

"Yeah, but if I pull out they'll find someone else." He sighed. "I'll do it."

"What do you need from me?"

"I don't think I can go in with any backup — human or technological. If they search me and find a bug or tracker then it's all over. And there'll be no cavalry in Croatia."

"What about the phone that Amar gave you?"

"They didn't give it a second look. But they took it off me. And ran a metal detector over me."

"How are you getting to Croatia?"

"Private jet to Zagreb, he said. Back tomorrow afternoon. Hopefully."

"And assuming you pass the test, he'll give you the contract?"

"Apparently. One third of the money up front, transferred to an account of my choosing."

"We've already set an account up in the Cayman Islands in the name of Harry Cartwright. That account feeds into accounts that lead eventually to Frederik Olsen. It's likely that Smit will run checks."

"That should do nicely," said Shepherd.

"I'll text you the details. Look, the Smit side is going well but we need something concrete to tie in Jansen."

"Like what? Smit on tape saying that Jansen is the client? Because I don't see that happening at the moment."

"Ideally a face to face with Jansen," said Button.

"How the hell am I supposed to do that?"

"I'm just saying. In a perfect world . . ."

"Yeah, well the world isn't perfect," said Shepherd.

"Just play it by ear, that's all I'm saying. See what you can do."

Shepherd ended the call and lay down on the bed. He put his hands behind his head and stared up at the ceiling.

The Range Rover turned off the main highway and drove down a single-track road for a mile before turning again. They stopped at a gate set into a wire fence. A second Range Rover pulled up behind them. Two armed guards cradling AK-47s walked towards the car but the driver wound down the window and said something to them in Croatian and they nodded and waved them through. The road dipped down and Shepherd realised they were in a quarry. It seemed to be disused as there was no equipment and no one appeared to be working.

Shepherd had been picked up at his hotel by two men in a Mercedes and driven to a private airfield where Smit was waiting inside a Gulfstream jet. They had flown to a small airfield in Croatia where two more heavies had been waiting with two black Range Rovers. Shepherd had climbed into the back of one and had expected Smit to join him. In fact Smit got into the second car and it was one of the heavies who sat next to Shepherd. The heavy had said nothing on the drive from the airfield to the quarry. He had turned his head away from Shepherd and just stared out of the window.

There were three SUVs parked in a line at the entrance to the quarry and the Range Rover pulled in behind them. Smit climbed out and Shepherd joined him. Shepherd looked around at the granite walls. "This isn't the best place for a long shot," he said.

"Don't worry about it," said the Dutchman.

"I thought I was here to show you my sniping skills," said Shepherd.

"You clearly are an expert sniper, the way you answered my questions was proof of that. I need you to show me your competence with explosives."

"Who is the target?" asked Shepherd.

"You'll be told that once we have confirmed that you are the man for the job," said Smit.

"And how do I do that?"

Smit walked over to one of the SUVs, a black Toyota. A heavyset man in a black leather jacket pulled open the rear door and stepped back. Smit took Shepherd over and showed him what was in the back.

"Are you serious?" said Shepherd. The rear of the SUV was filled with boxes of electrical equipment and C-4 explosive. "You want me to build a bomb?"

"Not just a bomb, my friend," said Smit. "An IED that is remotely primed and detonates either on a timer or when the car is in motion."

"I can tell you how to do it, why run the risk of building one?"

"As I said, it's not about talking the talk, it's about walking the walk. And if you truly know what you are doing, there is no risk."

"There is always risk," said Shepherd. He took off his coat and handed it to the man in the leather jacket.

"This is Dvorko," said Smit. "He'll be watching you."

Shepherd nodded at Dvorko. "You know IEDs?"

Dvorko grinned, showing a large gap between his two front teeth. "Some." His head was shaved and there was a thick rope-like scar above his left ear; his left cheek was pockmarked with scars that looked like they might have been caused by shrapnel.

"Do me a favour and shove that in the car while I see what we've got here," said Shepherd.

Dvorko opened the front passenger door and tossed the coat in while Shepherd ran an eye over the plastic boxes in the back of the vehicle. There were several types of detonators, mercury tilt switches, a range of batteries, half a dozen mobile phones, and handfuls of integrated circuits.

Smit flipped open a black plastic case and waved his gloved hand at the contents. "You are familiar with C-4, of course?"

"Sure," said Shepherd. "But the British version is PE-4. C-4 is ninety-one per cent RDX — Research Department Explosive — five per cent dioctyl sebacate as the plasticiser, two per cent polyisobutylene as the binder and just under two per cent mineral oil." He picked up one of the blocks. It weighed about half a kilo and was just under a foot long in an olive-coloured wrapping. "This is military grade C-4, packaged as a demolition block. They call it an M112." He gestured at the case just as Dvorko rejoined them. "They put sixteen of the M112 blocks into this carrying case with four priming assemblies and sell it as a demolition charge assembly." He put the C-4 block back into the case and took out one of the priming assemblies. "This is the detonating cord capped with a booster at each end. It's good kit this. The best."

Dvorko nodded. "We get it from the military."

"What about you?" Smit asked Shepherd. "Where do you get your explosive from?"

Shepherd tapped the side of his nose. "Trade secret, Lucas." He looked over at Smit. "What is it exactly you want me to do?"

Smit pointed over at a car on the other side of the quarry. It was a rusting white Volvo with its engine hood propped open. "Prepare an IED that can be remotely primed. Have it set up so that it will explode when the car is in motion. But have an override trigger so that it can be remotely detonated." Smit smiled. "Obviously we cannot have someone driving the car."

"Obviously," said Shepherd. "Lucas, what's going on here?"

"We need to be sure that you are able to use an IED, should that be necessary."

"It would be a big help if I knew who the target was."

"We need to know first that you have the requisite skills."

"And blowing up a car will prove that?"

"Of course."

Shepherd shrugged carelessly. "Fine. How big an explosion do you want?"

"Enough to be sure of killing the occupants."

"You've got it," said Shepherd.

He took a deep breath, composed himself and reached for a roll of wire. He worked quickly and efficiently, initially putting together a simple circuit of a mobile phone and a battery, hooked up to a test bulb. He used a battery soldering iron and had to choose between three types of solder, which he figured was a test because he saw Dvorko nod his approval when he picked up the Kester brand. When he had finished he tested the circuit by calling the number. After one ring the bulb glowed. He smiled to himself. That was the easy part. He put together a second circuit, this one with a battery and a timer. He removed the bulb and replaced it with the second circuit. He checked the circuit, then rang the phone again. This time as soon as the phone began ringing the timer began to tick off the seconds.

Shepherd stepped back so that Smit could see the circuit, then he switched the timer off. His third circuit would contain the two detonators but for testing purposes he replaced them with bulbs. He assembled the circuit, set the timer for one minute, and called the number. The timer started immediately the phone rang, and exactly one minute later the two bulbs winked on.

Shepherd rubbed his chin as he looked through the various components that were available. There were several makes of reed switch that were activated when a magnet came into the vicinity, and mercury tilt switches that were activated by movement. He looked over at Smit. "We could do this a number of ways," he said. "A lot depends on how much access I would have to the car."

"Explain?" said Smit.

"Well, if I could have some time with the car, then the best way would be just to wire the main circuit into the car's ignition system. That way the bomb will only go off when the engine is running. If I've only got limited access then some sort of motion-activated component would be best. Say the mercury tilt switch. The bomb could then be placed on the chassis or under a wheel arch."

Smit nodded. "Let's assume you have access. But go for the movement option."

"Okay," said Shepherd. He took one of the mercury tilt switches and soldered it into the detonator circuit. When he had finished he stepped back so that Dvorko could check his work.

"It's good," said Dvorko.

"And you wanted an override circuit?"

Smit nodded.

Shepherd put together a separate circuit connecting the battery to a second mobile phone and the two light bulbs. "If I do it this way, a call to this mobile will detonate the bomb no matter what else happens," he said. "There's no safety. I wouldn't recommend doing it that way. Mobile phones can sometimes go off on their own and if that happens . . ."

"What do you suggest?"

"Wiring the second phone circuit into the first one, so calling the second phone won't have any effect unless the first phone has activated the circuit."

"Let's do that," said Smit.

Smit and Dvorko watched as Shepherd modified the circuit. When he had finished he showed them how it would work. He called the first phone and the timer started. "At this point the bomb is in the car and is now active. One of two things will activate the device. You can either call the second phone in which case the bomb will explode immediately. Or if the car is in motion, if it accelerates quickly or brakes suddenly, the mercury tilt switch will activate the circuit." He twisted the mercury tilt switch, allowing the mercury inside to connect two prongs that then activated the circuit and the two bulbs winked on.

Smit looked over at Dvorko and the Croatian nodded.

"Right, time to do it for real," said Smit.

"Seriously? You want me to blow up the car?"

Smit grinned. "Walk the walk."

Shepherd sighed and reached for a detonator. "Suit yourself," he said. "But it seems like a waste of perfectly good explosive."

"You'll forgive me if I give you some room," said the Dutchman. He walked away and lit one of his small cigars.

Shepherd looked at Dvorko. "Are you staying?" he asked.

Dvorko grinned. "Looks to me like you know what you're doing."

Shepherd removed the two bulbs and soldered in two detonators in their place. He put the soldering iron down. "I'd be happier connecting this to the explosive in the car," he said.

"You and me both."

Shepherd nodded at the black plastic case. "Bring two of the blocks, yeah?"

He carefully rolled up the circuit and placed it on one of the plastic lids and carried it over to the Volvo. He placed the circuit carefully on the roof and pulled open the rear passenger door. Dvorko came up behind him, a block of C-4 in each hand.

Shepherd took one of the blocks and inserted one of the detonators into it, pushing it in as far as it would go. He took the second block and pushed the remaining detonator in. He could feel his heart racing. Without the C-4 in place, the worst that could happen would be a loud bang. But now the device was capable of blowing the car, and them, to pieces. He carefully lifted the circuit off the roof and leaned inside the car. He placed it on the back seat, figuring that as it was only a test he didn't have to go to the bother of concealing it. He closed the door gently and walked back to Smit's car with Dvorko.

"That was nice work," said the Croatian.

"Thanks," said Shepherd.

They reached Smit, who was halfway through his cigar. "Done?" he asked.

"Done," said Shepherd.

Smit looked over at Dvorko for confirmation. The Croatian nodded. "Let's do it, then," said Smit.

Shepherd took the first phone and made the call. He let it ring three times and then ended the call. On the far side of the quarry, the timer was now running. Shepherd put the phone down and looked at his watch. He waited until a minute had passed before nodding. "That's it. The device is now active." He picked up the second mobile phone. "Do you want to do the honours?"

Smit took the phone from him.

"Just press redial," said Shepherd.

Smit blinked, then made the call. Less than a second later the Volvo exploded and all three men ducked down behind Smit's car. Pieces of metal rained down around the burning shell and a plume of thick black smoke rose into the air.

"Nice," said Smit.

"Happy now?" asked Shepherd.

"Yes, I think so," said the Dutchman. "It's time to talk business."

Smit and Shepherd travelled back to the airfield in separate cars, and during the flight back to Amsterdam Smit sat at the opposite end of the Gulfstream, smoking a cigar and studying spreadsheets on a laptop. They took separate cars back to the house in Amsterdam and Smit waited until they were back in the secure room before telling Shepherd what he already knew — that Vladimir Putin was to be the target.

Shepherd feigned surprise. "It can't be done," he said.

"Of course it can," said Smit. He lit a cigar. "Anyone can be killed."

"He's one of the most protected men on the planet," said Shepherd.

"Yes, but even he has to go out sometimes. And you are one of the best snipers in the world. He has to move around by car and any vehicle is vulnerable."

"You think I'll be able to plant a bomb in Putin's car?" He shook his head. "Cloud cuckoo land — that's where you live."

"Of course you won't get anywhere near any of his cars," said Smit. "But a man like Putin has a schedule drawn up months in advance. So if you know where he is going to be, you can make plans."

"And where is he going to be? You obviously have something in mind."

"London. In three weeks' time. He will be attending the G8 meeting."

"Three weeks? That's not long enough. Something like this, it'll take months of planning."

"The planning has been done. All we need is for someone to execute it."

Shepherd frowned. "What the hell are you talking about? Whose plan?"

"This has been in the works since last year. We know the hotel he will be staying at and have been able to plan accordingly. We had someone lined up but it fell through."

"Fell through how?"

"That doesn't matter," said Smit. "But the plan is a good one. It will still work. And you are just the man we need."

"You keep saying 'we'. Who is 'we' exactly?"

"The client," said Smit. "You don't need to know his name. But the money is in place. Three million euros. One million when you agree to proceed, two million when the task is completed."

"This isn't how I work. Normally I do the planning, I decide where and when."

"I understand that. But that's one of the reasons why the contract is of such high value."

Shepherd shook his head. "No, the reason the contract is expensive is because of the target. It's a career-finisher. A last hurrah."

"What do you mean?"

"Whoever kills Putin will have to disappear for ever. The Russians won't forgive or forget, they'll be on his trail for ever."

"Not necessarily," said Smit. "Putin is a dictator and dictators are never loved. Once he is dead he will be swiftly replaced. And I doubt his replacement will be out for revenge."

"The king is dead, long live the king?"

"Exactly," said Smit. He flicked ash into a crystal ashtray. "So you will take the contract?"

"I will," said Shepherd. "But the fee is five million euros. Two million up front."

Smit's eyes hardened. "The fee is three million."

"Then find someone who is prepared to do it for that. If you want me it's five. And from where I stand, it doesn't look to me as if you have too many options."

"You are not the only contract killer out there."

Shepherd smiled. "I know that. But how many are available right now? And how many would be prepared to accept a target like Putin? And how many of those would be prepared to step into someone else's plan?"

Smit stared at him with unblinking eyes.

"And let's not forget all the money you've paid to get to this point. If you don't find someone to do the job, all that money will have been wasted. You've got three weeks to find someone. And you know you need a pro. I'm here. I'm available."

"But you are expensive."

"You get what you pay for." Shepherd shrugged. "Look, it's your call. I'm not haggling, I've told you my price. If you can pay it then we can move forward. If not, then it's been nice knowing you."

"Except that now you know who the target is."

"But that's all I know. And trust me, I'm not the sort to go running to the cops."

Smit's eyes narrowed. "This is not how I normally do business."

"I guess not. But this is a bit of a special case, isn't it?"

Shepherd flew back to London late on Sunday evening. As he passed through immigration his mobile beeped to let him know he had received a text message. It was Button. *I'M OUTSIDE.*

She was waiting for him at the wheel of a white Audi. "I thought I'd debrief you and give you a lift," she said as he climbed in.

"It's on," he said. "Smit has confirmed that Putin is the target. And he already has a plan. The problem is, he won't tell me what it is yet. He says he'll give me the information closer to the time."

"But it's definitely London?"

Shepherd nodded. "For sure. In three weeks, he said."

"Then the options are limited. Putin is flying in solely for the G8 meeting. He'll fly in, be driven from the airport to the hotel, then spend the day at the meeting before flying out later that night."

"They tested me on sniping and explosives. It's only a hunch but I wondered if they plan to use an explosion to change his route, send him down a street where I'll be waiting with a rifle. Smit said they know the hotel Putin will be using which means they can work out possible routes."

"That still leaves a lot of possibilities. When will he fully brief you?"

"He didn't say. He said he'd pay the deposit into my account. Maybe that'll be traceable?"

"I seriously doubt it," Button said, driving out of the airport and joining the main road into London. "We'll try, obviously. But I doubt the money will come from a Lucas Smit account marked 'payment for Putin assassination'. We need something tangible, Spider. A recording. Proof."

"My word isn't good enough?"

She laughed. "You know as well as I do that we don't want you in court. Especially not a court in Holland." She tapped the steering wheel as she drove. "Let's see what he does next," she said.

"He won't say anything over the phone, Charlie. He's as paranoid as hell. Wouldn't travel in the same car as me and the only time he'd say anything was in this secure room in his house."

"I'll talk to Amar to see if he has any bright ideas." She flashed him a sly look that he pretended not to notice. "How did you get on with Faith?"

"She was good. Very professional."

"Pretty girl."

He looked across at her. "I'm assuming that's why you used her."

"It was," she said. "Most definitely."

O'Brien and Walsh arrived in Paris expecting to be met by Harper. Instead, they were greeted by a car service driver. He was one of Harper's ex-para mates, now working on the Circuit, and picking up a very nice pay packet for five minutes' work — holding a placard with O'Brien's cover name on it, handing them two train tickets to Berlin and telling them to look out for another driver with a similar message there. It was almost a nine-hour train journey and on arrival in Berlin, the man waiting for them handed them a new pay-as-you-go mobile phone with one pre-programmed number, and two more rail tickets on a local stopping train to the grimy East German town where Harper was waiting. Tired, hungry and frustrated, O'Brien looked ready to explode with rage, but the bearer of the message merely shrugged and then vanished into the crowds. The two men made their bad-tempered way to the platform for their train, and as they were about to discover, it was a journey that took two more hours, in an outside temperature that was well below freezing. They didn't see the two Billys behind them, making sure that they weren't being followed or accompanied by heavies.

As soon as O'Brien boarded the local train, he phoned the pre-programmed number and launched into a foul-mouthed tirade at Harper.

Harper didn't apologise. "It's a necessary security precaution so don't get your knickers in a twist. Your security is normally your own concern but I need to reassure myself that I'm not jeopardising my own security by doing business with you. Okay?"

"I hate feckin' trains," said O'Brien. "If you'd wanted me in Berlin I could have just flown to Berlin."

"My men have been making sure that you are not being followed. If you were, we would not be having this conversation. I'm now happy to go ahead with our business and once you reach your destination, I assure you that you will find that your little bit of discomfort has been worthwhile. But if you're that unhappy you can just fuck off back to Ireland."

He broke the connection before O'Brien could reply.

Two minutes later and O'Brien called back. "Okay, okay, we'll be there," he said.

"I'm here, ready and waiting," said Harper.

While awaiting their arrival, Harper gave the heavies their final briefing, with Zelda translating for him. "All I need you to do," he said, "is stand outside the steel doors and look menacing. Don't speak even if spoken to, and don't let anyone near the building unless I give the okay."

Paying cash, he had booked the two men a twin room at the best hotel in town — though that wasn't saying much. Hansfree had already installed listening devices in it so they could monitor the New IRA men's conversation. Harper's last preparation before they arrived was to slip the Makarov into his shoulder holster, under his jacket. He wasn't expecting trouble but that didn't mean he wouldn't be prepared for it.

By the time the two men drew up in the taxi that Harper had sent to collect them from the station, they had been travelling for over sixteen hours and O'Brien in particular was in an even filthier mood that was only partly eased by the large glass of schnapps that Harper thrust into his hand. Walsh looked grey with cold as he clutched the briefcase he was holding protectively to his chest. A steel chain connected the handle to his wrist. Night had long since fallen, plunging the temperature even lower and Harper could see the American trying to suppress his shivers.

"We're very hungry," Walsh said. "We've been travelling for ever."

Harper nodded, putting on a sympathetic expression. "We'll have some food shortly, but let's take care of our business first."

Instead of leading them down the stairs at the back of the office, he steered them back out of the front door and made them walk up the narrow, cobbled street at the side, into the teeth of the wind-driven snow flurries that stung their skin like handfuls of grit. Thick icicles hung from the gutters above them and their footsteps rang like iron on the frozen ground. Harper hid a smile as he heard Walsh slipping and sliding on the ice in his expensive, leather-soled shoes and finally taking a

222

crashing fall. He picked himself up, cursing, and dabbed at blood seeping from a graze on his hand with his handkerchief. The two hulking bodyguards loitering by the steel doors, stamping their feet against the cold, stood to attention as Harper and the two men approached, but as instructed, they remained silent and made no move to help Walsh as he struggled the last few yards.

The two Germans stepped aside only enough to let them through in single file, once more blocking the view of the inside of the storeroom from anyone passing by, though only the most desperate need would have brought anyone out on to the streets on such a freezing night. The bodyguards swung the steel doors shut behind them as Harper led the others into the weapons store but the temperature was barely any warmer inside.

Harper gestured towards the crates at one side of the room. "Those are yours," he said.

O'Brien was about to pick up one of the AK-47s when Harper grabbed his arm. "I thought you said you were professionals," he said. "If that ever falls into the wrong hands, one fingerprint will be enough to earn you twenty years in jail." He held the box of disposable gloves out to him. "Wear a pair of these."

O'Brien glared at him, but did as he was told. He checked several of the weapons and nodded with approval.

Walsh had also pulled on a pair of disposable gloves and while O'Brien showed off his skills with an AK-47 by stripping it down and then reassembling it, Walsh checked the contents of the crates, counting the rifles, grenades and slabs of plastic explosive.

"I hope you're not going to want to count the ammunition as well," Harper said, "or we'll be here all night. Trust me, it's all there. I'm hardly likely to be trying to cheat you on this when we have a much bigger deal in the offing."

O'Brien was just finishing reassembling the AK-47, but as he snapped the breech shut, his expression changed as he realised he had caught the forefinger of his disposable glove in the breech. As he tried to jerk it free, there was a tearing sound and the glove ripped.

"If that finger has touched the breech," Harper said, "you'd better get polishing because if the shipment gets intercepted, even a partial print could be enough to get you banged up."

O'Brien pulled a handkerchief from his pocket and began rubbing frantically at the breech and barrel.

"I hope there's no DNA on that handkerchief," Harper added, maliciously twisting the knife. "And while you're at it, you'd better check that there isn't a bit of the glove still trapped in the breech, because that might be carrying a partial of your forefinger too."

Despite the cold, beads of sweat were now standing out on O'Brien's forehead and he directed a look of pure evil at Harper, but did as he said. It took him another minute before he could work the breech open and remove the fragment of rubber glove that was indeed trapped there.

Walsh was now so cold that his teeth were chattering and he shot Harper a grateful look when he suggested completing their business somewhere warmer. He led them back to the office, sat them down and poured them both another glass of schnapps.

"So," Harper said, "we just need you to arrange collection of the weapons and then, providing there are no hitches at that stage, phase one will be complete."

"The collection would have been a bit easier and a bit quicker if I hadn't had to divert my men to Paris on what turned out to be a wild feckin' goose chase," O'Brien said, glaring at him. "I've already sent them to Berlin but to get them here's going to take at least another two hours."

Harper shrugged. "I apologise for the inconvenience, but I had to reassure myself that you were as professional about your security as I am about mine. My men were observing you and carrying out counter surveillance at each stage of your journey to ensure that you were not being followed." He looked at his watch. "Rather than waiting here in the cold for them, I suggest we go to the hotel I've booked for you. It's not quite up to the standard of our hotel in Monte Carlo, but at least there's hot food and a warm fire."

The hotel seemed to double as the local nightclub and the bar was packed with what looked to be a broad cross-section of the area's lowlife humanity: petty criminals, thugs, gangsters, prostitutes, drug dealers, and less easily definable types. Just like a Wild West saloon, the place fell silent as Harper and the two men entered, with every head turning to stare at them, probably assessing whether they were undercover cops, rival gangsters, or tourists who had strayed into the wrong part of town: turkeys ripe for plucking. Seeing no obvious threat or opportunity, the locals resumed their conversations while Harper settled the men at a corner table, bought them some beer and more schnapps and ordered them some food. As they sat there, to O'Brien's mounting irritation, Walsh kept his chained briefcase on his lap and was constantly glancing around.

"For feck's sake," O'Brien said. "Will you stop feckin' fidgeting? You couldn't be more conspicuous if you'd walked in stark bollock naked."

When the food arrived — steaming bowls of soup with black bread — O'Brien sniffed at it apprehensively.

"It's Kohlsuppe — cabbage soup," Harper said. "It's a German speciality and tastes better than it sounds."

They sat mostly in silence, eating, drinking and watching the lowlifes. They had been there almost three hours when O'Brien's mobile rang. "They're at the station," he said, handing Harper the phone.

Harper gave them directions, then drained his drink and stood up. "Let's go."

By the time they got back to the weapons store, a white van was already parked outside. Zelda's thugs still stood, impassive, by the steel doors.

"Jesus," Walsh said, pulling his coat tighter around him. "Do Germans never feel the cold?"

At a nod from Harper, the thugs swung the steel doors open as the van backed up to them. As he walked inside with O'Brien and Walsh, Harper eased his jacket open a fraction, feeling the reassuring weight of the Makarov under his arm. He stood to one side, assessing the two solidly built Irishmen who had emerged from the van. Harper's experienced eye noted that one of them had a pistol tucked into his waistband under his windcheater and Harper kept a wary eye on him, but the Irishmen only seemed focused on the weapon crates. As they began to screw down the lids, Harper held up his hand. "Just one more formality, before we go any further. I take it you're happy with the shipment? In which case, the balance of the price — a hundred thousand euros — is now due."

Walsh glanced at O'Brien for approval, then unlocked his briefcase and took out a bulky manila envelope. Harper opened it, riffled through the thick stack of five-hundred euro banknotes it contained and then slipped it into his jacket pocket. It took no more than five minutes to load the crates and the drivers then set off at once on their journey to whatever port they had chosen. O'Brien and Walsh did not expose themselves to unnecessary risks by going with them.

The hidden trackers would reveal every step of the route taken from the weapons store in Germany, through the ports where they would be shipped and received and on to the hides and weapons caches in the "bandit country" of Northern Ireland and the Republic where they would be concealed. All Harper needed to do was hand the thumbdrive over to Button when he got back to the UK.

Harper returned Walsh and O'Brien to their hotel and then took his leave of them for the night. After listening in on their bugged conversation in their hotel room before they went to bed that night, Hansfree reported to Harper that the only reservation they appeared to have about him or the Katyusha deal was whether a rocket that had been manufactured more than twenty years before would still be in working order.

Shepherd's phone rang and he picked it up. The number was being withheld but that was by no means unusual in his line of work so he took the call anyway. "Yeah?"

"Mr Shepherd." The caller was jovial, the emphasis on the Mister and it wasn't a question. The voice was just upper class enough to be annoying but Shepherd still couldn't place it.

"Who is this?" he asked.

"How quickly they forget," said the man. "It's Jeremy, Dan. Long time no talk."

Shepherd cursed under his breath. Jeremy Willoughby-Brown. MI6 and a long way down his list of people he wanted to talk to.

"I'm busy," said Shepherd coldly.

"We're all busy these days," said Willoughby-Brown. "That's what happens when the threat level is raised to critical."

"What do you want, Jeremy?"

"A chat," said Willoughby-Brown.

"About what?"

"Not on the phone, old lad. Face to face, if you don't mind."

"I don't have time for cloak and dagger, really. I'm working my balls off at the moment. If you need to talk to me you're going to have to do it through Charlie. Lines of communication and all that."

"Unfortunately that's not possible. As you'll understand once I've briefed you."

"You're Six. I'm Five. You don't brief me, Jeremy. If you've fucked up again and you need someone to pull your nuts out of the fire, you need to use the correct channels."

Willoughby-Brown chuckled. "I do love it when you go all macho on me," he said. "Now be a good chap and stop fucking around. Meet me at the bandstand in Battersea Park."

"When?"

"Now would be good," said Willoughby-Brown. "I'm in the area and it's a short walk from that lovely two-bedroom flat of yours. I do envy you the view of the Thames. There's something so relaxing about overlooking the water, isn't there? Soon as you can, Dan, it's getting a bit chilly."

The phone went dead and Shepherd cursed again. The last thing he wanted was a face to face with Willoughby-Brown but the fact that the MI6 man knew his number and where he was staying meant there was something major going on. He grabbed his overcoat and headed out.

Willoughby-Brown had been right about the weather turning cold and Shepherd's breath feathered around him as he walked across the park. The sun was just starting to go down and the street lights were coming on. Willoughby-Brown was sitting on a bench, smoking a small cigar. He was wearing a brown raincoat with the collar up and a red scarf loosely tied around his neck. He didn't get up or. move to shake hands, he just waved with his cigar for Shepherd to sit next to him.

"You're looking fit," he said. "Still doing that running thing with the rucksack full of bricks?"

"Not so much these days." Shepherd folded his arms and waited for Willoughby-Brown to get to the point.

"You did well at King's Cross. That could all have gone very badly."

"Right place, right time," said Shepherd.

"More to it than that, I'm told," said Willoughby-Brown. "First-class surveillance followed by some very heavy action-man stuff. I'd tip my hat to you, if I were wearing a hat."

"Could have gone a lot worse."

"Killed two of them with your bare hands." He took a pull on his cigar and blew smoke. "I've seen the CCTV. You were a machine. How much of that is training, and how much is natural ability?"

Shepherd didn't answer. He looked around the park, wondering if Willoughby-Brown had come alone. He couldn't spot any tails.

"Serious question, Dan. Was it training or some inborn killer instinct?"

Shepherd shrugged. "Six of one . . ."

"I often wondered if I'd have made it into the SAS. I was quite fit, back in the day."

Shepherd laughed out loud and Willoughby-Brown turned to look at him.

"Seriously, I was a bit of a runner. Played cricket. Did a bit of orienteering at university." He patted his expanding waistline. "I've put on a bit of weight since then, obviously."

"Obviously," said Shepherd, trying not to laugh again. "What do you want, Jeremy?"

Willoughby-Brown took another drag on his cigar and blew smoke as he continued to stare at Shepherd. "You know Alex Harper," he said eventually. It was a statement, not a question.

"Sure. Lex used to be my spotter in Afghanistan."

"Seen much of him recently?"

Shepherd shrugged. "We haven't really kept in touch."

"He lives in Pattaya these days. Thailand."

"Yeah, I think I heard that."

Willoughby-Brown chuckled. "You have an eidetic memory, you never forget anything you've seen or heard."

"It's not perfect, by any means," said Shepherd. "Can you get to the point?"

"Is he still a friend?"

"We were close in Afghanistan. Had to be. A spotter is a sniper's most valuable asset. If you're not a tight team it won't work."

"I wasn't asking for a history lesson, I'm asking how close you are now."

"He's not on my Christmas card list, but if he called me up and wanted a pint, I'd go."

"You know he's a big-time drug trafficker now?"

Shepherd shrugged but didn't say anything.

"He was in Spain for a while, hanging out with the Costa del Crime mob, putting together cannabis deals out of North Africa. Things got a bit hot for him in

Spain so he relocated to Thailand. Lives quite the life out there, I'm told."

Shepherd shrugged. "Like I said, we're not that close any more."

"I wish I could say the same for Charlotte Button."

Shepherd's jaw dropped. "What?"

"Ah, now that you most definitely didn't know, did you? They're as thick as thieves, those two. Have been for a while now."

"Bullshit," snarled Shepherd.

"Not jealous that the fragrant Ms Button's affections now lie elsewhere, by any chance?" said Willoughby-Brown, smirking.

"You can be a pompous shit sometimes," said Shepherd.

"I find your reaction interesting," said Willoughby-Brown. "Frankly, it's more of an overreaction."

"I just want you to come to the point," sighed Shepherd.

"All in good time," said Willoughby-Brown. "What I have to tell you mustn't be rushed. I'd hate there to be any misunderstandings."

"Here's the thing, Jeremy. I don't trust you. I didn't trust you in Sierra Leone and I didn't trust you in Cyprus. So forgive me when I don't believe it when you start bad-mouthing my boss, a woman I've known for more than five years and who is one of the best bosses I've ever worked for."

"I thought you'd say that," said Willoughby-Brown. "Bear with me." He took out his mobile phone and sent a text message.

"What are you playing at?" asked Shepherd.

"You'll see in a minute or two."

"See what?"

"Dan, just wait, all your questions will be answered."

Shepherd wanted to stand up and walk away but there was something about Willoughby-Brown's demeanour that made him reluctant to leave.

In the distance a siren burst into life. Overhead a passenger jet headed towards Heathrow. Shepherd looked at his watch and then scanned his surroundings. He spotted the man immediately. He was in his mid-fifties, greying hair, rectangular-framed spectacles and wearing a dark blue overcoat. The man's gloved hands were swinging as he walked which suggested a military background, but Shepherd knew that he had joined the Security Service soon after leaving university and had never worked anywhere else. Once he'd spotted the director general it was easy enough to see his bodyguards. There were three. Two ahead of him and one following. The one following was in his twenties, wearing headphones and carrying a skateboard. There was a man about a hundred yards from Shepherd, wearing a light raincoat and carrying a briefcase in his left hand. To his right was a woman, hard-faced and holding a Harrods bag. All three were good but the fact that they were all matching their pace to the director general's and their eyes were constantly on the move marked them out as his protection team. In the old Cold War days almost no one knew the identity of the Director General of MI5 but in the brave new world of the Internet and social media, he had his own Wikipedia page and often appeared on television.

While the new openness had been widely welcomed it also meant that the man was now vulnerable to anyone with a gun or knife who wanted to try his luck.

The man in the raincoat nodded almost imperceptibly at Willoughby-Brown as he walked by the bench and twenty seconds later the director general stood in front of Shepherd.

"Mr Shepherd, good to see you again."

Shepherd got to his feet. He had met the director general several times during his career with MI5, but never one to one. It was usually at briefings where there would be more than a dozen men and women in suits and Shepherd was acting as backup to Button.

"I've been following your career with interest," said the director general.

Shepherd waited to see if the man expected a handshake but the gloved hands remained resolutely at his side. "Thank you, sir."

The man with the skateboard had placed it on the path and was trying a few tricks. He seemed to be quite good at it.

"I know how close you are to Charlotte Button, and I understand that what we are asking you to do is uncomfortable. But I want you to know that Jeremy Willoughby-Brown has my full authority on this. He is speaking with my voice."

Shepherd's mouth had gone dry and he had trouble swallowing.

"This is a very difficult situation, Mr Shepherd. The reputation of the service is on the line. You need to bear that in mind at all times. Discretion is of the utmost

234

importance. A lot is riding on you and Mr Willoughby-Brown."

"I understand," said Shepherd.

"I hope you do," said the director general. He sighed. "It's a mess, Mr Shepherd. The worst mess I have come across in thirty years." He shook his head sadly. "You know someone, you think you can trust them, and then this happens." He shrugged. "Anyway, I'll leave you with Mr Willoughby-Brown. You have a lot to discuss." He walked away, his arms swinging at his side. The skateboarder picked up his skateboard and walked after him.

Willoughby-Brown took out his pack of cigars and lit one.

"What the hell's going on?" asked Shepherd.

"The DG wanted you to know how important this is," said Willoughby-Brown.

"How important what is? You still haven't told me what this is about."

Willoughby-Brown blew smoke up at the sky and then smiled. "Charlotte Button has been running an off-the-books assassination operation and she has been using it to take revenge on the people who killed her husband."

Shepherd felt as if he had been punched in the stomach. He saw a look of satisfaction flash across Willoughby-Brown's face and he fought to keep his face impassive. "That sounds unlikely," he said.

"Doesn't it just? But it's true."

"It's impossible. How could something like that go on without anyone knowing?"

"Oh, the powers that be know about the assassination unit. It's the revenge killings that took us by surprise."

"You're talking in riddles," said Shepherd. "Just say what you have to say."

Willoughby-Brown's eyes narrowed and he took his time drawing on his cigar and blowing smoke before continuing. "From time to time there are people that the British government would rather weren't around. Now back in the golden age, it was your old regiment who took care of business. It was mainly the Irish problem back then. Your boys would find an IRA arms cache and put it under observation, pissing into plastic bags for as long as it took. Then when the boyos came along for their guns, they'd be dispatched with a minimum of fuss."

"Shoot to kill, you're talking about. That's not really assassination. It's one group of soldiers shooting at another. They call that combat."

"Well, we could argue semantics all night," said Willoughby-Brown. "But the simple fact is that the SAS killed at least fourteen members of the Provisional IRA and the Irish National Liberation Army that we know about. There were probably a lot more. All well before your time, obviously. But I've no doubt that you heard the war stories."

Shepherd shrugged but didn't say anything. He was still trying to process the little hard information that Willoughby-Brown had given him. Charlotte Button was running an assassination squad? He couldn't see how that could possibly be true.

"It wasn't just the SAS, of course. The RUC had its fair share of shoot-to-kill operations, but more often than not they were fed intel by the regiment or the spooks. It was all very murky. But because it was the IRA getting killed, and because they were murderous bastards in the main who thought nothing of bombing innocent women and children, no one really cared."

Willoughby-Brown took another long pull on his cigar and tried, and failed, to blow a smoke ring. "It was Gibraltar where the shit really hit the fan, of course," he carried on. "March 1988. What was that, eight years before you joined?"

"Thereabouts."

"You probably came across the guys who did it, right? Operation Flavius. Three IRA terrorists shot dead by the SAS on The Rock."

"They were planning a car bomb," said Shepherd.

"No argument here, Danny boy. But there was no bomb and the three Irishmen were unarmed when the SAS shot them. The inquest and the European Court of Human Rights declared the killings lawful, pretty much, but the country's *Guardian* readers had a field day. So the SAS was told in no uncertain terms that such shoot-to-kill operations were off limits, at least on British soil. The problem is, HMG still had enemies who couldn't be dealt with by conventional means. So another way had to be found."

He took another long draw on his cigar, and this time his smoke ring stayed together for a second or two before dispersing. "Even before Gibraltar, HMG knew it had to get the shoot-to-kill operations off the books.

With the SAS in charge, the state was liable, and the state could be sued. HMG needed plausible deniability, it needed to be able to say, hand on heart, that the British government was not in the assassination business. That meant setting up a funding system that was totally independent of the state. And back in 1997, when we first met, that's what I was tasked with. I didn't know the full story, back then. I was just a small cog in a big machine."

"The diamonds," whispered Shepherd.

"Yes, the diamonds. You never let me forget about those diamonds, do you? I'm sure you thought that I'd pocketed them myself."

"The thought had crossed my mind," said Shepherd.

"I was under orders to return the diamonds to London," said Willoughby-Brown. "But obviously I couldn't tell you that. At the time even I didn't know what they were to be used for. It was a need-to-know operation and apparently I didn't need to know. The diamonds were sold and the money placed offshore in secret accounts. Over the years that money has been used to fund the assassinations that HMG wants to be distanced from."

"And who decides who gets killed?"

"The people who care most about what happens to this country." He grinned. "Which rules out the politicians, obviously. It happens at a very high level, but behind closed doors."

"And whose idea was this?"

"To set it up? I don't know. But you have to remember where we were back in 1997. John Major

238

was on the way out and Tony Blair was on the way in. The heads of Five and Six could see the way things were going. They knew that our enemies would see a Blair government as a weak one and that there had to be something put in place to maintain our security. But it had to be something that could be plausibly denied by everyone involved. The director general has to be able to stand up in front of parliament and deny that MI5 carries out assassinations. The prime minister has to be able to assure parliament that the British government does not assassinate its enemies. Under the system put in place, that can happen and there's no comeback."

"Does it have a name?"

"Not officially. Insiders call it The Pool."

"Because?"

"No one seems to know. Could be because one of the first guys they used was based in Liverpool. Could be because there was a pool of killers that could be drawn on. All freelancers, all experts in their fields."

"And they knew who they were working for?"

Willoughby-Brown shook his head. "It was all done at arm's length. The decision would be taken, the name would be passed to whoever was running The Pool, and the contract would be placed. There was no paper trail, no money trail, nothing written down." He took another pull on his cigar and blew a tight plume of smoke up into the air. "Don't get the wrong idea, Danny boy," he said. "The Pool wasn't on the rampage. Most years it wasn't used. But every now and again when it looked as if the security of the country was at risk, The Pool would take care of it."

"I'm really not buying any of this," said Shepherd.

"I'm not selling it," said Willoughby-Brown. "But the fact that the DG bothered to haul himself out of his nice warm office to come and talk to you should demonstrate that this is all very real."

Realisation finally dawned on Shepherd. "Charlie is running The Pool?"

"Yes. She has been for the last two years. The Pool has been more active recently with what's been going on in Syria. There's a real danger that returning jihadists will wreak havoc here in the UK, so it's sometimes felt appropriate to make sure that they don't return."

"So they're assassinated?"

"The legal and political boundaries are blurred, Danny. Our enemies have blurred the conflict. IEDs, terrorist attacks, flying planes into towers. You can't fight enemies like that and follow the Geneva Convention. The old rules don't apply to modern warfare, and this is a war, make no mistake about that."

"And how come Charlie is handling this?"

"She asked for the job. Well, that's not actually true. You can't just apply to run The Pool, because it doesn't officially exist. But now, looking back, it's clear that she manoeuvered herself into the position where she was the obvious choice when her predecessor retired. It seems they actually had to persuade her quite strongly to take the job but again, with hindsight, it's what she was after all the time. You know her husband was murdered, obviously."

Shepherd watched Willoughby-Brown's face carefully, trying to assess how truthful he was being. Shepherd had been in Button's house when her husband had been murdered by an al-Qaeda assassin, a Palestinian by the name of Hassan Salih. Salih had been hired to kill Button and had come perilously close to achieving his objective. In the process, he had knifed Button's husband to death and managed to stab Button herself before Shepherd had stepped in to end it. "I'm guessing you know full well that I was there when it happened, Jeremy," he said.

Willoughby-Brown grinned. "It's not generally known, obviously. Everyone was very impressed with the way Charlotte dealt with it. Straight back to work after the funeral. She was offered counselling and all that new age nonsense but she turned it down. Nose to the grindstone, not easy when you're a single parent." He waved his cigar at Shepherd. "As you know, of course."

"Get to the point, please," said Shepherd. "I'm assuming there is one."

"Charlotte wanted the job so that she could abuse The Pool. She's been using freelancers to take out anyone and everyone involved in the murder of her husband."

"I find that hard to believe. Seriously. No one spotted what she was doing?"

"No one knew. Not until recently, anyway. There's no fiscal supervision of the accounts. There can't be, the accounts are totally outside the government's sphere of influence. It's not as if they can send in Ernst & Young to carry out an audit, is it? And there's no paper email trail of Pool operations. It's all done face to face. A couple of people have a chat and they talk to Charlotte and Charlotte gets the ball rolling. There are no checks and balances."

"Then it's a bloody stupid system," snapped Shepherd.

"It was based on trust," said Willoughby-Brown. "No one ever thought that someone would use The Pool for their own ends."

"And your proof is what?"

"Five of the men involved with the group behind her husband's death met untimely ends. Two were medical, but The Pool is expert at making deaths look like natural causes. One was a car accident but again The Pool contractors are proficient at death by car. The other two were up-front shootings and that's what opened the door."

"So it's circumstantial?"

"No, Danny boy, it's not circumstantial. Give us some credit. Some of the contracts have to be briefed overseas and we've matched her travel arrangements to several of the deaths. We've also gone through her phone and computer records with a fine-tooth comb. She's bloody adept at covering her tracks, obviously, but we've got enough to prove what she's up to. The first killing was a Moroccan who supplied Salih with the French passport that he used to get into the country. That was one of the road accidents. Found

242

dead behind the wheel of his car after it had crashed into a tree. Allegedly. The medical one was here in the UK. The Pool always has to be careful on its home turf, obviously. Button used one of her regulars, former SAS as it happens. I doubt you know him, long before your time. They call him The Doc. He was a medic in the regiment and now he puts his medical knowledge to good use. He killed a Palestinian who was given citizenship in the late nineties. Guy by the name of Hakeem. He should never have been allowed in but there was a bit of a rush back then. Turns out he was a bombmaker in Israel, responsible for dozens of civilian deaths. We're fairly sure that Hakeem helped Salih and Charlotte found out. And bang, another one bites the dust. Supposedly a heart attack but we dug up the body and we're fairly sure it was induced. That's The Doc's speciality."

He blew another half-reasonable smoke ring before continuing. "There was another killing in the UK. An RTA. Ran off the road and into a ditch. The passenger drowned. Apparently. The guy was a British-born Muslim, name of Mazur. His pal, Tariq, was killed trying to attack Button. We believe that Salih used Mazur and Tariq and that Charlotte found out. Mazur and Tariq were no great loss, it has to be said, they'd both been in al-Qaeda training camps in Pakistan and had been groomed as Shahids. Suicide bombers." He forced a smile. "Can't help wondering if the two of them are up in heaven now with their forty-two sloe-eyed virgins."

"I think you'll find it's seventy-two," said Shepherd.

"Whatever, I don't see it happening, do you?"

Shepherd shrugged. "All this, it's still circumstantial," he said.

"Which is why you and I are having this conversation," said Willoughby-Brown. "One of the freelancers she used was Alex Harper. She sent him to kill a Dubai cop by the name of Mohammad Aslam. It was a shooting, made to look like a carjacking. Aslam died and so did one of his wives."

"You're sure it was Harper?"

"No question," said Willoughby-Brown. "He flew into Dubai a week before the killing and flew out that afternoon. He used a different name and was on an Irish passport. But we've seen the picture in the passport and it's Harper."

"Lex isn't a hired killer," said Shepherd.

"He is," said Willoughby-Brown. "I can understand you don't want to believe it, but it's the truth. He's out in Germany as we speak on an operation for The Pool."

"A legitimate operation? Sanctioned?"

"This one is, yes. Two Irish terrorists who've been planning a spectacular in the UK for some time."

"Now we're assassinating the IRA?"

"Not the IRA, a splinter group of the Real IRA. Real bastards. HMG can't afford to have all the work that's been put into the peace process going to waste. If there were to be a Republican bombing campaign on the British mainland, or even in Ireland, it would be catastrophic to the economy, to the political structure. Which is what the bastards want, of course. So don't shed any tears for them. They don't deserve it."

244

"But this isn't a rogue operation? Charlie was given the job and she's hired Lex?"

"That's right. The present operation isn't an issue. But we need you to go out and talk to Harper. He needs to come in and tell us everything he's done for Charlotte. If he does that, if he cooperates fully, then he won't be charged with any offence. He gets an absolute get-out-of-jail card."

"And if he refuses?"

Willoughby-Brown flicked away what was left of his cigar. It spun through the air with a shower of sparks. "Then we'll pass on the details of the Dubai killing to the authorities there and won't resist extradition."

"He lives in Thailand."

"Well I think you'll find the Thais will resist extradition even less than HMG would. Either way he'll be taken to Dubai in chains and probably never see daylight again." He shrugged. "But it won't come to that, I'm sure. You just have to explain that Charlotte was acting without the required authority and that he was compromised as a result. He doesn't owe her anything. Neither do you."

"He might not see it that way."

"Then it'll be his call. Look, Charlotte is going down for this. Harper can either help or hinder." He stood up. "I need you to go to Germany and talk to Harper. And not a word to Charlotte."

Shepherd nodded.

"I'm serious. You've signed the Official Secrets Act and it covers everything the DG and I have said today.

You pass one word of it to Charlotte and you will go to prison, I promise you."

"Thanks for the vote of confidence, Jeremy. It's good to know you've got my back."

"I have, actually. It just might not look that way at the moment. I'll get a ticket and a hire car arranged for you, along with details of Harper's whereabouts. I'm sure you can fix up your own hotel arrangements. Okay, I'll bid you good night. Call me as soon as you get back." He handed Shepherd a crisp white business card with just his name and mobile phone number. "I know this has come as a shock to you, but believe me, it's for the best." He flashed what he obviously thought was a comforting smile, then turned and walked away, heading in the same direction as the director general.

Shepherd watched him go. "Prick," he muttered under his breath.

Harper had a brief meeting with O'Brien and Walsh over a breakfast of black bread, cheese and sausage washed down with coffee. "So," he said. "Are you guys ready to move to phase two?"

O'Brien nodded. "We want two Katyushas."

"Good man," Harper said. "When can you give me the advance payment?"

"Not so fast," said O'Brien. "We'll be wanting to inspect one to make sure it's still viable before any more money changes hands."

"Of course, that's easily arranged," Harper said nonchalantly, while privately praying that Zelda would be able to carry out her end of the bargain.

246

"When?" asked O'Brien.

"I'll see what I can do. But it will cost you."

"Cost me what?"

"Fifty thousand. Euros."

"Feck that."

"That's how much it'll cost to set up an inspection. It shows you're serious. Don't worry, the money will go towards the final purchase price." He shrugged. "Take it or leave it."

"We'll have the money. Now when can we see the goods?"

"In a day or two," said Harper. "It's going to take some arranging, you realise that? We can't just go down a dark alley and let one off."

"So you're saying you can't do it?"

"No, I'm saying it'll take time. You two should book into a hotel in Berlin. Set up the money and I'll contact you as soon as I'm ready. You're sure you'll have the money?"

"Don't worry about the cash," said Walsh.

"By the way," Harper said, "it's none of my business, I know, but that chain on the briefcase? It's a serious mistake in my view. All it does is draw attention — from police and/or criminals — to the fact that you're carrying something of high value." He paused. "And a chain wouldn't deter me or any serious criminal from taking the briefcase. I wouldn't even bother cutting the chain, I'd just cut your hand off instead."

After O'Brien and Walsh had left for the train station, Harper's team removed all the office equipment and every other trace of the building's temporary occupants, including the half-empty bottle of schnapps and the glasses that had been used. They went into rubbish bags that they would be dumping in a bin or skip somewhere on the other side of town as they drove away. When they shut the door on the building after a last careful check, the building looked exactly the same as it had done before they had moved in.

Shepherd was eating a bacon sandwich and watching Sky News when his intercom buzzed. He checked the monitor by the door. There was a motorcycle courier standing outside, holding a large manila envelope. The courier took off his full-face helmet and smiled for the camera. "Delivery for Mr Shepherd." He was in his mid-twenties with ginger hair and slab-like teeth.

Shepherd buzzed him up and waited by the open front door. He signed for the package and opened it as he sat down in front of the television again. There was a UK passport and driving licence with his photograph and his date of birth minus one year, in the name of Peter Parkinson. There was a printout with details of Lex Harper's movements over the past week and a copy of the passport he was using. He had booked into the Hotel Adlon close to the Brandenburg Gate. There were several surveillance photographs of Harper in Germany meeting with different people, and another printout detailing their names and backgrounds.

His main intelligence guy was Hans Hirsch, who had a German father and English mother. Hirsch had spent most of his childhood in the UK and joined the army at twenty-one. He had lost both hands when he picked up an IED in Bosnia but the prosthetics he had been given meant he could still do pretty much anything an able-bodied person could do. He was a member of the anonymous collective who carried out pro-bono hacking activities around the world when he wasn't being paid by people like Harper. He wasn't at all inconvenienced or shy about the loss of his hands, going so far as to adopt the nickname Hansfree.

There was considerably more information about a woman called Sally Sheldrake, who for some unexplained reason often went by the name Maggie May. It was probably her Security Service background, thought Shepherd, as he read her file.

Another former intelligence expert on Harper's team was Billy Walker. He had worked for 14 Int in Northern Ireland in the latter stages of the Troubles. He was a linguist and was fluent in several European languages as well as Russian and Arabic. When he wasn't working he lived like a hermit in an isolated cottage on the Yorkshire moors.

The final member of Harper's team was another Billy — Billy Hall. He was ex-SRR, which was based in Hereford like the SAS, but after he had left, Walker had relocated to the Dominican Republic with a wife half his age.

Shepherd automatically memorised the facts and photographs and when he'd finished reading the files he burnt everything in the kitchen sink and washed the ashes away.

His phone rang an hour after the courier had delivered the files.

"All good?" asked Willoughby-Brown.

"I wouldn't say good, but yes, I've read the files."

"As soon as I've nailed down Harper's location I'll send you over," said Willoughby-Brown. "He's moving around a bit at the moment but it'll be Germany, almost certainly Berlin."

"And how do I explain it to Charlie?"

"You don't have to," said Willoughby-Brown. "She's under observation twenty-four seven and I know what she's doing even before she does. When I'm ready to send you over, she'll find herself very busy. She'll have no idea that you're out of the country. And if she does get in touch, I'm sure you'll think of something to say. You've made a career out of telling lies, haven't you?"

"Go fuck yourself, Jeremy."

"There's no need to be like that, Danny boy. This is all for the greater good."

Shepherd hung up and tossed the phone away.

Harper drove his motorbike to Berlin and booked into the Hotel Adlon. It was on the Unter den Linden Boulevard, facing the Brandenburg Gate. It was discreet, opulent and eye-wateringly expensive. He helped himself to a bottle of champagne from the minibar before showering. He went out and used the credit card to buy himself a new wardrobe including a black Hugo Boss suit and dress shoes, jeans and an Armani leather jacket, mindful that Button had said that money wouldn't be an issue.

Zelda came to see him early in the afternoon and they sat in the lobby and drank tea from delicate

250

porcelain cups and nibbled freshly made finger sandwiches.

"My clients want to see one of your Katyushas before they'll go ahead and complete the deal," Harper told Zelda. "Do you have somewhere secure where that would be possible?"

"I know just the place and it's not far from where the Katyushas are being stored. We can use the old Soviet airfield at Finsterwalde. It's about an hour and a half's drive south of Berlin."

"Is it safe and secure?"

"No one goes there; virtually no one has gone there since the Berlin Wall came down. After the reunification of Germany, the West German government has spent billions wiping out every trace of the Russian presence in the cities of the former DDR, but in the rural areas they've done little or nothing to remove them."

"And the local people?"

"They have a schizophrenic attitude to the past. They prefer to pretend it never existed and the remaining Soviet installations and buildings are not only unused by them but avoided as well. I can drive you there this afternoon, if you want."

"Perfect," Harper said. "And do you have someone who can show them how the weapon works?"

She nodded. "I know a technician who was part of the crew who worked on them and fired them, though only on the ranges, never in action." She sounded almost wistful as she said it.

After they had finished their tea and sandwiches, they went outside and climbed into Zelda's car, a brand new white Audi R8 Coupé, and drove south through grey, sleety drizzle.

Finsterwalde was a few miles from Cottbus in the south east of the former DDR, but as they approached the airfield, Harper saw a newly restored art deco control tower and a light aircraft taking off from the runway. "Hold it," he said. "I thought you said this place was abandoned."

"It is," Zelda said. "They reopened it with a shortened runway about fifteen years ago and rebuilt the control tower, and a few civilian planes use it, but that's not the part we're going to. The rest of the Soviet airfield, including all the hardened aircraft shelters and the underground hardened munitions bunker where the nuclear weapons were stored, has been abandoned and fenced off ever since the Soviets left in 1992. That was a sad day," she added, her eyes misting over at the thought.

"For you, Zelda, maybe. For the rest of the world it was a good excuse for a party." Another thought struck him. "The nukes aren't still there, are they?"

Zelda gave a derisive laugh. "Of course not, even the West German government was not dumb enough to leave them untouched. More's the pity." She turned off the autobahn, drove a couple of miles along a minor road and then turned off on to a grassy, overgrown track and bounced and jolted away across a field and through a small wood. She came to a halt at a rusting, padlocked gate bearing a death's head sign and the caption ACHTUNG MINEN.

"And the mines?" Harper said.

Zelda gave an airy wave of her hand. "There may still be some, but not on the paths we shall use."

Harper tried to look reassured. They climbed over the gate, pushed their way along a bramble-clogged pathway and into dense birch woodland. She paused as they emerged into the open, gesturing to her right towards a strange-looking construction: three pairs of tall concrete columns, perhaps thirty feet high, supporting a flimsy corrugated roof. Beyond them was a massive concrete structure like a truncated pyramid. The face of it was painted in fading camouflage with newer graffiti tags spray-painted on it, and the top was covered by an earthen mound from which trees were now sprouting. In the centre of the concrete facade were two massive steel doors, at least eight inches thick, one of which hung open. A few feet inside, just visible in the gloom, was another set of double doors.

"This was the nuclear bunker," Zelda said, "where the weapons and missiles were stored. It was built to with-stand even a direct hit by one of your nuclear weapons."

"Sure, you keep believing that. And it's just left open for any kids to wander into?" Harper said, pointing towards the graffiti.

She shrugged. "Like I said, it's been abandoned for over twenty years."

"It'll take a hell of a lot more than twenty years for the radioactivity from those nukes to decay. You can't really be thinking of holding the demonstration here?"

"Of course not," she said, guiding him on along an overgrown concrete track leading away from the bunker. The track, its concrete surface cracked and pitted, and so strewn with weeds, fallen branches and debris that it was now barely distinguishable from the forest floor that surrounded it, split and split again, each branch ending in a concrete pan and a Soviet hardened aircraft shelter, still standing and apparently little altered by the passing decades. The super-strong reinforced concrete structures had been designed to withstand a direct hit by a 500-pound bomb or a near miss by a 1,000-pounder; everything, in fact, short of a nuclear blast. Modern precision-guided missiles would have obliterated them, but since the Cold War had never turned hot, their defences had never been tested in war and the Hardened Aircraft Shelters and most of the surrounding infrastructure of crew quarters and equipment and weapons stores was still in place. As Harper looked around him he had the feeling that the military airfield was merely in suspended animation, only waiting for the return of the squadrons of Russian Migs in order to spring back into life once more. He shivered; it was a place of ghosts and bad memories, but it would suit his purpose well enough to overcome those superstitious feelings.

Zelda was studying him thoughtfully. "You feel it too? Here the past seems very close at hand, *ja*?"

He nodded. "But only one of us thinks that's a good thing."

"But, just the same, it is perfect for what we need for your clients?"

254

"I think so, yes. I'll have my surveillance team check it over, and then we should be good to go. Is Thursday too soon for you? The day after tomorrow."

Zelda grinned. "I don't see why not."

Billy Big, Billy Whisper and Maggie May spent most of Wednesday exploring the Finsterwalde base and keeping it, and particularly the hardened aircraft shelter where the demonstration was to take place, under observation. Apart from a couple of kids hurling stones against the steel doors of the nuclear bunker, there was no sign of anyone, suspicious or otherwise, and they reported back to Harper that it was safe for him to go ahead.

Harper phoned O'Brien's hotel shortly after six. "We're on for Thursday," he said. "You'll be picked up at your hotel after breakfast. Make sure you have the cash with you."

"No problem," agreed O'Brien.

The two Billys picked up O'Brien and Walsh at their hotel in a rented Mercedes G-class SUV. The men climbed into the back of the vehicle. Walsh was carrying a briefcase, though this time it wasn't chained to his wrist.

"Mr Müller said we are to check the money," said Billy Whisper.

"What?" said O'Brien.

Billy Whisper repeated what he'd said but his voice was so quiet that neither man could make out what he'd said.

Billy Big twisted around in the driving seat. "We need to see the money," he said.

Walsh held up the briefcase. "It's all here."

"We need to see it," said Billy Big. "Mr Müller insists."

Walsh put the briefcase on his lap and clicked open the two locks. He lifted the lid and held up a bundle of €500 notes.

"Fifty thousand euros," said Walsh.

"Doesn't look much," said Billy Whisper.

"Yeah, well fifty grand is only a hundred notes," said O'Brien. "That's why the euro is the criminal's currency of choice." He laughed at his own joke as Walsh put the money back in the case and clicked it shut.

They drove in silence to the old airfield where Harper was waiting with Zelda. Billy Whisper climbed out of the front passenger seat and Harper took his place. O'Brien and Walsh flashed Zelda inquisitive glances but Harper didn't introduce her. Then O'Brien noticed the shady-looking, badly dressed men wearing cheap sunglasses who were staking out the area.

"Who the feck are they?" growled O'Brien.

"Ex-Stasi," said Harper. "Security."

"This better not be a set-up," said O'Brien.

"Why would I be setting you up, Declan? I make my money by selling you the gear, not by stealing fifty grand off you. Speaking of which . . ." He held out his hand. Walsh opened the briefcase and handed the money to Harper. He flicked the notes with his thumb, then nodded. "Let's rock and roll," he said, slipping the money into his jacket.

Billy Whisper and Zelda got into her Audi and they followed the SUV down a rough track and through a metal gate that stood open, its padlock having been severed by the bolt cutters that one of Zelda's men was holding.

Harper turned to face the two men in the back. "You're getting the executive treatment today, normally we would have to walk."

Zelda drove on across the weed-strewn wasteland of crumbling concrete, past the massive nuclear bunker and along the track to one of the hardened aircraft shelters. Four more of her ex-Stasi cronies were standing around the HAS, once more in near-identical dark suits and dark glasses.

The steel doors of the HAS were shut, but as Zelda pulled up in front of it, they were slid open a couple of feet with a deafening squeal of protesting metal that set the birds perched in the trees to flight. While Harper made for the HAS, studiously ignoring the Stasi goons, O'Brien and Walsh climbed out of the back seat and looked around.

Walsh left the briefcase on the back seat. He suppressed a shiver as he stared at the thick, damp-stained concrete walls. "And what the heck is this place?"

"An ex-Soviet airbase," Harper said, pausing in the entrance. "We won't be disturbed here."

Zelda led the way into the building and as soon as they were inside, two of her ex-Stasi henchmen slid the heavy steel doors shut again. The clang as they met made Walsh jump. A generator stood at the far end, its engine running, powering the lights that illuminated what the men had come to see. Covered by an old camouflaged tarpaulin, the Katyusha rocket was spaced across three folding tables that had been erected in the middle of the empty shelter. Behind the table, dressed in an immaculate white lab coat, and presiding over his apparatus like a stage magician preparing for a show, stood a stoop-shouldered, wispy-haired, middle-aged man, who Harper assumed was the weapons technician.

The atmosphere inside the shelter could scarcely have been more tense. Harper was confident that his surveillance team would give him ample warning on his phone if any danger threatened, but Walsh and O'Brien, shut off from sight and sound of the outside world, sealed in the tomb-like concrete bunker, looked increasingly nervous. Walsh directed baleful looks at Harper and at the two ex-Stasi men at the doors, who returned the glares with interest, hitching up the supposedly concealed weapons they had stuffed in their waistbands.

"Let's all relax, shall we?" Harper said. "We're here to do business. Zelda? Can we get the show on the road?"

She nodded to the technician who, after a theatrical pause, dramatically flung back the tarpaulin cover that had been concealing the weapon. The malevolent-looking cylindrical rocket, still with its Soviet markings in Cyrillic script, was about fifteen feet long, with four large and four smaller fins interrupting the sleek lines of its gunmetal-grey casing, which culminated in a needle-sharp point. At the back of the rocket was the booster, shaped like a large calor gas cylinder with a broad conical exhaust jutting from it. There were two other items on the tables: a large heavy-duty vehicle battery and a box with switches and illuminated dials, and wires connecting it to the rocket.

The technician waited while O'Brien and Walsh walked right around the rocket examining it minutely. Walsh steeled himself to touch it gingerly with his fingertips, as if frightened that a mere touch would be enough to detonate it. As they stepped back, Zelda gave another nod and the technician connected the control box to the battery. As soon as he did so, the lights on the control panel began to blink and flash, and the rocket started to make a bleeping sound. It increased rapidly in volume, going from the bleep to a high-pitched whine that set Harper's teeth on edge. "Jesus, Mary and Joseph," he said, pressing his fingers into his ears. "Every dog for twenty miles must be howling by now." The noise still kept increasing, finally peaking in an ear-piercing, teeth-rattling, banshee wail. Inside the bunker, with the sound reverberating from the closed steel blast doors and the concrete walls and roof that were several feet thick, the noise was almost unbearable.

Yelling to make himself heard above the din, the technician told them in heavily accented English that the rocket had already gone through its various self-analysis systems and was now ready to fire. He gestured towards the control box. "If I was now to press this red firing button," he said, moving his finger towards it, "the propellant in the body of the rocket would ignite and after flying for thirty metres the warhead would become live. In fact, if I were to press this button now we would all be dead before we could blink."

Nervous even before the demonstration had begun, deranged by the appalling noise and terrified by the thought that the rocket might explode, Walsh was now close to total meltdown. He began screaming at the technician to turn it off, then sprinted for the steel doors and began scrabbling at the locks with his hands, trying desperately to get out of the shelter. The ex-Stasi men looked to Zelda for guidance and then took his arms and pinned them to his sides to stop him opening the doors, which only increased his panic and frenzy, and it was all they could do to hold on to him. Even O'Brien was white-faced, with sweat breaking out on his brow.

Harper had heard and seen enough and shouted to the technician to shut the rocket down. The technician hesitated, first looking towards Zelda for her approval. With a faint smile on her face, apparently impervious to the dreadful howling noise of the rocket, she was watching Walsh, who was still trying to wrestle free of the ex-Stasi men and drag the steel doors open, and did not at first see the technician's mute appeal for her assent.

Harper shouted at him again. "Shut it down now!"

The technician flicked a couple of switches on the control box, shutting down the power. The bowel-loosening howling noise wound its way back down through the octaves and finally ceased altogether. The sudden silence was almost as shocking as the terrifying noise that had preceded it.

Walsh regained his composure and shook off the two men holding his arms.

"So, you can see that it works," said Harper. "Time for you to pay the piper and we'll talk about delivery."

O'Brien shook his head. "All we've seen and heard so far is something that looks like a rocket and makes a loud whining noise," he said. "We need to see the thing fired. We have to know that they function. I'll look a right prick if I ship them over to Ireland and we find out they don't work."

Harper thought fast. "We're not test firing pistols here. These are very valuable and expensive items of equipment and I'm not in the habit of firing one just for the entertainment of my clients. Besides, even out here it's likely to attract attention. These are not pop-guns. When a Katyusha rocket detonates, the explosion can be heard several miles away and it will bring police and army buzzing around us thicker than flies on a corpse."

"It's a deal-breaker," said O'Brien. He looked over at Walsh and Walsh nodded in agreement.

Harper took Zelda to one side. "What do you think?" he asked.

"You're right, we can't do a live firing here," she said. "But there may be a solution. The Bundeswehr — the

261

German army — inherited a very large number of Katyushas left over from when the NVA — the old East German regime's Nationale Volksarmee — was disbanded. As I'm sure you know, all weapons have a certain shelf life and, as with all other military equipment, they have to stage regular test firings to reassure themselves about the weapons' continued viability. I'm sure it will be possible for us to view one of these firings. Let me see when the next one is."

"You can get us in?"

"I've got good army contacts." She nodded at the two men. "Think that'll be good enough for them?"

"It'll have to be," he said. He went over to O'Brien and Walsh. "I can get you into a test firing. But it'll take time. And money."

"We'll wait," said O'Brien.

"Here? Or in Dublin?"

Walsh and O'Brien looked at each other. "We can stay tonight, but if it looks as if it's going to be more than a few days we'll head back to Dublin," said Walsh.

"How much is this going to cost?" asked O'Brien.

"Let me find out what we can arrange, then we'll discuss the cost," answered Harper.

O'Brien nodded at him. "Call us when you have a date. But we don't pay anything until we've seen one go bang."

"Deal," said Harper. He told the two Billys to run them back to their hotel.

"What do you think?" Zelda asked as they watched the SUV drive away. "Will they come back?"

"For sure," said Harper. "They want what we've got."

"And you're going to let them take the Katyushas to Ireland? You know the damage they can do, Lex?"

"They won't get anywhere near Ireland, trust me. They'll be stopped at the docks in Germany. Maximum publicity, maximum embarrassment, but we'll have our money so all's good."

"We could have just taken the money off them today."

"Fifty grand? That's nothing. There's more to come, Zelda. And this isn't just about the money. There's more going on here."

"I don't suppose you'd tell me," she said, and laughed.

"I could tell you," said Harper. "But then I'd have to kill you."

Her eyes narrowed as she looked at him. "When some people say that, they're joking."

Harper grinned and pinched her arm gently. "So am I," he said.

She shook her head. "I'm not so sure," she said. "So I'd rather not know."

He laughed out loud and hugged her. Then he took out the 50,000 euros and gave them to her. "Here, have this on account."

"You're a sweetheart, Lex," she said, and kissed him on the cheek.

Shepherd had arranged to meet Jimmy Sharpe in the Prince Albert pub, on Albert Bridge Road, a ten-minute walk from his flat. Sharpe was perched on a stool by the bar and Shepherd joined him. Sharpe was already halfway through a pint of lager and Shepherd slipped on to the adjoining stool and ordered a Jameson with ice and soda from a barman.

"Thanks for coming," said Shepherd, clapping Sharpe on the back.

"No problem," said Sharpe. "I've not much on at the moment anyway. Mainly admin. So is this about the Liam thing?"

"No. I've had to put that on hold, but if all goes to plan I'll be in to see the Leeds cops on Monday. This is something else."

"I'm all ears."

Shepherd's drink arrived and he took a sip before quickly filling in Sharpe about his meeting with Willoughby-Brown. Sharpe listened in silence, but by the time Shepherd had finished his brow was furrowed and he was staring at him in amazement.

"Bloody hell, that's a turn-up for the books," said Sharpe once Shepherd had finished. "But I have to say, I've never trusted the fragrant Ms Button." He drained his glass and waved at the barman for a replacement.

"She's been a good boss," said Shepherd. "Always had my back."

"Because you've always done exactly what she wanted. Plus she needs you."

Shepherd shrugged. "You never really liked her though, to be fair."

"Because I never fell for her charms."

"But I did, is that what you mean?"

"You did tend to be a lovesick puppy around her," said Sharpe. He held up his hands when he saw the angry look flash across Shepherd's face. "Don't take offence, I just meant you were always closer to her than I was."

"She's been a good boss, Razor, and now I'm supposed to betray her."

"From what you've said, all they want you to do is contact Harper and get him to come clean."

"It sounds simple enough, I know. But she's my boss. And a friend."

"So tell her what's going on."

"I can't say anything to her, Willoughby-Brown has made sure of that. The DG is watching over my shoulder, if I try anything like that they'll hang me out to dry."

"You could just tell Willoughby-Brown to go fuck himself."

"And then what?"

"The Met will always have you back at the drop of the proverbial hat. And the National Crime Agency would snap you up." The barman put Sharpe's pint down in front of him and Sharpe nodded his thanks.

"If it was just Willoughby-Brown then maybe," said Shepherd. "But this is official now. The problem is that if I refuse to help them then they can get me for obstruction of justice or even conspiracy. Hell's bells, it could even be considered treason. And if I try to warn Charlie then at the very least it'll be a breach of the Official Secrets Act. That would mean prison, and after that no one would touch me with a bargepole." He grimaced. "I'm between a rock and a hard place."

Sharpe grunted and sipped his pint.

"That bastard Willoughby-Brown has had it in for me for years. And that's despite the fact that I helped haul his nuts out of the fire last year."

Sharpe raised an inquisitive eyebrow.

"One of his assets got caught on the Pakistan-Afghanistan border and I went in to rescue him," said Shepherd. "Almost bought it myself, and this is the way he shows his gratitude. It stinks, Razor."

"Yeah, well you know as well as I do that these days it's every man for himself. It's the same in the cops." He took another pull on his pint, then wiped his mouth with his sleeve. "What do you want from me?"

"I just wanted to tell someone, that's all. But even telling you is a breach of the Official Secrets Act. I don't know, Razor. It's burning me up inside and I just wanted to share."

"I don't have to hug you, do I?"

Shepherd chuckled. "No, that'd be above and beyond."

"Because I will, if it'll help."

"You're an idiot. But thanks." Shepherd leaned over and clinked his glass against Sharpe's. "I'm going to have to work this out myself."

"What's your plan?"

Shepherd sighed. "Willoughby-Brown wants me to go over and talk to Harper in Berlin. I have to go. And I'll have to talk to him. But other than that . . ." He shrugged. "I just hate going behind Charlie's back."

"Like you said, you don't have a choice."

"Yeah, but that doesn't make me feel any better about it."

"If it wasn't you, it would be someone else."

"I bloody well wish Willoughby-Brown had gone to someone else."

"He picked you because you're close to her, I suppose."

"To be honest, it's because Harper's a friend. Lex isn't the sort of guy who takes kindly to strangers. I'm assuming Willoughby-Brown knows that."

"What's Harper's story?"

"He was a spotter with me in Afghanistan. He was a youngster then, with the paras. He could have joined the regiment, no question, but he chose the dark path."

"The what?"

"He took to crime, like a duck to water. Armed robbery at first and then he moved on to trafficking. Marijuana, mainly."

"And this guy's a mate?"

"We go back a long way. It's not as if we hang out, I see him once in a blue moon. But other than the fact he's a career criminal, he's a good guy. So yeah, he's a mate. Doubt he'd offer me a hug, though."

"And do you think he'll turn on Charlie?"

"I don't know. Like me, he'll be between a rock and a hard place. And they really could put him away for a long time, if they wanted. Lex is careful, but if they put the full resources of MI5 on him, he wouldn't last long."

"In a way that'd be the best thing all round," said Sharpe. "If he gives evidence against her, you'll be well out of it."

"I'll still be the one who betrayed her," said Shepherd.

"You're going to have to stop beating yourself up about this," said Sharpe. "If she's done what they're saying she's done, she's only getting what's coming to her. You're just the messenger."

"I doubt she'll see it that way," said Shepherd. He downed his drink and slammed the glass down on the bar. "I think I'm going to get drunk, Razor, and I'd appreciate your company."

"I'm here for the duration," said Sharpe. "So long as you're paying."

Harper booked the suite next to his for Hansfree and Zelda to use as a base. They went to work on his laptop, researching in the BRIXMIS files for any weapon ranges that the Bundeswehr might be using to test fire rockets like Katyushas. Within a few hours they had come up with the answer.

"Just as we thought," said Zelda, "the Bundeswehr have a large stockpile of Katyushas, and according to the BRIXMIS files the only range in the whole of Germany where they can be safely fired is the one on the Letzlinger Heide, north of Magdeburg. Luckily the BRIXMIS files contain details of the location of an observation post — an old hide overlooking the firing range that the BRIXMIS agents used to observe Soviet weapons' tests and Warsaw Pact manoeuvres during the Cold War."

Hansfree nodded. "All we have to do is establish when the Bundeswehr are next going to be carrying out a test firing of a Katyusha and then get O'Brien and Walsh in position to watch it."

"How do we do that?" asked Harper.

Hansfree grinned. "My five-year-old niece could penetrate the Bundeswehr's regular signals traffic and there's no reason why they would go to top secret encrypted mode when talking about routine firing tests and exercises. They might even circulate a schedule — 'green armies' often do that so that interested parties from other branches of the armed forces can send observers."

"Brilliant," Harper said. "See what you can find out, together with anything else you can discover about the range and the surrounding area, and meanwhile, I'll send the two Billys and Maggie May to do some ground reconnaissance."

Harper phoned Maggie May and gave her directions to the firing range, then went down to the bar for a couple of beers while he waited for Hansfree and Zelda to work their magic. In less than an hour his mobile phone rang.

"Good news," said Zelda. "There's a test firing in two days. Saturday."

"And that's definite?"

"Hansfree managed to get sight of an email from the commander of the Bundeswehr Artillerietruppe — that's the unit which is actually carrying out the test firing," she said. "And the confirmation of that is that the range officer has helpfully posted a list of scheduled firings with their dates on the range's website. I guess so that the locals aren't taken unawares."

Harper grinned. "Excellent." He phoned O'Brien at his hotel and told him to prepare for a demonstration on Saturday. "And don't forget to get the money in place," he said. "This has been dragging on long enough."

Willoughby-Brown had at least done the decent thing and booked Shepherd a business class flight to Berlin Tegel airport. He was through immigration in a matter of minutes and as he only had a carry-on bag, he was driving into Berlin less than an hour after the plane had landed. Shepherd had booked a room at the Berlin Marriott, a ten-minute walk from the Brandenburg Gate. He checked in and phoned Harper's number.

"Lex, how the hell are you? It's Spider."

"How did you get this number, mate?"

"It's a long story. I'll explain when I see you. I need to see you, right away."

"I'm not in the UK."

"Yeah, I know that. I'm in Berlin."

There was a short pause and Shepherd knew that Harper was wondering what the hell was going on. "That's a coincidence," said Harper eventually, his voice loaded with sarcasm.

"Obviously not," said Shepherd. "Look, I'm staying at the Marriott. Can you pop around? Beers are on me."

"I'll call you back," said Harper, and the line went dead.

Shepherd couldn't blame Harper for being suspicious. He just hoped he'd call back sooner rather than later. He tossed his phone on to the bed and picked up the room service menu. As Willoughby-Brown was paying, he figured he owed himself a decent steak and the most expensive wine on the menu.

Harper stared at his phone, deep creases across his forehead.

"Problem?" asked Zelda, looking up from the computer.

Harper forced a smile. "Just that an old friend has arrived in town unexpectedly," he said. He scratched his chin. "Very unexpectedly, as it happens."

He phoned Maggie May. "I need to see you and the two Billys in reception, as soon as possible."

"We're on our way," she said.

Harper ended the call and smiled at Zelda. "I've got to go out for a while," he said.

"Anything I can help you with?" she asked, sensing his unease.

"I think it's okay," he said. "I'll soon know, one way or the other."

Harper called back just as it was starting to get dark outside.

"I thought you'd forgotten about me," said Shepherd.

"Yeah, well, I'm in the middle of something," said Harper. "This isn't the best time."

"It's important, Lex. I wouldn't be here if it wasn't."

"I get that. Right, so here's how it's going to go down. Do you know Tempelhofer Park?"

"The former airport? Sure. It's not far from my hotel."

"That's the plan," said Harper. "I want you to turn left out of the hotel, then left and left again so that you go right around the block. Look like maybe you're confused. Then head north to the park. Not far from the terminal building you'll see a place on the airstrip where skateboarders hang out, doing their jumps and stuff. Hang around there."

"Why the cloak and dagger?"

"Just humour me, mate. You'll see me soon enough."

The line went dead. Shepherd walked to the park, rehearsing what he was going to say to Harper. It was going to be a tough sell. Harper was very much his own man and a free agent, not the type who could be easily pressured. Shepherd was sure that was why Willoughby-Brown had chosen him to do the dirty work; at least Shepherd was a friendly face.

Tempelhofer had been a functioning airport until 2008. After it was closed the government couldn't think of another use for it and eventually declared it a park for use by all. The main terminal building — constructed by the Nazis — had once been one of the twentieth largest buildings in the world. Shepherd pulled on his coat and went downstairs. He walked across the park to the skateboarding area and spent almost half an hour watching a group of grungy teenagers practising their art before taking out his phone and calling Harper. The call went straight through to voicemail. He waited another fifteen minutes and then walked back to his hotel.

Shepherd had been back in his hotel room for almost an hour before his mobile rang. It was Harper. He took the call. "What's up, Lex? What was that little excursion about?"

"Do you know you're being followed?"

"Don't fuck with me, Lex, I'm not in the mood."

"I'm serious. Two guys. Pros. I mean, real pros. Both white, in their forties, look like they've been around the block."

"Heavies?"

"Well they're not choirboys, but they're bloody good."

"If they're that good, how come you spotted them?"

Harper laughed. "Because I'm better. Seriously, these guys are good. They never looked at you, not once. They're obviously communicating but it's not verbal, must be some sort of clicker system. So they're not with you? They're that relaxed I wondered if they had your back."

"Nothing to do with me," said Shepherd, his mind racing. How the hell had he not spotted a tail? Counter surveillance was second nature to him, and had been ever since he had started working undercover.

"The big question of course is are they following you, or whoever you're pretending to be?" said Harper.

Shepherd had already realised that. Were his followers after him because he was Dan Shepherd, or were they tailing The Dane? And if it was him rather than his legend, who had sent them? Was Willoughby-Brown checking up on him, confirming that he did actually contact Harper.

"What do you want to do?" asked Harper.

"I dunno. Let me think."

"Yeah, well think all you want, mate. But there's no way I can meet you with them around."

"I'll shake them off."

"I don't think it'll be as simple as that, mate. Like I said, they're good."

"Definitely only the two of them?"

"Two that I've seen. But good point, maybe there are more and they're even better. What's the story, Spider?"

"It's complicated."

"Yeah, well I'm in the middle of something pretty fucking delicate here and I don't want you fucking it up for me."

"I get that, Lex." He cursed under his breath. Was it Smit? Was Smit having him followed?

"I've got an idea," said Harper.

"I'm listening."

"I'll have them picked up and worked over. Find out who they are and we'll take it from there."

"Are you up for that?"

"Anything for a mate, you know that. And I'd like to reassure myself it's nothing to do with me."

"I'm sure it isn't."

274

"Yeah, well I'd prefer that from the horse's mouth. You know, this would be a lot easier if you just told me why you wanted to meet."

"That's got to be face to face. Has to be."

"You've been in the secret squirrel business for too long," said Harper. "Okay, I'll set something up and get back to you."

"When?" asked Shepherd, but the line had already gone dead. He sighed and tossed his phone on to the bed. The last thing he needed just now was a tail. But who the hell was it? And what did they want? Strictly speaking he should call Jeremy Willoughby-Brown but he couldn't bring himself to do it, especially when the watchers could well be reporting back to him. He smiled to himself as he stared through the window out over the city. It was a funny old world where he trusted a criminal and supposed assassin more than an MI6 officer, but that's the way it was.

Shepherd woke to the sound of his mobile ringing. It was Harper. "Wakey, wakey, rise and shine," he said.

Shepherd sat up and ran a hand through his hair. "What time is it?"

"Eight. Looks as if you've got two two-man teams on you — midnight and midday are the changeovers."

"You're sure?"

"Of course I'm sure. There's one outside in a grey Mercedes as we speak. His partner is off getting a coffee."

"What's the plan?"

"Grab yourself some breakfast. We'll leave it until eleven because they'll be at the end of their shift. Leave the hotel, go left for about two hundred yards and then cross the road. Take the first right. There's a row of shops there, keep going until you see a church. Huge place with a spire and a graveyard. Walk through the graveyard, keep going straight and there's a rear entrance to an alley. Take a left down the alley and keep going until you hit the main road. Turn right."

"Bloody hell, Lex, what is this? A magical mystery tour?"

"I need to split them up so we can take them separately," he said. "You don't need to do anything, just follow the route exactly as I said. No looking behind you, no counter surveillance, no funny stuff. I'll send you a message when we're done or if there's a change of plan. Got it?"

"Got it," said Shepherd.

"Eleven sharp," said Harper. "Be there or be square."

Shepherd left the hotel at eleven o'clock on the dot. He'd eaten breakfast in the hotel coffee shop, helping himself from a buffet that ran for almost thirty feet with dishes laden with cold meats, sausages, cheese, boiled eggs, cereal and fruit, along with a dozen different types of bread and rolls. He had no missed calls or messages on his phone, which was a relief. He dreaded an urgent summons from Button because with the best will in the world he was at least four hours from London, door to door. There was a chill wind blowing down the road

276

and he turned up the collar of his leather jacket and thrust his hands in his pockets.

If there were watchers in a grey Mercedes he didn't see them or the car. He followed the route laid out by Harper, keeping his head down as if deep in thought. He walked purposefully, but not too quickly.

He looked right and left before crossing the main road, and still didn't see anyone on his tail. But then they must have been professionals because they had tailed him all the way from London without him knowing.

He walked by the row of shops. If he'd been in counter-surveillance mode he'd have been checking for reflections and doing the occasional double back, but he just walked along with his head down. The church was a good choice. They'd almost certainly split up because two men walking through a graveyard would be too obvious. One would probably head around the perimeter, the other would follow but at a distance.

As he left the graveyard he saw a windowless van parked down the alley. He turned his back on it, wondering if it was his tail but immediately dismissing the thought because there was no way they could have predicted the route. It was more likely to be Harper's team. He walked along the alley. A woman in a fur coat and a very small dog on a leash walked towards him. She smiled, showing unnaturally white teeth, and wished him a "*Guten Morgen*". He reached the road, turned right, and carried on walking.

It took him an hour to follow the route that Harper had given him. During that time he didn't see anyone following him, but then he had deliberately not been looking.

Shepherd's mobile beeped to let him know he'd received a text message. He put down the remnant of the club sandwich he'd been eating and picked up the phone. It was Harper. *SHE'S A FRIEND.*

He was still frowning at the message when there was a soft knock on the door. He padded over and checked the peephole. There was a dark-haired woman in her thirties standing in the hallway, staring back at him as if she knew she was under scrutiny. He took off the security chain and opened the door.

"Let's go," she said. Shepherd recognised her from the file that Willoughby-Brown had given him. Sally Sheldrake.

"Can I at least put some shoes on?" he asked, glancing down at his bare feet. She nodded and he headed back into his room and sat down on the bed. "Do you have a name?"

"You can call me Maggie," she said.

"Well, nice to meet you, Maggie," said Shepherd, slipping on his shoes. "How long have you known Lex?"

She ignored his question and looked at her watch, a plastic Casio. "Clock's ticking," she said.

Shepherd was having trouble placing her accent. English, for sure, but there was a faint Scottish burr in there somewhere, and maybe a bit of Irish brogue.

"Don't suppose you'll tell me where we're going?" said Shepherd as he stood up and grabbed his jacket.

"You'll know soon enough," she said. She looked at her watch again.

Shepherd drained his coffee mug and nodded. "Okay, I'm ready."

They went down in the lift in silence, and she led him across reception and outside. She had a white Mercedes saloon in the car park and they climbed in. There was a SatNav in the dashboard but she didn't turn it on. She drove like a professional, smoothly and efficiently, rarely touching the brake pedal unless it was to stop at traffic lights.

"I get the feeling you're not one for small talk, Maggie," said Shepherd.

"I'm just a hired hand," she said. "I don't know you, you don't know me, we're both professionals doing what we're being paid to do."

"So a date's out of the question?"

Her head swivelled and her mouth dropped in surprise until she realised he was joking. She smiled despite herself as she concentrated on the road ahead. "You're not my type," she said.

"See, now there's something we could talk about," said Shepherd, settling back in his seat. "What sort of guy do you go for?"

"The strong silent type," she said. "With the emphasis on the silent."

"Ever been married?" he asked.

"You don't give up, do you?"

Shepherd chuckled. "Lex said you were a friend. I've known Lex a long time and I respect his opinion."

"That's good to know," she said. "What about you? Married?"

"I was."

"You left her?"

"She died," said Shepherd. "Road traffic accident."

She looked across at him, clearly wondering if he was serious. She could see from the look on his face that he was. "Sorry to hear that."

Shepherd shrugged. "It was a long time ago."

"Kids?"

"A boy."

"Single parent? We've got something in common."

"Yeah?"

"Yeah. Mine's six."

Shepherd smiled. "Ah, six is a good age. They still love you at six, and they think you're the smartest human being in the world. Enjoy it while you can, because by the time they hit sixteen you'll be the idiot who nags them to make their bed. What happened to the father?"

"Still with his family. His real family. I was just a . . ." She shrugged. "To be honest I don't know what I was. Right up until I fell pregnant he was going to leave his wife and be with me. Soon as he saw those double blue lines he told me that he owed it to his wife and kids to be with them."

"Bastard," said Shepherd.

"Yeah. Bastard. But what can you do? I've got a beautiful little boy who I love with all my heart, so as far as I'm concerned I came out ahead." She looked across at him, eyes narrowing. "I hope you're not playing me," she said.

"I wouldn't dream of it," said Shepherd. "I just like to know who I'm working with."

"We're not working together," said Maggie. "We're just helping you out, that's what I've been told."

"That's pretty much it," said Shepherd. "How much did Lex tell you?"

"That you're being followed and we want to know by who and why."

"And what did he tell you about me?"

"That you're a friend in need."

"That's it?"

"That's it," she repeated. "That's all we need to know."

They drove the rest of the way in silence and eventually reached a brick-built factory on the outskirts of the city, surrounded by a wire fence. Shepherd's German was just about good enough for him to tell from the posted signs that the factory and land were for sale. By the look of the weather-beaten signs it had been up for sale for a while.

"There's a key in the glovebox," Maggie said. "Can you deal with the gate?"

Shepherd opened the glovebox and took out a key attached to a metal globe, the paintwork scratched so badly that rusting metal was showing through. He climbed out of the car and jogged over to the two twelve-feet-high gates that were fastened with a length of chain and a large padlock. He undid the padlock and pulled out the chain before pushing the gates open. He stood to the side and waited until Maggie was through before relocking the gates and getting back into the Mercedes.

Maggie drove around to the rear of the factory where there was a small car park, the tarmac pitted and erupting like infected skin. There was a windowless Renault van parked next to a delivery bay, along with a Range Rover, another Mercedes, an Audi and a high-powered BMW motorcycle. As Maggie and Shepherd got out of their Mercedes, a door opened on to the delivery bay and Lex Harper walked out. He was wearing blue overalls and black gloves. He waved when he saw Shepherd, then hurried down a concrete ramp and hugged him. "Long time, no see, mate," he said.

"Yeah, it's been a while," said Shepherd. "You're still in the Land of Smiles, right?"

"Most of the time," said Harper. He nodded at Maggie. "Do you want to keep an eye on the main gate, just in case?"

"We weren't followed," she said.

"I'm sure you weren't," said Harper. "But better safe than sorry."

Harper waited until Maggie was out of earshot before turning to Shepherd. "They're Russians," he said.

"Foreign Intelligence Service?"

The Foreign Intelligence Service — the Sluzhba Vneshney Razvedki — was Russia's overseas intelligence agency, the equivalent of Britain's MI6. It dealt with mainly civilian matters while the Glavnoye Razvedyvatel'noye Upravleniye concerned itself with military cases. Both agencies were staffed with former KGB agents.

"Apparently not," said Harper. "They're with the Presidential Security Service. The guys who guard Putin. That's all they'll tell me so far. They won't tell me why they're on your case. I don't think they're lying."

Shepherd sighed. "I think I know." His mind was racing though he forced himself to at least appear calm. He had wondered if Willoughby-Brown had organised the surveillance to check that Shepherd was following instructions, but Russian spooks was far more worrying.

"I don't suppose you want to tell me why they think you might be a threat to Putin?" asked Harper.

"Is that what they said?"

"No, I'm just guessing. These guys only have one function and that's to protect the Russian president. They wouldn't have been following you for fun. So what's it about? A Five case?"

"Officially I can't tell you anything, Lex, you know that. But yes. Like I said, I know what it's about."

"What do you want me to do with them?"

"What do you mean?"

"Don't be coy, Spider. Do you want me to take care of it?"

Shepherd realised what Harper meant and he reached out and put a hand on his shoulder. "Hell, no. Just let them go. They didn't get a look at you or your team?"

Harper shook his head. "We're clean. The snag is if we let them go they're going to be wondering who roughed them up."

"They might think you're German security services?"

Harper laughed. "Yeah, or maybe they'd think we're working for the Tooth Fairy. They were following you and they get picked up and questioned. How are they not going to think you're behind it?"

Shepherd shook his head. "How about this? Rough them up a bit more, ask them questions that lead them in a different direction?"

"A plot to kill Merkel, you mean?"

"Something like that."

Harper shrugged. "That might work. We've only been speaking to them in German."

"Didn't realise you spoke German."

"I don't, but I know a man who does. Yeah, we could set something up. A phone conversation they're not supposed to hear. Get creative." He gestured at the door. "Anyway, it's time that the dog saw the rabbits. Put this on." He handed Shepherd some overalls and a black wool ski mask. Shepherd slipped them on. There were small holes for his eyes and mouth in the mask, but other than that his entire head was covered. Harper pulled on a similar mask and then took him up the ramp to the metal door and beckoned for Shepherd to follow him inside. The door led to a short corridor painted a pale green with bare wires hanging from the ceiling where once there had been lights.

There were doorways leading left and right into offices that had long since been stripped and abandoned. The corridor opened into the main factory area. Like the offices, the workspace had been stripped of anything of any value, there was just a bare concrete floor, brick walls, and girders overhead. Light came in through large Plexiglas skylights in the roof. The floor was dotted with droppings from the pigeons that were nesting up in the girders and there was a strong smell of cat piss that had Shepherd wrinkling his nose.

There were two men tied to chairs that had been placed back to back and about ten feet apart. They were both big men but neither appeared well muscled. They looked like bodybuilders who had gone to seed, flabby arms and guts that spilled out over their thighs. They were naked. Their legs had been bound to the chairs with grey duct tape and their hands with plastic ties behind their backs; there were cloth gags in their mouths. One of them had tattoos all over his back and shoulders, mainly religious in nature. There was a large crucifix between his shoulder blades and a Virgin Mary on one shoulder. Both men were bruised and bloodied but when they turned to look at Shepherd they glared at him with undisguised hostility. Shepherd was grateful for the overalls and ski mask but as he stood watching the two captives he consciously changed his posture, dropping one shoulder and turning his feet inwards. A good watcher could recognise a target as much from body shape and movement as the face.

There were three other men in identical overalls and ski masks standing around. Harper nodded at one of the men who then stepped forward and pulled the gag from the mouth of the tattooed captive. The man barked questions in German that sounded fluent to Shepherd. The captive replied in German, but with a heavy Russian accent. Shepherd's German was basic at best but he heard the words *Sicherheit* — security, *Präsident* — president and *Russisch* — Russian.

The questioning went on for a few minutes, interspersed with slaps and punches.

Several times he heard the name Olsen. Shepherd's cover name. They were on the trail of the man they thought was after Putin — unless they knew that he was an undercover MI5 officer passing himself off as an assassin. There were questions that he would have liked to ask, but he couldn't do that without going through Harper and he didn't want to do that.

Eventually Harper said, *"Das ist genug."* That's enough. The man replaced the gag as Harper indicated for Shepherd to follow him outside. Harper took him down the corridor and pushed open the metal door as he took off his mask. "What do you think?"

Shepherd removed his own mask and shoved it into the pocket of his overalls. "I've never seen them before. But they look the part."

"That's what I thought. Did you follow what they were saying?"

"Some of it," said Shepherd. "Basically they were just following orders. They'd been told to follow me and report back to Moscow."

"That's right. They don't know why, the orders came from their direct boss and he wasn't that forthcoming. They just had your name and a photograph and had followed you from London."

"London, not Amsterdam? You're sure about that?"

"They were on your flight."

"Shit. Do you know how long they've been following me?"

"They said three days."

"Okay, that's not so bad. But it's still not good."

"They think your name is Frederik Olsen and that you're Danish."

Shepherd grinned. "Easy mistake to make."

Harper chuckled. "I'm guessing that's your cover, right? Don't suppose you want to tell me what Frederik Olsen is doing that's got the Russians all hot and bothered?"

"They're just on surveillance, is that right?" said Shepherd, ignoring the question.

"Yeah, but they were told to be on you like flies on shit. That's why we were able to pick them up so easily." He shoved his ski mask in the pocket of his overalls. "Now you and I need to talk."

"Not here," said Shepherd. "Can we go somewhere quiet?"

"I'll run you back to your hotel, how about that?"

"Sounds good to me."

"The drinks are on you."

"Seems only fair."

They stripped off their overalls and dropped them over a rail by the loading bay before heading for the cars. They climbed into the Audi and drove to the gates. Maggie already had them open. Harper wound down the window.

"I'll take Spider back to his hotel, make sure Hansfree doesn't lose it. You know how he hates Russians."

"I'll keep a leash on him," laughed Maggie.

Harper drove on and she pulled the gates closed behind them.

"She's fit," said Shepherd as they drove away from the factory.

"I could put a good word in for you if you wanted," said Harper. "You've a lot in common."

"Yeah, she said. We're both single parents."

Harper looked across at him. "She told you that?"

"Sure. You sound surprised."

"Maggie isn't a great sharer. You must have made a good impression." He turned the Audi onto the main road back to Berlin.

"When will you let them go, the Russians?" asked Shepherd.

"Soon as you've left the country. You're going to have to disappear in London, you know that? They'll be looking for you."

"Not a problem," said Shepherd.

"And why exactly do the Ruskies think you're Danish?"

"It's a long story."

"Yeah, well we've got time."

"And it's an MI5 operation."

"Mate, I think I've earned the right to know what the hell's going on," Harper said. "It's a bit late to be getting coy with me."

"Between you and me, right? Don't let me down."

288

"Fuck me, Spider, it's me you're talking to. Who am I going to tell? I just need you to put me in the picture so I can protect myself and my team."

Shepherd took a deep breath and exhaled slowly. Harper was right. If it wasn't for him, Shepherd wouldn't have known about the tail. "This Frederik Olsen is a contract killer. They call him The Dane. No one knows what he looks like; he's the original mystery man. Very choosy about his jobs, never misses, all that crap. He screwed up in the Gulf and is behind bars. I'm pretending to be him to entrap a guy who's intent on having Putin killed."

"He's in good company," said Harper. "That guy has enemies around the world."

"This is very much personal," said Shepherd. "He blames Putin for shooting down that passenger jet over the Ukraine. His daughter was on board. The guy's mega rich and is prepared to pay whatever's necessary to get his revenge."

"Is that right? He blames Putin for shooting the plane down?"

Shepherd nodded.

Harper grinned as he stamped down hard on the accelerator. "He couldn't be more wrong."

"What, you think the Ukrainians did it again?"

"It was never the Ukrainians. And it wasn't a missile."

"You know something, Lex, or is this one of your conspiracy theories?"

Harper's grin widened. "Saying something is a conspiracy theory doesn't mean it's not true. Some

289

theories are true, some aren't. Sometimes conspiracies happen and sometimes they don't. Did you see the photographs of the wreckage? Along with those lovely shots of the local peasants looting through the luggage?"

"Sure."

"Then you'll have seen that the damage to the cockpit was side on. You could see the holes."

"Sure. Shrapnel damage from the missile."

"Except that an SA-11 anti-aircraft missile doesn't strike side on or from below. It arcs above the target and then homes in from above. You know that as well as I do. They're designed to target fast-moving fighter jets, so they don't target the cockpit or the engines, they zoom in and explode about twenty metres above the target, blasting out red hot metal everywhere. The whole plane would have been peppered with holes — but it wasn't. The damage was focused on where the pilot was."

"But the plane was blown apart."

"It was pressurised. You shoot a pressurised plane and it explodes. Bang! But the only place showing shrapnel damage was the cockpit. So how come there were holes in the cockpit? I'll tell you why. Machine-gun fire. From a jet. Thirty-millimetre calibre, probably."

"Lex, why would a fighter shoot down a passenger jet?"

"Who installed the Ukrainian government?" Harper took his right hand off the wheel and held it up to stop Shepherd before he could answer. "Obama, that's who. America pulls the strings."

"So the Ukrainians shot the plane down for the Americans?"

Harper put his hand back on the wheel and shook his head. "It was a CIA plane, but flying out of the Ukraine. The Yanks run the Ukraine and can do what they want in the country's airspace. A CIA jet went up and Bob's your uncle. The plane is shot down and before the wreckage even stopped smouldering the US was accusing the Russians of supplying the Ukrainian rebels with a Buk system. They get to damn the rebels and the Russians at the same time. Turned the whole world against them. It was the perfect black flag operation."

"And do you have proof?"

"The damage pattern on the fuselage of the jet for one. And contacts."

"Contacts?"

"I've a pal in the Foreign Intelligence Service. He says he knows for a fact that the CIA did it."

"Lex, mate, of course a Russian spook is going to say that."

"He's a pal, Spider. There's no reason for him to lie to me."

"Maybe he's not lying. Maybe he believes it. But that doesn't make it true."

"Suit yourself," said Harper. "There's none so blind as those that will not see. Mate, the CIA are a law unto themselves. Just because they do something doesn't mean the president told them to. Hell, the CIA kills America's presidents."

"Your Kennedy conspiracy theory?"

"Not just Kennedy, mate. They were full-on to kill Nixon as well."

Shepherd sighed. "Okay, I'll bite. Why did the CIA want to kill Nixon?"

"Nixon wanted American troops out of Vietnam, he wanted to up the SALT talks with the Soviet Union, and he wanted to build bridges with China. The CIA wanted none of it so they hatched a couple of plots to assassinate Nixon and install Spiro Agnew as president."

"And you know this how?"

Harper leaned towards him and dropped his voice to a whisper. "Contacts, mate. Guys who know."

"More Russians?"

"Can't tell you, mate, but these are guys who were in the loop back then. They were all geared up to fire a missile at Nixon's vacation home in Key Biscayne, down in Florida, until someone got cold feet. And they planned to stage a gunfight and have him shot in the crossfire."

Shepherd laughed. "Oh, come on, Lex."

"I'm serious, mate. It was all set up to take place at an anti-war convention in Miami back in 1972. The CIA had the gun ready; they had a guy ready to do the job, but he pulled out when he found out who the target was."

Shepherd shook his head and sat back. "You make me laugh sometimes."

Harper shrugged. "Fine. Don't believe me. But you've seen governments do enough shitty things to know that anything is possible. Look at all the lies that were told to get us to go to war with Iraq. And for what? Oil, mate. Pure and simple. That was the only reason we toppled Saddam. He had the oil and the Americans wanted it and Tony Blair did what he had to do to get us to back Bush. Shooting down a passenger jet is small fry compared to invading a country. So the guy who wants to kill Putin is after the wrong guy. If anyone, he should be after Obama."

"I'll be sure to tell him."

Harper indicated a left turn. "My hotel's straight on," said Shepherd.

"I'm not going to drop you at the door, mate," said Harper. "Just in case the Ruskies are mob-handed. I know a quiet little bar near here where we can have a chat and you can get a taxi back to the hotel."

"I don't need to go back," said Shepherd. "I'll go straight to the airport."

"Probably best," said Harper. "What about your bag?"

"Nothing in it I need," said Shepherd. "I travel light."

Harper grinned. "You and me both."

The bar was little more than a concrete windowless bunker set at the end of a car park big enough for a couple of dozen cars. There was a line of Harley-Davidson motorcycles near the entrance and a couple of battered BMWs. There was a flickering neon sign over the door with the name of the bar but Shepherd's German wasn't good enough to translate and he didn't want to ask Harper.

"It's a bit rough and ready but at least there's no chance of you being recognised here," said Harper as they climbed out of the Audi. "Locals only."

"How come you know Berlin so well?" asked Shepherd.

"I've been here quite a lot over the last couple of years," said Harper.

"For Charlie?"

"Sometimes."

Harper pushed open the door and rock music spilled out, so loud that he felt his stomach tremble. AC/DC. "Highway to Hell". They stepped inside. There was a long bar in front of them where a barman the size of a small tank was polishing a glass in shovel-sized hands.

"Bloody hell, he's big," muttered Shepherd.

"That's why there's never any trouble here," said Harper. He waved at the barman. "Hey, Klaus, *Wie geht es dir*?"

"*Es geht*," replied the barman dourly. He had jet black hair tied back in a ponytail and a goatee that glistened as if it had been oiled. He was wearing a black T-shirt that showed off his bulging forearms and tight black jeans. Shepherd quickly decided that "the bigger they are, the harder they fall" really didn't apply to Klaus. It would take a small army to take him down.

"Jameson?" asked Harper.

"Yeah. Ice and soda."

"What is it with you and Irish whiskey?"

"I got a taste for it working undercover in Ireland."

"North or south?"

"Both. East and west, too."

294

Harper grinned. "Grab a seat and I'll get the drinks in."

There was a pool table at the far end of the bar and the bikers had gathered around it. The youngest was in his sixties but they were all dressed like Hell's Angels, leather jackets with a leering flaming skull on the back. Only one was drinking beer from the bottle, two appeared to be on water and the rest were drinking from coffee mugs. They looked over at him uninterestedly and Shepherd smiled, nodded, and headed for a corner table, sitting down under a framed Black Sabbath poster.

There were only two other customers in the bar: two middle-aged women in short leather skirts who looked as if they charged for their company by the hour. One had badly dyed frizzy blonde hair and the other seemed to be wearing a wig that had slipped to one side. They both smiled hopefully at him but he pointedly ignored them.

The AC/DC song came to an end. There was an old-fashioned Wurlitzer jukebox and one of the old bikers went over and chose another track. Aerosmith. He did a little soft-shoe shuffle as he went back to his friends.

Harper returned, smiling at the two middle-aged hookers as he sat down. He raised his beer mug to Shepherd. "Good to see you, mate."

"You too, Lex," said Shepherd. He picked up his glass and clinked it against Harper's. They both drank, then Harper waited for Shepherd to get to the point.

Shepherd took a deep breath, knowing it wasn't going to be easy.

"There's a problem, with Charlie," he said.

Harper's eyes tightened fractionally, but he didn't say anything.

"She's been doing some wet work off the books, pursuing a personal agenda, and she seems to have involved you."

"Bollocks," said Harper dismissively.

"There's a lot you don't know about Charlie," said Shepherd.

Harper grinned. "Back at you, in spades."

"She's been using you, Lex."

Harper laughed out loud, then leaned forward and lowered his voice. "She's been paying me, mate. And she pays well. I do the dirty little jobs that HMG doesn't want you to do."

"Off-the-book jobs, that's what she told you?"

"She was always up front, Spider. The jobs I do can never be traced back to HMG."

"Dubai, two years ago. You killed a cop by the name of Mohammad Aslam. It was a shooting, made to look like a carjacking. You killed Aslam and one of his wives."

Harper's eyes narrowed. "Now how the hell do you know that?" he asked. "Not that I'm admitting anything, of course."

"How do you think I know, Lex? She lied to you. The government had no issues with Aslam. He was no threat to the UK, he didn't appear to be active in any terrorist organisation. He was a husband and a father."

"He was al-Qaeda, she said."

"He was a cop and a bent one, but he wasn't a terrorist. Charlie sent you to kill Aslam because he was involved in the death of her husband." Shepherd saw the look of surprise flash across Harper's face. "You didn't know about Charlie's husband?"

"Her personal life is nothing to do with me," said Harper. "She hires me, she pays me, end of story."

"Her husband was a civilian but he was butchered by an al-Qaeda assassin. I know because I was there. I couldn't do anything about her husband but I saved Charlie and killed the guy. She was using you to get revenge, Lex. She wanted Aslam dead because he helped facilitate an operation that ended with her husband being killed."

"So he was a bad guy?" Harper shrugged. "No one's going to give a shit."

"That's bollocks and you know it. You could go down for murder, Lex. They could turn you over to the Dubai cops and you'd never see the light of day again."

"And by 'they' who do you mean, exactly? You?"

"It wouldn't be me, Lex."

"Five? The Home Secretary? The PM? Who exactly is going to grass up an assassin hired by the British government?"

"You weren't hired by the government, Lex. You were hired by Charlie. She paid you with government money, sure, but it wasn't an official operation. It was personal."

"Do you know why I'm here, Spider? Did they tell you what I'm doing?"

"Taking out a couple of Irish terrorists."

"Who have been designated as valid targets, right? Targets for assassination."

"It's a grey area."

"Fuck that," said Harper. "The government wants them dead and they've tasked me to do the dirty work. And the lovely Charlie was the conduit. Do you think they're going to let me stand up in court and explain exactly how that cosy little relationship worked?"

"We're going around in circles here, Lex. The fact is that Charlie has been using you to exact revenge. Any protection you thought you might have had is gone. She's in big trouble and unless you come clean now, you'll go down with her."

Harper grinned and shook his head. "Mate, you have no idea how the world works."

"This is from the top, Lex. The Director General of MI5 wants her gone."

"Yeah, well good luck with that. And who's going to be sticking the knife in? Who's running you?"

"A guy called Willoughby-Brown. MI6."

Harper nodded. "He's the prick that got you in that jam last year, right? When you got caught on the Pakistan-Afghanistan border?"

"He wouldn't be my first choice, but you play the hand you're dealt."

"I need another drink," said Harper. He went to the bar and ordered another Jameson and soda and a beer. A new track started on the jukebox. Bon Jovi. "Living on a Prayer".

Shepherd knew that Harper was playing for time but there was no point in rushing things. He waited until he'd set the fresh drinks on the table and sat down before leaning forward. "You're going to have to give evidence against her, Lex. That's the only way you're going to get out of this clean."

"Is this you talking, Spider? Or that prick Willoughby-Brown?"

"I'm not happy about this, Lex. On any level."

Harper snarled but didn't say anything.

"They ordered me to come and talk to you, Lex. I'm damned if I do and damned if I don't. The DG is watching every move I make. They told me what to tell you, and I'm to go back with your response. That's my role, end of."

"You could have just told them to go fuck themselves."

"Then I'd be out of a job. And probably facing a prison sentence. You know how the world is, these days."

"I know how your world is," said Harper. "Full of pencil-pushers and slippery pole-climbers covering their arses."

"Those pencil-pushers and pole-climbers rule the world," said Shepherd. "And if they get you in their sights, they will take you down."

"I've got options," said Harper.

"Like what?"

"Mate, I can disappear at a moment's notice. I can step off the grid and you'll never find me."

"Cambodia? Vietnam? Laos? You think you can hide there?"

Harper laughed. "That's not my style, mate. If I thought for one moment that the shit was going to hit the fan then Lex Harper would just vanish. And I wouldn't be in South East Asia. I've already got half a dozen US identities fixed up. Passports, driving licences, bank accounts, all legit. I'd be in the US of A, and no one would ever find me. How many illegals do they have living there? Millions. And they can't even track them. With the right paperwork — which I have — they'd never find me. I'm not stupid, Spider. I plan ahead."

"I'm sure you do," said Shepherd. "But what about right and wrong? She broke the law. Again and again. For no other reason than revenge. Think about that."

"Fuck me, right and wrong? Are you serious? Why did we invade Iraq, Spider? Revenge. Because George Bush Junior wanted revenge for the way Saddam Hussein thumbed his nose at George Bush Senior. The son wanted to finish what the father had started. And the oil, of course. We went to war for revenge. Iraq was nothing to do with 9/11. You know that. I know that. The Yanks know it. But we still went to war. So don't talk to me about right and wrong." He shook his head and took a long pull at his beer. "I can't believe you of all people are going after Charlie. After everything she did for you."

"She was my boss, but that doesn't give her the right to bend the rules."

"No, but it gives her the right to expect your loyalty. She saved your life, Spider. She did what she had to do to pull your nuts out of the fire. And if she hadn't bent the rules, you'd have died out there. They'd have put you in an orange jumpsuit and hacked your head off with a rusty blade."

"What the hell are you talking about, Lex?"

"She didn't tell you?"

Shepherd shook his head.

"Then maybe she should have." He drank and then slammed his glass down on the table. "She moved heaven and earth to get you out of that shit-hole and this is how you thank her?" He leaned closer and lowered his voice. "There was an al-Qaeda paymaster by the name of Akram Al-Farouq out there with you, right?"

"She told you that?"

"She knew that locating Al-Farouq was the key to rescuing you. And she knew that an imam up in Bradford had links to Al-Farouq. The imam's name was Mohammed Ullah, a Bangladeshi-born Brit. Al-Farouq had been sending money to Ullah, and Ullah had been sending out jihadists for training. Charlie tasked me with getting Ullah to tell me where Al-Farouq was." He sat back in his chair and pointed a finger at Shepherd. "She didn't send a memo to her boss, she didn't consult the director general, she didn't stick her thumb up her arse and worry about right and wrong or what was legal and what wasn't, she just called me up and told me to do whatever was necessary to locate Al-Farouq. And do you know what I did, Spider?"

Shepherd shook his head. "No, and I don't want to know."

Harper sneered and leaned forward again. "Well I'm going to tell you," he said. "You need to know what was done in your name. I beat the bastard black and blue and he wouldn't tell me. I poured petrol over him and threatened to set him on fire, and he wouldn't talk. He was one tough son of a bitch. So you know what I did?"

Shepherd shook his head.

"No, of course you don't. Because Charlie didn't want you to know. I picked up one of the imam's friends. One of the jihadists that he'd sent for training. He was like a son to Ullah. Shakeel Usmani his name was. I killed him, in front of Ullah. I shot him three times. Bang, bang, bang. Groin, chest, throat. Then I watched him bleed out on the floor. Then I told Ullah that Usmani had told me all about Ullah's three wives. One of them, the youngest, was six months pregnant. I told him that if he didn't give up Al-Farouq I'd kill all his wives, all his kids. I'd kill them one by one and I'd do it in front of him." He sneered at the look of disgust on Shepherd's face. "I would have done it, too, because I'd put your life above all of theirs. That's how Charlie felt too."

"What happened? To Ullah?"

"He told me what I needed to know."

"Then what?"

"Then I slotted him. What the hell do you think I did? He told us how to reach Al-Farouq and I shot him and buried him next to his little jihadist mate. And up until this moment I hadn't given either of them a single thought. That's what I did for you, mate. And it was Charlie who asked me to do it."

"For money?"

"Sure I was paid, but I'd have done it pro bono if she'd asked. That's what you do for your friends. The point is, she saved your arse by breaking the rules. And now you want to kill her for it."

"No one's talking about killing her."

"You know what I mean. You need to back off, Spider. You owe her. She deserves better than this."

Shepherd sighed. "If I could, I would. But I've been given my instructions."

"By this Willoughby-Brown prick?"

"If it hadn't been him it would have been someone else."

Harper glared at Shepherd, then shook his head angrily. "I can't believe you're doing this. Where's your loyalty?"

"It's not about loyalty, Lex."

"It is. You just don't see it. What the hell does this Willoughby-Brown want me to do?"

"To tell us what you've done for Charlie. Assignment by assignment."

"So that he can work out which ones were official and which weren't?"

Shepherd nodded. "And he says that if you do that, you walk. You get a free pass. For anything you've done. It's a good deal, Lex."

"It's not a good deal for Charlie, is it?"

Shepherd didn't say anything. He was still trying to understand what Harper had told him. He'd had no idea that Charlie had used Harper to help free him in Pakistan. Or the price that had been paid.

"You have to tell this Willoughby-Brown to go fuck himself," said Harper.

"I can't," said Shepherd. "It's my job." He grinned. "You can, though. If that's how you want to play it."

"Friends are more important than work, you know that," said Harper. "Hell, you were Sass, Spider. You know about loyalty. Or at least you did. You know I'm going to have to tell her, right?"

"You can't say a word to Charlie about this," said Shepherd.

"I can do what the hell I want, I didn't sign the Official Secrets Act. Maybe down the line we'll laugh about this over a drink but right now I'm really pissed off at you as well as this Willoughby-Brown."

"Don't go shooting the messenger, Lex."

Harper laughed harshly. "If I shoot anyone, it'll be Willoughby-Brown," he said. "He's no idea of the danger he's put me in. I'm in the middle of a life-or-death operation. He presumably knew that and didn't care. Not only that, he let you come here with Russian spies on your tail. Have you any idea how much shit I could have been in if they had followed you to me? And now he wants me to turn grass and spill my guts to bring down Charlie? That's not going to happen."

"I figured you'd say that," said Shepherd.

"But you still came?"

Shepherd shrugged. "A rock and a hard place," he said. "Just don't take it personal."

Harper raised his glass. "We go back a long way, you and I," he said. "But this, it's pissing me off."

"So what do we do?"

"You don't have a plan? The great Spider Shepherd has nothing? All those years playing secret squirrel and you haven't got a wizard wheeze tucked up your sleeve?"

"Is there any way you can tip her off, through a third party? So that she doesn't know it's come from me or you?"

"Anonymous, you mean?"

"Anonymous wouldn't work. But someone else who's worked for her. Tip them off and get them to feed it back to her."

"And then what?"

"I don't know. Maybe she runs? Maybe she does a deal? I'm just testing the water here, Lex. You know more about what she's done than I do."

"I don't think she'll run," said Harper. "She's smarter than that. She'll protect herself."

"So find a way of tipping her off. And maybe warn anyone else that's done work for her that MI5 will be on their cases."

"And what about you?"

Shepherd raised his glass. "I'll tell Willoughby-Brown that you told us all to go fuck ourselves, and that if I go near you again you'll put a bullet in my head."

"Think he'll buy it?"

"Frankly, I'm getting to the stage where I don't care one way or another."

"You know, mate, you do have options."

"Dropping off the grid? That's not going to happen."

"I mean in the private sector. Fuck the secret squirrel stuff. Fuck the cops. Come and work with me."

"Smuggling drugs and killing people? I don't think so."

"Private intelligence, mate. Knowledge is power and these days people pay a lot for the right sort of intel. You think it's only the security services and the cops who run undercover operations? I could introduce you to some very heavy hitters who would pay you big bucks to do pretty much what you're doing now. Without the back-stabbing."

"I'll think about it," said Shepherd.

"No you won't," said Harper. "You're too attached to your white hat and sheriff's badge."

Shepherd grinned. "You say that like it's a bad thing."

Shepherd arrived at the airport an hour before the next BA flight to London but it was full and he couldn't get on board for love nor money. There was a flight to Manchester shortly after that and a couple of flights that would get him to London with a connection, but eventually he decided to wait for the next direct flight. He helped himself to a beer and a sandwich in the business class lounge, then found himself a quiet corner and phoned Jamie Brewer.

"What's up, Spider?" asked Brewer.

"I need a favour."

"Ask and ye shall receive."

"I'm flying back to Heathrow from Berlin in a couple of hours and I want you to check for a tail."

"Something spooked you?"

"Just a feeling," lied Shepherd. "Can you get someone to take a look when I arrive? Watch me all the way back to my flat in Battersea."

"No problem," said Brewer. "Give me the address."

Shepherd gave him the address of the flat and his flight number. "Can you keep this off the books, Jamie?"

"No sweat, I'll call you once you get home."

Shepherd ended the call and sipped his beer thoughtfully. The Russians knew where he lived, that was almost certain. They'd been following him in London before he flew to Berlin, so they had to know about the apartment in Battersea. The problem was that he couldn't tell Button that he knew he was being followed without telling her that he'd been in Berlin, and that was out of the question. He didn't want to tell Willoughby-Brown either. This was turning into a nightmare and just at that moment he had absolutely no idea how he could get out of it.

Shepherd didn't see any watchers at the airport, nor did he spot Brewer's men, but his phone rang five minutes after he'd unlocked the door to his Battersea flat. It was Brewer. "You're all good," he said.

"Thanks, Jamie."

"One of my guys was right behind you in the black cab queue. And I've had a man outside your place from the moment your plane landed."

"You're a star."

"What do you want me to do? I can keep the team on you overnight."

"Nah, it's good," said Shepherd.

"So how was Berlin?"

"Bloody cold," said Shepherd.

"Used to be a fun city before the wall came down, I'm told. Okay, I'll stand my guys down."

"And mum's the word?"

"I've put it down as a training exercise."

"I owe you," said Shepherd.

"We're quits if you'll forget about me farting in the van."

Shepherd laughed. "Done deal," he said. He ended the call and made himself a cup of coffee before phoning Willoughby-Brown. "He isn't up for it," he said. "Said he'd kill me if I went near him again."

"Empty threat," said Willoughby-Brown.

"He was pretty pissed off. But yeah, I don't think he meant it. But it shows his depth of feeling."

"The guy's an idiot. I make one phone call and he and his team get picked up by the Berliner Polizei."

"He probably figures HMG won't risk the bad publicity. British assassins planning to kill Irish terrorists on German soil. The *Guardian* will have a field day."

"I don't think anyone gives a shit what the *Guardian* thinks these days," said Willoughby-Brown. "But point taken."

"Now what?" asked Shepherd.

"Let me give it some thought, I'll get back to you," said Willoughby-Brown. "And remember what I said. Mum's the word."

Shepherd spent an hour on the sofa watching Sky Sports but as the sky outside darkened he figured he could do with some exercise. He changed into sweat pants and an old T-shirt and went for a run around Battersea Park. The street lights had come on and other than a few dog walkers the park was quiet. He did a couple of slow laps and then a series of sprints, and by the time he'd finished his shirt was soaked and he was panting like a sick dog. He spent a few minutes stretching before doing a series of press-ups and sit-ups and then heading back to his flat. After showering and changing into clean clothes, he dropped down on to the sofa and flicked through the TV again but realised there was nothing he wanted to watch. One of the downsides to working undercover was that it involved spending long periods with absolutely nothing to do. He had to avoid friends and family and his usual haunts, because being recognised by the wrong person at the wrong time could spell the end of months of work.

He sat up and ran his hands through his hair. He needed to be around people, he realised. He needed the buzz of conversation, he needed to be able to see and hear other people and not just on a television screen. He picked up his coat and headed out, walking through the streets towards the river. Ahead of him he saw a pub called the Lighthouse and he decided to go in. He took off his coat and sat at the bar. He ordered a

Jameson and soda with ice and nibbled at peanuts while he waited for it to arrive.

He heard a girl to his left curse and turned to look at her. She was in her late twenties or early thirties, pretty with dark skin and near-black eyes that suggested Asian heritage. She had short curly black hair and was wearing a brown leather bomber jacket over tight Versace jeans; a Louis Vuitton bag was slung over her shoulder. She was glaring at an iPhone and as Shepherd watched she cursed again and banged it face down on the bar. The barman placed Shepherd's drink in front of him and asked the girl what she wanted.

"A new bloody phone," she said. She sighed and then flashed him a smile. "A Kir royal, please." The barman went off to make her drink and she sighed again. "Bloody phone," she muttered.

Shepherd couldn't place her accent, but there was a hint of American in there somewhere. "Problem?"

"I'm supposed to meet a client here but he hasn't shown up and my phone has packed up. I don't think it's the battery, I charged it up this morning." She tilted her head and smiled. "I don't suppose you'd let me make a call on yours, would you? It's local. I'll reimburse you."

Shepherd laughed and took out his phone. "Have it on me," he said, handing it to her.

"Thank you so much, you're a lifesaver," she said. She put her bag on the bar and took out a matching purse. Then she took out a dozen or so business cards and flicked through them, selected one and carefully tapped in a number. She mouthed, "Thank you so much," as she waited for the call to be answered. She slipped off her stool and walked away as she began talking. "It's Julia, I'm here, where are you?"

She frowned as she listened. "I know, I know, I'm so sorry, my phone just died. Where are you?"

She turned her back on Shepherd but he could just about make out what she was saying. Whoever she was supposed to be meeting wasn't going to be turning up but had left several messages. She rescheduled for the following day before apologising again for her phone not working.

Shepherd sipped his drink as she came back. She slipped on to the stool next to his and put the phone down in front of him. "I can't thank you enough," she said. "He had to cancel. If I hadn't called him I'd have been waiting all night."

"Happy to help," said Shepherd, putting the phone into his pocket.

The barman placed her drink in front of her and she nodded her thanks. "To be honest, I'm happy to have the night off. It's been work, work, work ever since I got here." She held out her hand. "I'm Julia," she said.

"Harry." They shook hands.

"Like Prince Harry?"

"The same. Though obviously I'm a few years older than him."

"So what do you do, Harry?"

"Marketing," said Shepherd. "Promoting energy companies mainly."

"Sounds interesting."

"It's not. What about you?"

"Website design, mainly. If you've got a website and you want to get more traffic from the various search engines, I can get you all the traffic you want. There's a team of us over from Brazil working on a project with a large electronics retailer."

"You're Brazilian?"

She shook her head. "No, but we're based there. The owner of the company is Brazilian and he doesn't like to travel. So he stays put and sends his team out." She drained her glass. "Can I buy you a drink? It's the least I can do."

Shepherd looked at his watch. It was just after nine and he had nothing else planned. And it had been a long time since an attractive woman had hit on him.

"Oh shit," she said, putting her hands up to her face.

"What?"

"You think I'm a hooker."

"Of course I don't!"

She shook her head. Her cheeks had flushed red. "You do, I saw it in your eyes. A woman on her own in a bar offers to buy you a drink, of course you're going to think I'm a prostitute."

"Julia, I swear the thought hadn't even crossed my mind. I was just thinking it's getting late."

"You have to be somewhere?"

He smiled. "Actually I don't. So yes, please. A whiskey and soda would be great."

"You know what, I haven't eaten yet and I'm famished. I was going to take the client for dinner on the company credit card — why don't I take you?"

"Are you allowed to do that?"

She laughed. "If it makes you feel any better we can split the bill. Have you eaten?"

Shepherd hadn't. He'd been planning to microwave a Marks and Spencer ready meal when he got back to the flat. He had the choice of sausages and mash with onion gravy, fish pie or Thai green curry. "I haven't, and yes, I'd love to."

She smiled. "I'll even let you choose the restaurant."

She held his look a second or two longer than necessary, and alarm bells began to ring in Shepherd's head. He was realistic enough to know that he was a good-looking guy but the girl was a good ten years younger than he was and pretty enough not to have to be picking up guys in pubs. The phone conversation had been good but had sounded staged and he was pretty sure there had been no one else at the other end of the line.

Shepherd had decided on the Gaslight Grill, a trendy steak restaurant at the back of the Lost Angel bar, a short walk from his apartment. He'd been there a few times and always enjoyed the food. The maître d' recognised him and complimented him for finally bringing a pretty girl with him. "Mr Cartwright usually dines alone," he said to Julia.

"It's because I promised to split the bill," she laughed.

He showed them to a corner table. The next hour went quickly. The steaks were as good as ever, she chose a Chilean red wine that complemented the food perfectly, and by the time their coffee arrived the restaurant's mirrored doors had been opened up to combine the dining area with the cocktail bar. She was funny, smart as a whip and several times she reached over and touched his arm or the back of his hand. She laughed easily, and despite his reservations about being set up, she made him smile, too. But the more she flirted with him, the more certain he became that her meeting him in the pub hadn't been an accident.

When the bill came Julia took out her credit card but Shepherd insisted and paid with cash. "I haven't enjoyed myself so much in years," he said. "I've had a pretty shitty time over the last couple of days and I needed a break."

"Happy to have helped," she said. "I'm in town for a few more days so we could do it again, if you like."

Shepherd nodded. "Yeah, that'd be cool." He wondered for a moment if he'd been wrong and it really had been a chance encounter.

She pulled out her purse and gave him a business card, then took out a pen and scribbled a phone number on the back. "That's got my Rio details and that's my UK mobile."

Shepherd took the card and stood up. He followed her outside. "Where are you staying?" he asked.

"I'm at the Premier at County Hall," she said. "Cheap and cheerful but to be honest it's just a place to crash. You?"

"I've got a flat not far from here," he said. "To be honest, I only went out for a walk." He looked at his watch. "Five hours ago."

314

"You could invite me in for coffee," she said, and then immediately laughed. "There you go, now you'll be sure I'm a hooker. How about this?" She put her hand over her heart. "I solemnly swear that no matter what happens, no money will change hands."

Shepherd smiled at her, sure now that she was up to something. "You're funny," he said. He could think of only two reasons why she would be so keen to get him alone. She was either planning to rob him, or hurt him. And she'd already seen that he didn't have much cash in his wallet.

"I'm serious."

"About the coffee? Or the money?"

She linked her arm through his. "Both," she said. She gave his arm a squeeze and Shepherd flashed her a grin that suggested he had fallen for her charms. There was only one way to find out what she was up to and that was to take her back to his flat and see how it played out.

Shepherd unlocked his front door and tapped in the four-digit code to stop the alarm system from buzzing.

"This is nice, Harry," said Julia, walking over to the floor-to-ceiling window and looking out on its view over the river.

"The view? You hardly notice it after a while. And I'm sure Rio's stunning. Do you want a coffee? Or wine?"

"Wine would be good."

"Red? White?"

"Surprise me."

"I'm a fan of red but I keep it in the fridge."

"You rebel."

"I just like cold red wine. Is that okay?"

She laughed. "That's fine." She was still standing at the window but turned and took off her coat and tossed it on to an armchair. "I just love this view."

Shepherd took a bottle of Rioja out of the fridge and two glasses. He poured the wine and went over to the window and gave Julia her glass. She sipped it and nodded her approval. "Cold is good," she said.

"I drink it with fish, too."

She laughed. "You really are a rebel." Before he knew what was happening she had moved towards him and was kissing him full on the lips. His left hand was still holding his wine but he slipped his right hand around her waist and pulled her closer. She moaned and pressed herself against him but then he shivered and gasped as her wine spilled down his back.

"Oh my God," she said, stepping back.

He laughed. "That's one way of ending a kiss."

"I'm such a klutz. And look at the floor. I'm so sorry, it'll stain." She stared in dismay at the red wine pooling on the wooden floor.

Shepherd put his glass down on the coffee table. "It's varnished, it's okay." He was fairly sure that the spill hadn't been accidental. She was making her move.

She headed over to the breakfast bar. "I'll clean it up, you change your shirt. And that will stain, so I owe you a new one." Shepherd went to the bathroom as she picked up a cloth from the sink and went to mop up the spilled wine.

"It's a rental flat, don't worry," he said as he grabbed a towel. He peered around the door so that he could catch her reflection in the window. She was bent over his glass and pouring something into it from a small bottle. She shook the bottle and then used her finger to stir the wine. As she straightened up, Shepherd pulled back, smiling to himself. She'd put something in his drink, obviously, but why? Was he a random pick-up and she just wanted to rob him? Or had she targeted him as Frederik Olsen, hired killer? Or Dan Shepherd, MI5 officer?

He dried himself, took a clean shirt from his wardrobe, checked himself in the dressing-table mirror and then practised his most winning lovelorn smile and went back into the main room. She was just finishing up wiping the floor. "I think it has stained it, a bit," she said.

Shepherd took the cloth from her. "Don't worry about it, really." He picked up his glass and took it and the cloth over to the sink. "See what music you want," he said, nodding at the stereo. As she went over to look at the extensive CD collection in a rack above a Bang & Olufsen stereo system, Shepherd turned and as he tossed the cloth on to the draining board he poured most of his wine down the sink. He raised the nearly empty glass to his lips as he turned.

"The music's yours?" she asked.

"Yes," he lied. In fact the CD collection, along with almost everything else in the flat, had been carefully selected by Damien Plant, one of MI5's top dressers. Plant's department supplied homes and offices, vehicles, furniture, clothing and jewellery along with faked photographs and documentation, everything needed to pump life into a legend.

"I wouldn't have pegged you as a Santana fan."

"Have been for years," he said, raising his glass to her.

She slotted the Santana CD into the stereo and picked up the Rioja bottle. "Let me top you up," she said.

He walked towards her and faked a stumble. "Whoops," he said.

"Careful, we don't want another spillage," she said, and slopped more wine into his glass. She was smiling but the flirtatious look had gone from her eyes and had been replaced with something colder and more clinical.

"I don't normally get as drunk as this," he said, slurring his words a little.

"Maybe sit down?" she said, putting the bottle and her glass on the coffee table.

Shepherd sat down on the sofa. He figured he'd go with the flow just to see what she had planned. The fact that she'd put something in his drink suggested she wasn't going to pull out a gun and shoot him. He started blinking rapidly and put a hand up to his head. "Sorry," he said. "I guess I drank too much."

She smiled sweetly and took the glass from his hand. "Well, it is a good wine."

"Yes, but normally I can hold my drink better than this." He forced a smile. "I can barely keep my eyes open."

"Have a nap. I'll enjoy the view." She put his glass down next to hers and walked over to the window and looked out over the river, but Shepherd could see that she was checking out his reflection. She kicked off her high heels.

"No, I'll be okay," he said, made as if he was trying to get up and then slumped back on the sofa. He allowed his eyes to close and then he breathed heavily for the best part of a minute before he heard her pad over the wooden floor. He heard a rustle as she picked up her bag and a thud as she placed it on the coffee table. He heard rustling and then a thwack-thwack sound. He opened his eyes a fraction and saw that she had put on a pair of blue latex gloves and was putting on a hair net. As he watched she reached into her Louis Vuitton bag and took out a roll of silver duct tape, followed by a plastic bag and a large syringe. Whatever she was up to, it had been well planned.

She walked over to the front door and he realised she had an accomplice. His heart began to race. Maybe he'd been a bit too clever playing her along.

He stood up as she opened the door. There was a man standing there, short and heavily built in a leather bomber jacket and cargo pants. Shepherd knew that he'd have to act fast because one against two was never a good idea, even if one of the two was a pretty girl. He moved quickly but it was a big flat and the man was inside and Julia was closing the door before he reached them.

It was only at the last minute that the man saw him coming but Shepherd was already throwing a punch that connected with the man's chin and slammed him against the wall, knocking the wind out of him.

The girl screamed and scratched at his eyes but he ducked back and her nails missed him by inches. She screamed again but before she could lash out once more he punched her in the solar plexus and she fell to her knees, gasping for breath.

The man scrambled to his feet and Shepherd turned to face him. The man's face had gone blank, his eyes focused on Shepherd, his lips forming a tight line as he breathed in and out slowly through his nose. His left leg moved forward, his right heel went up and he bent slightly at the knees. His hands went up in the air and then came down, his elbows tucked into his sides. His shoulders were relaxed and his chin was down. His hands were in front of his face as if he were holding an invisible basketball. As soon as he saw the hand movement Shepherd knew what to expect. Krav Maga, the martial art developed by the Israeli Army. Everyone who studied Krav Maga was taught the same movement. It was a way of relaxing the shoulders and getting the hands to the correct position, and it was a dead giveaway as to what would happen next. Krav Maga was terrific for self defence, the fighting stance meant the man could react quickly to any aggressive move Shepherd made. But in this case the man was the attacker and any movement he made would involve him driving off the back foot.

He launched a punch at Shepherd's head and Shepherd took a step back, but the man followed him and before he was aware of what was happening, the man had kicked him in the stomach and Shepherd was slammed against the wall, gasping for breath. That hadn't been a Krav Maga move, he realised. He was going to have to focus.

He pushed himself away from the wall and put his hands up. "We don't have to do this," said Shepherd.

The man flashed a half-smile but didn't say anything. Shepherd could feel the man's confidence. He knew he was good. But that confidence would be his undoing because he didn't know how good Shepherd was.

Shepherd threw a punch at the man's face and he backed away but Shepherd used his momentum to launch a kick. However, the man kept moving backwards and easily avoided it.

The man's right hand dropped and started to move inside his jacket and Shepherd realised he had a concealed weapon, probably a gun. He faked a kick and the hand twitched back into a defensive position.

Shepherd jabbed with his left hand then punched hard with the right, but the man blocked it and kicked Shepherd in the chest. Shepherd saw the kick coming and managed to start moving backwards, which took some of the sting out of it, but he still staggered back, his arms flailing for balance.

The man reached into his jacket and started to pull out a handgun. Shepherd launched himself at the man and managed to grab the weapon as it emerged from the jacket. He caught a glimpse of a grey Glock and his left hand locked on to it as his right hand went for the man's throat, pushing him against the wall. Shepherd's fingers tightened around the man's voicebox but he was strong and he began to swing the gun around towards Shepherd's face. The man started to grin with triumph and Shepherd could see his finger tightening on the trigger. Shepherd released his grip on the man's throat and grabbed for the gun, twisting it towards the man's chest as the trigger finger twitched. The gun roared and the bullet ripped up through the man's chin and out of the top of his skull, erupting in a hail of blood and brain matter. Shepherd staggered back as the man slid down against the wall leaving a wet red smear glistening on the wallpaper.

Shepherd heard a noise behind him and turned to see the girl getting to her feet. Her back was close to the breakfast bar and they both looked at the knife block at the same time. She grabbed a large knife and held it low with the blade raised.

Shepherd moved back, knowing that she had the advantage. She slashed the blade, left and right, and moved forward. She handled the knife professionally, no question of that. Holding the blade up meant it would be harder to block any blow. If he did try to block it and got the timing wrong she'd cut his hand or worse.

He didn't bother saying anything to her. There was no point. She wanted to kill him, no question, and she'd either succeed or he'd stop her, there was no other possible outcome.

The knife slashed again and he moved backwards. There was nothing close by that he could grab to protect his hands. Nothing he could throw at her.

Slash. Slash. Then two more in quick succession. Slash. Slash.

Each time she slashed, Shepherd had no choice other than to move back and he knew that he was running out of space. At the rate she was moving his back would be up against the wall in a few seconds and then he would have nowhere to go.

She lunged forward and this time Shepherd didn't move back, he twisted to the side but not quickly enough and the blade sliced through his shirt and he felt a searing pain as it bit into his flesh. He kept turning, ignoring the pain, and span around, raising his left arm and smashing his elbow into the side of her head. There was a satisfying cracking sound and she fell backwards, arms flailing as the knife span from her hand. She was totally off balance and Shepherd reacted instinctively, stepping forward and punching her in the face with all his weight behind the blow. She crashed backwards and her head hit the coffee table before she flipped over on to the floor. She lay still and Shepherd could tell from the unnatural angle of her neck that it was broken. He wasn't sure if it had been the punch or hitting the table that had killed her but it didn't matter. She was dead and he wasn't. Shepherd stared down at the body. He was angry more than anything. Angry at her stupidity and angry at whoever had sent her to kill him. It was all so bloody unnecessary.

He picked up her handbag and riffled through it. No knife. No gun. But there was a vial of tablets. He tossed the pills and the bag on to the sofa. The plan had obviously been to pump him full of sleeping pills and put the plastic bag over his head. Shepherd had to admire the professionalism. He picked up his phone and called Charlotte Button.

"Well, will he live?" asked Button. Shepherd was sitting on a stool as a doctor attended to the wound on his stomach. The cut wasn't deep and the doctor had cleaned it and closed it with Steristrips.

"He'll be fine," said the doctor, a woman in her thirties who had arrived with Button and two men in grey suits who had zipped the bodies of Shepherd's attackers into black plastic bodybags. Ten minutes later another man had arrived. He had used a digital camera to take a photograph of the dead couple's faces and a portable LiveScan machine to take their fingerprints and he was now sitting on the sofa tapping away on a laptop.

"Will I be able to play the piano again?" joked Shepherd, pulling on a fresh shirt.

"Clearly your sense of humour hasn't been damaged," said Button. She showed the doctor out and then went to the kitchen area to make two cups of coffee. She gave one to Shepherd. "How did it happen?" she asked.

The two men were moving through the room, collecting the wine bottle, the knife, and the woman's belongings and placing them in a black rubbish bag.

Shepherd sipped his coffee. "I met her in a pub, around the corner. The Lighthouse. I had a few drinks, we had dinner. She came back with me."

"That's not like you."

Shepherd laughed. "When did you become an expert on my social life, Charlie?"

"She is pretty, I suppose." She grimaced and corrected herself. "Was pretty, I should say."

"She was good. She was funny, she was attentive."

"And you thought you'd pulled?"

"I had a pretty good idea what was going on," he said. "But the man caught me by surprise. The plan was to give her enough rope, but then she let him in and the dynamic changed." He shrugged. "He was going to shoot me, I didn't have a choice. She was an accident, sort of. I didn't mean to kill her."

"And she knew you as . . .?"

"Don't worry, I stayed in character. I used the Harry Cartwright legend we set up for the Battersea flat. Told her I was in marketing."

"And she said she was what?"

"She said she was from Brazil and worked in website design. A group of them were over here on a job. She said she was staying at the Premier Inn at County Hall." He fished her business card out of his pocket and handed it to Button.

Button studied the card and then turned it over. "This is her UK number?"

Shepherd nodded. "She said her phone wasn't working. I let her use mine."

"What happened when you got back to the flat?"

"We had a drink. I saw her put something in my glass. I pretended to drink it. She thought I'd passed out and then she let the guy in. I hadn't reckoned on that."

The man with the laptop looked up. "Facial recognition has given us a match," he said. "The girl's Maya Katz. She's Israeli. Former army, former Mossad, now freelance."

"Does she work for Smit?" Button asked him.

"She works for the highest bidder," he said. "But no intel that she's connected to Smit."

"What about the man?" asked Shepherd.

"Nothing yet."

"So what do you think?" Shepherd asked Button. "I doubt she took offence at anything I said to her in the pub."

"Someone paid them, that's for sure," said Button. "The question is, who?"

"It has to be the Russians, right?" Shepherd knew that it would be a lot simpler if he told her about the two Russians who had been following him in Berlin, but that was one can of worms he didn't want to open.

"To be fair, you have acquired a fair number of enemies over the years."

"Yeah, but it's a hell of a coincidence that they send someone to kill me now, a couple of days after I get back from Amsterdam. And just after Smit's money has gone into my account."

"I'm not arguing with you. I'm just saying, we don't know for sure."

"Well, with the greatest of respect, we need to find out PDQ because if it was the Russians who put out the contract on me, what's to stop them sending someone else?"

Button nodded. "You're right, I'll put out some feelers."

"I'm serious, Charlie. I was lucky today. I might not be so lucky next time. I'm going to have to move out."

"No argument there," she said. "I'll get something fixed up. Now, let's think this through. If it is the Russians, they must know that there's a plot to kill Putin. And they can't have plucked your name from the ether. Assuming that they were sent to kill The Dane, that could only have been because they connected you to Smit."

"So if they know about Smit, presumably they also know about Max Jansen."

"In which case, the easiest way would be to take Jansen out of the picture. No client, no payment, no contract." Button wrinkled her nose. "That would be the simplest option, I suppose. Rather than taking out anyone who accepts the contract. That'd be a never-ending job."

"Maybe they know about Smit but don't know who he's acting for."

"You're suggesting that MI5 knows something that the Russian Foreign Intelligence Service doesn't?" she said. "Unlikely."

Shepherd knew that she was right. "I suppose it depends on how good their Dutch sources are."

"As I said, I'll put out some feelers," said Button. "My worry is that if we ask the Russians too many questions, they'll put two and two together."

"Maybe that's no bad thing," said Shepherd. "If they don't know already, maybe tipping them off means they'll just cancel Putin's visit."

"I think they would prefer it if the Dutch authorities put Smit away."

"In a Dutch prison? Aren't they like hotels? Cable TV and weekends with the families?"

"I'm not going to argue prison conditions with you," she said, standing up. "You're going to have to leave this flat, obviously. Tonight. Anything you can't carry we'll have moved for you. The flat you used in Hampstead is still there and we've kept the John Whitehill, freelance journalist, legend up and running. Credit cards, driving licence, everything is still current."

"I'll miss the river view," said Shepherd.

Button ignored his attempt at humour. "Now, what do you want to do protection-wise? I can put a team on you, if you want. I wouldn't want anything to happen to my favourite officer."

"I bet you say that to all your people."

Button smiled sweetly. "I do actually. But in your case, I mean it."

"I'll be okay," said Shepherd. "Just find out what the hell is going on."

Saturday night was cold and frosty. It was 3 a.m. when Zelda and Harper left their hotel in a green Mercedes SUV. They had ordered flasks of coffee and a dozen sandwiches from room service because there'd be no refreshments on offer at the firing range. Harper was happy enough to let Zelda drive. She and Hansfree had been busy over the previous forty-eight hours and had been able to provide Harper with almost everything he could possibly need. They had produced a mass of information about the range and its test-firing procedures, from the details of the unit carrying out the firing to the number and frequency of guard patrols around the perimeter of the range, and had even found out the name of the range's safety officer. The two Billys and Maggie May had also been hard at work, travelling the chosen approach route, checking lines of sight from the observation post and following the various escape routes detailed in the BRIXMIS reports, in case Harper and the New IRA men were compromised as they observed the firing. Harper's original plan had been to watch the firing from the road but with the information Zelda and Hansfree had come up with, he figured he could get the IRA men much closer to the action.

They picked up O'Brien and Walsh from their hotel. They were accompanied by a single bodyguard, a big man in a heavy overcoat and a fur hat with ear flaps on his head.

"Who's that?" asked Harper, winding down his window.

"Just one of the boys," said O'Brien.

"Why's he here?"

"What's the problem? There's plenty of room."

"I'm not happy about dealing with people I don't know," said Harper.

"His name's Joe and he's part of my security team."

"Is he carrying?"

"A gun? How would he get a gun?"

"You won't mind if I check for myself, then," said Harper. He climbed out and patted him down, paying particular attention to the man's armpits and waist, then bending down and checking for an ankle holster. The man was clean.

"Happy?" asked O'Brien.

"I am now, yes," said Harper. He got back into the front passenger seat while the three IRA men climbed into the back.

There was minimal conversation with O'Brien and Walsh as they drove south-west out of the city. They muttered among themselves and O'Brien responded to Harper's occasional attempts to start a conversation with his customary monosyllables. About ninety minutes after they left the hotel, Zelda was driving along the autobahn a few miles west of Magdeburg, while Harper was reading a large-scale map and counting down the autobahn distance markers. On spotting what he was looking for, he told Zelda to turn off on to a barely discernible track down the embankment. They then drove very slowly and without lights along a series of dirt and grass tracks across heathland and through oak woodlands and scrub birch, avoiding any roads and circling around any signs of habitation. Occasionally when the track was too difficult to follow from the car, Harper got out and went ahead of the SUV, guiding it on foot.

Eventually he signalled to Zelda to stop in the middle of a small copse of silver birch trees and high-growing shrubs and heather. Harper made a careful check of the immediate area, then nodded to himself. Hansfree, Billy Big, Billy Whisper and Maggie May had done a very thorough job and found the perfect position, where the trees would give them cover from the air, and the surrounding shrubs would shield them from any prying eyes on the ground.

It was still dark outside. Harper grabbed a flashlight, left Zelda and the New IRA men in the vehicle and disappeared to make a thorough check of the surrounding area. He returned forty-five minutes later, got back into the SUV and quietly closed the door.

"Well?" O'Brien said, still limiting his conversation to words of one syllable.

Harper smiled. "All good," he said. "We're a few hundred metres from the range firing point. There are a couple of sentries mooching about, but they're not straying far from the cosy stove in their guardhouse and everywhere else looks pretty quiet. So, there's nothing to be done until the firing starts in a couple of hours. I suggest that we all try to relax and get some rest."

"Relax? Rest?" Walsh said. "How the hell are we expected to do that? We're in the middle of a goddam German army base. If we're spotted, we're done."

"Your friend seems a little tense and overwhelmed by it all," Harper said to O'Brien, his voice affable. "Technically speaking," he went on, "we're not actually in the middle of a goddam German army base, we're seventy or eighty metres outside the perimeter fence of a firing range." He paused. "If that helps at all."

Harper was dozing when he was jerked awake by a voice bellowing from a tannoy on the range. "*Achtung! Achtung!*" Harper yawned and stretched, then glanced at his watch. It showed the time as six fifteen. The dawn light was beginning to strengthen and for the first time they could see what lay around them. To either side was heathland and scrub, punctuated by more scattered copses and clumps of trees. Although the view ahead of them was partly blocked by the trees and shrubs that were giving them cover, they could see that these thinned out rapidly. Beyond the perimeter fence, they gave way to a vast plain, criss-crossed with dirt tracks that were rutted by the tyre marks of heavy vehicles and the tracks of tanks. Shell craters also scarred the plains almost as far as the eye could see, each one marked by a corona of sandy soil flung out by the blast. There were smashed buildings and vehicles that had been used as targets, which stood gaunt and derelict at intervals, the ground around them scorched and blackened by fire.

Closer to them was the range firing point, with just behind it a massive concrete blockhouse. At a more respectful distance there was a cluster of other low concrete buildings, including the guardhouse where two sentries stood huddled against the cold, stamping their feet and blowing on their hands. Behind the guardhouse there was a tall concrete observation tower, rising five storeys high, like the lift shaft of some never-built apartment block. A rough wooden building, like a birdwatchers' hide, had been erected on top, presumably to give the watchers some shelter from the elements.

Harper turned to survey the three men in the back seat. Pale and unshaven, none of them was a pretty sight. "I've got some coffee and sandwiches," he told them, opening his bag and passing one of the flasks into the back. "We've got three quarters of an hour before the test firing, which is scheduled for seven o'clock. If you need to stretch your legs or take a piss, now is your moment, but stay close to the car out of sight and don't slam the doors as you get in or out, or we'll have half the Bundeswehr round our ears before you can say a Hail Mary."

He passed Zelda a coffee, poured himself one and demolished a cheese sandwich in three bites. "Zelda," he said, as the metallic voice began echoing from the tannoy again, "translate everything they're saying, will you, so that we can all keep up with the commentary?"

When he'd finished his coffee, Harper asked Zelda to open the sunroof on the vehicle. "Is it not cold enough already, without that?" O'Brien said.

Harper shrugged. "We'll get a much better view of the rocket being launched if we sit on the roof. We'll not all fit but there'll be room enough for me and you." He clambered out through the sunroof and O'Brien followed him. He sat down gingerly on the roof and almost fell off it in shock as he raised his gaze and saw how close they were to the Bundeswehr troops preparing the range for the test firing. Harper heard the click of the door as Walsh got out of the car and stood next to it, peering through the bushes towards the range.

Harper and O'Brien watched intently as the Germans prepared to fire the rocket. Harper was just as interested as the Irishman. He'd fired off plenty of RPGs and Milan missiles in his time, and had even seen the impact of Katyushas at close to first hand, but he'd never actually seen one launched before.

They saw a couple of Bundeswehr soldiers using a mechanical sweeper to brush the firing point clear of litter and debris from previous firings. An officer strutted out to inspect the area then gave a curt nod, and heavy, armoured steel blast walls began to rise out of the concrete, raised hydraulically around the firing point to shield the watchers from the ferocious blast of the rocket's thruster as it ignited.

A strange-looking hybrid vehicle then emerged from a concrete shelter at the far end of the range buildings and was driven slowly towards the firing point.

"That's a Stalin's organ," Harper whispered to O'Brien. "A BM-21 Grad rocket launcher on a Ural-375 six by six chassis. Just imagine them raining down on the Square Mile of the City of London instead."

O'Brien's face creased into a smile and he moistened his lips with the tip of his tongue, like a snake tasting the air, looking for prey.

"Best of all," Harper added, revelling in his role as weapons super salesman, "as you saw in the demonstration that Zelda laid on at Finsterwalde, you don't need a launch vehicle to fire them, just a battery, a control box and a launch ramp that you can even improvise from a length of metal gutter or a couple of steel rails."

As the BM-21 approached the concrete firing position, a second truck came into view, following close behind the first and carrying what Harper and O'Brien could clearly see was a Katyusha rocket, painted in disruptive pattern camouflage, but otherwise identical to the one they had seen at Finsterwalde airbase. After much to-ing and fro-ing amid clouds of diesel smoke and bellowed orders reverberating from the tannoy, the launch vehicle was finally reversed into position to the satisfaction of the range officer, with the rear of the firing tubes a few feet from the steel blast walls.

A few minutes later, two soldiers dressed in Bundeswehr camouflaged uniforms and supervised by a junior officer, began removing the rocket from the cradle holding it on the back of the support truck. They loaded it at once into one of the central rocket barrels on the BM-21 and the officer plugged in the electrical connections. Still watching intently from their hide, Harper, O'Brien and Walsh could hear the familiar high-pitched whine, rapidly building to a piercing howl. Less nerve shredding than in the close confines of the hardened aircraft shelter, it was nonetheless still a frightening sound.

The soldiers and the officer made some final checks and then after more shouted orders relayed over the tannoy, they and all the other range personnel took cover in the concrete blockhouse. After a final check round the guard posts surrounding the range, the metallic voice booming from the tannoy began the firing countdown.

"Funf! Vier! Drei! Zwei! Eins! Feuer!" At the command *"Feuer! — Fire!"* a wisp of flame came flickering from the tail of the rocket, immediately followed by a cloud of dark-grey smoke and a searing tongue of flame. An instant later, with a deafening

335

bang, the rocket left the barrel and disappeared down the range with a terrifying howling sound.

Seconds later they could see in the distance a huge volcanic-looking eruption, a boiling cloud of angry red flame, black smoke, clods of flying earth and lumps of shattered rock as the warhead impacted and exploded in the target area. This was followed by the sound of a faint bang and a pressure wave that tossed the tree branches and leaf litter around and raised small dust devils from the dirt on the range. As the smoke from the blast cleared and the debris came spattering down for a quarter of a mile in all directions, they could see that the Katyusha had blown a huge, smoking crater in the ground while the shrapnel from the blast had gouged deep, vivid, black furrows into the surrounding dun-coloured grassland.

Everyone watching from the SUV had been transfixed by the speed, power and ferocity of what they had just witnessed.

"Feck me!" O'Brien said at last. "I've seen explosions enough in my time, but I've never seen anything like that before."

"And that was only one Katyusha," Harper said. "Just imagine the impact if you fired all forty tubes at once." He took a sideways glance at O'Brien. "But that would take rather more millions than perhaps even your American friend could afford."

Before O'Brien could answer, there was a sudden torrent of shouting from the tannoy.

"Quick, get in, we've been spotted," Zelda shouted.

336

Harper looked away from the site where the rocket had impacted and caught sight of Walsh who had moved away from the SUV to find a better vantage point. Carried away by the excitement of the rocket launch, he had then wandered out into the open at the edge of the copse of trees, placing himself in full view of the command post.

As O'Brien scrambled over the roof of the SUV and dropped back through the sunroof into the back seat, Harper jumped down on the driver's side and opened the door.

"Move over, Zelda," he said. "I'll drive." He slid into the driving seat as the New IRA bodyguard got into the back seat behind him.

Walsh, ashen-faced with fear, came running back through the trees and reached the rear door on the passenger side. He jerked at the handle and clambered into the back seat just as a Bundeswehr truck appeared, driving fast towards them along a track leading from the range. Without a second's hesitation, Harper gunned the engine, span the wheel and drove flat out, head-on towards the truck in a nerve-jangling game of "chicken". At the last possible split second, he rammed on the brakes and ended up bonnet to bonnet within a couple of feet of the army vehicle. He whipped the Makarov out of his shoulder holster, leaned out of the window and using his left hand, took aim and shot out one of the tyres and the radiator on the truck.

As troops armed with rifles began to spill from the back of the truck, Harper slammed the SUV into reverse gear, stomped on the accelerator and reversed away from them for a hundred yards, then jammed on the SUV's handbrake, slewing it into a high-speed U-turn. He then floored the accelerator while the car was still turning and drove hell for leather away from the range area, bouncing and bucketing over the tracks they had crept along the night before. Only when they had hit the autobahn and put another twenty kilometres between themselves and the Letzlinger Heide range did Harper reduce his speed.

He glanced at the others in the rear-view mirror. O'Brien was chewing gum as he stared ahead, a vein pulsing in his temple. Walsh was once more hunched, pale-faced and silent, and though his face looked impassive, Harper could hear the fast, nervous drum of his fingertips on the armrest. Even Zelda, normally stolid and phlegmatic whatever the circumstances, looked shaken.

"If those soldiers had fired, we would all have been killed," she said as she caught his eye.

"Relax, there was never any danger of that," Harper said. "Peacetime soldiers only carry their weapons loaded when they're firing their weapons on the ranges, and they weren't firing rifles today, just a Katyusha. They have to get a senior officer's permission to load and fire and by the time they had done that, even if permission was granted, we would have been long gone."

A couple of hours later they were in a decrepit café in a rundown area of Magdeburg. As soon as they had carried their cups of grey, thin-looking coffee to a table away from the counter, Harper rounded on the American.

"You put us all in jeopardy with that stupid stunt you pulled. I told you to stay close to the car and keep out of sight, and what did you do? You wandered out into the open like a dumb American tourist gawking at Buckingham Palace on a Sunday stroll round the sights of London." He looked around the table, eyeballing each of them in turn. "I told you all before that there can be only one boss and that is me. You do as I say or take the consequences." He turned back to the American. "Your money saved you this time, but bodyguard or no bodyguard, it won't save you the next time you screw up like that."

He let the silence build for a few minutes, then spoke again, softening his tone. "However, that's all water under the bridge now. We've some business to conclude and we don't have to be best friends to do business together, do we? I hope you and your organisation are now convinced that we can supply these weapons, and indeed any others that you might want. And having seen that impressive demonstration this morning, I'm sure you'll agree that despite the Katyusha rockets' age, they will still launch and detonate to quite spectacular effect." He glanced around the table. O'Brien gave a nod in agreement, and although Walsh was still glowering at him, he didn't voice any dissent.

"So, once the next tranche of the money has been paid, all that remains to be settled are the arrangements for the final handover of the weapons," Harper said.

O'Brien glanced at his American backer, noted his angry expression and said, "We'll just need a moment for a word." O'Brien and Walsh then got up and walked out of the café, standing on the street outside while they argued with each other. Their bodyguard remained where he was, giving Harper his best hostile bouncer's stare.

Harper pulled a face as he sipped his coffee and then pushed the cup away from him. He could see the two men's profiles through the frosted-glass window at the front of the café. They were animated, the smaller figure of Walsh waving his hands for emphasis as he said something, but Harper then saw O'Brien stabbing his stubby finger into the other man's shoulder, emphasising a point. A couple of minutes later the two men filed back inside. Walsh, looking close to tears, took his duffle bag off his shoulder, placed it on the floor and then slid it across to Harper with his foot. He picked it up, opened the top and looked at the bundles of notes inside. He ruffled through a couple, checking they really were notes and not just one-hundred-dollar bills at either end and a wad of paper in the middle, then he closed the bag and put it back on the floor at his feet.

"Right then," Harper said, "the arrangements for the handover."

Despite close questioning from O'Brien, Harper discussed only in the broadest outline the method by which the Katyushas would be moved from the secret, ex-Stasi stores where they were held.

"That's our business and our problem to deal with," he said. "Your only concern should be how the items can be safely dispatched onwards to the Republic of Ireland or wherever it is you're going to ship them to. So . . . we will transport the goods to a suitable trans-shipment point within Germany. The items will be delivered in environmental packaging only, i.e. camouflaged plastic weatherproof covers as part of a cargo of plastic piping of the same length and diameter as the goods themselves. The paperwork will be supplied by us and will show that we are moving pipework for export. On the day of shipping, you will travel to Berlin as before. Today is Saturday, so it will be early next week. I suggest you stay in Berlin but it's your call. We'll rendezvous with you and bring you to the site where you will be able to check that the cargo is as per specification and then pay in full the final settlement for the goods. They will then be released to you and you will be responsible for onward transportation of the goods to whatever destination you wish to choose. Okay?"

O'Brien and Walsh nodded.

"Pleasure doing business with you, gentlemen."

Alexei Klimov was a big man, as all Russians seemed to be. Charlotte Button had never met a small one, nor a thin one, at least not within the intelligence services. Klimov was waiting for her on a bench overlooking the Thames and beyond that the London Eye, the giant Ferris wheel that gave tourists one of the best views of the river and the city.

341

As she walked from her car she saw two men who were definitely bodyguards and possibly a third. All male, all wearing raincoats, and all, like Klimov, big men with weight-lifters' shoulders. Klimov nodded but didn't smile as she joined him on the bench. She was wearing a beige Burberry raincoat with the collar up and carrying an umbrella because the leaden sky was threating rain.

"I do hope you're not going to stab me in the leg with that," he said, nodding at the umbrella.

"That's a Bulgarian trick," she said. "Besides, we do our best not to kill people on our own turf. That's the downside of a free press, of course."

The Russian chuckled. "Free press? That's as much a non sequitur as military intelligence. It's been a long time since there was such a thing here, Charlotte, and we both know it. It went the way of free speech." He shrugged. "Listen to me, getting all political." He looked around. "Do you ever wonder how many spies have met here, by the Thames?"

She laughed. "A lot," she said. "Spies, criminals, journalists, lovers. It's a popular spot."

"If it were Russia in the old days, we would have planted permanent listening devices in the benches. All of them."

"How do you know we haven't?" she asked.

"Because this is England," said the Russian. "It would require too much paperwork."

She chuckled softly, then leaned closer to him. "We need to talk, Alexei."

"Definitely," said the Russian. "Do you want to, go first, or should I?"

"I was the one who asked you out, have you forgotten?"

Klimov inclined his head slightly. "Then by all means go first."

"Yesterday a couple of hired killers tried to murder one of my officers. Came close to succeeding, too. We haven't been able to ID the man but we did identify a Maya Katz. She's Israeli. Former army, former Mossad."

"They can be dangerous, the Israelis. And Mossad, well they're a law unto themselves."

"I said former Mossad, Alexei. She works for the highest bidder. And I have it on very good authority that she has done work for the SVR in the past."

"Do you think the SVR paid for this Katz to attack your man? It sounds unlikely."

"No, Alexei. I don't think the SVR would have any interest in my man. But the Federal Protective Service, well, they might. You see, your people might not have realised that he was my officer. They might have thought he was a threat to your president. And they might have decided that a contract killer was fair game."

"Now I'm confused, Charlotte. Katz is the contract killer, you said?"

"My officer is pretending to be a contract killer. Katz and her partner tried to kill him. I think whoever gave them the contract didn't realise that the man was my officer. I am pretty sure they believed his legend."

"Which is?"

"Frederik Olsen. He's known in the business as —"

"The Dane," Klimov finished for her.

"You're well informed," said Button.

The Russian sighed. "I'm afraid this is going to get rather complicated, Charlotte."

"So Katz and her partner were working for you?"

He smiled thinly. "You know I couldn't possibly admit that."

"This is unofficial. Off the record. It goes no further than me."

Klimov looked pained. "We both know that is not true, Charlotte. You say unofficial but I really doubt that you are permitted to meet an agent of the Russian Federal Protective Service without informing someone."

"Well, yes, obviously I have to say that we met, but I don't have to go into details. I need to know what's happening, Alexei. I need to know if my operation has been compromised."

Klimov slowly reached inside his overcoat and brought out two photographs; black and white headshots. He passed the first one to Button. "Oleg Gruzdev. He had been with the protective service for more than ten years. He was a good man. He had two children; one of them is about to join the army. They found him under a bridge. His wallet was left on the bridge so the German police suspect suicide. There was no note, of course." He passed her the second photograph. "Leonid Yelagin. He'd only been with the protective service for two years but he was a rising star. He had good family connections, too. He was due to

344

get married later this year. His fiancée's family is also very well connected. That might well cause you problems in the future, Charlotte."

"And this involves me how, Alexei?"

"Please don't be coy with me, Charlotte. We've known each other far too long to be playing games. Leonid and Oleg were following your man. They knew him as Frederik Olsen. They disappeared while they had him under surveillance."

Button frowned. "But they died in Germany, you said."

"Exactly."

Button shook her head. "I'm sorry, but that doesn't make any sense. My man hasn't been to Germany. He's in the UK, which is where your assassin tried and failed to kill him. He's been back and forth to Holland but that's it."

"He was in Germany, Charlotte."

"I wonder if it's another Frederik Olsen. The operation we're running is complicated. My man is using another man's identity, there might be someone else doing the same thing."

"Now I'm even more confused, Charlotte. You have a man pretending to be The Dane and as such he has been hired to kill our president? Is that the position?"

"Well, yes. But no. Obviously he's not going to kill Putin, that goes without saying. Olsen is behind bars in the Gulf. We're trying to nail the man who has commissioned the assassination."

"And at no point did you think of informing the Federal Protective Service?"

"It's early days yet. We have it under control. There is absolutely zero risk to your president and we are perfectly capable of resolving this long before he arrives."

"We should have been notified," said Klimov.

"You want to be notified every time we hear of a threat to one of your people? We'd be on the phone to you every day."

"We're talking about the president," said the Russian. "Would you be so reticent if the assassin had been hired to kill the American president? I don't think so. Do you mind if I smoke?"

"No, of course not," said Button. "It's a free country." She smiled to show that she was joking.

He smiled back, took out a pack of cigarettes and lit one, being careful to keep the smoke away from her.

"So your man was being tailed by my men. They thought he was a Danish assassin. You're telling me he was one of your men undercover. Fine. I accept that. But who killed Leonid and Oleg? Did this Parkinson do it?"

"Parkinson? Who the hell is Parkinson?"

"That's the name your man used to check into the hotel in Berlin. Peter Parkinson."

"Alexei, I can assure you, hand on heart, that my man was not in Germany. And I have never heard the name Peter Parkinson before. My man is Harry Cartwright."

"His real name?"

She smiled tightly. "Obviously not. That's his operational name."

Klimov reached into his coat pocket and pulled out a third photograph, larger than the head and shoulder shots of his agents. It was a surveillance photograph taken with a long lens of Spider Shepherd walking out of what was clearly the Marriott Hotel in Berlin. Button swore in a way that she hadn't sworn in years, so vehemently that even the Russian was taken aback. He grinned. "You and I should play poker some time," he said.

"Can I keep this?"

"Be my guest."

Button put the photograph away. "Frankly, Alexei, I have no idea what is going on. Perhaps you can tell me. What was he doing?"

The Russian shrugged his massive shoulders. "Your man checked into the hotel. He went out for some fresh air and so far as we can ascertain he met with no one. If you are asking me to surmise what happened, perhaps his excursions were counter surveillance. Some time later my men went missing."

"If that's true, it had nothing to do with my people, I swear."

"So who then?"

Button frowned. "I wish I knew, Alexei. And you're absolutely certain he met with no one?"

"Oleg reported in two hours before he went missing," said Klimov. "It appeared to him that your man was waiting for something. Killing time. Then he went out. That's when they vanished. They turned up dead twenty-four hours later."

"So you think he led your men somewhere and they were taken?"

"That seems obvious to me."

"I say again, Alexei, it was none of my doing."

"Who then? The BND?"

The Bundesnachrichtendienst was Germany's foreign intelligence service.

"Unlikely," said Button.

"What about Smit?"

"You know about Smit?"

"Of course we know about Smit. How do you think we found out about Olsen or whatever your man is called?"

"So you think that Smit might have had your men killed?"

"If he thinks they were on to him. Yes, I suppose so."

Button smiled thinly. "Do you think that perhaps what happened in Queens had him spooked?"

The Russian's eyes narrowed. "And what happened in Queens?"

"Now who's being coy?" said Button. "A contract killer by the name of Rob Tyler was killed. We believe that Smit had hired him for the Putin contract. That's how we managed to get our man inside. With Tyler dead, Smit needed a replacement and we gave him one."

Klimov rubbed his square chin. "Without admitting to anything, let's just say that yes, Smit had every reason to be concerned. He could have had your man watched and they spotted my men."

"That sounds reasonable," said Button.

"But what doesn't sound reasonable is that your man was in Berlin without your knowledge. Do you usually keep your officers on such a loose rein?"

"You can be sure that's something I'll be taking up with him," said Button. "But for now, we need to do some serious talking."

"That's why I'm here, Charlotte."

Button decided to walk back to her office. She needed time to think. She had spent more than an hour on the bench talking to Klimov and was just as confused as she had been when the Russian had dropped his bombshell about Shepherd being in Germany. She could think of only one reason why Shepherd would visit Berlin, and that was to see Alex Harper. There was no way that could have been a coincidence. But why would Shepherd want to talk to Harper? Button knew they were friends and had served in the army together, but it didn't explain the flying visit to Germany and it most definitely didn't explain the use of a legend. Towards the end of the conversation, Klimov had produced a copy of the passport that Shepherd had used when he had checked into the hotel. Button hadn't asked how he'd managed to obtain it but it was clearly Shepherd's photograph, although the date of birth was off by a year.

The discussion with the Russian had been full and frank but she was sure that he hadn't told her everything. That was fair enough because Button hadn't told him everything, either. She hadn't mentioned Alex Harper and she certainly hadn't told

349

the Russian what Harper was doing in Germany. She had been more forthcoming about the plot to assassinate Putin, although she had insisted that at no time had the Russian president been in any danger, and nor would he be. Everything would be done and dusted long before he set foot on British soil.

Klimov had pretty much confirmed that the Russians were responsible for the killing of Rob Tyler in the States without actually saying the words. He was a lot more hesitant about discussing the attack on Shepherd in Battersea.

"You know I can't say anything about that," he had said, smiling grimly. "An attack on a British citizen on British soil. That could not possibly be condoned."

"Let's talk about her without talking about Russia," Button had pressed. "She was former Mossad?"

"Israeli Army followed by Mossad where she became by all accounts a very skilled assassin. One of their best, especially when a honey trap was needed. Her speciality was the Black Widow thing, sex followed by death. Then she went freelance. She's in quite some demand. Female contractors are few and far between. I'm surprised you haven't come across her. She has no political affiliations, she will work for whoever pays."

"Why, Alexei? Why on earth would a British civil servant have need of a hired killer?" she had asked in mock astonishment. It took him a couple of seconds to realise that she was joking, and he laughed along with her.

His laughter turned into a coughing fit and for a few moments he was close to choking, but he banged himself hard on the chest, recovered and smiled. "Charlotte my dear, one day you'll be the death of me, I swear."

Shepherd left Sharpe in the car while he went into the Leeds police station. He asked to see DS Drinkwater and had to wait almost an hour in reception before the door opened and DC Allen beckoned to him.

"Sorry, we've had a targets meeting that went on for ever." He grinned mischievously. "But you'll be glad to know that overall, recorded crime in Yorkshire is down twelve per cent, year on year."

"Well done you," said Shepherd. "Will they give you a gold star?"

Allen grinned. "The key word there is recorded. The trick to getting the stats down is to just record fewer crimes. Turn break-ins into insurance claims and don't bother to charge shoplifters." He held the door open for Shepherd. "We'll be using the second interview room on the left."

The door to the room was open and DS Drinkwater was sitting at the table, engrossed in his smartphone. He didn't look up when Shepherd entered, nor when he sat down opposite him. Only when DC Allen came in and closed the door did the detective look up from his phone.

Shepherd knew that the man was being deliberately rude but he didn't rise to the bait and smiled politely. He had a black leather document case with him and unzipped it and took out the results of his surveillance on the minicab office, a dozen photographs in all. He placed them in front of Drinkwater who looked at them but made no move to touch them. Shepherd also had a printout with the names, addresses and dates of birth of the Yilmaz brothers.

"These are the guys that Aidan Flynn buys his drugs from. They run a kebab shop and a minicab business that they use to shift the drugs around town." He tapped one of the photographs. "This is Yusuf Yilmaz, the older brother." He tapped another of the photographs. "This is Ahmet. It's a tight operation, which is probably why they've stayed under the radar. All their drivers are Turks and from the look of it a lot of the drivers are related, by marriage if not blood."

"How do you know they're Flynn's suppliers?" asked Drinkwater, his eyes on the photographs.

"I just know," said Shepherd, figuring it best not to go into details.

"That's it?" said Drinkwater. "That's all you have?"

"You've got details there of a major drug distribution network."

"No, what I've got here is a load of photographs of taxi drivers and allegations about two brothers who run what appears to be a legitimate business. Two businesses. A takeaway restaurant and a minicab firm. There's no evidence of any wrongdoing."

"I bought an ounce of cocaine off them."

Drinkwater's eyes narrowed. "And where is this cocaine now?"

"It can't be used as evidence in any case, there's no chain of custody, not one that would stand up in court, anyway. But take my word for it. You call that number and ask for Yusuf and within the hour the drugs will be on your doorstep."

"Yes, but a reasonably small amount. And you've given nothing to me that shows that the Yilmaz brothers are behind this. For all we know, they might be totally unaware of what's going on."

"I spoke to Yusuf."

"In person?"

"Yes."

"I don't see a photograph of you talking to him."

"On the phone."

"So not in person. There's no evidence that it was Yusuf Yilmaz you spoke to. And you can't even produce the cocaine you say you bought from him. You've got nothing here, Mr Shepherd."

"Aidan Flynn buys his drugs from the Yilmaz brothers. That's a fact."

"So you say. But I doubt that he'll go into a witness box and confirm that. Look, I do appreciate you bringing this information in and I'll be sure to pass it on to our drugs squad." He began gathering up the printed sheets and photographs.

"Whoa, hang on a bit," said Shepherd. "What about Liam?"

"What about him?"

"Does this mean you'll be dropping the charges?"

"Mr Shepherd, all you've done here is given me rumour and supposition. I'll pass it on to the relevant department but that doesn't change the fact that your son was caught in possession of a Class A drug."

Shepherd held up his hands. "What is it you want from me, DS Drinkwater? What do I have to do to get you to drop the case against my son?"

The detective placed the papers and pictures back on the table. "I need a real case, Mr Shepherd. Something I can take to my bosses with all the ducks lined up in a row. A case, open and shut." He gestured at the papers and pictures in front of him. "This is supposition. I want real hard evidence and I want it against a serious villain, not the owner of a pissy little kebab shop."

"Okay," said Shepherd. He picked up the papers and put them back in his pocket. "Just give me some time," he said.

"To do what?" asked the detective.

"To put something together."

"I can't wait for ever," said Drinkwater. "The Crown Prosecution Service is already snapping at my tail."

Shepherd doubted that was true. In his experience the CPS rarely went looking for work, it was all they could do to keep up with the files that kept hitting their desk. But there was no point in calling the detective on a lie. "Can you give me a couple of weeks?"

"I'll give you one week," said the detective, folding his arms. "Five working days. Then I'll send your boy's paperwork to the CPS."

Shepherd had to fight the urge to launch himself across the table and grab the man by the throat, but he forced himself to smile. "Okay, I'll see what I can do."

He stood up and gathered the papers and pictures up. Drinkwater left the room leaving Allen alone with Shepherd.

"He's a bit curt, I know," said the detective.

"Must be a pleasure to work with," said Shepherd.

"He's a stickler for the rules and doesn't have much of a sense of a humour, but he never puts a foot wrong," said Allen. "You know that if you're on an investigation with Paul then every box will get ticked and every base will be covered. The CPS love him. Every case he gives them is airtight. He has a one hundred per cent conviction record and pretty much everyone he charges pleads guilty eventually."

Shepherd put the paperwork in his pocket.

"I'm sorry about your lad," said Allen. "If it were down to me . . ." He shrugged.

"Thanks," said Shepherd.

The detective showed Shepherd out. As he said goodbye at reception he gave Shepherd his business card. "If there's anything I can help you with, give me a call," he said.

"He's serious about the week?" asked Shepherd.

The detective looked pained. "I'm sorry."

"Better pull my finger out, then," said Shepherd. He headed out of the police station.

"How did it go?" asked Sharpe as Shepherd climbed into the Mondeo.

"Not great," said Shepherd.

Back in her office in Thames House, Button sipped a cup of tea and took out the photo of the passport that Klimov had given her. It was definitely a photo of Shepherd, and a recent one by the look of it. She wrinkled her nose as she stared at the photograph.

"What the hell are you playing at, Spider?" she whispered.

The fact that Shepherd had been in Berlin at the same time as Alex Harper was clearly no coincidence. But if it had been in any way connected to the ongoing case, he would have cleared the trip with her first. The fact that he hadn't set all sorts of alarm bells ringing in her head.

She needed to get the passport checked but she had a feeling that it wouldn't be straightforward. She called up the departmental staff list and went through it, looking for someone who had never met Shepherd and who knew their way around the agency's computer system. She smiled when she got to the name of Liz Calder. She had joined from university and was still at the enthusiastic stage, working long hours without complaint and always keen to take on extra tasks. Her degree was in computer science and she was near fluent in French, German and Italian. Button called her extension and asked her to pop along for a chat. Five minutes later Calder was sitting in front of Button, a yellow legal pad on her lap and her pen poised. She was a brunette with porcelain skin and wearing a grey suit and what Button was fairly sure were Gucci heels. Button had read Calder's positive vetting report, which she had passed with flying colours, but what she was going to ask her to do wasn't about loyalty to her country.

"I need you to do something quite sensitive for me," Button began. She passed over the photocopy of the passport. "I need you to check him out. Criminal record, school, university, travel, birth certificate, the full Monty. But I need you to be careful. Very careful. I think there might be something a bit special about the paperwork."

Calder frowned. "Special?"

"Just a feeling," said Button. "So I need you to do all the checks once or twice removed. Use proxies, whatever you can do so that none of the checks can be traced back to you."

"That's easy enough to do," she said.

"You're going to have to be really careful, Liz," said Button. "If I'm right then there could be all sorts of flags, visible and hidden. Softly, softly. For instance I'd really like to know how many passports have been issued in that name and who countersigned the original application. Also the passport is supposed to have been manufactured three years ago. I doubt that's true."

Calder nodded and made a note on her pad. Computer files on government databases could be flagged so that when anyone opened them, their details would be sent to whoever had flagged the file. Sometimes the flags were clearly marked but flags could also be hidden so that the file could be read without the reader ever knowing that they had been identified and noted.

"I can't emphasise how delicate this is, Liz," said Button. "Anything you find out is for my ears only, nothing in writing and please tread carefully."

"I won't let you down," said Calder, nodding enthusiastically.

Button smiled and thanked her and tried to remember if she herself had ever been so young and enthusiastic. If she had, it was in another life.

"I've got to be honest, I don't see this working," said Sharpe. He and Shepherd were sitting in the Mondeo, down the road from the kebab shop. "He's going to want to see the cash up front. And I don't know about you but I can't get my hands on the sort of money he's going to want to see."

"You never know, maybe they'll take a liking to us."

"Yeah, and maybe we can hitch a ride on a flying pig."

"I don't have much choice, anyway. The cops say that Liam stays in the frame unless I come up with a bigger fish and they don't think that the Yilmaz brothers fit the bill." Shepherd shrugged. "What's the worst that can happen? He says no. And at least we'll get a look around inside."

Sharpe gestured at the kebab shop. "Then let's get to it."

The two men got out of the Mondeo and walked across the road. The kebab shop was fairly busy with three customers lined up at the counter and half a dozen schoolboys sitting at Formica tables as they munched on their kebabs. A heavyset Turkish man in stained chef's whites was slicing lamb off a rotating vertical spit with a knife the size of a machete and heaping it on to pitta bread. Sweat was dripping down his face and arms and he wiped his forehead with his sleeve as he worked.

358

"I could go a kebab right now," said Sharpe.

"Focus, Razor," said Shepherd. They went over to the door leading up to the minicab office. There was a metal intercom to the left of the door with the word MINICAB written in felt-tip pen on a single button. Shepherd pressed it. There was a small CCTV camera staring down at them.

"Where are you going?" asked a tinny voice.

"We're here to see Yusuf," said Shepherd.

"You want a cab?"

"No, we want to talk to Yusuf. Or Ahmet if Yusuf's not about."

"This is a cab firm."

"Yeah, I know. Look, we did business with Yusuf last week. Bought an ounce of Charlie off him. We really don't want to be talking about this with me on the street, do we?" He stared up at the CCTV camera and flashed it a sarcastic grin. After a few seconds the door buzzed and Shepherd pushed it open.

The door opened into a small hallway. There was a big Turkish man in a scuffed leather jacket standing halfway down the stairs glaring at them. "What the fuck do you want?" he said. He had a gold front tooth and his cheeks were pockmarked with old acne scars. He was the size of a large refrigerator.

"We just want a word with Yusuf," said Shepherd.

"You look like cops," said the man.

"Would cops be walking around with an ounce of Charlie?" said Sharpe, taking the drugs out of his pocket. "Now stop being a twat and let us up."

"I need to pat you down," said the man.

"You can suck my dick if you want, whatever makes you happy," said Sharpe.

Shepherd wasn't sure if Sharpe was playing the part of a drug dealer or if he was just pissed off, but either way his outburst did the trick because the heavy patted them down sullenly and waved them upstairs. They had to squeeze past him and he glared at Sharpe as if he would happily have ripped his head off.

At the top of the stairs was an equally large heavy with an equally sullen expression on his face. He opened a door and nodded for them to go through. The office overlooked the street and there was the odour of stale onions that reminded him of the smell of Jamie Brewer's surveillance van. There were two more heavies in the room standing either side of the door, their faces impassive and arms folded across their chests. One was bald, the other had thickly gelled hair; both had physiques that suggested they ate a lot of kebabs. Shepherd could see at a glance that they were big but they weren't hard.

As they stepped into the office, one of the heavies closed the door behind them. There was a man sitting in a high-backed executive chair behind a desk that was strewn with papers and files. There was a hookah pipe by the side of his chair and an overflowing ashtray close to his right hand. He was smoking a cigarette and he blew smoke as he stared at them. He was in his forties, not as big as the heavies but he still filled the chair. He had a square chin and a thick moustache that gave him the look of a Middle Eastern dictator. His purple shirt was open to the navel to reveal thick curly chest hair and a heavy gold chain with what appeared to be a chunk of jade hanging from it.

"Are you Yusuf?" asked Sharpe. They'd decided that the Scotsman would do most of the talking and that Shepherd would play the strong, silent type.

"Who wants to know?" asked the man behind the desk. He stabbed out what was left of the cigarette as if he were grinding it into Sharpe's eye.

"My name's Carrick," said Sharpe. "We're down here from Glasgow." He jerked a thumb at Shepherd. "This is Mac."

Shepherd nodded but didn't say anything.

Sharpe gestured at two wooden chairs. "You okay if we sit down? Feels like I'm in front of the headmaster here."

The man waved a hand at the chairs. Sharpe and Shepherd sat down. "You're Yusuf, right? Mac here spoke to you on the phone?"

Yusuf nodded and lit another cigarette.

Sharpe reached into his jacket pocket and took out the ounce of cocaine they had bought. He slapped it on the desk. "That is good Charlie," he said. "Seventy, eighty per cent."

"I'm glad you appreciate the quality of my merchandise," said Yusuf. He blew smoke up at the yellowed ceiling.

"I do," said Sharpe. "That's why I'm here. We'd like more."

The Turk grinned. "You have a heavy habit?"

Sharpe laughed. "Our regular supplier was in Manchester, but he got caught a few weeks back."

"What's his name?"

"Why does his name matter?"

"It matters to me."

Sharpe shrugged carelessly. "Marty Potter. Anyway, Marty's now out of commission and if I don't find someone to replace him, I'm dead in the water in Glasgow. I'll be out of business within the week."

"So what are you looking for?" asked the Turk.

"In the short term, two or three kilos, just to tide me over. Then if you can link me up with your supplier, probably ten kilos a month."

The Turk's eyebrows shot up. "That's a lot. That's a hell of a lot. Why can't you buy in Scotland?"

"Because I'd be buying from the competition and they're trying to fuck me over. Look, I'll pay you a finder's fee, whatever you want, if you can hook me up. And the first three kilos, I'll do through you."

The Turk frowned. "Do through me? What do you mean?"

"I'm going to be needing ten kilos a month and that's out of your league, right? No offence."

"You came to me," said the Turk. "If you want cocaine, I will get you cocaine. If you want heroin I will get you heroin. I will get you whatever you want."

"Excellent," said Sharpe, rubbing his hands together. "So do you have three kilos now?"

The Turk frowned. "Do you have the money now?"

"I can get it, no problem."

"You have it with you? In your car?"

"No, but I can get it within hours."

The Turk nodded. "So your money is in Glasgow?"

"Less than four hours up the M6," said Sharpe. "It's not a problem."

The Turk. "So get your money here and we'll talk."

"Do you have the gear?"

"I will get it for you. Once I have seen your money."

Sharpe smiled. "Well, the way we normally work is that we see the gear first."

The Turk opened his hands. "And the way I normally work is that I see the money first. Especially when the buyer has just walked in off the street."

"How about this," said Sharpe. "You make the introduction to your guy, I'll let him know that you got him the business. Maybe throw some commission your way."

"Commission?"

"How much a kilo? For the good stuff."

"Thirty eight."

"That's all good. So we'd agree to pay forty thousand a kilo and you take two off every kilo we buy. That's twenty grand a month your way just for linking us up."

The Turk looked at Shepherd. "So are you the muscle or the boss?"

"What do you mean?"

"In my experience if two guys come to a meeting and one of them does all the talking, the other one is either in charge, or he's the minder."

Shepherd smiled easily. "I'm the silent partner."

"Not Scottish?"

"No. Not Scottish."

The Turk nodded slowly and then looked back at Sharpe. "You bring me a hundred and twenty grand and I'll get you three kilos. You bring me four hundred grand and I'll get you ten kilos."

"That's not what we said," growled Sharpe. "You said thirty-eight grand a kilo."

Yusuf shrugged. "We can negotiate, for larger orders."

"Like I said, no offence, but I don't see you coming up with ten kilos." Sharpe looked around the office. "It's not like you're living the high life here, is it?"

"Appearances can be deceptive," said Yusuf. "Look at it this way. Your money is four hours away. The drugs are ninety minutes from here. The ball is in your court."

"How about this?" said Sharpe. "We go with you to where the drugs are, we take a look and if the gear is good, we get the money to you."

The Turk chuckled and opened the bottom drawer of his desk. He pulled out a Glock and waved it in the air, thankfully with his finger outside the trigger guard. "How about this?" he said. "You go and get your money as a show of good faith. You give me your money and I'll go and get the drugs."

"So you'll be using our cash for the buy?"

"What's the problem with that?"

"The problem is that if it's our money then we should be handling the buy."

The Turk pointed the gun at Sharpe and used it to punctuate his words. "You bring me the money and we'll talk. Otherwise . . ." He gestured at the door with the gun. "Go fuck yourself."

"How about this?" said Sharpe, unfazed by the weapon being waved around. "We bring the money and you take us to see your supplier. We all shake hands and from then on you take two grand for every kilo we buy."

"As I said, my Scottish friend, bring the cash and we'll talk."

Sharpe opened his mouth to speak but realised there was nothing he could say that would move things on. He stood up and nodded. "We'll be seeing you."

"I hope so," said the Turk, waving his gun at the door. "But I won't be holding my breath."

Sharpe and Shepherd left the office and went downstairs. Sharpe opened the door and stepped out on to the pavement. "See, I told you it wouldn't be easy," he said. "Do you mind if I get a kebab?"

"Are you serious?"

"I'm hungry. At least this way we walk away with something."

Shepherd shook his head and waved at the entrance to the kebab shop. "Knock yourself out."

Sharpe grinned. "Do you want one?"

Shepherd laughed despite himself. "Yeah, go on."

Button's phone buzzed. It was an internal call. She picked up the receiver. It was Liz Calder.

"I've had a good look at that passport," she said. "You said you didn't want a memo."

"That's right, Liz. Can you pop up now?"

"Absolutely."

In less than five minutes, the young officer was sitting opposite Button. This time her yellow legal pad was full of handwritten notes. She handed the photocopy back to Button.

"Right, so yes, your suspicions were correct. This is not a regular passport. In fact it was only issued last week, despite the date." She shifted in her seat and looked uncomfortable. "You're not going to like this unfortunately. Please don't shoot the messenger."

"Cut to the chase, Liz, please."

"Long story short, it's an MI6 legend."

The news hit Button like a punch to the solar plexus and she gasped. It was the last thing she had expected to hear.

"I know," said Calder. "It was the last thing I expected. And you were right. Pretty much everything connected to Peter Parkinson is flagged. That wasn't a problem, it just took me some time to find back doors. Okay, so there is no birth certificate, no police file, no tax records. There is no paperwork to go with the passport, it was just issued. I have an old school friend who works at the Passport Office and she was able to run a check for me. She said it came from high up in the Home Office. It's a genuine passport but can't be renewed. There are credit cards all issued on the same day as the passport but appearing to have been in effect for several years. Ditto a driving licence. It even has a few penalty points for speeding, which is a nice touch. The driving licence uses the same photograph as the passport, which frankly is a tad lazy. That was my first clue that this was a legend. Then I looked at the credit and debit cards and realised they used a bank that Six often uses."

"So it's circumstantial."

Calder shifted uncomfortably in her seat. "I'm afraid not. I have another friend, from my university days, who's over at Six. On the very QT I gave her the name and asked for a simple yes or no, would I be correct if I assumed it was one of theirs and she said yes. I know that perhaps I shouldn't have done that but I wanted to know for sure."

"Not a problem, Liz."

"She won't say anything, and really all she did was confirm something I already suspected."

"And other than that conversation, nothing else links back to you?"

"The two conversations, Passport Office and Six, but they were just chats and there's nothing official. All the database trawling was done through proxies, overseas mainly. There's zero trail back to me." She looked down at her legal pad, opened it and pulled out several photocopied sheets. "I've got credit card details that show he bought a return ticket to Berlin, business class. And a booking at a Berlin hotel." She gave the sheets to Button.

Calder looked pained and Button realised there was still something troubling her. "Is there a problem, Liz?"

Calder pulled a face. "Well, I know you asked me to check out the passport, and the date of birth, and so on. The thing is, I thought I'd run the photograph through our facial recognition system."

"That was very enterprising of you."

"And I got a hit."

"Yes. I'm sure you did. Don't worry, Liz, I think I know where this is going."

"So you know it's Dan Shepherd, an MI5 officer? I mean, his file is above my security clearance so other than the fact that he works for us I have no information."

Button nodded. "I did know, yes. And you did an excellent job, I must congratulate you on that. But now I'm going to have to ask you to forget it all. I'll take it from here."

"Has something bad happened?" asked Liz quickly. She grimaced and held up a hand. "I'm sorry, of course, I'll wipe it from my memory. And other than my pad here, I have no notes." She ripped off the top half dozen pages from her pad and placed them on Button's desk. "I'm sorry if I did something wrong by, you know . . ."

Button flashed the young officer an encouraging smile. "You didn't do anything wrong, Liz. The opposite, in fact. I wouldn't have given you the assignment if I hadn't wanted it done thoroughly. You've done brilliantly. Just leave it with me now."

Calder still looked uncomfortable but she nodded and stood up. She dropped her legal pad, apologised, bent down to pick it up, apologised again and hurried out of the office, closing the door behind her.

Button sat back in the chair and studied the photocopy of the passport. Peter Parkinson. MI6 legend. What the hell was Shepherd doing with an MI6-issued passport? And why had he flown to Berlin?

To see Alex Harper? And who had killed the two Russians? Had Shepherd gone rogue? She dismissed the thought immediately. He wasn't the type. Shepherd was the original straight shooter, a man with a moral code so firmly defined that at times it was a hindrance. Shepherd rarely broke the rules and on the few occasions he did, there was always a good reason for it. So what was he up to now? And who at MI6 was pulling his strings?

As usual, Harper took a long run through the streets surrounding the hotel early in the morning. Except where an op prevented it, the morning run had been an unbreakable habit of his since he'd joined the paras all those years before. He loved the stillness and the emptiness of the streets as dawn was breaking, and the coolness of the air. He ran the first five miles at a steady pace, his long strides eating up the ground, then ran the last mile flat out, finishing drenched in sweat and with his chest heaving. Back at the hotel, he showered, and was just drinking a cup of coffee when his mobile beeped to let him know he'd received a text message. It was from Button. Short and to the point, as always. *YOU HAVE MAIL.* He walked along the street to a Turkish-run newsagent and general store, with a couple of elderly computers in the back room, available for hire by the half-hour. When he checked the drafts folder, there was a message from Button: *I NEED YOU IN LONDON TODAY. REPEAT TODAY. LET ME KNOW YOUR LOCATION WHEN YOU GET HERE.*

He frowned. Button would not normally intervene in an operation once she had set it up and briefed him, preferring to keep a safe distance metaphorically and literally until the job was done. The fact that she wanted to see him at this critical stage suggested either that she had concerns or had unsettling intelligence to share. Or it was connected to Shepherd's trip to Berlin. If the latter, Harper knew he was in big trouble.

He phoned Maggie May and told her that he'd be unavailable for the next twelve hours but that she could keep in touch via text messages. Then he drove his bike to the airport and caught the first flight back to London. He usually travelled via Ireland but he figured that his MI5 Müller legend and passport would mean he could enter and leave through Heathrow without being compromised.

Harper had booked into a different hotel to the one he'd used during his last visit to London, but it was also in King's Cross, had no phone in the room and a shower cubicle that hadn't been cleaned in a year or so. But none of that mattered to him, all that mattered was that he wasn't asked for ID when he checked in and could pay in cash. There was a grubby plastic kettle and sachets of coffee and Coffee-Mate so he made himself a coffee while he waited for Charlotte Button to arrive.

He had drunk half of it when there was a soft knock on the door. He opened it and let her in. She was wearing a long coat that looked as if it was cashmere and had a black leather Prada bag with gold zips on one shoulder. "Welcome to my humble abode," he said, and waved for her to come inside. She looked disdainfully around the room and decided the wooden chair by the window was the best place to sit. It was cold in the room and she left her coat on.

"I've got the tracking details of the first consignment," he said, handing her a thumbdrive. "I know you don't like me teaching you how to suck eggs but I'd leave it a week or two until the Paddys add the stuff to their existing caches."

She smiled coldly. "Thank you so much." She put the thumbdrive into her bag.

"Is something wrong, Charlie?" he asked, sitting on the bed.

If anything her eyes got even colder as she looked at him. "I'm not sure where to start," she said. "Okay, let's kick off with what happened at Letzlinger Heide."

Harper grimaced. "Yeah, we had a bit of a problem."

"Didn't I make it crystal clear that you were to stay below the radar in Germany? There was a gunfight with German troops. Do you want to explain to me how that is staying below the radar?"

"I shot out the tyres of a truck. That's all. It wasn't a gunfight."

"That's not the point. The point is that you were supposed to maintain a low profile; now the Germans are worried that al-Qaeda are trying to steal a Katyusha. The shit has well and truly hit the fan."

"No one was trying to steal anything," said Harper. "The Paddys wanted to see one being fired. The best way to do that was to get them on a range."

"Alex, I can't believe how bloody irresponsible you've been. The contract was to take out O'Brien and Walsh."

"And to hit them financially. And discredit their organisation."

"But nowhere in that brief were you told to go to war with the German Army."

"It was a bit of rough and tumble, Charlie. Really. Nothing to worry about."

"And I'm far from happy with this whole Katyusha business," she said. "Why not just offer them RPGs? A ground-to-air missile or two. Something small."

"Because a Katyusha is big money. Look, Charlie, they're not going to get a Katyusha. Not out of the country, anyway. I'll take their money and the Germans can take the weapons. It'll all go to muddying the waters. No one's going to know what's going on or who's involved. And O'Brien and Walsh will be collateral damage." He grinned. "It's going to be fine, I promise."

"You say no one will know what's going on. But Zelda Hoffmann does. She knows everything."

"I've known her for years."

"She's an arms dealer who will apparently sell to anyone."

"That sort of goes with the turf," said Harper. "Arms dealers don't tend to pick and choose their customers."

"That's not true," said Button. "Any dealer would think long and hard before selling to al-Qaeda, for instance. In Europe and the States, anyway."

"They can buy from plenty of other sources," said Harper.

"But there aren't many dealers offering Katyushas. And Hoffmann was happy enough to agree to sell them to Irish terrorists. What if she's contacted by jihadists?"

"I think that's unlikely."

"Unlikely? I want a better guarantee than that, Alex."

"Why?"

"What do you mean, why?"

Harper's eyes narrowed. "That sounded like a threat."

"Hoffmann's the threat. She's not selling toys. A few Kalashnikovs, fine. But Katyushas? I'm sorry, that's just not acceptable. Suppose al-Qaeda or ISIS got hold of one? Can you imagine the havoc they'd wreak?"

"It's no different to the New IRA getting one. It doesn't really matter who is pulling the trigger, does it?"

"Perhaps not, but it does matter where those rockets are aimed. And if Hoffmann is selling them to people who might use them in the UK — or anywhere in Europe — then she is an enemy of the state."

She stared at him as she let the words sink in. "You're saying she'll be killed?" he said eventually.

"If she starts selling rockets to UK jihadist groups, then I wouldn't rule it out."

"That's not going to happen," said Harper flatly. "Zelda and I go back a long way."

"You're not the only contractor on my books," said Button. Her face stayed impassive for a few seconds, then it broke into what was meant as a reassuring smile. "But there's no need for it to come to that. The ones the New IRA are buying can be taken off the market. We can pass on the intel to the Germans and they can pick up the rest."

"You mean grass her up?" Harper shook his head in frustration. "She's helping me, Charlie. Where's your loyalty?"

"She's a threat," said Button.

"She's a friend. There's no way I'm going to throw her to the wolves. And not only that, who would ever trust me again if they heard that I'd betrayed her? The sort of jobs I do for you, I need support and backup. Who's going to help me if they know that at any point I could betray them?" He stared at her for a while but there was no clue from her face what she was thinking. "How about this? I'll have a word. I'll put her straight. I'll tell her she's not to sell big stuff to jihadists. How's that?"

"This isn't funny, Alex."

"I'm serious. You tell her what the ground rules are, I'll pass them on. I'm assuming that selling to ISIS in Syria isn't an issue. Or al-Qaeda in Africa? You're worried about home turf, right?"

"I'm worried about terrorist groups getting hold of weapons of mass destruction," she said.

"Then you need to be looking at the Russians and the Chinese and our own defence industry," said Harper. "Half the terrorist groups going have got weapons made by us. You think the government doesn't know that half the end-user certificates they see aren't worth the paper they're printed on? It was a French Exocet that sank the *Sheffield* in the Falklands War.

And it was an Exocet that hit the USS *Stark* in the Iran-Iraq War killing thirty-seven Yanks and I didn't see the Americans going to war with France."

"Zelda Hoffmann isn't a state-sponsored defence firm, she's selling dangerous hardware to terrorists who are a threat to the United Kingdom."

"Then I'll get her to stop. Trust me."

Button sighed. "Fine. Just make sure she knows that she's on our radar. Without telling her that you work for me, obviously."

"I'll get it sorted, Charlie. I promise."

She nodded slowly and he sensed that something else was on her mind. He had a horrible feeling he knew what it was but waited for her to say it. If he pre-empted her he'd only sound guilty, so he flashed her his most confident smile and stayed quiet.

"Is there something you need to tell me, Alex?" she said eventually.

"What do you want to know, Charlie? I'm an open book, you know that."

Button's eyes narrowed and then she nodded slowly. "I'm really not sure what to do about you," she said.

Harper smiled easily. "Something has clearly upset you, Charlie," he said. "And it's not just Zelda, obviously. So why don't you come straight out with it?"

"I know you saw Spider in Berlin," she said, her voice a low husky whisper. "What I don't know is why you didn't tell me."

The words hit him like a bucketful of ice-cold water but he just shrugged. "Nothing to tell," he said, his mind racing. Just how much did she know?

"So you did see him?"

Harper grimaced, realising that he'd just been played. She hadn't known for sure, but his slip meant that now she did.

"What do you want me to say, Charlie?"

"I want to know what the hell's going on. And I want it to come from you without me having to drag it out. You're working for me and one of the things I expect from my employees is loyalty. Let me rephrase that. I don't *expect* loyalty, I bloody well *demand* it. Now you don't seem to realise the deep pit of shit you've fallen into, but trust me, the only way to dig yourself out of it is to tell me everything."

Harper stared at her in silence, trying to work out exactly what she knew. She'd already fooled him once.

"Let me start with an easy one," she said. "Why was Spider in Berlin?"

"He wasn't there for you?"

"I think we both know he wasn't," said Button. "Now, I'm going to give you one last chance to come clean, but if you don't, it's going to get very messy from this point on."

Harper put up his hands, as if in surrender. "He wanted a chat. He called me up and asked for a meeting."

"He knew you were in Berlin?"

Harper thought back to his initial conversation but he couldn't for the life of him remember whether he had told Shepherd he was in Germany. "Hand on heart, I don't know. Maybe I told him where I was. I don't have his trick memory."

"Did he know why you were there?"

Harper shook his head. "No, and I didn't tell him." He saw the look of disbelief flash across her face and he put his hand on his chest. "Hand on heart, Charlie, I told him nothing."

"Do you think he knew already?"

Harper frowned. "I hadn't thought about that. Yeah, he didn't ask anything about what I was doing, so maybe."

"And when did he meet you?"

"Last Friday."

"Where?"

"We went to a bar. Had a few drinks."

"You didn't go to his hotel?"

Harper shook his head. "Definitely not. We met at a bar. I left, he made his own way back to his hotel."

"But you knew where he was staying?"

Harper nodded. "Sure."

"And you knew he was being followed?"

Harper swallowed but his mouth had gone dry and he almost gagged. He sipped his coffee and watched Button over the top of his paper cup. He was reasonably certain that Button already knew everything, but until he was sure he wasn't going to go running off at the mouth.

"You spotted he had a tail?"

Harper nodded again.

"Do you have any idea what you've done, Lex? Any idea at all? You killed two Russian agents. Members of Putin's protective team."

Harper's hand trembled slightly and he saw the look of satisfaction on Button's face as she registered his reaction. "I didn't have a choice," said Harper. "They were heavy hitters, they would have identified me and my team eventually. I couldn't take that risk."

"Spider got you into this. Why the hell didn't you say something to me?"

"Spider doesn't know they're dead," said Harper. "At least not from me." Harper tried to sip his coffee but his hand began to shake again so he put the cup down on the bedside table. "Look, he wanted to meet, I saw that he had a tail so I pulled in the two guys I spotted. I was worried that they might be on to me. I questioned them and during the course of the interrogation my team started to worry that they had been compromised. You know what bastards the Russians can be. None of them wanted to end up stashed in a kitbag in their bathroom."

"So you killed them?"

"We had a Chinese parliament and we decided it was the only thing to do."

"You can't go around killing people like that."

Harper flashed her a tight smile. "To be fair now, that's what I do."

"They're Russian secret service. There'll be repercussions."

"There would have been repercussions if we hadn't done it. They'd have tracked us down eventually. They'd have found out why we were there. And that would have opened one hell of a can of worms, wouldn't it?"

378

"That doesn't make what you did right. It doesn't even make it necessary."

Harper shrugged. "What's done is done. No use crying over spilt milk, et cetera, et cetera."

"You're a bit flippant about the death of two men, Alex." She looked at him for several seconds. "And Spider doesn't know you killed the two Russians?"

"Swear to God. I said I'd let him go back to London and then cut them loose. But after he went my team started to have misgivings."

"And despite the fact you knew who and what they were, you still killed them?"

"It was precisely because of who they were that we had to, don't you see that? They were pros. They'd have tracked us down one by one. At least this way we had a chance of getting away clean. Who else knows, Charlie? Who else knows what happened?"

"At the moment, only me. The Russians know that their men were killed. I mean seriously, Alex, a mugging and a suicide on the same day? Did you think you'd get away with that?"

"We were thinking on the hoof," said Harper. "We just wanted rid of them. With no witnesses, no one would know we'd been involved."

"And what about Spider? The two Russians who were following him both turn up dead on the same day. You didn't think that would put him in the frame?"

"He was back in the UK when it happened."

"In which case the Russians would think it was Five or Six."

"Not if they thought they were following an assassin who was planning to take a crack at Putin."

Her eyes narrowed and again Harper realised he'd said too much.

"So Spider told you what he was working on?"

Harper tried to look less tense than he felt. "We questioned the Russians, they said they had been told to tail a guy who was believed to be a threat to Putin. They didn't know he was Shepherd or that he worked for Five. At least if they did know, they didn't let on."

"They told you he was planning to kill Putin?"

Harper nodded.

"And what did Spider tell you?"

"Not much. But he confirmed what the Russians had said."

"So he knows that the Russians are on to him?"

Harper nodded again.

Button stared at him with unblinking eyes. The longer she didn't speak, the more Harper had to fight the urge to say something to fill the silence. It was an interrogator's technique, he knew, but knowing how it worked didn't make it any easier to resist. He reached for his cup and managed to take a sip of coffee without spilling any.

"And again, Spider didn't tell you what he was working on?"

"Not a thing. Is that what you're worried about?"

"I'm worried about two things, Alex. I'm worried about the fact that you didn't see fit to tell me that Spider had come to see you in Berlin. And I'm worried that you took it upon yourself to murder two members of the Federal Protective Service."

"I was wrong on both counts. I'm sorry."

Button didn't seem to hear his apology. "But here's the thing that's really worrying me, Alex. Why did Spider come to see you in the first place? He's on an active operation in the UK, so it must have been pretty damn important for him to fly to Berlin. It's time to stop playing coy and tell me what the hell is going on."

Harper stared at her for several seconds. "Fine," he said eventually. "I give up. I'll tell you everything. But you're not going to be happy."

"Alex, believe me, that ship has well and truly sailed. Now tell me everything, and be quick about it."

Shepherd left his flat wearing a sweatshirt and tracksuit bottoms. He had old army boots and thick socks on his feet. He always preferred to run in heavy footwear even though it was harder going. Moving into the Hampstead flat had been like returning to an old friend and he was glad to be back. He liked Hampstead with its quaint high street, its old-fashioned shops and bustling bars and restaurants. And the heath was a great place for a run. The flat was much smaller than the one he'd been given in Battersea. It was on the second floor of a block that had been built during the sixties to fill the gap left when two mews houses were demolished by a Second World War bomb. There was a small sitting room overlooking the street, a bedroom at the back, a small shower room and a kitchen that wasn't much bigger than the shower room. Button was right, the flat was up and running but the cable had been disconnected and there was no terrestrial television, but there was a good range of books to read so that wasn't a concern.

He jogged to the heath, then set off on his regular route: up North End Way and round the Hampstead Heath extension, a large open space to the north-west of the main heath, then he cut around West Meadow and down to Parliament Hill Fields. It was while he was cutting across the fields that he realised he was being shadowed by another runner. Several running clubs used the heath but the guy behind Shepherd wasn't one of the hi-tech trainers and Lycra shorts brigade, he was wearing a tracksuit and black Nikes and had a woollen beanie hat pulled low over his brow. He had an aggressive style, his arms pumping at his side with every step. He matched Shepherd's pace for a couple of hundred yards then started to gain on him. Shepherd could hear him breathing as he headed east to Duke's Field and he put on a spurt as he skirted the secret garden and headed north to Cohen's Fields. Shepherd took a quick look over his shoulder. The runner was only a dozen or so feet behind him. Shepherd hit the ground hard with his right foot, pushed off to the left and whirled around, his hands up to defend himself. He froze when he recognised the runner. Lex Harper.

"What the hell are you doing here, Lex?" he asked.

Harper grinned. "Just out for a run. Stretch the old legs."

"How did you know where I was?"

"It's me you're talking to, mate."

"I'll ask you again, Lex. How did you know where I was?"

"I found out where your phone was and I figured you'd be running on the heath sooner or later."

"Do you know where my flat is?"

Harper's grin widened. "I know the building, it'll take me a bit longer to find out the flat's number. Why, have you forgotten where you live?" He frowned. "What happened to the old rucksack? The one you filled with house bricks."

"I'm getting a bit old for the iron man stuff," said Shepherd. He put his hands up slowly, wondering if Harper was about to attack him. There was nothing in the man's hands but there was a heavy belt pack around his waist that could easily have contained a handgun.

Harper sensed his unease and his face broke into a grin as he put his hands on his hips.

"I hope you're not here to shoot me, Lex," said Shepherd.

Harper laughed and clapped him on the back. "Now would I do that?" he said. "I just need a word. And as I was in the area, I thought I'd strike while the iron was hot." He guided Shepherd over to a bench and they sat down. Harper looked around, checking for tails.

"There's no one on my case," said Shepherd.

"What, you move north of the river and they can't find you? They're Russian secret service, mate. If they want you, they'll find you."

"Charlie's fixed it," said Shepherd. "She's spoken to the Russians. They thought I was an assassin out to get

Putin. It was nothing personal. We're on the same side now."

Harper shivered. "Yeah, about Charlie . . ."

"What's happened?"

"She knows pretty much everything, mate," said Harper. "That's why I'm here. She called me back for a bollocking. Wanted to know why I hadn't told her that you'd been in Berlin."

Shepherd cursed.

"Yeah, she's not happy with you, obviously. She hasn't mentioned anything?"

Shepherd shook his head. "How the hell did she find out, Lex?"

Harper held up his hands. "Hey, don't be looking at me like that. I'm just the fucking messenger here. She called me back to London and knew everything already. There was no point in trying to lie to her, I'd have just been digging myself into an even deeper hole."

"When you say everything . . ."

"She knows about the Russians. She knows that MI6 sent you out to talk to me. She knows you're trying to set her up."

"I'm not setting her up. That's not what's happening."

Harper screwed up his face. "To be honest, mate, it is. They sent you out to Berlin to get me to give evidence against her. And now she knows."

Shepherd felt suddenly sick. He stood up and took a couple of deep breaths but that didn't make him feel better.

"There's something else you need to know," said Harper quietly.

"Bloody hell, Lex, I can't take much more of this," said Shepherd.

"I have to tell you," said Harper. "Those two Russians in Berlin. We had to off them."

Shepherd's jaw dropped. "Please tell me that's a joke."

"I had no choice. The others insisted on it."

"Your team? What the hell are they doing dictating to you?"

"It doesn't work like that," said Harper. "It's like when you were in the SAS. We have Chinese parliaments, everyone has a chance to say how they feel, everyone has an equal voice. My guys were scared of the repercussions and they decided the best way out of it was to kill them."

"Killing two Russian secret service agents was the best way out?" said Shepherd. "Are you insane?"

"Well, to be fair, mate, you did bring them to us, remember? This is all down to you."

"Fuck that, Lex," said Shepherd, exasperated.

"You know I'm right," said Harper quietly. "You led them to us. We nabbed them. At that point, even though they hadn't seen our faces, they would have been looking for us the moment we let them go. And you know what the Russians are like. Relentless. They would have found us and killed us."

"And now what? You slotted them and you think that'll be the end of it? They'll just send more agents."

"Yeah, but the ones they send won't know who we are or what we look like or how many of us there are. They've got nothing."

"They've got me, Lex. They were following me and now they're dead. Who do you think they're going to blame?" He paced up and down, his mind racing.

"That's why I'm here, mate. I know I flew off the handle in Berlin, but you need to know what's going on."

Shepherd sat down and folded his arms. "I'm screwed. That's what's going on." He looked up at the darkening sky. "I'm so screwed."

"You said Charlie had fixed it with the Russians."

"That's what she told me. But now she knows I lied to her." He shook his head and cursed again. "This is a fucking nightmare, Lex."

"Maybe that's how she found out about Berlin," said Harper. "The Russians told her."

"I guess so. When did you see her?"

"This afternoon. Straight from the plane to a hotel. I'm flying out tonight."

"And she contacted you yesterday?"

"You're wondering how long she's known?" He shrugged. "Couple of days, I think. She wouldn't have waited long before talking to me."

"I was attacked in London," Shepherd told him. "As soon as I got back. An Israeli contract killer. She botched it big time and I killed her. I had to tell Charlie, obviously. I didn't know it was the Russians who'd sent her, not then. But she ID'd the woman and went to see her contact at the Russian embassy. He told her that they thought I was an assassin hired to kill Putin. They didn't know I was MI5. But they do now." He cursed again. "I was on safer ground when they thought I was a contract killer. I could have just disappeared. But Charlie told them who I was, thinking that would help. But if they know that I'm responsible for the deaths of two of their men . . ." He shook his head. "I am so fucked."

"What about that MI6 guy who sent you out? Jeremy whatshisname? Can't he protect you?"

"He's a devious bastard only interested in his own career. I wouldn't trust him as far as I can throw him."

"Then maybe you need to talk to Charlie."

"After what I did? I betrayed her. She's not the type to forgive and forget."

"No, mate, you were told to do what you did. You couldn't say no. It's like being in the army — if an officer says, 'jump' the only thing you can say is 'how high, sir?' You didn't have a choice."

"I could have done what you did and just told him to go fuck himself."

"You're comparing apples and oranges, mate," said Harper. "I don't work for MI5 or Six or the cops. I work for Charlie. She has my loyalty one hundred per cent and I know that she has my back. But you work for MI5. They pay your wages. And if you refused you'd be out on your ear." He grinned. "Mind you, you could always come and work for me."

"Somehow I don't see that working," said Shepherd. He leaned back and rubbed his hands over his face. "I need to think about this," he said. "There's got to be a way out."

The two men sat in silence for a while, Shepherd staring up at the sky while Harper kept glancing around, looking for signs of surveillance. "So how's your boy?" he said eventually. "What's his name? Liam?"

"Yeah. He's okay." Shepherd shrugged. "Actually, he screwed up quite badly. Got caught with drugs at school. They expelled him and he's back in Hereford now."

"Sorry to hear that, mate. What the hell was he doing with drugs? He's what, sixteen?"

"Just seventeen. Drugs are everywhere now, you know that. His school is in the middle of the countryside and you'd have thought he was safe there, but . . ." He shrugged and didn't finish the sentence.

"So what's the story?"

"A pal gave him what he thought was cannabis to hold for a party. Turns out it was coke. Half an ounce."

"Bloody hell, kids are knocking around with that much coke? They must be getting too much pocket money."

"There's a lot of wealthy kids at the school. Overseas students. A lot of them have got more money than sense. Anyway, the school has a zero tolerance rule for drugs so they kicked him out. I got him into a school in Hereford, which means his grandparents can keep an eye on him, but that's not the major problem. The local cops want to make an example of him."

"He's seventeen, you say? He won't go to prison."

"If he does go down it'll be to a young offenders' institution," said Shepherd sourly. "His life'll be over, Lex. Even if he doesn't spend time inside, a conviction like that will haunt him for the rest of his life."

"Can't you talk to the cops? Professional courtesy, and all that?"

"I tried that." He sighed. "Here's the thing. They'll lay off Liam if I can give them a bigger fish. But I've gone as far up the food chain as I can — doing it off the books."

"I'll ask around, if you like. See what I can find out."

"Nah, it's okay. It's not your problem."

"Mate, the drugs business is a small world, especially up near the top. I'll just turn over a few rocks and see what crawls out. Where did the drugs come from, do you know?"

"Leeds. Two brothers. Turks. Yusuf and Ahmet Yilmaz. Yusuf is older by a couple of years. They run a kebab shop and a minicab firm. They use the cabs to deliver the drugs."

"Turks still run most of the heroin into this country, you know that. Cocaine's not really their thing. The Colombians control that and they get pretty heavy with anyone who tries to muscle in on their turf."

"I figured the Turks are just supplying what the market wants. I don't think they're big enough to be bringing the gear in themselves."

Harper nodded. "Sounds right. They'll probably be getting their stuff in Liverpool or Manchester, I'd guess. No point in them going farther afield. But there's a lot of Charlie in Scotland at the moment so they could be buying it from the Jocks." He patted Shepherd's leg. "I'm heading back to Berlin tonight, I'm still in the middle of that Irish thing but I'll make a few calls before I go."

"You don't have to do this, Lex."

Harper nodded. "I do, mate. It's what friends do. They help each other." He patted Shepherd on the leg again, stood up, and jogged away.

Shepherd sat alone on the bench, running through all his options. The problem was, they were few and far between.

Harper arrived back in Berlin early on Wednesday morning. He had kept his suite at the Hotel Adlon and he showered and changed before going to see Hansfree and Zelda. In Harper's absence, Hansfree had been hard at work on the BRIXMIS files and had identified a possible site for the weapons handover at a freight marshalling yard and loading ramp in the Michendorf Bahnhof — a sprawling network of railway tracks and sidings, flanked on either side by dense forest.

"If we do it early morning there'll be no one around," said Hansfree.

"Are you happy with that?" Harper asked Zelda.

"It's perfect," said Zelda. "What about the transport?"

"I'm going to suggest we leave the truck with them," said Harper. "You can take the cost of it out of my share. That way they can check the consignment without having to unload it."

"So my driver delivers it, and then what? Leaves?"

"Let's get Billy Whisper to drive the truck. He can leave with Hansfree. Can you arrange that?"

"Of course."

"For tomorrow?"

"They're already loaded and the driver is waiting for instructions."

Harper grinned. "Tomorrow morning it is." He looked at his watch. "I'll leave you guys to it," he said. "I've got some calls to make."

Button crouched, her hands up defensively. The Arab bared his teeth as he swished his knife from side to side. There was no way to run, the man was between her and the door. He took a step towards her and she took a step back. Her husband's body was to her right. Graham was on his back, his mouth open in surprise, his eyes wide, staring and lifeless. Between his body and the window was a desk with a computer on it. Button bent down, picked up her mobile phone and threw it hard at him. It hit him on the shoulder and went spinning behind him, shattering against the wall. Button started to move forward, ready to grab the knife, but he was too quick for her and he jabbed at her hand, just missing her. She grabbed a glass paperweight but the Arab lashed out again with the knife, catching her in the shoulder, cutting through her shirt and slicing into her flesh. She screamed and hurled the paperweight at him. It smashed into his jaw, breaking his two front teeth. He glared at her as blood trickled from between his broken teeth and ran down his chin and he raised the knife. He stabbed at Button and she turned to the side and grabbed at his wrist with her right hand but he was too quick for her and he jerked the knife back. The blade cut into her palm and she felt blood spurt between her fingers. She screamed, more from anger than from the pain.

The Arab said nothing as he slashed at her again with the knife. Blood was pouring from his mouth where she'd hit him with the paperweight but the only sound was a gentle whistling noise as he breathed through his nose.

Button glanced across at the desk and saw the letter opener that went with the paperweight, a steel blade embedded in a piece of carved crystal. She lurched towards it but the Arab anticipated her and he slashed at her, screaming. The knife caught her in the side, ripping into her flesh. She could feel the blade bite deep and she tried to twist away from the searing pain. She tripped over her husband's legs and went sprawling on her hands and knees.

She heard the Arab grunt and then fell forward as something thumped into her right shoulder. The thump was followed by a sharp pain and she realised that the knife was embedded in her shoulder. She screamed as he pulled the knife out and the serrated edge ripped through skin and muscle. Tears filled her eyes. She didn't want to die like this, cut to pieces in her own home. She screamed and rolled over. He was standing over her, blood dripping down his chin. Still he said nothing, though she could feel the hatred pouring out of him.

Button pulled her legs up and scrabbled away from him. She could feel blood running down her hip. He grunted again and slashed the knife at her legs. The tip nicked her ankle, drawing more blood. Button yelped and pulled her legs in close to her body.

She shuffled to the left and he moved with her, waving the knife menacingly. He lunged at her but as he did she lashed out with her right foot and managed to catch him in the groin with the heel of her shoe. The Arab grimaced and stabbed at her thigh. The blade went in deep and Button screamed in pain. She screamed again as he pulled the knife out and she saw blood spurt down her leg. She shuffled back to the wall and pushed herself up against it, then almost fell over as her injured leg gave way beneath her. She staggered along a bookcase, scattering books on to the floor. She grabbed at a book and threw it at her attacker as hard as she could. It hit him on the forehead and span across the room. He laughed at her and stabbed again and she jumped away.

The door was to her left, just a few yards away, but the Arab realised that too and he took a step to the side, blocking her escape. As he moved she saw Shepherd at the study window, a machine gun in his hands. For a brief moment they had eye contact.

"Down," Shepherd mouthed.

Button did as she was told and as she fell to her knees the window exploded and bullets raked across the Arab.

Button woke up, her chest heaving. Her face was bathed in sweat and she was panting. She wiped her face and rolled over to reach for the glass of water she'd left on her bedside table. She gulped some down, the images from the dream still racing through her mind. In her whole life she'd never been closer to death than on that day back in 2008. She'd survived but her husband hadn't, stabbed in the heart by the assassin who'd come to kill her. It had all been about revenge — the assassin had been paid to kill her by an old man who blamed her for the death of his sons. Button had learned a lot about revenge that day — the lengths to which people could go to right a wrong.

She put down the glass and lay on her back, staring up at the ceiling. Shepherd had killed the man who had tried to kill her. But that hadn't been revenge enough for her. The day that she'd stood next to her daughter and watched her husband's coffin be lowered into the ground, she'd silently sworn to herself that anyone connected to his death would die too. She'd made good on that promise. It had taken her more than five years, but she'd done it. Now they were all dead, and she felt not one iota of guilt. She felt the opposite, in fact. She'd carried out her promise. Everyone involved with Graham's murder was now dead. But still the dream came. Almost every night. Alcohol sometimes helped. A bottle of wine before bed seemed to keep the dream away. But not always. She took a deep breath and sighed, knowing that she wouldn't be able to sleep again. She turned her head and looked at the clock. It was just after six o'clock. The sun hadn't risen yet and she never liked getting up in the dark. She closed her eyes and tried to think happy thoughts. She thought back to the day that Zoe had been born, and the look of pride on Graham's face as he'd held her for the first

394

time. She smiled to herself as she relived the moment, then the realisation that he would never see the beautiful girl she had become hit her like a blow to the stomach and she rolled over into a foetal ball and sobbed into her pillow.

Shepherd's ringing mobile woke him. He opened his eyes and stared at the ceiling for a couple of seconds, wondering where he was and more importantly, who he was. Sleep was always a dangerous time for anyone in the undercover business because it was when you were most off guard. Hampstead. His legend was John Whitehill, freelance journalist, but he was also Frederik Olsen who was the man known as The Dane. And somewhere amongst all the lies he was Dan Shepherd, MI5 officer. He sat up and double-checked that the phone ringing was his own and not that of one of his legends. "Yeah?" he said as he rubbed the sleep from his eyes.

"Wakey, wakey, rise and shine." It was Lex Harper.

"What time is it?"

"It's intel time, mate. Are you awake?"

"Where are you?"

"Krautland. Listen, about that kebab thing. The brothers get their stuff from a gang in Liverpool. They drive over a couple of times a month."

"What stuff are we talking about?"

"Everything, mate. The Liverpool gang runs a one-stop shop operation, they sell everything. Coke, heroin, Ecstasy, dope, you name it, they'll price it for you. They bring it in from Amsterdam, usually on the Ostend-Felixstowe ferry."

"They're big?"

"Damn right. Third biggest in Liverpool and gunning for number two."

"They friends of yours?"

Harper chuckled. "Nah, mate. I'm friends with the number two gang. And I've done business with the top dogs. To be honest, they're all getting a bit fed up with this lot. They're getting a bit too big for their boots, if you get my drift. They're a nasty bunch and there have been a few shootings over the last month or so. So if you were to, say, talk to your cops and give them some intel on them, you'd be doing us all a favour."

"Sounds like a plan. How much can you tell me?"

Harper laughed. "Me, bugger all. I'm no grass. But there is a lad I'll send along to fill you in. His name is Justin. Justin Time, we call him, because he's always late. He's a Scouser but don't hold that against him. He's a good lad and he'll tell you anything you want to know. I've said you're a mate and to be trusted. He doesn't know who you are or who you work for and I've used that bollicky name you used in Berlin — Peter Parkinson. Wasn't he Spider-Man, by the way? Were they playing some bloody game with you?"

"Spider-Man was Peter Parker. And the legends are randomly generated. That's what they say, anyway."

"Yeah, well Justin thinks you're him and that you're a mate over from Spain. You'll have to go and see him in Leeds, he doesn't travel much. Hates flying, failed his driving test a dozen times so he gets around on public transport. He's a laugh but he's sound."

"What's he do?"

Harper laughed. "Best you don't know," he said. "Let's just say that he's bloody good with laundry."

Harper gave Shepherd a mobile phone number.

"Lex, thanks for this."

"No need for thanks, mate," said Harper. "It's like I said before, it's what friends do for friends." He ended the call.

"Is that him?" asked Sharpe, peering through the rain-splattered windscreen of the rented Ford Mondeo. A man in his twenties was standing in the doorway of a betting shop, his head down over a racing paper. They were in Leeds, not far from the railway station.

"Maybe," said Shepherd. He took out his mobile and rang Justin's number. Seconds later the figure in the doorway pulled a phone out of his parka pocket.

"Yeah?"

"Justin. It's Peter. We're in the blue Mondeo across the road from you."

Justin looked over, waved, shoved the phone and paper into his pocket and flipped up the fur-lined hood of his parka before jogging through the rain towards the car.

He climbed into the back and pushed the hood off his head, grinning. "Good weather for ducks, yeah?" His accent immediately betrayed his Liverpool origins.

"Justin, thanks for this," said Shepherd. He twisted around in the driving seat to shake hands with him. "I'm Pete. This is Ricky."

Justin shook both their hands. "Any mate of Lex's, as they say. He says you're Spider-Man."

"Pete Parkinson not Peter Parker," said Shepherd.

"Like the disease?"

"I guess so."

"My gran had that. Shook like she was being electrocuted. If we wanted to loosen the sauce bottle we used to give it to her to hold for a few minutes. Worked a treat." He laughed at his own joke and settled back in his seat. "So what do you need to know?"

"This gang, the ones who are bringing in stuff from Amsterdam, what can you tell me about them?"

"They're local, mainly, but they've got a few lads from Manchester with them. They came out of nowhere a couple of years back. I think one of them did time with a guy who worked for one of the Colombian cartels and they put together a coke thing. The Colombians get it to Amsterdam and this guy — his name is McLaren, like the racing car — has done a deal with this company here. They charge him two and a half grand a kilo, heroin or coke, cheaper for hash. Trucks drive straight off the ferries, up north and across the M62. Six hours on a good day. Dover's so busy there's next to no chance of being pulled. They're bringing in twenty or thirty trucks a day and they don't have gear on them all, so the only way they'd catch a delivery is if they had intel and the gang is as tight as a duck's arse so there's no one to grass them up."

"What about when it gets to Liverpool?"

"They've got a depot near the end of the M62. They unload the containers there and use vans to deliver the stuff to shops and restaurants. The drugs go out on the vans. But again, not all the vans. You'd never know if a van had heroin or coke or just chicken or fish."

"And the cops never raid them?"

"They've been turned over a couple of times but never found nothing. They've got cops on the payroll and I'd bet they're drugs cops. Probably got their own men in Customs and at the ports. Same as Lex, right? He's got cops on his payroll right across the country. Has to be that way."

Shepherd nodded. "I guess." He didn't want to hear any more. The less he knew about what Lex Harper got up to, the better.

"I heard that now McLaren's paying to put his people's kids in private schools and for them to go to university, just so they can get them on the graduate entry schemes. They're getting them into the cops and MI5 and Border Force and they pay them five times their salary to stay there and keep their noses clean. I swear to God, mate, it's that organised. They shell out a couple of hundred grand a year and they've got their own people, right at the heart of it. Long and the short of it, they're pretty much untouchable at the moment."

"Are you okay to show me the depot they use?"

"Sure," said Justin. "Head out the city, east, follow the signs for the M62."

The depot was on an industrial estate a few hundred yards from the end of the M62, on the outskirts of Liverpool. The estate was composed of a dozen featureless buildings of varying sizes, of which the depot was the largest by far. It sat in the middle of the estate like a mother hen surrounded by its chicks. The depot, and a car park large enough to take twenty or so container lorries, was surrounded by a wire security fence and the whole area was covered by CCTV. The only way in and out was through a metal gate that rolled back and forth to allow the trucks in and out. There were two uniformed security guards to check the paperwork of the trucks as they entered and left, and another to operate the electric gate.

There was a large loading bay on one side of the building where three large grey trucks were parked up with their rear doors facing the building. Men in white overalls were unloading boxes on to trolleys and wheeling them inside. On the other side of the building was a smaller loading bay with several vans parked next to it.

"So how does it work?" asked Shepherd.

He, Sharpe and Justin were sitting in their Mondeo in the car park of a unit that had a large FOR RENT sign across its main door. Justin was in the back.

"It's a legit business," said Justin. "It's been around since the seventies but they moved here a couple of years ago. They supply chicken around the whole of the north-west and down as far as Birmingham. Fish, too. Anything that needs refrigeration. There's dozens of trucks that pass through here each day, some from the Dover ferries, some from Felixstowe. The vans are refrigerated and the chickens are packed in boxes. The only way to check the truck completely is to take out all the chickens. But if they get above a certain temperature then Health and Safety steps in and declares the consignment unfit for human consumption and Customs has to stump up the money. But they're lazy bastards anyway. No one wants to be humping out dozens of cases of chicken. So ninety-nine times out of a hundred they don't even check. But where they're clever is that they only bring in ten or twenty kilos on a truck. That much gear is easy to hide. They build secret compartments into the trucks and Customs wouldn't see if they were looking right at it. The only way they'd ever get caught is if they had serious intel, you know, telling them that there was gear in a specific truck, but that's never going to happen. Even the drivers don't know when they're carrying gear."

Shepherd twisted around in his seat. "How come you know all this?" he asked.

"One of their guys had a falling-out with them and ended up working for us. Gave us the full SP."

"And you didn't think of shopping them to the cops?"

"There's no point. The gang's got an inside man in the drugs squad. Any time they start sniffing around they just stop the shipments. Then they get the all-clear and it starts up again. It's a sweet operation."

"So at any one time there's probably hundreds of kilos of drugs in there?"

"Yeah, but it doesn't hang around for long," said Justin. "The smaller vans move the chicken and fish around to the supermarkets and restaurants they supply, and they use the same vans to move the drugs."

Shepherd looked over at Sharpe. "What do you think?"

"It's a big operation," said Sharpe. "Plenty big enough, I'd say."

"Anything else you need?" asked Justin.

"Nah, you've done us proud," said Shepherd. "We'll run you back home."

Jeremy Willoughby-Brown pressed the remote to open his garage door and drove his Volvo carefully inside. There were four bikes parked to the left and a large lawn-mower to the right and there were only a few inches to spare if he wasn't going to scratch the paintwork of his car. He held the door close as he climbed out, then reached inside for his briefcase. As he straightened up he gasped involuntarily as he saw the figure standing in the open doorway. He held the briefcase up to his chest even though he knew it wouldn't even come close to stopping a bullet.

The figure chuckled. "Don't worry, Jeremy, I'm not here to shoot you," said the figure. "Not that I haven't thought about it."

The voice was familiar but Willoughby-Brown couldn't quite place it. He took a few hesitant steps forward and then realised who it was. "Shepherd? What the hell are you doing here?"

"Relax, Jeremy, that's not a gun in my pocket, I'm just pleased to see you."

"What do you want, Shepherd?"

"Oh, so now I'm Shepherd and not Danny boy. What's happened, Jeremy? Are we not best friends any more?"

Willoughby-Brown glanced anxiously across at the house.

"Don't worry, I won't keep you long," said Shepherd. "Emily will never know I've been here. She's probably helping Joshua and Jane with their homework." He smiled as Willoughby-Brown stiffened. "What, you think you're the only one who can get intel on people? I have to say I never pegged you for a married man. Not that I thought you were gay, just sort of asexual, you know? I could never picture any woman wanting you to climb on top of her."

Willoughby-Brown glared at him but didn't say anything.

"But here you are, married to a former stockbroker, father of two lovely kids at private school. The perfect family. And I love the Jeremy, Joshua and Jane thing. Maybe if you have another son, you could call him Judas?"

"What the fuck do you want, Shepherd?"

"I want a chat."

"You could have come to my office for that."

Shepherd shook his head. "I'm not going anywhere near your office," he said. He was wearing a long black overcoat and had his hands thrust deep into the pockets. The collar was turned up against the cold wind that was blowing down the street.

"So you just come to my home instead?"

Shepherd shrugged. "How does it feel to know that someone has been digging into your personal life, Jeremy? It doesn't feel good, does it? Bit like when you started talking about my two-bedroom flat and the view of the Thames. Just to let me know that you knew. But that didn't intimidate me, it just made me angry."

"Fine, message received loud and clear. Now I'll ask you again, what the fuck do you want?"

"I'm not doing your dirty work any more," said Shepherd.

"This is about Button?"

"Of course it's about her. If you want to bring her down, you can do it yourself. Lex Harper told me to fuck off and that's what I'm saying to you."

"Because?"

"Because I didn't join MI5 to shaft my boss, a boss who I also count as a friend. If she's broken the law then you can use someone else to put the case together because I'm not doing it. I take down villains and I take down terrorists, I don't take down friends."

"Even friends who break the law?"

"Like I said, if she's broken the law then you go and put a case together, but I don't want to be part of it."

"You don't get to choose your cases," said Willoughby-Brown coldly.

"Actually I do. I work undercover most of the time and I'm never asked to do anything that I don't want to."

"This isn't an undercover case."

"Yes, it is. You want me to screw over Charlie behind her back. You want me to look her in the eye and smile while at the same time I'm plotting with you to bring her down. And I'm here to tell you that's not going to happen."

404

Willoughby-Brown glared at him. "You do this and your career is over," he said quietly.

"No, it's not," said Shepherd. "I'll still have a career, it just might not be with MI5. I had a career before Five and I'll sure as hell have a career afterwards. If you want to get me fired, fine. We'll see how you get on at an employment tribunal. But you're not using me to take down Charlie Button. I'm done." He turned his back on Willoughby-Brown and walked away into the night, his feet crunching on the gravel drive.

Willoughby-Brown stood where he was, his heart pounding. He realised he was still holding his briefcase in front of his chest and he slowly lowered it. He took a deep breath, clicked the remote to shut the garage door and tried to smile as he headed towards his house.

Harper and Maggie May took a taxi to the city's nightclub area and it dropped them off outside a pretty rough bar that Harper was familiar with. The doormen greeted him with the traditional bouncers' scowl and they both checked out Maggie May's impressive legs and cleavage, which were very much on display, before waving them inside.

They found a seat at the table in a chill-out area away from the pounding house music on the dance floor, and drank a couple of beers as they surveyed the crowd. Eventually Harper found what he was looking for — a group of bikers who were all wearing filthy chopped-down denim jackets emblazoned with a lightning bolt motorcycle club insignia that looked to be first cousin to a Nazi swastika. They were loud and obnoxious and had carved out their own area in the bar. Most of the club's patrons gave them a wide berth except for the young girls in short skirts and cropped tops who allowed themselves to be groped and fondled in exchange for alcohol and the white tablets the bikers kept feeding them. Several of the bikers had shaved heads; they all had tattoos and were missing teeth and while they were all big and well muscled Harper knew that none of them would be a problem, one on one. They were pack animals. They lived in a pack and they fought in a pack, and that was always their weakness.

Harper sipped his beer and chatted to Maggie May as he waited, like a cheetah surveying a pack of wildebeest, waiting for one to leave the safety of the herd. There were two false starts when two of the bikers went to the men's toilets. The first time there were already two clubbers inside and the second the biker had been followed in by another man. It was third time lucky. The biker was just over six feet tall; his jacket sleeves had been hacked off to reveal his vivid full-length arm tattoos. His belt buckle was in the shape of a large razor blade and he had chunky metal rings on all his fingers, effectively giving him lethal, and legal, knuckledusters on each hand. He pushed a man in a black suit out of the way. The man turned and glared angrily but when he saw who had pushed him, he moved away quickly.

"That's the one," said Harper. "I'll be in and out in thirty seconds. If anyone looks as if they're going to follow us in, run interference."

406

Harper slipped on his gloves as he headed into the toilets. He would only have a few seconds to take the man out but he had rehearsed it in his mind and knew exactly what to do. He pushed open the door. There were two stalls to the left and a long stainless steel urinal to the right. The biker was standing in the middle of the urinal, playing a stream of urine in the general direction of the wall but not seeming to care how much sprayed over the floor. He took a quick look over his shoulder as the door opened but then turned back to the matter in hand.

Harper walked quickly across the tiled floor, grabbed the back of the biker's head and smashed it against the wall. The biker slumped to the floor and Harper helped him down, then stood over him and patted him down. He found a large folding knife in the back pocket of the man's jeans and he slipped it into a Ziploc plastic bag which he shoved inside his jacket. Then he grabbed the biker's hair and pulled out a clump, which went into a second Ziploc bag. Less than thirty seconds after entering the toilet Harper was heading out of the club with Maggie May and five minutes after that they were in a taxi heading back to the hotel.

Shepherd and Sharpe were sitting at a table furthest from the bar when Drinkwater and Allen walked in. It had started raining outside and Drinkwater shook out a large golfing umbrella before slotting it into a stand by the door. Allen had already spotted Shepherd and strode across the pub to shake his hand.

407

"Thanks for arranging this — I didn't want to do it at your station," said Shepherd, keeping his voice low so that Drinkwater wouldn't hear. "I owe you one."

"Paul's more than happy to hear what you've got to say," said the detective. "I told him you could deliver him a big score and he's been on tenterhooks ever since."

The detective sergeant walked over, his face impassive. Shepherd got the impression that he didn't smile much, but then detectives rarely did when on duty. Drinkwater made no attempt to shake hands. He nodded curtly at Shepherd and then gestured at Sharpe.

"And this is . . .?"

"An old colleague," said Shepherd. "Jimmy Sharpe."

"Less of the old," growled Sharpe.

"Jimmy's attached to the National Crime Agency."

"Then he won't mind showing me his warrant card."

Sharpe stood up, took out his warrant card and handed it over. Drinkwater studied it carefully, as if committing the details to memory, before passing it back.

"Scottish?" he confirmed.

"Aye. I voted for independence but what can you do?" said Sharpe. He sat down again. "Get the drinks in, Spider," he said, gesturing at his half-empty glass.

"What can I get you guys?" asked Shepherd.

"We're on duty. So an orange juice will do me," said Drinkwater.

From the look on his face it was clear that Allen would have preferred a beer but he asked for a coffee.

They sat down as Shepherd went over to the bar but stayed silent until Shepherd returned with their drinks and a fresh pint for Sharpe.

"So what have you got for us?" asked Drinkwater, getting straight to the point.

"It's good news," said Shepherd. "The Yilmaz brothers aren't as small time as you might have thought. They take a run over to Liverpool every two weeks to pick up their drugs from a firm there. Each trip it's a couple of kilos of coke plus heroin, Ecstasy and amphetamines. They pay in cash too, on the spot."

"This Liverpool firm is where?"

"The drugs are in a warehouse depot on the outskirts of the city. They bring them in from Amsterdam in refrigerated trucks full of chickens."

"Chickens?" repeated the detective sergeant with a look of disbelief.

Shepherd nodded. "It's clever. They've been doing it for years. They bring in a dozen or so trucks a day and distribute the chickens right across the north-west. Fish, too. It's a real business, the drugs side is the icing on the cake. The drugs are kept in the depot and they use the same delivery vans to move them as and when."

The detective sergeant frowned. "If you know this . . ." He nodded at Sharpe. "And the NCA knows what's going on, why haven't they been shut down?"

"Merseyside police have gone in a couple of times but both times the depot was clean. No drugs, no cash, no weapons. We think the gang has a man inside the drugs squad."

"A corrupt cop?" said Drinkwater.

"It wouldn't be the first time," said Shepherd.

"Well, we have to do something about that, right?"

"The problem with that is that a corrupt cop means Criminal Complaints. And if they're informed then they'll take over the investigation. With phone taps and bank records being checked, it could take years before they put a case together. And you'll get none of the credit. Worse than that, you bringing down another officer probably won't help your career prospects."

Drinkwater nodded slowly. "So what's your plan?"

"The way I see it there are two ways forward. We can bust the Liverpool operation but if we do that we're going to need to bring in the NCA. We can't use the Liverpool cops because they're obviously leaking like a sieve. Or we can just bust the Yilmaz brothers when they get back to Leeds with a delivery. That way it can all be handled by the West Yorkshire cops. No need to involve Liverpool at all. It'll be a smaller bust but still a few kilos, plus you'd get a decent proceeds of crime investigation going."

"That's why you're here?" said Drinkwater, looking at Sharpe.

"I can get the NCA moving, no problem," said Sharpe. "They'll arrange surveillance at the ports, they'll put the gang under the microscope, and they'll go in without the Liverpool cops knowing what's happening."

"And that would be an NCA case, not a West Yorkshire case?"

"I'd make sure you got full credit," said Sharpe.

"But it would be an NCA case?" repeated the detective sergeant.

"It would have to be," said Shepherd. "The geographic reach, for a start. Also, budget-wise. It'd be expensive. But it would be a great bust. This gang is bringing in hundreds of kilos at a time. Bringing them down would be a real victory. They'd be behind bars for decades and we'd be taking millions of pounds worth of drugs off the streets."

Drinkwater rubbed his chin. "Maybe we're better going for the brothers when they bring back a delivery," he said. "We'd have more control, less chance of anything going wrong."

It sounded to Shepherd as if the detective sergeant was trying to talk himself into it, so he said nothing. Frankly he didn't care which option the detective went for, all he was interested in was getting Liam off the hook.

"Plus we'd be striking when the iron is hot," Drinkwater went on. "They go to Liverpool every two weeks, you say?"

"Regular as clockwork," said Shepherd. "Every second Thursday."

"And when are they next due for a run?"

"Next week," said Sharpe.

"Let's go for that, then. How do we proceed?"

"You're sure about this?" said Sharpe. "You want to go for the small fry?"

"Not that small," said Drinkwater. "By keeping it in-house, we can make sure that nothing goes wrong. And we've got a major drugs problem in Leeds at the moment, so this will show that we're doing something about it. So what do we do?"

"It's simple enough," said Shepherd. "Jimmy and I can give you the intel and you just put a tail on the brothers next Thursday. If they visit the depot you'll know they have the drugs. You follow them back to the minicab office and Robert's your mother's brother, as they say."

Drinkwater frowned, not getting the joke.

"Bob's your uncle," said Sharpe, filling in the blanks.

"And how do I say we got the intel?" asked Drinkwater.

"Anonymous tip's the best way," said Shepherd. "Just say you caught the call, you used your initiative, blah blah blah."

Drinkwater nodded thoughtfully. "So no NCA involvement?"

"If that's the way you want to go, sure. We'll give you the intel and leave it at that. I just want to be sure that you won't be taking the case against my son any further."

"If your intel is good then I'll happily drop the case against him."

"No caution, nothing on his record?"

"It'll be as if it never happened," said Drinkwater.

Shepherd held out his hand. Drinkwater frowned, but then offered his hand and the two men shook on it.

"Thank you," said Shepherd.

"Just make sure he doesn't get into trouble again."

"Oh believe me, I've already read him the riot act and I'm watching him like a hawk."

Sharpe reached into his pocket and took out a thumb-drive. "That's everything we have," he said, passing it to Drinkwater. He gave him a business card. "Anything else you need, my mobile number is on there."

Drinkwater stood up. He hadn't touched his orange juice. "Okay, well thanks for what you've done. I'll take it from here."

Allen nodded at Shepherd, forced a smile, then followed the detective sergeant out of the pub.

"Well, that was interesting," said Sharpe.

"In what way?"

Sharpe gestured at the door. "Drinkwater. Graduate entrant, fast-track, won't drink on duty, stickler for the rules, pole up his backside, and yet given the chance between personal glory and shutting down a major drug route, what does he do?"

Shepherd knew the question was rhetorical so he didn't answer. He shrugged and sipped his whiskey and soda.

"I thought he would have gone for the big score," said Sharpe. "Caught me by surprise, that."

"There's not many would choose the greater good over personal advancement," said Shepherd. "He sees himself on the front of the local paper taking credit for a big drugs bust. And getting a congratulatory email from the chief constable."

"He would have got that in spades in Liverpool."

"A bird in the hand, Razor," said Shepherd. "And he probably doesn't trust us."

"I'm a policeman," said Sharpe with a grin. "I can be trusted."

"Yeah but he doesn't know us. For all he knows we're spinning him a line. This way he gets the local bust and the credit."

"And meanwhile tons of drugs keep coming into the country on those refrigerated trucks." Sharpe shrugged and sipped his pint. "Not everyone's as altruistic as you, I suppose."

"What do you mean?"

Sharpe raised his glass. "You know what I mean. If it was you, what would you have gone for?"

"I'm not looking for personal glory, Razor."

"Exactly. You're the guy in the white hat, the good guy, the Jimmy Stewart of law enforcement. You always try to do the right thing."

"And that's a problem?"

Sharpe grinned. "You tell me."

Shepherd was in the Hampstead flat when his phone rang. It was Button.

"There's someone you need to meet," she said. "Can you come to the Freemason's Arms in about half an hour?"

"No problem."

"It's a date then."

The line went dead and Shepherd frowned at his phone. She hadn't asked him where he was, which meant that she probably knew he was in London. Did she have him under surveillance? And why hadn't she told him who he was meeting?

414

He grabbed his coat and headed out. Button was already at the pub, sitting on the terrace with a big man who was wearing a black overcoat over a dark suit. Shepherd had a feeling he was Russian — a feeling that was confirmed when Button introduced him.

"Mr Klimov works for the Russian Federal Protective Service," said Button. "Specifically for the Presidential Secret Service."

Klimov stood up and the two men shook hands. The Russian had surprisingly soft hands for a man so large. "Pleased to meet you," he said. There was a hint of an American accent, though it was still easy to tell that he was Russian.

They sat down. Button hadn't introduced Shepherd, which meant either she didn't want the Russian to know his name or he already knew who Shepherd was.

"We thought we'd sit outside, it's a bit crowded in there and I for one could do with some fresh air," said Button. "I've been stuck in the office all week."

There was an opened bottle of Pinot Grigio on the table and two glasses, one empty and one half full. Klimov had a brandy glass in front of him and from the look of it Button and Klimov had been at the bar for some time. They had almost certainly been together when Button had called Shepherd. He wondered what they had been talking about and why she hadn't forewarned him that he was meeting a Russian agent. Button poured some wine into a glass for him.

"I've brought Mr Klimov up to speed, and he's happy with the way we are handling things," said Button.

"That's good to know," said Shepherd.

"I've explained that we are close to apprehending all the people involved, and that everything will be wrapped up before President Putin arrives."

"That's the plan," said Shepherd, nodding.

"Now for the sensitive bit," said Button. "The attack on you in the Battersea flat was, how should we describe it . . .?"

"Almost fatal?" suggested Shepherd.

She flashed him a tight smile. "Unfortunate," she said. "It was a misunderstanding. If anything it demonstrated how successful we were in establishing your legend."

"So Katz was working for the Russians."

"That cannot ever be officially admitted," said Klimov. "But I do offer you my apologies. Without any admission of guilt."

Shepherd shrugged. "Well, I apologise for killing your agent," he said.

"She wasn't our agent," said the Russian coldly.

"Semantics," said Shepherd. He sipped his wine and stared at the Russian over the top of his glass.

"As I said, it was a misunderstanding and one that will not be repeated. Mr Klimov is now fully in the loop and will stay there until the current operation is concluded."

The Russian nodded in agreement.

"Anyway, what happened can actually be used to our advantage," said Button. "Maya Katz killed the first assassin who took the Putin contract. Then she attacked you. That would be a good reason for you to make contact with Smit and to insist on a meeting."

"But that was a week ago. Won't he ask why I waited so long?"

"Lie. Tell him it just happened. Tell him you're in the firing line, which means someone must have talked. You know you didn't talk so it has to be him. You're angry, you want an explanation, and if you don't get one you're pulling out and keeping the deposit. You say you don't trust him so you want to meet on neutral territory, somewhere away from his house. He won't like an outdoor meeting but you stick to your guns."

"And I ask for more money?"

"More money and an assurance that Smit's organisation didn't betray you."

Realisation dawned. "And we bug the conversation?"

"We'll fix you up with state-of-the-art equipment."

"Smit will have jammers, guaranteed. He's not an amateur."

"We'll use solid state recording, we'll video him from afar with parabolic mics. And we'll have a team on the ground. Our people and Mr Klimov's."

"A joint UK-Russian operation?"

"We need to have the Federal Protective Service on board," said Button. "We're in this mess because we didn't keep our lines of communication open."

"We will not be in the way," the Russian said to Shepherd and flashed him what was supposed to be a reassuring smile but resembled a shark about to attack.

"You have every right to demand a face-to-face meeting after what's happened," said Button. "And any professional would be looking to increase his fee. Smit

417

will understand. And the time pressure means that he will have no choice other than to agree."

The Russian was nodding. "You must insist on a higher price. He will have to confirm that with the man paying the money. We will record that call and then we will have a case against them both."

Shepherd nodded at the Russian, then turned to look at Button. "Parabolic mics, you said. That means outside?"

"Again, you can play on your paranoia. You can say you don't trust him any more so you don't want to go to his house. It has to be outside. Somewhere public, somewhere with lots of escape routes, but somewhere where there aren't too many people. You can let him choose but really it isn't much of a choice. You tell us as soon as he suggests the place and we'll get it staked out. You tell him you're thinking of pulling out and he'll try to talk you out of it. His attempts to persuade you to continue should convict him. You can press him for details of the assassination, you can tell him you need to know exactly what the plan is before deciding if you will go ahead."

Shepherd nodded thoughtfully. It made sense. There was a logic to what Button was saying, and if he handled the meeting just right, Smit would talk himself straight into a prison cell. He would also implicate the father who was paying for the contract. "Sounds good," he said.

"You need to talk to Smit as soon as possible," said Button. "I'll start work on the surveillance team."

"As will I," said the Russian, flashing Shepherd another shark-like smile.

After the Russian had gone, Button ordered another bottle of wine.

"How much does Klimov know about the attempt on my life?" asked Shepherd.

"He thought you were an assassin planning to kill Putin, so in a way you were fair game."

"Assassination is okay now, is that what you're saying?"

"I'm just looking at it from his point of view."

"So it was him who gave the order?"

She shook her head. "He's a cog in the machine — a fairly important cog but still a cog. I don't think he even knew about it until I raised it. He spoke to Moscow and then confirmed it." She smiled. "Not in so many words, of course. They'll never admit to ordering a killing on UK soil. And I doubt that Klimov would have personally hired the assassins."

"No, but somebody did."

"And it won't happen again, not now that the FPS is involved. Klimov will report back that he met you and that he has been fully briefed. There won't be any more attempts on your life. Not from the Russians, anyway."

"I hope you're right," he said. "But I'm not convinced."

Harper and Maggie May picked up O'Brien and Walsh from their hotel at five o'clock in the morning. Walsh was carrying a black nylon holdall. The two men climbed into the back of the SUV.

"You won't mind if I check the money," said Harper from the front passenger seat.

"You're not getting paid until we've seen the rockets," said O'Brien.

"That's not a problem, but can the dog at least see the rabbit, as you English say?"

"We're fecking Irish," growled O'Brien.

"My apologies," said Harper. "A slip of the tongue. I sometimes realise my English is not as good as I think it is."

Walsh unzipped the holdall. Harper twisted around and reached inside, pulling out a wad of bank-fresh €500 notes. He flicked through the wad then pulled out a single banknote and checked it carefully.

"They're real enough," said O'Brien.

Harper nodded, gave the notes back to Walsh, and twisted around in his seat. Maggie May drove off. Harper dozed during the drive but woke with a start when Maggie May slapped him on the leg. "We're here," she said.

Harper opened his eyes. Ahead of them were the marshalling yards. There were hundreds of flatbed and boxcar rail wagons on the maze of branching lines and sidings, all waiting to be shunted into packages so that they could be distributed around the various other rail yards all over Germany.

"Where do we go?" asked Maggie May.

Harper pulled out his mobile and called Zelda. "We're here," he said. "Where are you?"

In the distance, headlights flashed twice. Before Harper could say anything, Maggie May was already heading towards Zelda's Audi.

The SUV parked next to the Audi and Harper and O'Brien climbed out. "Where's the truck?" asked O'Brien, looking around.

Harper went over to talk to Zelda. "The truck is about half a mile down the road," she said. "Billy Big and Hansfree are in a black Mercedes parked next to it."

O'Brien came up behind Harper. "Where is it? Where's the fecking truck?"

"Not far," said Harper. "We'll drive down."

O'Brien shook his head. "Nah, Michael can stay here with the money. I'll check the equipment. If it's okay you come back and get the cash."

"If that's what you want . . ." said Harper.

"That's the way it's going to be," said O'Brien emphatically. "We'll use her car," he said, pointing at the Audi.

"Fine," said Harper.

O'Brien went over to tell Walsh what was happening, then hurried back and got into the front of the Audi next to Zelda, leaving Harper to climb into the back. Zelda drove slowly around the cinder tracks in the freight yard towards a loading ramp. Towards the far end of the yard they could see railway workers coupling and uncoupling wagons and shunting engines clanking to and fro, but the centre portion of the complex seemed almost entirely deserted.

In the distance Harper saw a large grey truck with the name of a bakery firm on the side and a cartoon of a loaf of bread. Next to it was a black Mercedes.

The Audi parked alongside the truck. O'Brien looked over at the Mercedes. "Who are those guys?" he asked.

"Two of my team, keeping an eye on the truck," said Harper. "That's a very valuable cargo," he said.

"You're telling me," said O'Brien. "Tell them to piss off. I don't want them looking over my shoulder."

Harper got out of the car. He waved for Billy Whisper to get out of the cab of the truck and to join Billy Big and Hansfree in the Mercedes. O'Brien waited until the Mercedes had driven off before getting out of the Audi and walking over to the truck with Harper. Harper pulled open the truck's rear doors. Inside were the launchers, wrapped in green canvas held down with ropes. Either side of the launchers were green metal containers which held the rockets.

"I'm going to need to open some of the containers," said O'Brien.

"Help yourself, I'll give you a hand." Harper turned his back on O'Brien and took the biker's knife from his pocket. He pulled out the blade and in one smooth movement turned and slashed O'Brien across the throat. It was the most efficient way of doing the job. The thick coat meant that a stab to the heart would have been problematic at best, and by cutting the throat he was able to simultaneously ensure that there were no cries or screams.

Blood spurted down the front of O'Brien's coat. His eyes were wide and staring but the life was already draining from them. Bloody froth began to ooze from the gaping wound in his throat and then he sank to his knees, his arms loose at his side. Harper dropped the knife as he waited for O'Brien to die. It took no more than ten seconds. O'Brien pitched forward, twitched, and then went still.

Harper knelt down, taking care to avoid the pool of thick blood that was soaking into the ground. He took the Makarov from his holster and pressed O'Brien's lifeless fingers all around the gun. He ejected the clip and pressed that to O'Brien's fingers, then removed the first three rounds and one by one pressed them to his fingers before putting them back in the clip and slotting the clip back into the gun. He rubbed the handle of the gun roughly against O'Brien's palm to maximise the DNA transfer, then he carefully slipped the man's index finger on to the trigger. He slid the gun back into his underarm holster, then took out the Ziploc bag containing the hair he'd pulled from the head of the unconscious biker. He put the hair into O'Brien's right hand and made it into a fist. He stood up and surveyed his handiwork for several seconds, then carefully rolled the body over so that it was lying on top of the knife.

It wasn't a perfect crime scene by any means, but it would do.

He checked that he hadn't picked up any of O'Brien's blood, then went over to the Mercedes and climbed into the back.

Hansfree drove back to Zelda's Audi.

"All done?" she said.

"Yeah," said Harper.

"Seems a lot of trouble just to kill a man," she said as he climbed into the car.

"It's about telling a story," said Harper. "It's not just about the man, it's about wrecking his organisation."

"Best I don't know the details," said Zelda.

She drove him back to the waiting SUV and parked some distance away. The Mercedes was by the entrance to the yards, its engine running. "I won't be long," he said as he got out. Zelda kept her hands on the steering wheel and stared straight ahead.

Harper walked slowly over to the SUV. Maggie May gave him a wave and he waved back. Walsh wound down the window as Harper walked up to the SUV. "What's happening?" he asked.

"All good," said Harper.

"Where's Declan?"

"He's staying with the gear. I think he's frightened I might take it off him." Harper nodded at Maggie May. "You can head back to the hotel with the guys. It's been a pleasure, as always."

Maggie May climbed out of the SUV and blew Harper a kiss. "You've got my number."

"Damn right," said Harper. He waved her goodbye and she jogged over to the Mercedes and climbed into the back. Harper leaned through the window of the SUV and held out his left hand. "Give me the bag and I'll be on my way," he said.

"Not until I've spoken to Declan."

"You are the suspicious type, aren't you?" laughed Harper. "Okay, you can use my phone." He reached into his jacket, pulled out the Makarov, and shot Walsh in the face. Blood splattered across the rear window of the SUV and what was left of Walsh's head slumped back against the seat. Harper grabbed the bag with his left hand and pulled it from Walsh's lifeless grip. "Pleasure doing business with you," he said.

The Mercedes drove off. Hansfree would already be making the anonymous call to the authorities, tipping them off that he had heard a gunshot at the Michendorf Bahnhof yards. As Harper walked away from the SUV he tossed the gun into a clump of bushes. Even a cursory search would turn it up, leading the German police to the obvious conclusion that Declan O'Brien had shot his partner and had then been killed by a neo-Nazi biker who would no doubt proclaim his innocence loudly and often. It would be messy but the cops would be keen to tie it up as quickly as possible.

It was a short walk to where Zelda was waiting in her Audi. He climbed into the front and unzipped the bag to show her the money inside. She grinned. "Nice," she said.

"I'll leave it all with you," he said. "Transfer my share to my Singapore account."

"I love it that you trust me," she said.

He zipped the bag up and tossed it behind her seat. "Where would life be without trust?" he said.

"It does seem a shame giving up perfectly good weaponry for no obvious reason," she said.

"The cops will need the evidence," said Harper. "Plus you got a good price. A very good price."

She sighed wistfully. "I suppose so. Now where do you want me to drop you?"

"The airport," he said. "I'm out of here."

Zelda put the car into gear and pulled away from the kerb. "You're going to have to keep your head down for a while," Harper said to her.

"I know."

"I'm hoping the cops will think it was neo-Nazis who were selling the rockets. But there probably aren't too many dealers who can get their hands on them."

"Don't worry, Lex, I've plenty of friends in the Bundespolizei. I'm safe."

"And in future, be careful who you deal with."

"Dangerous men like yourself, you mean?" She flashed him a sly smile.

Harper chuckled. "I mean terrorists," he said. "Guns you can get away with, but explosives and heavy-duty stuff like the Katyushas, that's a whole different ball game. They're not going to let you sell stuff like that to the jihadists."

"Who do you mean by 'they', Lex?"

"The Americans. The Brits. The Europeans."

"Are you telling me something officially here, Lex? Are you warning me off?"

He smiled and shook his head. "I'm just a friend offering advice. This operation has been for the greater good; at the end of the day we've saved lives and made the world a slightly safer place."

"And made ourselves some money."

His grin widened. "Well, yes. I'm not arguing with you there. I'm just saying that in future, make sure the weapons you sell don't get used against friendly targets. If you're going to drag more of those Katyushas out of cold storage, make sure they go to Africa or the Middle East. I'd hate there to be . . . repercussions."

Zelda nodded but didn't say anything for a while. "I'm glad you're my friend, Lex," she said eventually.

"That's mutual, Zelda."

She dropped him at the airport with a kiss on the cheek. Harper took a flight to Warsaw, squashed into a seat next to a morbidly obese Pole who reeked of vodka, and spent the entire flight eating Polish sausage and dill pickles out of a waxed-paper carton. Escaping with some relief at the end of the flight, Harper bought a first-class ticket to Bangkok via Dubai and after checking in, he found an Internet terminal and slipped a couple of coins into the slot to buy himself ten minutes' access. He accessed the drafts folder that he and Button used to communicate, and left a one word message in it: *DONE*.

Two hours later he was settling himself in his seat in the first-class cabin and asking for a glass of champagne.

Amar Singh handed Shepherd an iPhone. "It's the same as the one I gave you at Heathrow," he said. "Records but doesn't transmit."

"He's suspicious of all phones," said Shepherd. "Even though we'll be outside, I'm pretty sure he'll just take it off me."

"Hopefully a bodyguard will take it and stay close," said Button. She was sitting on a sofa by the window, a cup of tea on the table in front of her. "If he keeps it on himself then it's even better for us, but that's probably unlikely."

They were in a modern hotel a short walk from Vondelpark, Amsterdam's largest park, the place where Smit had agreed to meet Shepherd. Or rather had agreed to talk with Frederik Olsen, aggrieved contract killer and the man who had signed on to kill the president of Russia. Smit had refused at first and had only agreed when Shepherd had said that if he didn't, he would pull out and keep the deposit.

"You can't do that, it's unprofessional," the Dutchman had shouted down the phone.

"What's happened to me is unprofessional, so if we don't meet now, it's all off," had been Shepherd's reply.

The Dutchman had sworn and hung up, but he had phoned back ten minutes later and agreed to meet the following day close to the east entrance of Vondelpark. The park was Amsterdam's equivalent to London's Hyde Park, full of dog walkers, joggers and rollerbladers year round, often full to the brim during a hot summer's day. There were frequent free concerts at the park's open-air theatre and bandstand, and lots of play areas for children. Like most of the country it was constantly fighting a battle against the encroaching sea and had to be pretty much rebuilt every thirty years or so to prevent it becoming one vast pond.

Shepherd had flown over on a KLM flight and Button and Singh had been waiting at the hotel.

According to Button there were already half a dozen MI5 surveillance people in place, along with an equal number of Russian watchers, and hi-tech parabolic surveillance microphones and high-definition video cameras had been set up on various buildings overlooking the park.

"Our second line of attack is your coat," said Singh, handing a black woollen overcoat to Shepherd. "See if you can spot anything out of the ordinary."

Shepherd had a good look and squeezed it between his fingers but nothing felt or looked unusual.

"The middle button is a microphone, but there's no way you can tell by looking at it," said Singh. "There's a small wire in the material of the coat that helps transmit the signal to a receiver in the heel of your shoe." He handed a pair of black shoes to Shepherd. "The wire looks like a thread so even if the button is pulled out it doesn't look suspicious. The heel is totally sealed and there is the capacity and battery to record for a week. There is a camera version but it's temperamental whereas this one is tried and tested."

"Can the signal from the mic be jammed?"

"It's possible but very unlikely as it's not on any frequency used by phones or regular bugs. It's more akin to Bluetooth. And it won't trigger a metal detector, no matter how sensitive."

Shepherd nodded and sat down to take off his shoes and replace them with the ones Singh had given him.

"You need to keep him as close to the perimeter of the park as you can," said Button. "The parabolic mics are good but the closer they are, the better. We'll have mics within the park but they'll be mobile and not guaranteed."

Shepherd nodded. "Got it," he said. He stood up and walked up and down. The shoes fitted perfectly. He pulled on the coat. It too was made to measure.

"Very smart," said Button approvingly.

"What if he takes the phone and the coat off me?"

Singh passed him a small key ring. It was a metal fob with the Danish flag etched into it. "Put your keys on that. As you leave the hotel, press it hard and that'll activate it. It's good for about twelve hours. The quality isn't great but it's okay within a few feet."

Shepherd looked at his watch. There was fifteen minutes to go before the agreed meeting time. "I should be heading off."

Button stood up. For a moment he thought she was going to hug him but she just smiled and held out her hand. "Good luck."

Shepherd was caught by surprise; it wasn't something she normally did. He shook hands with her.

"Break a leg," said Singh. "But please don't break any of my equipment."

Shepherd let himself out of the hotel room and headed for the lift.

Shepherd walked through the park, his hands in his pockets. It was a mild day, the sky was overcast and threatening rain but there was little wind to disturb the branches of the horse chestnut, plane and birch trees that dotted the park.

He saw Smit in the distance, and at the same time recognised four of the bodyguards from his house. Two of the bodyguards moved purposefully towards him and he stopped and waited. They said nothing to him but Shepherd knew the drill and raised his hands to be searched. One of the men quickly patted him down and removed his phone. "Wallet?" asked the heavy.

"I didn't bring it," said Shepherd. "I figured it would save time."

The man nodded. The other heavy stepped forward, pulling a portable metal detector from inside his coat. He quickly passed it over Shepherd's arms and legs, his front and his back, then nodded when it made no sound.

"Are we good?" asked Shepherd.

The heavy nodded and put away the metal detector. The two men moved to stand either side of Shepherd and they walked together towards Smit.

Smit didn't offer to shake hands with Shepherd. Instead he lit a cigar and waited until he had blown smoke before speaking. "This is very unprofessional," he said.

"Really?" said Shepherd. "Two words. Pot. Kettle."

The Dutchman frowned. "What are you talking about?"

"Why didn't you tell me about Rob Tyler?"

Smit frowned as if it were the first time he'd heard the name.

"Don't fuck me around, Smit," snarled Shepherd. "Rob Tyler. Former Delta Force. The guy who had the Putin contract before me."

Smit swallowed. "He became unavailable."

"He was shot in the face at point-blank range," said Shepherd. "And two days ago someone tried to kill me."

"Who?"

"A woman. An Israeli contract killer. Maya Katz. And some other guy we've yet to identify. They planned to make it look like suicide. Now you tell me, Smit, why anyone associated with this contract is being attacked? What the fuck is going on?"

"I've heard of Katz, but I've never used her."

"So who was using her? Has to be the Russians, right? The Russians know you've got the contract and they're killing anyone you give it to."

Smit shook his head. "That can't be right."

"Or are you in on it? Is this some sort of plan to take out contractors? Take out the competition so that your people get a bigger share of the work?"

"That's ridiculous," said Smit.

"Then what the fuck is happening, because I'm not imagining what happened to me and Tyler is most definitely dead."

Smit rubbed his hands together, his brow deeply furrowed. "I am shocked. Stunned. I don't know what to say."

"It's the Russians then. It has to be. Somehow they've found out that you have the contract."

Smit shook his head. "Impossible. I deal only with people I know and trust."

"You dealt with me."

"But you have a track record. You are a known quantity. I don't talk to strangers."

432

"Then maybe someone on your team." Shepherd gestured at the bodyguards. "Someone close to you."

"My men are hand-picked," insisted the Dutchman. "I trust them with my life."

"Well, I hope you've made good choices because if you're wrong . . ." He didn't finish the sentence.

"You will carry out the contract as agreed?"

Shepherd shook his head. "No, not as agreed. Not after what has happened. If the Russians know about me then my career is over. I have to go underground for the rest of my life and that's going to take a lot of money."

The Dutchman sighed. "How much?"

"An extra two million. And I want it now. Up front. Either that or we call the whole thing off."

"You can't do this," said Smit. "That's not how professionals work."

"I almost died, Smit. I almost died because you hired me. That gives me every right to walk away. If you want, I'll do that, I'll walk away now."

He turned to go. The Dutchman reached out and grabbed his arm. Shepherd stopped and glared at the man's hand. "Let go of me or I'll break it," he said quietly.

Smit released his grip on Shepherd's arm. "Look, I'll see what I can do."

"You'll have to do better than that," said Shepherd.

"It's not up to me. It's up to the client."

"How about this?" said Shepherd. "We go and see him together. He's here, right?"

"I'm not sure where he is. Meeting the client is out of the question."

"What about this, Smit? What if the client is involved in this?"

The Dutchman shook his head, confused. "I don't follow you."

"What if he's a set-up? What if the Russians are using him to test the water, to find out which contract killers are willing to take a shot at Putin. He offers the carrot and the Russians kill anyone who takes the bait."

"That's ridiculous," snorted the Dutchman.

"Maybe, but I'll soon know once I look the guy in the eyes. I need to see him. I need to look him in the eyes to see that he's serious."

"He is serious," said Smit. "As serious as cancer. His daughter died on that plane."

"Then he can tell me, to my face."

"That's not going to happ —" Smit's face folded in on itself in a bloody mass and almost immediately brain and blood and bone fragments sprayed across the grass behind him. Shepherd didn't hear the shot but that wasn't surprising because it would have come from hundreds of yards away and from high up. Even without a suppressor the wind would have whipped away most of the sound.

Smit slumped to the ground. His right arm twitched and then went still. Smit's two bodyguards started to run towards the body but realised immediately there was nothing to be done. They stopped and stared at Shepherd, obviously wondering if he was the one who had shot their boss. Shepherd held his arms out to the side, palms open, to show that he didn't have a weapon.

Then they started to look around, realising it was a sniper.

Shepherd stood where he was, his hands out. There was nowhere to run and no cover to hide behind. If there was a second shot it would already be on its way. He wouldn't hear it, the round would just blast through his head exactly as it had done with the Dutchman. It would be a messy death but a quick one. He doubted that Smit had felt a thing. Alive one second, dead the next. Shepherd realised he was holding his breath, bracing himself for a bullet travelling faster than the speed of sound. He exhaled. A second passed. Then another.

Off to his right, a woman screamed. He looked over in her direction, wondering if someone else had been shot, but she was staring at the body of the Dutchman, her hands over her mouth. The bodyguards turned on their heels and walked away. Shepherd thrust his hands in his pockets and did the same.

"It had to be the Russians," said Shepherd. "Had to be." He took off his coat and threw it on to the bed. "Where the hell is Klimov?" He was back in the hotel room. Button was there but there was no sign of Singh.

"Debriefing his team."

"Like hell he is," said Shepherd. "He's on a plane back to Moscow, mission accomplished."

"He's based in London," said Button.

Shepherd took off one of his shoes and kicked it across the room. It smacked into the wall and hit the carpet.

"How can you be so bloody calm?" said Shepherd. He kicked off the second shoe and it also hit the wall, harder this time.

"I'm guessing it's because a man wasn't shot to death in front of me," she said. "It's a shock."

"Damn right it's a shock," said Shepherd. "One hell of a shock for Smit. Why didn't you see this coming?"

"Dan, we don't know this has anything to do with the Russians."

"Oh, come on. Who else would have wanted Smit dead?"

"He hires contract killers — can you imagine how many enemies he must have made over the years?"

"And how many would have known he was going to be in Vondelpark today? And had enough time to get a sniper in place?"

"I accept the Russians are a possibility," said Button. "But we're going to need proof before we start slinging mud around. I'll talk to Klimov."

Shepherd shook his head in disbelief. "Why are you defending him, Charlie? He's already tried to have me killed and he's just murdered a man in public."

"I hardly think he pulled the trigger," said Button. Shepherd opened his mouth to reply but she held up a hand to silence him. "I'll find Klimov and talk to him," she said. "You stay here until Amar comes for his equipment then head back to London. The job's over. Done. Finished. Putin's visit can go ahead as planned."

"So all's well that ends well," said Shepherd, sarcastically.

"Don't start giving me grief over this," said Button as she headed for the door. "I'll talk to Klimov, I'll make enquiries, and we'll talk again when our heads are clearer."

"My head is perfectly clear," said Shepherd. He pulled open the minibar and grabbed two whiskey miniatures.

"You need to talk to Caroline Stockmann."

"I'm fine," said Shepherd. He twisted the tops of the bottles and poured them into a glass.

"Fine or not, your biannual psych evaluation is due. I'll arrange it."

Shepherd shrugged but didn't say anything. He turned his back on her and drank as he looked out over the street below. Button let herself out.

Charlotte Button walked out of the lift, across the reception area and through the revolving door that led outside. It was almost eight o'clock and home was at least an hour's drive away. She stood on the pavement trying to decide whether she should go straight home and cook or if she'd be better off grabbing a bite to eat in London. Lunch had been a Marks and Spencer sandwich at her desk. With the threat level at critical, long lunches were few and far between.

"Ms Button?"

She looked around, frowning. There were two men standing behind her, big men with the look of former soldiers. Close-cropped hair and rugged jaws but with thickening waistlines that their large coats couldn't conceal, which suggested it had been a few years since they had left the military.

"Yes?"

"You're to come with us," they said.

"I don't think so," she said.

The man who'd spoken looked pained. "Please don't make this difficult for us, Ms Button," he said. "We really don't need any grief."

The two men had made no attempt to identify themselves, which meant they weren't police officers, or even Special Branch. But she didn't recognise their faces so they almost certainly didn't work out of Thames House.

"Where are we going?" she asked.

"Somewhere quiet where we won't be disturbed," said the man.

There were two CCTV cameras covering the area and Button looked up at one, wondering who was watching her being picked up. "And under whose orders is this happening?"

"The DG," said the man. He took out a mobile phone. "I'm under orders to call him if you prove uncooperative."

Button looked into his eyes. They were blue and ice cold and he had no problem meeting her gaze. She nodded slowly. "If this is going to take some time, I'd be grateful if we could pick up a coffee and something to eat," she said.

"That won't be a problem, ma'am." He gestured for her to walk along the pavement. "We have a car waiting."

"I don't suppose you can tell me what this is about."

438

"I don't know, ma'am. I've just been told to deliver you."

She forced a smile. "You make me sound like a package."

The man didn't smile back and Button started walking. The two men fell into step either side of her.

The car was a black Vauxhall Insignia with darkened windows. The only man who had spoken opened the rear door for her and then climbed in next to her. A driver sat at the wheel and the other man got into the front passenger seat. The engine was already running and the driver edged the car into the evening traffic.

The man held out his gloved hand. "Your mobile, please."

Button knew there was no point in arguing so she pulled it out of her pocket and gave it to him.

The house they took her to was in Hampshire. Their route took them along unnamed roads and a single track that cut across farmland and was several miles from the nearest street lights. It was a large Georgian building set in several acres. There were three other cars parked in front of it. The man who had taken her phone escorted her out of the car to the front door. It was opened just as they reached it by a stern-faced woman in a grey trouser suit who had a holstered Glock on her hip. The man gave the woman Button's mobile phone and then went back to the car.

The woman took Button down a hallway lined with framed landscapes to a study lined with leather-bound books. "You're to wait here," she said.

Button smiled and thanked her. The woman left and closed the door behind her. There was a desk and several overstuffed leather armchairs. French windows overlooked a terrace, and beyond that were formal gardens.

Button took off her coat and sat down. All she could do now was wait.

Button sat alone for almost two hours before the door opened. She had been reading a two-year-old copy of *Country Life* to pass the time and it slipped from her fingers as she stood up and recognised the woman standing in the doorway. Patsy Ellis was probably the last person she would have expected. Ellis was holding a bottle of wine in one hand and two glasses in the other. She smiled at Button.

"I come bearing gifts," she said. Her face broke into a smile. "Actually, I figured we could both do with a drink."

"Patsy, what a lovely surprise," said Button, getting to her feet. The two women air kissed. It was a surprise, and not an unpleasant one. She and Ellis went back many years, and early on at least Ellis had been something of a mentor.

The two women sat down, smiling like the old friends they were.

"I didn't think it would be you," said Button.

"They wanted a friendly face. Obviously." Ellis handed her a glass. She showed Button the bottle. "Chardonnay. Screw top, I'm afraid."

"The DG doesn't want to do his own dirty work, is that it?"

"You clearly don't know the DG the way that I know the DG," said Ellis. She unscrewed the top of the bottle and poured wine into their glasses. "He's perfectly capable of getting his hands dirty. To be honest, I think he quite likes it."

She raised her glass. "Good to see you, Charlie. It's been too long."

"Hasn't it just," said Button. They clinked glasses and drank, watching each other warily. Ellis was an old friend but in view of what had happened, friendships could be fragile. "How are things these days at the JIO?"

Ellis had left MI5 a few years earlier to join the Joint Intelligence Organisation, the agency which was responsible for assessment and forward planning. It offered advice and support to the Joint Intelligence Committee that oversaw the work of MI5, MI6 and GCHQ. No one knew moreabout the workings of the British intelligence agencies than Patsy Ellis.

"Interesting times," said Ellis. "No question of that."

"Tell me about it."

"I could, but then I'd have to kill you," said Ellis. She grimaced. "Whoops. That's probably not in the best possible taste, all things considered."

"You've got to keep your sense of humour," said Button. She sipped her wine. It was perfectly chilled and she had to fight the urge to gulp it all down.

Ellis waved a languid hand at the French windows. "Why don't we take our wine outside and enjoy the evening air."

"So they can get a clear shot?"

Both women smiled as they picked up their glasses and stepped out on to the terrace. There was a large circular glass-topped white wrought-iron table with four matching chairs and plump green cushions. They sat down and surveyed the garden. To their left was a rockery of ferns and small plants, and to the right was a line of apple trees. Down at the bottom was a gazebo and Button saw two men in dark overcoats sitting together. One of them was smoking.

"This is lovely, isn't it?" said Ellis. "Have you been here before?"

"Twice," said Button. "But not recently."

"It doesn't get much use these days," said Ellis. "They used to debrief Russian and East German defectors here, years ago. They'd stay for months at a time."

Button looked up at the darkening sky. The brightest of the stars were already visible. "I read a thriller once," she said. "Brian Freemantle was the author. His hero was Charlie Muffin. Ever read him?"

Ellis shook her head. "I was never one for fiction."

"Not even Le Carré?"

Ellis shook her head again.

"You don't know what you're missing, Patsy. This book, I forget the title, was about a defector being debriefed in a house much like this. The defector had a friend, a countryman, who had also just defected and for some reason had to come and talk with him. Maybe that was a condition of him defecting. The friend was an astrophysicist and they spent hours sitting in the

442

garden, talking. Eventually they realised that the astrophysicist was working out the location of the safe house by looking at the stars."

"Is that even possible?"

"I suppose so. I'm not sure how accurate it would be. But in the book the astrophysicist does it and they send in a rescue squad or a hit team."

"How does it end?"

Button shrugged. "I can't remember, it was so long ago." She sipped her wine. "Of course these days they'd find the house with satellite surveillance or a drone or a GPS tracker."

"It's a different world, that's for sure," said Ellis. "It used to be that human intel was the be all and end all. Now it's GCHQ and websites and search engines and email and phone monitoring. We have so many CCTV cameras we can follow people right across London without ever leaving our office."

"A brave new world indeed. George Orwell got it right, pretty much."

"George Orwell wrote *Nineteen Eighty-Four*," said Ellis. "It was Aldous Huxley who wrote *Brave New World*." She raised her wine glass. "English Literature at Oxford."

Button clinked her glass against Ellis's. "Mathematics at Bath."

"Lovely city," said Ellis.

They sipped their wine. Both men in the gazebo were smoking now, the red tips of their cigarettes moving up and down like fireflies.

"So how does this story end, Patsy?" asked Button.

"How do you think it ends?"

Button shrugged. "Not with a court case, obviously."

Ellis laughed. "Perish the thought."

"It's a tough one, isn't it?"

"The toughest. It's not as if you can get a spare bedroom in the Ecuador embassy, is it? I suppose the Russians . . ."

Button shuddered. "Don't even say that in jest."

"You see, you're not a traitor. You're not a double agent. It would be hard to argue treason."

"I was carrying out government policy most of the time."

"Yes, well, certainly, but not all the time, and that's where you crossed the line."

"No one was ever targeted who didn't deserve it," said Button.

"Again, no one is disputing that. The world is probably a safer place because of the actions you took. But that doesn't mean you should expect a medal. We both know what you did, Charlie. And, hand on heart, if I'd been through what you've been through, I can't say I wouldn't have done the same. If my husband had . . ." She put up a hand and waved away the rest of the sentence. "Best we don't go there."

"How is Tony?"

"Good. Not happy that I'm here with you instead of being at the theatre with him."

"Are you missing anything nice?"

"*Evita*. He's taken Hannah."

"And how is she now? She must be what, twenty?"

"Twenty-one. She got a 2:1 from Cambridge and is planning to work in the City after a gap year."

"You did well with Hannah. Lovely girl."

"Thank you. Yes. She's done us proud." Ellis swirled her wine around the glass. "You used government money and personnel to deal with personal matters," she said eventually.

"It's a grey area, though."

"Very grey," agreed Ellis.

"The funding has always been off the books," said Button. "And the personnel were freelance."

"You're splitting hairs," said Ellis. She grinned. "Splitting grey hairs, I suppose."

"The government has always had plausible denial," said Button. "Nothing was ever written down."

"So there are no notes? No emails? No written record?"

Button shook her head. She sipped her wine and watched Ellis over the top of her glass.

"So what is your insurance, Charlie? What do we need to be worried about?"

Button shrugged but didn't say anything.

"I'm not recording this, you know that."

Button smiled. "Some things are better not said."

"Because they might be taken as a threat?"

Button shrugged again and sipped her wine.

"There's no paper or email trail, obviously. But I'm thinking that someone with an eye to the future might record the odd conversation, either phone or face to face. The occasional briefing. Plus, of course, a diary would be very revealing, wouldn't it?"

"I couldn't possibly comment," said Button.

"And D-Notices aren't much use in this brave new world. Details of a government-sanctioned assassination unit would go global within minutes. Especially if there was a list of targets. It would be —"

"Embarrassing," Button finished for her.

"Dangerous, I was thinking. Countries who thought we were their friends might start reassessing their relationship with us. Then there are the legal implications. You can imagine the lawyers piling in, can't you?"

"Again, I couldn't possibly comment."

"And I'm assuming that there wouldn't just be one copy in a safe deposit box somewhere. And I don't doubt that you've left an envelope with a close family friend to be opened in the event of your demise."

Button sipped more of her wine.

"More likely on a website somewhere that requires you to visit it on a regular basis. If you don't log in, the information there is made public."

"It's the Internet age," said Button.

Ellis sighed. "I'm guessing you have all your bases covered, as our American cousins are so fond of saying. So where do we go from here, Charlie?"

"The ball's in your court, to use another sporting metaphor."

"There'll be no charges, obviously. No one wants you in court, even a secret one. But you can hardly continue as if nothing has happened."

"I'm happy enough to resign," said Button. "It would be nice if I could keep my pension."

"Resigning for personal reasons?" Ellis nodded. "I think that would work."

"I could do some charitable work," said Button. "Something with animals, perhaps."

"I didn't realise you were into animals."

"I'm not, really."

Ellis chuckled softly. "I don't think anyone expects you to start working for the RSPCA," she said. "In fact, I've been authorised to suggest that you continue doing what you have been doing, but in a freelance capacity."

Button's eyes widened. "Are you serious?" she asked, her voice barely above a whisper.

"Are you telling me you hadn't considered something along those lines?"

"Of course. But not with Her Majesty's Government's approval."

"Who said anything about approval?" said Ellis. "That's not what I said. I'm simply passing on the suggestion that you might consider going private. You have to leave MI5, Charlie. You know that's a foregone conclusion. But if you decided to go private, you wouldn't meet any resistance. The opposite, in fact."

Button smiled. "I'm listening."

"Off the record, there might well be occasions when HMG would put work your way — at arm's length, of course."

"Of course," said Button.

"Your company would not be paid, of course. Nor expenses reimbursed. We couldn't afford a paper trail."

"That makes sense."

"But in return for the occasional pro-bono contract, as it were, HMG would allow you the freedom to operate pretty much without impediment."

"That's an interesting proposal."

"The world has changed, Charlie. And the pace of change has picked up. When those fanatics raided the offices of Charlie Hebdo and massacred all those French cartoonists, they took it to a whole new level. HMG is now even more committed to The Pool. Plus, there would be the possibility of you receiving intelligence from us that might be helpful in your operations."

"And how might that work?" asked Button.

"Every now and again we could get together for a little chat. Share a bottle of wine. Shoot the breeze, put the world to rights."

"And you'd share intel with me?"

"I don't see why not. So long as national security wasn't compromised. And we would assume that you would never take out a contract that clashed with HMG's intentions."

"I don't see that being an issue, Patsy."

Ellis raised her glass. "Then I don't see we have a problem," she said.

Button raised her glass and clinked it against Ellis's. "Here's to the start of a long and mutually beneficial relationship," she said.

Ellis grinned. "We can but hope," she said.

"They're coming now," said Allen. He was sitting in the back of the Mondeo. Sharpe was in the driving seat and

448

Shepherd was sitting next to him. Allen had a transceiver in his hand and a wire running up to the earpiece in his right ear.

"There they are," said Sharpe.

Heading down the road towards them was the white van belonging to the kebab shop.

The Mondeo was parked in the car park next to a doctor's surgery that gave them a reasonable view of the kebab shop and the minicab office above it.

It was just after eight o'clock in the evening and Ahmet had left in the van at four o'clock for the ninety-minute drive west along the M62 to Liverpool. A West Yorkshire Police surveillance team had shadowed him to the depot; a simple matter as they knew exactly where he was heading. The same team had followed him back, but again they were able to keep their distance. Yusuf had remained in the minicab office but his eldest son had gone with Ahmet.

Ahmet brought the van to a stop outside the kebab shop. Yusuf's son climbed out, went around to the rear of the van, pulled the doors open and took out a large box labelled FRESH CHICKEN.

"There we go," said Shepherd.

Yusuf's son took out a second box and slammed the door shut. Then, instead of heading into the shop he went to the door that led to the stairs up to the minicab office. He pressed an intercom button and looked up at the CCTV covering the pavement. A couple of seconds later he pushed the door open and went inside.

"They're getting ready to go now," said Allen.

"They'd be better waiting for Ahmet to go up and join his brother," said Sharpe. He held up his hands. "But then it's not my gig."

Half a dozen armed police came down the road towards the kebab shop in black suits, bulletproof vests and Kevlar helmets. In the midst of them was an officer holding an enforcer, a bright orange battering ram capable of smashing open the most reinforced of doors. It weighed sixteen kilos but in the right hands could generate a force of three tonnes.

Two of the armed cops went into the kebab house. The rest positioned themselves either side of the minicab office door. Two grey Mercedes-Benz Sprinter vans came down the road. No sirens or flashing lights, but at speed. They pulled up in front of the kebab house and half a dozen constables in fluorescent jackets piled out and headed inside.

"It's going to get bloody crowded up there," said Sharpe. He laughed. "And here comes the detective sergeant."

A Vauxhall Astra pulled up with Drinkwater in the front passenger seat. With him were two uniformed senior officers, a chief superintendent and an inspector. Drinkwater was wearing a stab vest over his suit and had a police cap bearing the insignia of the West Yorkshire Police, which Shepherd thought was a nice touch. The three officers climbed out of the Astra and headed inside.

"That's it then," said Sharpe. "All's well that ends well."

450

"The DS looks like the cat that got the cream," said Allen.

"He'll have his moment in the limelight," said Shepherd. "But at the end of the day, it doesn't count for much. They'll go down but other dealers'll take over from the Yilmaz brothers."

Allen took out his earpiece and coiled the wire around the transceiver. "Seems a pity we didn't shut down the Liverpool end," he said.

"It's in hand," said Sharpe.

"Seriously?" asked Allen.

"Sure. I'm not one to let good intel go to waste. We'll let the furore over this die down and then the NCA'll move in." He twisted around in his seat. "I can get you in on it, if you want?"

"You can do that?"

"No problem at all. I'll get you attached to the team closer to the time." He grinned. "If nothing else, it'll piss off Detective Sergeant I Don't Drink On Duty."

"Speaking of which, why don't we retire to the pub?" said Shepherd.

"I'll drink to that," laughed Allen.

Charlotte Button was pouring herself a glass of chilled Pinot Grigio to go with the smoked salmon she had prepared for herself when her doorbell rang. She frowned and looked at her watch. It was almost ten o'clock at night and she wasn't expecting visitors. She opened a cupboard next to the fridge. There was a CCTV monitoring system there with a large LCD screen showing the views from the eight cameras that covered her property. There was a man standing on her doorstep and as he turned to look up at the camera she realised it was Shepherd. She took a deep breath, closed the door and took a long sip of wine before carrying the glass to the front door. She faked surprise as she pulled the door open. "My goodness, you don't usually make house calls."

"Can I come in?"

"Of course you can," she said, pulling the door open. "I've just opened a bottle. Would you like a glass?"

"I'm driving," he said.

She closed the door and took him along to the kitchen. "Coffee then? I've got one of those coffee machines that George Clooney uses."

"Coffee, then. Please."

He stood by the kitchen island as if unsure where to sit.

"Pull out a stool," she said. "Are you hungry? I've just thrown a salad together."

He shook his head. "I'm not hungry."

"I do hope this is personal and not official," said Button.

"What do you mean?"

"I mean . . ." She shrugged. "It doesn't matter."

Shepherd frowned. "You thought someone might have sent me? To do what?"

"I said it doesn't matter. Pull out a stool and sit down. I'll get your coffee."

Shepherd pulled a copy of the *Daily Mail* from his pocket and tossed it on to the kitchen island. "Did you read that?"

"The paper? Of course. I read half a dozen papers a day. Personally, I prefer the *Telegraph*."

"Don't play games with me, Charlie. You're better than that. You know exactly what I mean. Max Jansen killed himself. The guy who wanted Putin dead hanged himself yesterday in his garage. Hanged himself and left his car engine running, just to make sure. Except we both know that he didn't kill himself."

Button turned her back on him and busied herself at the coffee machine. "I'm not sure what you want me to say," she said.

"The Russians killed him. Just like they killed Lucas Smit. And you didn't lift a finger to stop them."

"They both died in Holland," she said flatly. "Not my jurisdiction."

"That's a cop-out and you know it. And there's more than that. You set up Smit. Worse, you used me to set him up."

He sat in silence while she made his coffee. When she'd finished she handed him the mug and sat down on the other side of the kitchen island with her wine.

"You know I'm leaving?" she asked.

He nodded. "And Jeremy Willoughby-Brown is taking your job. I can't tell you how happy I am about that."

"He's a little shit."

"You know he was using me?" asked Shepherd.

453

She smiled over the top of her glass. "Of course I know. I know he sent you to Berlin to talk to Harper. You should have come to me then." She shrugged. "But I understand why you didn't."

"Rock and a hard place," he said.

"You can't ever trust him, you do know that?"

Shepherd nodded and sipped his coffee. "Yeah, I know."

She sighed. "Smit and the father, they were the price." Her voice was little more than a whisper, as if she were in the confessional baring her soul to a priest.

"The price?"

"The price for you to stay alive. The Russians were going to kill you for what you did to their men in Berlin."

Shepherd opened his mouth to argue — he hadn't killed the Russian agents in Berlin, that had been Harper's work. But he realised that he had led them there so the Russians would hold him responsible.

"The only way to get them off your back was to give them Smit and the father," Button continued. "I'm far from happy about it, but I did it. To be honest, they would have done it with or without my help, so at least this way you're safe. They've called off the dogs."

"I suppose I should be grateful for that."

She shrugged. "You're welcome." She took a big gulp of wine.

"So they're firing you?"

"It's a mutual decision. I get to keep my pension."

"That's it? No comebacks?"

"Comebacks? What do you mean? Prison time? You thought they'd put me on trial?"

"After what you did, yes. Maybe. I suppose they couldn't afford the publicity, right?"

She smiled. "It's more complicated than that."

Realisation dawned and Shepherd nodded. "You know where the bodies are buried?"

"Figuratively and literally," said Button.

"And they let you walk?"

"Like I said, it's more complicated than that. Why are you here, Spider? What do you want from me?"

"I want to know what happened. I want to know why you did what you did."

She looked at him, her eyebrows arched. "Seriously?"

He waved his hand dismissively. "I understand, of course I do. They killed your husband, you wanted revenge."

"It's the most visceral of urges," said Button. "Someone hurts you, you hurt them back."

"Sometimes you forgive and forget."

Her eyes narrowed. "Screw you, Spider."

He put up his hands. "I didn't mean I expected you to do that. I'm just saying, not everyone exacts revenge."

"How did you feel when your wife died?"

"Angry. Hurt. Lost." He shrugged. "That hasn't changed over the years. She was the love of my life."

"And Sue died in a senseless accident, right? No one to blame. Except herself, perhaps? She lost concentration and went through a red light. Now imagine there had been someone to blame. Worse, what if someone had deliberately murdered your wife?"

"That's not what happened."

"I know that. I'm talking hypothetically. Suppose someone had killed Sue, wouldn't you have lashed out?"

"I can't answer that," said Shepherd.

"Can't, or won't?"

"How many people did you have killed, Charlie? As revenge?"

"A handful. And every one of them deserved it, Spider. I was sure, I was a thousand per cent sure in every case. There were no innocents. Every one of the bastards deserved what they got."

"If you knew for sure, why not have them arrested, put on trial? Let the authorities deal with them?"

Button put down her glass and stared at him. "Dan Shepherd, whiter than white, always wearing his heart on his sleeve, always taking the moral high ground. You think I don't know, Spider? You think I don't know what you did? You and the galloping major? Back in 2011?"

Shepherd's jaw tightened but he said nothing.

Button smiled. "You work for me, Spider. You've worked for me for a long time. I know everything there is to know about you. Every breath you take, every move you make, every bond you break."

Shepherd stared at her, trying not to show any emotion but knowing that she knew that every word had struck home.

456

Button smiled. "Lisa O'Hara. Real IRA enforcer. A right bitch, as they say."

She waited for him to speak, but he couldn't. He didn't know what to say. Or how to react. He had never suspected that Button knew about Lisa O'Hara.

"Major Gannon remained outside in his car while you did the dirty deed," said Button. "Of course it only needed one man because O'Hara would never in a million years have expected to be shot in her own home. Not by a serving MI5 officer, anyway. Did she say anything, Spider? Did she beg for her life when she saw you standing there with a gun?"

Shepherd took a deep breath and exhaled slowly. "She didn't believe I'd do it."

"Well she read you wrong, didn't she? Two shots. One in the chest, one in the head."

"She put a bomb in my car. She could have killed Liam and Katra and she didn't care. She targeted my family."

"That's right," said Button. "She did. And you killed her. Without a second thought."

Shepherd shook his head. "Actually I thought long and hard about it."

"But you still killed her."

Shepherd flashed her a thin smile. "Yes. Yes, I did."

"And no regrets?"

"No, I've got regrets. But she deserved to die and it was only right that I was the one to pull the trigger. I'm not proud of what I did. But she looked me in the eye and said that she was a soldier in the Real IRA and that she was at war with the occupying forces, of which I

457

formed a part." He shrugged. "She was a soldier and she died like a soldier."

"We know that's not exactly true, is it?" said Button. "You ambushed her in her own home and shot her while she was kneeling on the floor, unarmed."

Shepherd looked away, too embarrassed to lock eyes with her, knowing she was right.

"Don't get me wrong, Spider," said Button quietly. "I understand why you did it. I empathise. In your place I would probably have done the same. But at least give me the respect of understanding why I did what I did. And perhaps even offer me a little empathy. Because at the end of the day, we're not that different, you and I."

Shepherd sipped his coffee. She was right. He had killed Lisa O'Hara in cold blood. It wasn't something he thought about much. Immediately afterwards he'd disposed of the weapon and the clothes that he'd been wearing, and he'd never spoken of what had happened to anyone, not even the Major. Shepherd's memory was pretty much infallible but that didn't mean he couldn't lock things away. What had happened to Lisa O'Hara was in a part of his memory that he rarely visited.

"Don't worry," said Button. "Your secret is safe with me."

"I'm not worried," said Shepherd. "Knowing and proving are different things."

"Exactly," said Button. "But you're assuming I don't have proof. A video of you entering the cottage and leaving several hours later. And being driven off by

Major Gannon." She shrugged. "But maybe there is no video. And maybe the gun was never recovered."

Shepherd stared at her, his heart pounding. "What gun?"

"The hypothetical Glock that you might or might not have used."

"I doubt there would be any prints on this hypothetical gun."

"I'm sure there wouldn't be. But if there was a video showing you disposing of the weapon that killed Lisa O'Hara, that would be fairly conclusive, wouldn't it?" Button smiled and raised her wine glass. "Anyway, this is all hypothetical, isn't it? All I'm saying is that you and I are similar in many ways. We believe in right and wrong and the greater good and all that, but we both know that sometimes you have to do things for personal reasons. That's what I did, Spider, and I'm not apologising for it. A line has been drawn and now it's time to move on."

Shepherd sipped his coffee and said nothing. He was trying to come to terms with the fact that for the past four years, Button had known that he had killed Lisa O'Hara. She had known and said nothing. But did she have proof? Had there been someone watching the cottage, someone that neither Shepherd nor the Major had seen? Someone who had been able to follow him when he'd disposed of the gun?

"Oh come on, Spider," chided Button. "Relax. It's all good. It's probably for the best, anyway. I wouldn't want to be in the hot seat when the shit hits the fan in the UK, and it will eventually. I'll be better off in the private sector. And frankly, so would you."

Shepherd raised his eyebrows. "Are you offering me a job, Charlie?"

"Why not? It pays a darn sight more than government work. There's no pension, but no tax either, so swings and roundabouts."

"You think this is funny?" asked Shepherd.

Button's eyes hardened. "No, I don't. We're playing big boys' games here, we both know that. I'm moving on, and yes, I'm a bit concerned that I'll be in uncharted waters. But I'll survive. Maybe even prosper. The question is, Spider, what are you going to do? Willoughby-Brown is no great fan of yours, you know that?"

"I'd gathered as much, yeah."

"So do you want to work for him? Do you want him watching your every move, waiting for you to slip up so that he can haul you over the coals?"

Shepherd shrugged. "I could always go back to police work," he said.

"The National Crime Agency? That'll go the same way as SOCA. Too many cooks, too many pencil-pushers."

"So what are you saying? I should leave MI5 and become a professional assassin?"

"Would that be so bad, Spider?"

"Killing for money? Are you serious?"

"Most of the work is government-sponsored," said Button. "We're not criminals. We're doing the work that governments need to be distanced from. Terrorists,

460

mainly. The sort of people the world is better off without. And it isn't just about killing individuals, it's about destroying networks. We're at war, Spider. And in that war, some soldiers wear uniforms and some don't. But they're doing the same job — trying to make the world a safer place. If you work for me, you'd be making a difference. A real difference."

Shepherd took another sip of his coffee, then nodded slowly. "Let me think about it," he said.